Trolley

A Soylent Publications release

Copyright 2011 Grig Larson
Cover art and design by Christine Larson

All rights reserved.

ISBN: 978-1-4507-7521-2

Trolley

DEDICATIONS

This book is dedicated to Christine, the love of my life, and to the best and most understanding son on the planet, Christopher. I'd also like to deeply thank Chance and Scarlet, whom I love like daughters, and the best assistants I have ever had. This book would not have happened without all of you.

Anya and Rogue, thanks for holding up my lantern when things were darkest. Many thanks goes to Kory and Alison, as well as the rest of MSD, who gave me guidance and support at many conventions, as well as WTMI out of GenCon. Thanks to Bruce and Cheryl, who supported my first writing endeavor, kept me from being homeless, and told me not to quit my day job. Thank you, Suzi, for putting up with all the crap surrounding my first book; there is a spot in Goth heaven (if there is one) for you. And to the beta readers, thank you for your wisdom and edits. To the Punk Walrus fans, thanks for sticking with me, especially April, who is better than any DVD commentary.

Last but not least, I bow humbly before all the unsung heroes of fandom conventions: the volunteers who work tirelessly to to run them. They pull off some of the most amazing parties, events, and programming. Like watering holes for us struggling artists, they give us the support, late-night banter, and sage advice on how not to be a douchebag guest. It is my hope that I honor your sacrifices in sanity and vacation time during my continuing journeys among you literary carny folk.

This book was written entirely on Open Source software. OpenOffice, gedit, and NotePad++ provided a writing environment on the Ubuntu and CentOS Linux distribution. In addition, GIMP was used to do some of the graphics. Please support Linux, Open Source software, and the Electronic Frontier Foundation.

TROLLEY

One
Bleeding Dreams

Heather January was dangerously deep within the gears. One false slip and she would be crushed and extruded as if inside a butcher's grinder. The gears had been disengaged, in this part of the machinery, anyway. Their imposing heavy metallic presence in cramped space barely offered any room for a full-sized adult, which is what made her ideal for this kind of work. At 12 years of age, she was small and agile in comparison to the Professor. She couldn't even see the access panel anymore as she tilted her lantern to see what she was working on. The polished gears of her recent handiwork lay side by side in stark contrast to the ancient, darker, and time-worn gears they connected to. Like two worlds that perfectly meshed together; Heather was always in awe at this part of the machine. The mechanisms all hung around her like organs of some living thing in suspended animation.

"I don't see anything unusual," she shouted against the surrounding thumping and ratcheting noises. This part of the assembly had been disconnected, but the rest of the root machine was still running all around her, just outside her field of vision. Those boundaries were incredibly dangerous, with spinning wheels, razor-sharp belts, and steam pipes so searing, they would burn through paper in a matter of seconds. Clouds of steam wafted around like ghosts as her damp shirt clung to her like a second skin. "If the jam is taking place here where we're connected to the root machine, it's going to require a complete disassembly."

"That is bad news," the Professor said from the other end of the access panel. "I have looked over the diagrams and if you're by one of the titanium cogs near the huge clock spring we replaced last year...that's where I have determined the problem to be."

"It *has* to be here," Heather shouted in agreement. She could only see half the clock spring in the dim light, but she had tapped it with a hammer and determined something was not quite right by the way it rang. "I saw the diagram myself, and I can't see where else the problem would be."

"Well..." said the Professor in sarcastic shock. "Glad to have *your* approval..."

Heather rolled her eyes. "I didn't mean that you *needed* my approval. I am just *agreeing* with you."

"That's also unnecessary. Look at the block reduction assembly as it connects to one of the larger bronze flywheels near one of the pipes. It should be below your left foot."

Heather looked down at her grease-stained toes and shifted her legs back and forth, shining her lamp into the darkness. Drops of oil-stained sweat rolled off her face and disappeared in the inky space below her. "I don't... see a gear reduction box. You sure?"

"Quite sure. It would be one of the larger ones, like a two by three foot box with steel cladding."

Heather looked at the empty space. "There's a huge hole here where I could see it fit... wait a minute, I see some bent support rods! And a sheared bolt!"

"What's below it? Can you see any wreckage?"

Heather "I can't see down there, it's too dark below where I am. I'll have to climb down — "

"**No!**" the Professor said. "Just come back up. I'll get a rope, and you can lower the lantern. I don't want you down that far. Don't be a Chip LaCroi with this!"

Heather cringed at the name Chip.

Chip LaCroi was a fictional character of the "League of the Brave," a popular comic book series that the citizens of her city read and enjoyed. Everyone also assumed Heather, like most children, enjoyed the stories as well. But Heather felt Chip was no more than a stereotyped, hapless, yet stupidly brave boy who always got into scrapes and escapades. But, by the end of the story, Chip always managed to find some poorly-contrived, "nick of time" idea to save him. If this were one of his comics, Heather thought, he would have done something stupid, like toss in his wrench and jam up the works just before he was shredded. But the reality was that gears this large had been running for centuries, if not longer, and if something as small as a brass wrench would have clogged it up, they would have long since been replaced. No, these were titanium gears that were dozens of feet tall and must have weighed uncountable tons. They would squish the wrench like it was clay, where the hot remains would clatter down into some oil-pan to be drained out later.

"You're just like Chip..." adults would say in a patronizing tone one normally uses on small children. "Your little tomboy is so cute..." they would say to her mother. Well, they used to, until Heather got older and Heather's tomboy mentality was starting to wear thin on people's sense of proper behavior of young women. But instead of quietly shaming Heather, the scorn only made her more determined to be "one of the boys." So, two years ago, Heather became an assistant to a local theoretical mechanics professor of high degree, helping him solve the many mysteries that mechanics still had yet to uncover. Of course, there was always danger. Heather's biggest advantage had been her size and her quick reflexes, but one false move and she would be gristle and bone ground into thousands of random gears.

Heather was no Chip. This was reality where people died.

"I think it will be okay," Heather said, lowering herself onto her belly and hanging the lantern even further. As she peered down, she saw a small green glow that was so faint, she had to look at it with the corners of her eyes to even get a fix on it. It appeared to be a puddle, but how large a puddle was hard to say because she couldn't tell how far away it was. "I think we have some loose trolley down here...!"

"Then get **up!**" the Professor shouted. "I am not losing you to trolley gas!"

"Relax, it's really far away — " Heather started to say, but was interrupted by an uncomfortable groan that shuddered the gear on which she lay. Heather had worked with machines for years, and she knew from experience what sounds are normal versus sounds that were dangerous. This sound echoed all around her and was the very scary sound of metal fatigue. Even the distant thumping of the root machine seemed to pause to get a better listen.

"What was that?" asked the Professor.

"I'm coming up!" Heather shouted. She scrambled to her feet and started to climb back up to the access panel. But the gear she was using to hold her footing was starting to turn. "Oh no..." Heather realized.

When the grunts and rumbling suddenly started all around her, Heather January realized that something had gone horribly wrong. Her lantern, which had been propped up on one of the clock springs, rattled and shattered against the wall of a ventilation shaft, snuffing out all light but the glow from the access panel above. Her perspective shifted and she realized she was falling backwards into the huge machinery blindly. She desperately tried to right herself, but only managed to twist sideways as a piece of her shirt got caught in a worm gear and stripped it off her arm like butcher paper. A spinning fly rod struck her hard on her temple. She tried to grab its axle to steady herself, but it only pulled her forwards and into a much darker part of the machine. As Heather slid near a huge set of gear teeth, she kicked backwards trying to get away from the crushing death that spun in front of her.

Heather screamed with fear some of the strongest and most vulgar curse words that came from deep within her gut. She tried to grip onto something to delay the inevitable grinding of flesh and bone. As she scrambled to find a handhold among the spinning wheels, a thin gap of metal pinched the palm of her hand like a pair of scissors, tearing off a strip of skin from her wrist to the edge of the middle finger. Blood and oil squirted into her eye, stinging and partially blinding her.

"What's going on in there? Get out of there *now!*" asked the Professor from the access panel opening, shouting over the ratcheting noise.

"Fucking shit gears turned on and are fucking killing me!!" Heather screamed, watching her toes disappear into the shadows of the gears. She hoped that the death would be quick, and tried not to think that it would probably take agonizing seconds of bone crunching up her legs and abdomen before she lost consciousness. Her life flashed before her eyes as raw fear erupted from her chest in wailing terror.

Something clattered out from behind her, followed by the most horrible of shuddering noises that surrounded her. The entire assembly shook, and her ears rang with the cruel deafening sympathy of a dying machine. The cold slithering edge of a huge gear tooth brushed against the top of her big toe as she braced for the initial pain. But just as the lower gear scraped her heel, and she felt the tops of her feet bending inwards, the machine stopped and became deathly quiet. The silence was quickly replaced by the rising hiss and squeal of a huge number of pipes.

The machine was trembling under the strain. Axles were creaking under the tension and the entire structure flexed under the stress. Quickly, Heather scrambled backwards towards the freedom of the access hatch and climbed with a swiftness she didn't know she had.

"Quickly!" the Professor shouted. "I can't hold these gears back for long; it's connected to the root machine! It's going to break!"

Heather lunged for the door and gratefully felt the Professor's bony hands grip her elbow joints. She scrambled at the edge of the access hatch, but her hands were slippery and greasy with oil and blood. She felt a tightening fear of desperation as all the scrambling in the world did nothing but slowly let her drift back into the machinery.

"You've gotten heavier..." the Professor grunted. "I can't get the proper leverage to lift you out!"

A green glow started to fill the chamber. The power of trolley, the green mineral which powered all machinery in the world, was growing. It was gaining power under the pressure, and whatever the Professor had jammed into the gears was about to snap.

"Get me out of here!" Heather screamed. Her eyes were wide with panic. **"I'm slipping; don't let go!"**

The Professor strained; his arms were bony and weak, and a stone star necklace he wore was banging against her face. Steam started to fill the chamber as the creaking grew louder. Then there was a deep pop, and as the gears started to churn again, a huge part of the pallet escape wheel snagged its hooked tooth on Heather's overalls.

"Fuck I don't want to die! Don't let go!!!" Heather screeched. She felt the Professor's grip slide off as she was quickly sucked back into the spinning metal. Her head jammed between the unforgiving teeth of two large gears and started crushing as her neck snapped. Hot blood and brains oozed down her back with a shifting crunching sound. Her stomach was torn open by a pallet spring, and as her mangled body became one with the machinery, she felt pieces of her curl up into wadded mats of gristle and broken bone. Her screams turned to juicy and meaty gurgles drowned out by the humming of gears catching up for lost time. The last thing that she saw before her eyeballs popped was trolley, glowing green and pulsing with a radiance that enveloped her like some kind of huge sucking monster. As her sight dimmed, a battery containing the fuel turned to face her, and she saw one huge gray-green eye with a kidney-shaped lens stare right through her and into her gut; drinking her blood with ratcheting sucking noises.

Heather awoke screaming, clutching her stomach. It took her several seconds to adjust to the darkness as her conscious mind started to assemble her bedroom section by section, replacing the sucking fear of grinding death with the reassurance of a stable reality. The green glow was replaced by the gas street lights from outside, and the gears replaced with knotholes in the wooden panels of her walls.

Morgana turned on their oil lamp by her bed. "Oh for goodness sake, Heather!" she complained.

Heather's screaming became choked by her swelling throat as she gasped for air. Her eyes were wide with panic; her face glistening with sweat and painted with wet strands of her short blond hair.

"Mother!" Morgana said with an annoyed urgency. Her twin sister's night terrors were becoming more frequent now. Morgana had complained before that she was losing her beauty sleep, that she was even starting to get bags under her eyes like old people did. She got up and sat beside her sister, hugging her loosely out of sense of show and duty rather than love.

Heather gasped and clutched her stomach. She pulled aside her blanket and looked at her bed, startled to find the sheets spotted with blood.

"Uh oh..." Morgana said, recoiling at the sight of the stain. "Did someone stab you?" She looked confused and frightened.

"B-Blooooooodddd!!!" Heather screamed. **"Mother!!!"** She screamed hysterically while Morgana dove off Heather's bed into her own, where she curled up and hid under her covers.

"Okay okay okay..." said their mother from their parent's bedroom, "I'm coming!"

Heather stared at the spots of blood in her bed. As her night-mares faded into the waking world, her own reality was starting to spawn its own nightmare. She was still disoriented and con-fused, not knowing if her dreams were escaping and killing her from the outside now. The green glow of trolley was still fresh in her mind, looking back at her like... some all-watching eye. It was otherworldly and horrifying. There had been other dreams late-ly, too. There were dreams of a stone table, vaulted ceilings, and strands of lights that twisted and danced. There were people with-out eyes, with glowing green pus draining from their eye sockets, shouting her name slowly. But apart from the occasional falling to the floor, the pain and damage from night terrors were all un-real until now. Looking at the blood around her legs, she realized that her dreams were coming out of her body and tearing at her flesh. They were crawling out of her belly and dragging her insides with them. Heather didn't know what to do but shriek and wail while her mother thumped down the hallway towards their room with increasing urgency.

"This scream is different," her mother whispered to herself as she burst into their room, her nightgown untucked and flailing. She shone her oil lamp on Heather's sweat-soaked face, and her chest tightened by the look of terror in her daughter's eyes. "Mother is here," she said, "mother is..." Then her oil lamp spotlighted Heath-er's nightgown right between her legs.

Morgana tossed her covers aside from her own bed. Her face was wet with tears and confusion. "She's *bleeding*, mother! Her nightmares became *real!*" she cried out in horror. Up until now, the nightmares Heather described were always something that only ended in screaming, crying, and incessant rocking until their moth-er calmed her down. The appearance of blood now added to the horror as fresh as the first time Heather screamed herself awake a few months ago.

"Mother what's happening to me...?" Heather asked, shaking in fear and confusion. Her nose ran in sticky strands like it did when she was still a toddler and she sniffled in her sobs. She spread her nightgown apart, looking at her legs and bed sheets.

"Ohhhh..." Rose January, mother of four, had known that this day would come soon. Her daughters were fraternal twins; yet despite being the same age, they were as different as black was from white. There seemed to be a kind of cruelty in Heather showing signs of being a woman first, given that Morgana was the more feminine one, and Heather still looked like a small boy. She wondered how long it would be before Morgana had a similar incident.

"Get some rags. Hurry." Rose shouted to Morgana.

Morgana thought her mother seemed awfully calm for blood, but the girl ran as fast as she could to the kitchen.

Heather wasn't afraid of blood; she had actually seen her own spilled blood, even recently, from various cuts and scrapes she received in the normal daily tasks of her machine work. She had a fairly fresh scar down the back of her leg and another near her neck from a few years ago where the doctors feared she would die from blood loss. A few splotches of blood on her legs should not have alarmed her. It was the fact that she awoke with it from one of her night terrors, and that it reached into the darker parts of her mind, scarring her deeply. Just like a bad oil leak from the center of an engine, something was very wrong at the core.

"What's the problem, Rose? Another nightmare?" asked Heather's father as he stumbled into the hallway. Bruce January worried that this would be another night of lost sleep. Already, his coworkers had commented on his sluggish responses and mathematical mistakes. His daughter was strange enough without this new phase where she now screamed at night. "She takes after her aunt," he admitted with worry to Rose aloud one night.

"It's a womanly problem, father," she said with a mix of amusement and exasperation. "Go back to bed."

"A womanly problem?" Heather wondered what that meant as her father blushed and quickly turned around, heading back to his bedroom. "What do you mean, mother?"

Her mother gently lifted up Heather's nightgown, and looked at the spotting on the sheets. "Honey, is this... the first time this has happened to you?"

The blood had an unusual smell. "No, I have been cut lots of times. But never when I got cut in my dreams did I wake up with blood on my — "

Rose chuckled. "No, I mean... bled from your more... private areas."

Her privates? Heather felt a rise of panic from her throat. Her mother was certainly taking this well, and it never occurred to her that one could... *bleed*... from there. Before Heather could ask any more questions, Morgana ran back in, her normally graceful gait thumping on their wooden floor in haste. "I have some wet rags. I brought some bandages and some alcohol to sterilize the wound." Morgana had received good grades in her basic first aid classes. "Is she... did her dreams...?"

Rose chuckled. "No. No, I have been suspecting this would happen some day, only I didn't think so soon. Morgana? Go boil us some water for tea. Heather and I have some... delicate matters to discuss."

"Did she get stabbed? Who stabbed her?" Morgana pleaded. "How come they stabbed her and not me? Did they rob us, mother? Did they come in through the fire escape and rob us?"

"No, no dear. Morgana, listen... this is a... private thing between Heather and I right now."

Morgana's eyes lowered. "Is she in trouble...?"

"No no!" Rose laughed. This was not how she had been told of the womanly curse. She recalled her own discovery one day after coming back from school and thinking she had soiled herself. Her mother had handled it with grace and tact, but had never brought it up again. Rose knew this speech would someday have to be passed on to her girls, but she assumed that she would have more time. As small as Heather was, she did not expect her, of all people, to become a woman at this early age.

"Is it the dreams?" Heather asked, her voice barely a whisper. "Do they become real if I have them too many times?"

"Is my sister going to die?" Morgana asked. She seemed more interested than afraid. "Are my dreams able to kill me, too?"

Rose thought this was getting out of hand quickly. "Oh, Morgana, *nobody* is going to die! Now, sweetie, you go down and have yourself some sweets. I'll be downstairs in a little bit to — "

Heather gasped. "How come *she* gets sweets and *I am* the one cut and bleeding?"

"Heather? You're trying my patience. Morgana? **Out!**"

Once certain that Morgana had left, Rose sat down with Heather and said, "I will give you twice the number of sweets before bed. But I need to talk to you about... what just happened."

"It's dreams, isn't it? The medicine the doctor gave me didn't work, and now my dreams are going to kill me when I sleep..." Heather sobbed into the rag her mother had handed her. The dreams had been ongoing for about a month, and the sedative that the doctor had prescribed had done little to alleviate them. It only ended up making Heather groggier and more disoriented when she was awake.

"Heather, dear Heather," she took the rag from her daughter and looked down at it with an amused smirk. The innocence of youth. Rose rolled the cloth into a familiar shape and sighed at the fact this would become routine. "This is not... well, shouldn't be the reason for your dreams. But... did you have a nightmare about being crushed again?"

Heather nodded. "And that green eye. Trolley was coming to get me."

"The stone table? The people trying to cut you open with a golden knife? The huge monster scraping behind a wall?"

Heather shook her head. "Not this time. Just the huge eye. That huge... staring fish eye..."

Rose sighed deeply. "I think maybe when your semester with the Professor ends this year, we should send you to a normal school. I think the Professor's lessons are scrambling your delicate female brain."

"Noooo!" Heather whined. "I don't *like* public school!"

"Heather, I think that place you work in has... scared you. I mean, you work with gears and trolley and oil and come home all dirty and greasy and covered with who knows what. You're 12 now, Heather. It's time to think about your future. Your future... as a woman."

"Please don't make me go to public school, please?? All the girls hate me... and I hate all of them, too!"

"Heather... you're growing up now... and maybe it's time you stopped playing around with machines and — "

"Nooo!"

"Heather?" Rose said sternly, "Listen to your mother. You are becoming a young woman and it is inappropriate to get dirty and messy anymore. Now, your father and I have been very lenient with you. We let you have your way, and allowed you to become an assistant to a professor who would provide you with proper lessons, but... it's time you start acting and dressing like..." Rose looked at her daughter. A small, dirty blond waif with grease behind the ears. She still looked more boy than girl. She sighed. "What am I going to do with you?"

"Don't take me away from the Professor..."

"These dreams would stop, dear..." Rose said, trying to make it sound tempting.

Heather stared at her hands twisting in her bed sheets. "Then... then I'll keep the bad dreams. Even if they make me bleed." Heather started to cry, and wipe her face with the rags.

Rose sighed. Heather was no fool, unlike her sister. "Heather, those dreams may be many things but... okay, first? I want you to stop wiping your face in those particular rags. We need to have a little... woman to girl talk."

An hour later, when Morgana dared come back upstairs, she saw her sister with the biggest look of dumb shock on her face.

"You didn't eat *all* the sweets, did you?" Rose asked, even though she knew the answer right away without needing to turn around to look.

"No..." Morgana lied through colored teeth.

"Uh huh..." Rose said. "Well, tomorrow, I am going to get more, and Heather will get to choose what flavor and what kind."

"Uh...!" Morgana began, but cut herself off with her mother's stern glare.

"To bed. All lights extinguished!" Rose demanded, and as Morgana jumped into her bed, the lights dimmed. Her mother took the teapot and teacups they had shared, and closed the door quietly behind her as she left.

After a few fidgeting minutes in the dark, Morgana rolled to her side and looked at Heather. She could see from the light from the street lamps that spilled from the outside that Heather was still sitting upright.

"Are you gonna be okay?" Morgana asked.

"Yeah..." Heather replied glumly. "I guess."

"What happened? Why are you bleeding...?"

Heather thought of a million different things in her head, and not one of them could come up with a reply. She was numb with shock about what her mother had just told her about being a woman, the change of life, and new types of complicated undergarments she was going to have to wear. She wasn't allowed to tell Morgana, either, even if she knew *how* to explain it to her. She couldn't quite fathom what her mother had just said; up until now, she seemed a perfectly normal and rational a person. It was unreal; as unreal as the dreams, and the only consolation she had was that it was going to happen to her sister eventually. She hoped the shock of blood would shatter her perfect frilled lace universe.

"I... I don't know," Heather finally said.

Morgana, full of spunk with sugar, was beside herself. "You don't *know*? Was it the dreams — "

"No, it wasn't the dreams. Okay? It was... something else. Something that will make you not want to be a woman. *Ever.*"

Morgana scoffed. "Pfft. I highly doubt that! I am going to be a woman just like Anna Demure!"

Anna Demure was another famous character in the series of comics from "The League of the Brave." Morgana was completely in love with the League, along with what Heather called all her annoying girly friends. They would talk endlessly about the plots, the books, the comics, and the actors who would come to town once a year and put on a huge show for a week that ended with a noisy parade. Morgana desperately wanted to be the beautiful research assistant, Anna Demure, a woman talented in wooing men with stunning good looks that matched her brains. Even though Heather despised Chip now, at one time — long ago — she had secretly been intrigued with him. As the young assistant of the League, known for his small stature and mechanical skill, Heather identified more with his boyish manners. But any mote of interest in the League was wiped clean when Morgana spoke about the main star of the League, Lance Worthingheart.

"I will get a man like Worthingheart, who will adore me and — "

"I am going to be sick," Heather said sternly. "I hate that League stuff. They are all fake. I don't know why you don't see that. Can't we talk about something else for a change?"

"I was on the parade float with Worthingheart..."

"I know, I *know*, Morgana. Jumping sparklers, Morgana, I am so sick of you retelling that story and every time, that insipid man gets closer and closer to you — "

"He is *not insipid!*"

Heather chuckled. "Do you even *know* what insipid means?"

"Yes," Morgana lied. She paused in thought. "It means something very naughty!"

Heather shook her head. "You don't even know what naughty is. My whole knowledge of naughty things... was just matched thought for thought tonight..."

"What do you mean?" Morgana asked, sitting up.

Heather lay back down in her bed. "Go to sleep, Morgana."

Morgana was in no mood to sleep for the rest of her life. "I am going to marry a handsome man, and you... who are you going to marry?"

Heather stared at the ceiling in the dark, peering up at the hinged panel above her bed. It covered the entrance to an attic she wished she could crawl in and hide. "I don't want to marry anybody."

Morgana gasped. "You don't want to marry *anybody?*"

"Why should I?"

"B... because... you... you *have* to marry someone! Who is going to take care of your needs?"

"Look, Morgana. The real world is not all fun and games and Lance Worthinghearts and Anna Demures. Every weekday, I go down to the market square and pass the lives of our city's finest citizens, and each and every one of them is deplorable and miserable. I see men in pubs drinking to forget their wives and their needs. I think most of them want to murder their wives in their sleep, and I think a few of them have actually done it!"

Morgana gasped. Her sister was always saying such shocking things. "That's horrible. You're making that up!"

Heather reflected how many times she had said that very thing with her mother in the last hour. Women *bleed* every *month*? Why in the world would that happen? "I am *not* making it up, Morgana, and for the women? Hah! They are also miserable and needy; trapped in loveless marriages with no ways to change anything. They just have babies and those babies grow up to be drunks and harlots — "

"Heather!" Morgana gasped in shock at the vulgar words.

"Well, that's what they are. And that's what you'll be: looking for a man to take care of you, and while he drinks himself to forget, you will be selling yourself on the street."

Morgana threw herself back into bed. "You're such a horrible person to say those bad words. I can't believe you're my twin sister."

"Fraternal twin. We are not the same like the Covesh twins, Dawn and Dara. Those are identical twins. You are so different than me!"

Morgana slammed her head into her pillow. "I know I know... but I don't even know how we can be related. You're so... mean and bitter."

Heather shrugged. "I am, and I have a lot to be bitter about."

"It's that professor you work for. If you went to public school, you'd be a much nicer girl."

Heather sat up angrily and looked at the dim figure of her sister from the fire escape window light. "Professor Gaylord is a decent man. Sure, he can be gruff, but work is work. And I like working for him. He's not married, he's going to stay single the rest of his life —"

16

"That's what makes *him* so mean —"

"No, it's what makes him a *professional!*"

"So why do you have those night terrors, then? Huh? And sometimes you call out his name." Morgana noticed the pause. "Yeah, didn't know I knew that, did you? Well it's true — "

" — it is *not* — "

"It's most certainly true, Heather. Your bad dreams that you claim are about green trolley monsters with tentacles and giant gears and huge fish eyes and all those things to mother and father are things you made up, aren't they. *You* are dreaming of the *Professor*, aren't you??"

Heather wanted to punch Morgana hard in the mouth. "You be quiet. It's not like that! He is my *teacher* and I have no feelings for him like you do for that... Worthing git!"

"Yooou are in love with the Professor..."

Heather seethed.

"Yooou — "

"If you say one more thing, I am going to make *you* bleed from your privates."

Morgana gasped at the deep, guttural horror of that kind of talk. "I am telling *mother* what you said — "

"Go ahead. You do that. I'll tell her you hump your pillows when you talk about Worthingheart. In the dark."

Morgana was stunned into silence, but Heather could feel the waves of shame crash against her sister's stomach. "Now who is the one with the secret, dear sister?" she said, cruelly. But instead of anger, all she heard was her sister slowly starting to cry. Heather listened to the pitiful weeping of shame for a few minutes before she couldn't help herself, and she wiggled out of the bed, not yet used to the feel of the new garment used to capture the blood that her mother had provided her. She waddled over to her sister, and with great difficulty, knelt by her bed, and stroked her hair.

"I'm sorry, Morgana. I... I didn't mean that..."

Morgana simply wept in response. It was an annoying, wet, snotty kind of crying; the kind of weeping she usually did after being spanked or yelled at by one of their parents. Heather's heart could not turn cold against her own sister weeping with such defeated tones, and felt a little scared that she might have gone too far. She soothed Morgana's hair back, wiping away her tears with the edge of the bed sheet.

"I'll share some of my candy with you tomorrow, okay?"

Morgana nodded with a tense face and sobbed a little more.

"I won't tell mother, okay?"

Morgana nodded in response, and her weeping tapered down to sniffling. Heather hugged her sister and rocked her a little.

Morgana broke the silence with her concerns. "I don't like it when you have bad dreams. I don't... I don't want you to be scared to death. I don't want your dreams to kill you."

"They won't, Morgana. I'll be fine."

Morgana smiled, wiping her face with a sleeve. "You sure?" she asked.

Heather stood up, and stroked her sister's hair one last time. "Good night, Morgana."

"Good night, Heather." Morgana thought it would be best to say something supportive, just to be safe. "I hope you don't have bad dreams, sister."

Heather waddled back to her bed. The irritating garment was going to take a bit of getting used to. "Me too, Morgana. Me too."

But Heather did not go back to sleep that night, just to be safe.

wo
A Sudden Journey

"You don't say?" said the Professor. The man never suspected that he would be speaking to Heather about such personal feminine matters, much less during his morning tea. His implied hints to change the subject went unheeded and he found himself unable to finish his breakfast, especially when catching a glimpse of the raspberry jam.

Professor Drake Gaylord was a well-traveled man of scientific importance in southern Palachia. A retired member of the Queen's Royal Scientific Society, the Professor had a long history of impressive credentials. He had taught in places as high as Upper Palachian University, and traveled the world from the niches of the mountainous and rugged Rokasia down to the remote flat tundra of southern Yurpa. He had crossed the seas, flown in great airships, and dined with the greatest minds of all Palachia. The League of the Brave and royalty themselves scraped and bowed in their attempts to impress him. While his worthy accomplishments left many a man humbled with quiet reflections, the Professor found his twilight years to be filled with jaded bitterness. Nothing impressed him. There were no more miracles of nature, nor great feats of mankind for him anymore. There was only rot in one form or another. The only thing in his world that remained constant was the pumping of the world's heart through the machinery that he had spent his life's purpose focusing upon.

The Professor's lab was in a large building that was mainly sparse due to the noise of the "root machine," a connection to the machinery that powered their world from the Sky Ring, which hung high in the air, to the center of the world where heat and fire lived. One side of his lab was exposed to the gigantic gears and coupling rods that slowly rotated throughout the day. It was not unlike living next to the insides of a giant watch. It was here he had decided to retire, and only required the help of an assistant to do his day-to-day work so he had more time to do research. In his retiring years, he was convinced boys were rude and arrogant, refusing to learn or respect their elders. He ~~never~~ hadn't brought on boy assistants since his teaching days, preferring instead the quiet subservient manner of women to do all the cleaning and cooking for him. But this didn't always work as well as he liked, either.

Heather was the first assistant he had in a while that actually cared about the machines around her. Unlike most girls her age, she was unafraid to get dirty, curious about her surroundings, and asked intelligent questions. And while she was generally quiet and obedient, today was not turning out to be one of those days. Normally the two of them would spend time discussing topics like engineering and politics, but today the Professor was starting to realize that he might lose his best assistant to the allure of ball gowns, bustles, and parasols. It reminded him of his last promising student, whom he lost nearly a decade earlier to the same problems.

Heather was looking over a large cog, and wiping at it with a rag. "And every 28-30 days, I will have to wear sanitary garments for when the bleeding comes," she said in disgust. "Honestly, I had no idea this was normal and I still think she's pulling my leg. Have you ever heard of such a thing? I mean, wouldn't I eventually bleed to death?"

In fact, while the Professor was aware that such a thing did exist, he was also under the pressure of common manners to never mention it; something Heather's mother neglected to emphasize, apparently. The plumbing of the fairer sex was a matter best left discussed in medical terms or not at all. "I *have* heard of such things. Generally it's not spoken about in common discourse. So we shall follow this example and turn our talk to the mechanical business at hand. What do you think of these gears that came by parcel post after you left last night?"

Heather eyed a gear, scanning for any variance in the cog's teeth. Her skills had become very refined; she could tell just by an alteration of metallic sheen that a cog was poorly tempered. This gear, a counterfeit from the west, was one of many recent problems. They were trying to see if they could correct the flaws or at least melt it down for scrap, but the bands of dull matte among the shine of poor polish did not give them hope. Despite the material distractions, Heather had not heard the Professor's last remark, and kept on with her fascination of what she had just learned about adult women. "Mother also said it wasn't to be told to anyone, not even my own *sister*... I wish it were not so. Did you know that all women have this? Even Morgana is going to have it, which is just too rich. Wait until this happens to her. Can you imagine? She'd spend days complaining the discharging colors didn't match her new petticoats."

The Professor slapped down his morning paper on the work bench. "Morgana will deal with it as she deals with all adversarial things in her life; real or imagined. But as I said, I would rather discuss these gears we have been getting from the latest Iron Horse shipment from the west! I cannot abide by these poor standards in conversation or gears. What is your opinion?"

Heather was not pleased that she was not allowed to discuss her new menstruation issues, because she considered the Professor to be an honest scientific resource. However, she was quickly allured by the Professor's desire for her opinion. "I don't even think we can smelt them down. Too many impurities." She tossed the gear back in the packing crate, and shuddered at its incorrect metallic tone as it landed; she could even tell it was off-key. "Are the entire lot like this?"

"The first few gears I pulled seem to be from the same batch. There are too many carbon impurities that suggest a sloppy drop-forged process. I have sent out an announcement to the university, and the Palachian business community is awaiting my judgment. If I say they can't even be salvaged from scrap, they may choose to ignore it. Merchant relations with the west are already strained, and an outright rejection of this matter may be considered too risky. I may have to tell them we can use this for scrap, but still apply political pressure in the form of saying that much will be lost in additional refining processes."

Heather rolled her eyes. "I say tell those brown-eyed bastards to — "

"Heather January? Do not refer to the west in racial stereotypes. It is poor form and the speech of the gutter-born ignorant. They are Rokasians: a proud people not immune to sarcasm and racism in all its forms."

Heather swallowed her bitter comments. The last few weeks had been tense in the lab. The Professor had been getting odd letters in the pneumatic tube mail, and he seemed more and more concerned about what was going on in Rokasia. While she knew substandard gears were a problem, some part of her felt there was something more that itched at the Professor's skin. Rarely was the Professor stern with her so quickly, and she really needed to be on his good side since she had to get some paperwork approved about schooling.

Heather had been allowed to avoid traditional schooling by being an assistant to Professor Gaylord for the past few years. She hated public school, and the school system didn't have a high opinion of her, either. She asked too many questions, and had a "stubborn mind." They didn't like girls to ask so many questions of mathematics and mechanics, and the teachers they assigned to the girls were content with rote memorization and no actual hands-on work except when it came to sewing, washing, and cooking. Heather was the only girl she knew of who had actually touched gears on a daily basis. She was constantly repairing broken things in the house, and had the innate spatial concept common of a high-level engineering student. She frequently took tests on her own using the Deosil-Widdershin frames; a set of exam machines where hundreds of gears spin in all their own directions, and you had to determine if one gear spun one way, what way would another gear in that set spin? She had gotten so skilled at it, that she could tell what test she was going to get simply by the hole patterns in the exam plates that set the machines. So the concept of test on washing powders with various cloths or how many tubers one could add to a standard stew without turning the broth into wallpaper paste were mental torture left for the dulled minds of idiots like her sister. In order for her to be allowed to work with the Professor, she had to have various papers signed, and the Professor was rather negligent of turning things in on time. "Bureaucracy jams progress," he would say, "as paper makes a terrible lubricant." Paperwork made him irritable and difficult to deal with, and one of Heather's jobs was to make sure the Professor dotted his I's and crossed his T's, so to speak. The normal royal and government paperwork seemed to make sense to her, which often made the Professor joke about her sanity.

"They have a new truancy ruling," Heather said. "I need you to stamp this card with your educator's wax signature that states you are an accredited professor and not someone who makes me repair fan belts in a workhouse."

"Ah, the wheels of education have many gears..." the Professor said, but did not seem to change his interest in the subject as he scraped the filings from one of the western gears and looked at it under a microscope. "Oh, this explains a lot. I can imagine that they have no real tempering process. I think they just pour these molds and stamp them. Just look at these markings."

"I will look at them if you get your wax seal while I confirm your suspicions."

"Very well. I suppose I must have you..." the Professor grumbled and started rummaging through his desk drawers.

Heather was peering at the poor alloy grain structure of the shavings when there was a familiar "thump" of metal on wicker, followed by a clatter. She looked over at the end of the room at the pneumatic tube basket, and saw that mail had come in. One of her jobs was to fetch and sort the mail the Professor received on a daily basis. So far today the mail flow had been slow, so this was a bit of a welcome distraction.

"Mail," Heather said, strolling purposefully towards the basket, giving an a subtle extra emphasis on how important she was.

The Professor looked up from his rummaging. "... what stamp is it again?"

Heather opened the tube and slid out a very strange scroll. "The educator's seal!" she called out absently, as she cracked the seal and unrolled the scroll on a small work table. The wax was a strange green color, different from the ordinary dirty brown that made the usual seals. The scroll was soft and did not feel like the standard seaweed parchment, either. And when she looked at the writing, she sighed as it was not in the Queen's Language. The letters looked like small doodles one made when testing the nib of a new quill or fountain pen. They were small and complicated, but flowed together. At the bottom, someone had drawn a picture of a knife with similar lettering on the blade. She guessed that one of the archeology professors had found something, and had sketched it out to give the reader an idea of the shape. Normally these types of scrolls had pictures of mechanical items, not things like swords and knives.

"Professor?" she called out.

"I know I had the seal here somewhere!" the Professor called out from a back storage room.

"You have it in your main desk in the back, next to the work table," she shouted as she shook her head. "I'll get it. Here, you got another one of those weird letters!"

The Professor came from the back, and pulled his spectacles from his waistcoat pocket. "Weird letters?"

"Yeah, like... Rokasian? Something like that? There's a picture of a knife, looks like a double-edged sword of some kind but the measurements he gave are smaller."

The Professor peered at the lettering. "No no... this is not Rokasian. It's..." he stopped in mid speech and left the words drift silently from slowly moving lips. Heather knew this meant he was trying to make sense of something completely nonsensical, or translating something.

"Yeah... Korrr..ise...Korisan?" Heather asked. When she did not get a response, she shook her head. "One of those ancient tongues, anyway. The seal was green, and the mark was definitely Rokasian. Not sure about that knife, though. I have never seen anything like that in one of your letters."

"Oh... my..." the Professor said as he continued reading the scroll. Heather started at his face and screwed her expression in thought. She had seen him angry, jovial, and even a little sad. But this was not an expression she had seen before. It seemed almost... shocked. Around his neck, he had a small stone star, which he absently started to twirl in his fingers.

"What is it?"

The Professor dropped the scroll back on the work table and started to search his bookshelf. Heather had seen him do this when lost in thought, but now he seemed disoriented in urgency as he let books fall to the floor in his rapid quest. Was he shaking slightly?

"Professor...?" Heather asked in an annoyed tone as she picked up after him. "Really, this is a little dramatic don't you — "

"Why don't you shut up for once," the Professor snapped back at her. Heather held back a gasp as the burning comment spread from her ears into her chest. The Professor was rarely so directly rude to her.

"I-I was only trying to pick up aft — "

"Picking up books is your job, and you can do it without speaking unless you want to be sent home early, little lady!"

Heather gasped again, this time she couldn't help but let it escape. She had to suppress the knee-jerk reaction to cry, which she had a lot of difficulty with lately. And it wasn't the first time the Professor responded to her in a feminine form that day. First, he wouldn't talk about "women's plumbing," and then he just called her "little lady" in a severely patronizing tone. When Heather first started, the Professor didn't seem to care what sex she was. He even called her "the lad" to colleagues occasionally, which Heather secretly loved. She hated being a girl and hated its underpinnings and until that day, she loved the Professor for not thinking of her as the lesser sex. But as she stammered to think of a response, she found herself staring dumbly as the scattered books and trying to hold back a tear.

The Professor noticed the pause. "If my tone seems stern it's because I am very busy trying to find — "

"The book you want is **prob**... I mean... most likely in that shelf over there."

"What in the world is the Korisan Tome of... what is it doing over there??"

"You asked me to organize the books a few months ago, remember? I put it with K for Korisan."

The Professor frowned as if he'd been stung by an insect but was far to refined to jerk violently. "There is no K in the Korisan language!" he said angrily as he strode over to the shelf Heather pointed to.

"No, but there is in the *Queen's language!*" she shouted back. She felt two betraying tears streak down her cheeks and she wiped them away violently with her sleeve.

For the next few hours, Heather tried her best to busy herself and stay out of the Professor's way. He had translated whatever he needed to from the scroll, and then placed it in his jacket pocket. That was also unusual, as he never put anything away with any sort of care or purpose unless it was dangerous or very, very important. The rest of the day he was lost in some kind of shuffle, pulling out everything from books on Zoology to maps of places from nearly everywhere. And as he collected works, he wrote down notes in that same mysterious language in his small moleskin notebook. Heather surmised quickly that he didn't want her to know what he was doing.

"I am going to ask you... nicely... to not read my notes," he said with a forced grin, snatching his notebook from the workbench. He paused, as he seemed to sense he had hurt Heather's feelings, but didn't really want to actually make amends as much as hope they would fade away.

"I can't read Korisan," she offered in a polite attempt to calm the tense moment. "I just think it's a pretty language."

"Well then, I am glad the language meets your feminine standards. Perhaps if another ancient people wrote pictographs of lace, ribbons and colorful birds, you would find their culture *beyond* praise!"

"I am not one of *those* girls!" Heather balked.

"Eh," the Professor responded. "I can see it now. First comes... the blood. The change. Then comes the painted face, the bustles and skirts, the endless prattle about boys, and suddenly I don't have an assistant anymore, but someone who tries to manipulate me and weeps at the slightest hint I didn't notice their new hair curl!"

"I am *not* like my sister! I was *never* — "

"Eh! It all changes. I have seen it happen. Soon, you grow a pair of breasts and your brain turns to mush. Just as well. It looks like I am going to have to make an extended trip for several months, and I have no use for you here. I will sign you up for one of the local schools, and you can be more with your kind."

Heather felt her face grow hot with anger and resentment. "What? No!"

"And why not? By the time I come back, you won't even be angry. You'll be at the local soda merchants, chatting it up with the other girls on bustles and garters and 'Oh I wish I had a waist thin enough for a man to grasp with one hand!' It's all the same. I've seen it before."

Heather's face twisted in revulsion. "I would rather slit my own throat! I hate those — "

"You hate them now. But once the blood leaves your brain every month, you'll barely have enough intellect to tell square tooth from a ratchet tooth. Your long, flowing hair would get tangled in the gears anyway."

"I *hate* long hair!" Heather pulled at her own short hair as proof.

"I want you to prepare my trip on the Iron Horse right away as one of your last tasks. I am going to Plana Halo in Rokasia. I want to stay at the Ching Lee Hotel. it won't be listed in most of the major listings, but write it down. I want a room with a study with *no* windows. There is no known departure time. You still have enough blood in your brain to get me a trip planned out, right?"

Heather stomped off. "I have *more* than enough blood in my brain!"

"Yes yes..." the Professor said dismissively.

"Please don't send me to a public school, I *hate* it there!"

"That's what my last female assistant said. Then one day, she got all hot and bothered that I didn't notice how she had curled her hair, or decorated the edges of her eyes with grease pencil. Started weeping. That's when I realized why women are not allowed in universities!"

"I am *not* Anna!" Heather stomped. She had heard tales about the last assistant the Professor had. Anna had flowing handwriting where she put circles on top of the letter "i" and signed her name with hearts. "I am different than Anna! I don't like makeup, I don't wish for longer hair — "

"You will soon enough! No no, apparently your body will go through the change and soon you won't know a gear from a cog. You won't care, either."

"I *won't...*" Heather stomped defiantly.

"For example, isn't it odd that I asked you to do a simple task, a task you would have previously found easy and satisfying, but now that you're a young woman, all you choose to do is bicker with me? That's the kind of changes I am talking about, and if you can't get me an Iron Horse ticket and a reservation, I will dismiss you to the nearest dress shop in the market square!"

"Ching Lee Hotel in Plana Halo, I remember!" Heather pouted. "I'll get you those reservations..." She felt trapped. If she argued, she'd be accused of petty feminine bickering, and if she didn't, the Professor would assume he was right. Either way, she had to figure out a way to get out of going to public school.

The last time she set foot in a public school was two years previously. The Professor stood by her side when she had to hand them paperwork showing she would be tutored by one of the largest brains of southern Palachia.

"You are asking Heather to be your assistant?" the principal asked, incredulously. He was an unkind man, Heather remembered. She had been sent to him many times before when she attempted to correct her teachers, and a whipping wasn't doing as well as it did with the other girls.

"Yes," the Professor answered impatiently, "I am not in the habit of repeating myself. Should I speak louder each time?"

"No need," the principal answered uncomfortably. "It's just a little surprising, given her... academic problems."

"She's smart and has an engineer's mind."

"Professor Gaylord... she's a *girl*..."

The Professor scoffed with wide eyes. "Well, I am glad you pointed that out. I wouldn't want to court a small *boy* by accident."

The principal bristled. "I wasn't accusing you of — "

"No, but your manner implies it. I am well aware that she is a girl and that she has academic issues, but let me ask you, what is the highest level of math you teach?"

"We teach differential calc — "

" — to *girls*?"

The principal smiled and calmed himself. "Professor, we are men of education — "

The Professor looked deeply annoyed. "I know I am, but you are an administrative ink blotter. Please do not refer to me as a member of your kind of guild."

"... men of educational direction. What use is abstract and higher math to a girl? All she needs to do is count stitches and price bows — "

"And that is why she's my assistant. She is none of those things! She is a child of science, mechanics, and a rational mind. No wonder she didn't get along here, because this building is devoid of those things. You are a diploma mill paid for by the Queens treasury to keep all the same-sized cogs churning in unison. Men become servants of the Queen, women become servants of the men. At least I get someone so starved for knowledge that she hungers at my every word. Back when I taught at the universities, I couldn't even get a single young man interested in those things. These men came from your schools. So when I get a child thirsting for knowledge, I wouldn't abandon them to your dry teats. Boy or girl. Just do what you're trained to do: sign the forms, stamp the seals, and Heather will cross your doorstep no more."

Now it seemed all those promises Heather kept in her heart, the heart that swelled with pride that she was more than just a silly girl, were dashed. Her body was betraying her. The second she started some horrific cycle that sets her to womanhood, all the gains she had worked for in the last years were lost. She remembered when she could hold her head up high, mistaken for a lad, passing by those stupid frilly flowers that were destined for servitude. She strode past all men and women with an air of purpose. Now that purpose was gone.

"Have you made those reservations yet?" the Professor asked.

"I am looking up the timetables!" she lied, and then went to go actually do what she claimed to have been doing. She didn't know how the Professor would even do even the simplest of menial tasks without her. Every day, there were letters, paperwork, orders, and ledgers to fill. There were parts to clean, cogs to check, and countless mechanical repairs that they encountered in all the tests and experiments. "I don't know if we have current timetables, the only ones we have are — "

"Don't bother! Just ask for the next trip out to Plana Halo!"

The Professor didn't even know it didn't work that way. The Iron Horse was the large train connected Upper Palachia with Eastern Rokasia, and was the quickest way to get there across the shallow western sea. Unlike traveling by ship, access was strictly controlled as passengers were treated as "specialized cargo," and like all cargo, you had to have paperwork for each end. You couldn't fill out a form for the Iron Horse with a ticket that had, "next one available" as a departure time. As she looked over the form, she noticed a lot of blanks that needed filling. "What will you be doing when you're th — "

"Mind your own business, Heather January!"

Heather gritted her teeth. "When I fill out the form, they ask for the nature of your tr — "

"Tell them I am planning on taking a nice vacation on a beach! Don't tell them a damn thing. I am going on holiday. Doesn't matter what I am doing. Just get the ticket request sent at all speed!"

"Yes, sir!" Heather crudely filled in the blanks on the request form, using a mock exaggeration of the Professor's terrible handwriting. "And what about the hotel?"

"They won't ask."

"It's on the form. You are traveling across countries, they want to know where you are staying — "

The Professor ran up to Heather and stood inches from her face. "If the form asked you to describe your *menstrual cramps* would *you* put it on there?"

Heather was shocked. "Um..." she said, shaking in fear. Then she started bawling. She knew it made her look weak, but she couldn't help it. She cried like her sister did when she dropped a slice of cake on the floor.

"What... what what is this?" The Professor was agitated, as this simple request was getting more and more tangled in Heather's insolence.

"Stop *yelling* at me! I am doing the best I can, don't you see I'll *miss* you?"

The Professor gasped in dramatic astonishment. "You'll *miss* me? Sure you won't miss all the skipping school and all that?"

"I don't want to go and be a girl. I want to work with **you**!"

"But you **are a girl**, Heather January! You have no life here. No future in science or math or ... or mechanical things!"

"That's not what you said when you took me from the school, remember?" She wiped snot on her sleeve absently.

"Oh that is just vile, miss. Those same sleeves are coated with industrial lubricant."

Heather started sobbing again. "Please stop being mean to me, you've never been mean to me like this! I haven't even been this mean to **you!**"

"I..." the Professor stopped, despite himself. He swallowed his anger, desperately trying to gain control over what he thought was the dealings with an insane person. "I am... sorry. Just... don't take it personally. I can't take you with me, obviously, and you can't stay here alone. I have no idea when I'll be back. It could be weeks, months even."

But Heather didn't hear him. All she heard was "stay here alone." And suddenly, some part of her didn't feel so bad. A plan started to form...

Three
Heather's Lonely New Life

People from the lower levels of the Palachian cities were considered a dangerous lot. Mainly laborers and manufacturers, they were a motley mix of various expatriate nationalities, illegitimate offspring, and criminal elements that formed the bowels of civilization. Heather's middle city level was a few levels above what was considered "safe enough for an organized constabulary," so her worries of remaining hidden were mainly lawmen of various types more than any criminal element. Criminals were fairly rare, making the constabulary more aloof and nonchalant than some of their harder working brethren below. During the working hours, her main concerns with being out of school were the police and truant officers.

Heather had seen the truant officers on patrol, but as usual, they were more interested in getting free drinks than keeping an eye out for small urchins skipping school. They never looked for children among the utilities and gangplanks; those places were hot and humid, and their heavy felt uniforms were often too hot and stiff for running after people in such environments. The constant hissing and rumbling also disguised footsteps and the clouds of steam that condensed near cold ventilation ducts often obscured everything in a clingy fog. Heather knew the maps of all the local utilities like she knew the veins on the back of her hand, which helped if she had to suddenly change course, or had to run through them blindly. She made sure to vary her course with every trip she made, and spent the hours alone on utility catwalks and gangplanks near the stone ceiling of her city. There, partially obscured by giant street lamps, she would sit and look over the usual sights one can see of a city up high in its rafters. But it was difficult to stay so close to the realm of smoke and fog for more than an hour before one's lungs became clogged with the slime and grease mixed with the slithering mists. So she had to keep moving. Sometimes she'd stay in one of a few vacant buildings, or curl up in space between two large pipes and catch a snooze in the lazy heat. She had enough sense to know when workers were about, or notice the telltale signs of someone else who was not supposed to be in hidden places. Even though criminals were rare, she knew they still existed, and would not think twice about harming a small person such as herself.

While Heather did her duties planning the Professor's trip down to the smallest details, she skipped one vital task: she did not sign herself up for school. The Professor was so busy with something that upset him greatly, that he only asked her about it twice, and each time Heather made an excuse she needed something from him which he had forgotten. And as he was focused very much on packing and leaving, he never remembered to follow up on the school paperwork. When she got the ticket back for the Iron Horse which, to her surprise, did accept "next departure available" she knew the Professor was really leaving. Amid holding back her tears, the Professor shook her hand, and said he liked working with her, and he would give her high marks and hand over transcripts when he returned. It was insultingly formal, given the several years they had known one another. Heather felt he had dropped her like some wrench socket he didn't need anymore. The Professor stayed behind at the lab for another few days, and then he was gone.

Heather was now an illegal free agent; she was a minor youngster who did not go to any school. As far as anyone knew, she still worked at the lab. Even her parents, concerned with the hustle and bustle of their daily lives, barely noticed Heather's stoic mood. For the first few days, she hid in some areas she knew were secret to everyone but steam and ventilation personnel. Normally, she would have been considered bold and free by the romantic fiction of the time, but she was very realistic about her situation. Unlike the

35

famed gypsy lifestyle of some of the lowest levels of Palachia, she did not have the luxury of a lax social climate run by corrupt and lawless sections of civilization. She lived in the middle levels where people were poor enough to work for their wages, but paid enough taxes to support essential sanitation and constabulary services. Before, she always had the luxury of providing papers to any truant officer who might have stopped her. Signed and stamped by the Queen's Regent Education Department, she always had a small passport to travel as she wished. Usually she was on errands for the Professor, and the small booklet gave her a sense of security as she passed by adults with wandering eyes. In the years she had worked for the Professor, she was only stopped a few times by a new officer in the force who didn't know her face. Now she could not risk being stopped, so she was very cautious. She still had the passport, but it would expire at the end of the week. And if she was caught with no schooling to claim her... she had no idea what would happen to her, but it was probably very unpleasant.

After a few days of eating some stolen cheese and hard tack from her home pantry while pretending to be at work, Heather felt she had to keep moving forward with her plan. The atmosphere of the hidden areas of civilization was dangerous if she wasn't careful, and she knew every day was a risk of being discovered, or worse, attacked by unsavory men who prowled the areas away from the prying eyes of the law. Her mother was beginning to suspect something, too, as Heather's clothing was always far dirtier than normal, and Heather feared her mother would complain to the Professor that her daughter shouldn't be allowed to work in such conditions, given her "new feminine issues."

Heather didn't exactly know what she was doing. She didn't reveal to anybody her plan, because she wouldn't have had a good answer if anyone had asked. Apart from her family she had no friends, as being a tomboy was considered incredibly mortifying for a girl her age. Thus, nobody else would notice her missing. She knew one thing: she would *not* be forced to wear dresses at some dreadful public school like her sister. She was not going to waste her days learning how to cook, sew, dance, and service her future husband in some premeditated destiny set for all women in her society. But what would she do instead? She felt the Professor's lab would be unoccupied, and since he had left in such a hurry, he had most likely neglected to tell anyone he was leaving. The only neighbors they had were a small dance studio at the other end of the building, and one of the floors below the lab housed a small law office. Behind them was a large cannery. The Professor was so dour and cheerless to their neighbors, they never came round except, perhaps, to investigate a noise that had been going on for days. He was even less friendly to their landlord; a woman so scared of the Professor that she only communicated via notes slipped under the door. For right now, Heather had to pretend the Professor was still working in his lab and too busy to see anyone. But after that... what?

Heather had lain awake in bed the night the Professor let her go and hatched a plan. After staying hidden for a few days, she was going to pretend to continue working for the Professor, forge some education paperwork, and then spend the entire time in the lab learning as much as she could about anything and everything mechanical or scientific. She felt if she proved herself as a competent engineer, she would not be asked to act like a lady. And then when the Professor returned, he would see she wasn't some silly little girl with schoolgirl crushes and affections for things named after candy.

Heather knew the Professor would have closed off all the major access points, such as the main door, the service entrance, and probably even the ventilation windows. All were simple common sense security precautions, so she didn't even try those entrances. But she knew his absent mindedness would probably preclude some of the less obvious accesses to the lab. If she could get in through a ventilation shaft next to the root machine or even one of the flues, she could get inside and open up a more convenient way to get in and out.

Down an alley behind some steam pipes there was a hole in a vent grating that was not large enough for a normal person, but for Heather's size, it was just big enough. Or it used to be. In the last few months it seemed her hips had gotten a bit larger than she realized, and this was unusual for her since she was always a little on the undernourished side. Her chest had been getting a little raw and sore as her work shirt rubbed at new developments beneath that alarmed her. Her mother had suggested she start wearing a small camisole, but the very thought of wearing something so feminine, even under her work clothes, was repugnant. The last month it seemed like her whole body was rebelling against her: cramps, bleeding, sore chest, and her pants weren't fitting so well. So when her skin scraped across the ragged rusty edges of the vent grating, she winced and trembled, which only seemed to make the problem worse. She managed to keep down her swearing, as she didn't want people to see where the voice was coming from, but it was a difficult task.

Eventually, using a piece of scrap metal, Heather bent back the sharper edges of the grating and lowered herself down into a small metal box that connected some of the lab's machinery to the pressure vents. There was a huge set of gears and mechanics connected to the root machine she could cross, and her footsteps would be masked by the distant rumbling and clicking that sounded day and night. After her eyes adjusted to the light change, the glow of trolley in batteries cast enough of a dim twilight that helped show her where she was. She quietly tip-toed across the metal, gingerly distributing her weight to make sure the small wooden support struts didn't give way from under her. The root machine innards had gaps that went high above her head through the city levels to the surface, and below her, they went down deep beyond all comprehension. Things that fell down those gaps were things you never saw again, and she did not want to be one of them. When she got to an access panel, it was trivial to pop the rusted screws from the other side with her thumb, but she didn't catch the metal sheet that covered it in time, and cringed as it fell away and clattered a dozen feet below. She stayed still, peering into the darkness, wondering if anyone heard her.

After a few minutes of breathless silence, it didn't seem like anyone had noticed. Heather crawled out the hole and lowered herself down. She had no idea what lay below her. She couldn't see in the pitch black, and she heard the metal plate had struck something complicated when it fell, possibly a work table covered with various objects. When she last left the lab, she remembered that the area was clear and free, but she didn't know what the Professor had moved when he packed for his trip. Usually when he was busy trying to find something, he'd leave the lab in complete disarray. He'd move storage chests, tables, and even entire rows of bookshelves around. As she dangled from the edge of the access shaft on the wall, she swung the tips of her toes in the darkness, hoping to touch something, like the edges of a shelf she had assumed would still be there. Nothing but air met her swinging.

After a few minutes of trying to figure out what she should do, the edges of the shaft started to cut into her fingers. Her nerve of just dropping down straight would have to be resolved because now she couldn't climb back up without a severe amount of pain. She braced herself, and let go, intending to drop straight down.

Despite her intentions, both hands did not commit at the same time. Heather swung wildly to one side and then dropped at an awkward angle into the unknown. She hit something solid to her left, which spun her backwards. The back of her legs hit something else, and for a brief moment she felt the solid floor of the lab hit her back ribs and shoulder blades. Before she could even think to protect her head, her neck and the back of her skull smacked the granite floor with a loud crack.

Heather's next memory was a huge array of lights sparkling in front of her. She didn't know how long she lay in the darkness. Maybe only moments, possibly minutes, or longer. She tried to get up, but more stars swam into her vision with accompanying blinding pain. While she expected to be hurt from the fall, she was not prepared for this level of disorientation. She was aware of a loud ringing in her ears as she rolled back in forth in confusion. Her neck was stiff and felt oddly out of joint. Her stomach heaved in protest as she moved her head, and she wasn't sure if she had vomited or not. She tried to crawl around in the complete darkness, but couldn't get a bearing on where she was in the lab, so after a few minutes of confused stumbling, Heather just lay down and tried to quell the panic.

Eventually, she felt more at ease, and tried to assess the situation. She was in complete darkness on a hard granite floor. Her voice was hoarse and she realized she might have been screaming. Her hair was sticky and crusty, but from what, she couldn't tell. Her whole body ached like she'd been beaten, and as she tried to sit upright, her stomach lurched like she had been spinning around too fast like she did when she was little. And much to her annoyance, she realized she was crying. With much difficultly, she tried repeatedly to stand up. It wasn't easy at first; she had no visual points of reference, and her internal balance was all but gone. Heather stumbled around on her shins and knees until she crashed nosily into the metal access panel strewn on the floor. She dimly realized that a quiet entrance to the lab was now ruined; however nobody seemed to be coming right away to see what the fuss was about. Would someone check on the commotion and then see how badly she had injured herself? While she would have normally considered this a good thing, she realized this would complicate matters; she didn't know if she really wanted to explain how she had gotten that way even though she had a right to be in the lab, technically. Whatever had happened, she was on her own and had to get out of this mess without an adult's help.

After a few more wobbly minutes, she moved to hold herself upright on the edge of a work table, resting across it for stability. She felt a little better, and once she was sure she could keep upright without much assistance, she started to feel her way around the room.

Heather was well aware of the layout of the lab's walls and its surroundings, easily navigating around large pipes and shafts that ferried steam, provided ventilation, or were part of some mechanical equipment. The first thing she needed to do was establish a light source, but the lab had gas lighting, and the gas had likely been cut off at the main valve in the Professor's absence. She also didn't want to alert anyone she was there by suddenly lighting up the entire room. While she probably could have spent half a day feeling around for candles and phosphor sticks, she knew an easier way.

Trolley.

Trolley was the power that fueled the entire world. An alluring yellow-green mineral that glowed brightly, the heat it gave off was used to generate steam that powered everything from the small trams that crisscrossed Palachia to the massive machinery that operated the Sky Ring. Whenever there was something not moved by a person or an animal, trolley was behind it in some way. Due to its volatile nature, it was mined from only a few places, and was considered extremely dangerous for good reason. The Professor had drilled this into Heather's brain for weeks until she couldn't help but recite the rules set to an ancient rhyme as she stumbled in the dark for the large metal storage vault.

> *Trolley is mined from the shallow seas,*
> *And gives us the power to do our deeds.*
> *If trolley is used in your working day,*
> *Remember these rules, and respect their way.*
> *Trolley must be sealed away from air,*
> *Or harm will come to those who are unaware.*
> *Trolley must be kept from the Sky Ring's domain,*
> *For the light from the clouds will kill and maim.*
> *Trolley must be respected as if it's alive,*
> *Or misfortune will befall all who survive.*
> *Trolley is mined from the shallow seas,*
> *And gives us the power to do our deeds.*
> *If trolley is used in your working day,*
> *Remember these rules, and respect their way.*

Heather's fingers found the cold metal latch of the storage locker. She hoped the Professor hadn't fixed the broken latch as he kept saying he would for the last few years and was rewarded when, after a few shoves, the heavy titanium lid opened and warmed her face with a familiar yellow-green light.

Several dozen batteries lay on the bottom of the box, wallowing in a thick yellow-green mist. That mist was dangerous, Heather knew, because it meant one of the batteries had cracked and the trolley had been exposed to air. Trolley exposed to air would quickly degrade and form an acidic and poisonous mist that would slither around the floor and burn the ankles of anyone unfortunate enough to share a room with it. Breathing in trolley gas was an excruciatingly painful way to die. Legends of trolley miners exposed to it ended with their fellow comrades beheading them in order to spare them the agonizing last few minutes of having one's lungs eaten through their chest from the inside. In a more diluted form, trolley gas was also highly flammable. Thankfully, the mist in the storage chest quickly sealed the trolley from the air. As long as Heather did not fall in the storage chest or throw an open flame into it, she would be safe.

The only thing worse than exposing trolley to air or flame was exposing it to "lectromag," a strange and unknown substance that naturally occurred in the sky on the surface of the world. A strange blue/white color, it was considered the snake that hunted trolley from its burrows. When lectromag came in contact with trolley, the explosion was so massive, that it dwarfed all common sense. Even in minute amounts, trolley that had come in contact with lectromag had been known to dig craters miles wide and hundreds of feet deep. Luckily, one of lectromag's properties was it could not function underground naturally, and it could not be stored. This was why most all civilization migrated deep below the surface, and the scant rural towns on the surface had no modern conveniences that trolley provided. Surface people had to work from fuel provided by wood and coal which was both dirty and inefficient. It was because of lectromag that trolley was almost exclusively mined by divers in thick suits underwater. Trolley was never brought to the surface unless it was sealed tightly in mineral oil within titanium canisters.

Shallow seas and flooded mines held vast undersea factories that sized, processed, and sealed trolley in a safer form known as "batteries."

But Lectromag was far from Heather's mind as she looked at the trolley mist that oozed inches over her light source. She eyed a few of the batteries, picking the brightest one. Using a pair of tongs on a winch, she gently removed the heavy cylinder from the locker, and held her hand near it to gauge the amount of heat it was giving off. The cold metal surface of the battery told her that this particular container was safe, and when she was certain the last remnants of trolley gas had fallen from it, she gently carried it over to a work table.

"It never gets old," Heather thought to herself as she looked into the small glass window that held the mineral. Even though the glow was fairly dim, in the surrounding darkness, it shined like a luminescent jewel, bathing her dirty face in a steady greenish glow.

Heather surveyed the lab in the monochrome green light. It was a mess. The Professor must have left in a hurry on his last day, given the litter on the floor and the scattered arrangement of the furniture. She hoped that he forgot to lock some of his cabinets as well, as this would make her plans easier. The glow from the battery, along with the light from the storage locker, was enough for her to complete her chosen tasks, and one of the first things she did was to look for his seals.

After an extensive search, she concluded that the educational seals were missing. The Professor had most likely taken them with him, and while this was a disappointment, Heather had predicted this possibility and had an alternate plan at the ready. In the desk drawer were a few seal imprints in wax the Professor had already made but never actually used. Sometimes it was to test a new wax, but the Professor also had an absent minded habit of making various letters, sealing them, and then never sending them. Heather retrieved a few that she needed and set to work.

Using a fine plaster compound, she made a reverse cast of the wax seals and set them to dry. She then took her battery and hooked it up to a metal casting mold. She carefully turned the dial on the battery, making the trolley inside contact two copper plates within the device. As the trolley touched the oxidized metal, its glow brightened and the battery heated up significantly. She connected this to the bracket in the smelting mold, and set it aside on a fireproof area of the work bench.

Heather then set to work cleaning the rest of the lab up. Her head stung something fierce, and at times it was difficult to move or stand because she would become dizzy or nauseous. She tried her best to clean her hair up in the lab sink, but it was difficult to wash her hair as the bump on the back of her head hurt with sharp pains from even the slightest touch, and even lightly pressing the wound made her sick with pain. She thought of a dozen stories to explain the injury to her mother when she got home, but couldn't seem to concentrate on forming a good story. Often, she had to sit and rest until the spots of lights stopped, or until the room stopped spinning. She had never felt this way before, and was more than a little scared.

When Heather was done cleaning her hair, she closed the trolley storage chest, and was able to find a few phosphor sticks and some candles. After lighting a few hand lanterns, she set to work moving equipment back to a more efficient location about the lab. As she was putting away some of the Professor's books, she came across a few about Korisan and Rokasian languages. Intrigued, she set them aside in a different pile to read later. Using a grease pencil and some scrap paper, she made notes on which books had been moved and which ones might be missing. She didn't have a mental map of all the books the Professor had, since it appeared that he had several thousand volumes in the lab alone, and twice as many in his apartment upstairs, plus a few areas she knew of in storage at the local bank vaults. But she did notice some gaps, and since she had alphabetized them herself, she was able to make some pretty good guesses as to which ones he'd taken with him.

Heather figured out that the Professor had taken a few archaeological lore books with him, along with a few slim books of his own notes, written in cryptic languages, like Korisan and Roka-sian. During a few minutes in thought while redressing her head wound, she decided that the best place to start her own lessons was to learn these languages. She figured this would impress the Pro-fessor greatly when he returned and he would eat his words about her wanting to learn them because they "looked pretty." The mem-ory of her slip up made her cringe. Above all, she would be able to read his notes, which she considered to be of great future value. It was difficult to decide which books she should start with, because unlike children's books, there was no "My First Korisan" with pop-ups and pictures. Trying to think back on how she had learned to read, she remembered teaching her sister with small, easy-to-read books. Often, they were books about "The League of the Brave," which had a lot of action in their comic panels, and the dialogue could be inferred from the action. Unfortunately, there were no Korisan comics, either. All Heather knew about either language that was Korisan was both a subset and a root to Rokasian. To learn one was to learn the other eventually, but she decided to start with Korisan, because like reading books on older machinery, one could learn about new machinery by knowing where it originated from, even if it had evolved. Sadly, there were even less Korisan books, so she set aside a few books that looked simpler in both languages to cross-learn them.

After a few hours of janitorial work, the mold she had set aside was hot enough to melt a small amount of copper. Usually, this process was used to recreate gears or cast a brace on an existing broken gear. Instead, Heather was going to recreate the stamping heads that created the wax impressions. She added a few copper in-gots and checked on the plaster casts. Given that she was working with trolley closely, she didn't bring over the lanterns, but tested a few gas lamps along the walls, and was happy to see that the gas was still flowing, for now. She took the plaster, holding it over a lantern flame until the wax from the wax seal melted and ran out, leaving a negative impression. Carefully, she cleaned out the remaining wax with a small copper brush, and set it aside.

When the copper ingots became liquid and flowed easily in the bowl, she carefully poured the molten copper into the plaster casts and set them aside to cool on a warming plate overnight. She didn't want them to cool too fast, as it might crack the plaster mold or damage the fine detail of the stamp. Before she left, she wound all the clocks and swept up a little. She then made a mental note to *really* give the shop a good cleaning before she started on her journey to prove to the Professor, to prove to *everyone*, that she was born to be an engineer.

As she left the lab, closing the door behind her, she carried a spare key out with her. She said goodbye to the Professor as if he was still there, in case anyone was watching, and locked the door behind her.

The trip home was painful. Her thoughts were dull and faded and her head throbbed mercilessly. On the way to the house, she decided to explain her injuries with something generic and stupid-sounding, thus eliminating the need for complicated stories.

Her mother nearly screamed when she pulled back the makeshift bandage Heather had made. The doctor was summoned at once.

"I was on market square..." she said to the doctor. "... and I was hit on the head from behind. I think I was hit by someone carrying a large packing crate." When asked about witnesses or who saw her or could anyone describe how she was hit, she would say it was difficult to remember and she wasn't even sure how she got home. Or who bandaged her up. Oh woe was her.

"This is very serious," the doctor said. "This is a severe blow to the head, and I can see down to the skull. She split her skin here and here. It's like she must have fallen pretty hard. Look at her back."

Heather cringed, but disguised it as pain. She hadn't thought about the other wounds. Again, she used the "I don't recall, it's all a blur." But this didn't work out as well as she had planned. The constabulary was summoned. Despite her best efforts, Heather's lie was becoming very complicated, and she didn't want that at all. The rather bored and slightly irritated lawman took down notes, but he dismissed her as a silly girl who probably fell or something, which upset her parents, and so the rest of the evening, Heather was forced to listen to her parents, the doctor, and two policemen argue about what was to be done.

The doctor said that the wounds were indicative of being attacked by a thug. The policemen said that nothing of value was stolen, and they didn't have proof she was attacked by anyone. Her father said that she had nothing of value, but the thugs probably didn't know that until after they had searched her. Heather still stuck to her story that she didn't have any memory of what happened. She kept it as bland and repetitive as she could, stating she just walking down market square, pain in the head, crowds of people, and her stumbling home. Sometimes she would also add disoriented comments about not remembering what the police were doing there.

In the end, there was nothing but frustration on both sides. The police established a written case report, and said an investigator would be sent round later in the week. The doctor said Heather would have to stay in bed for the next week, at least. This caused more problems.

"I have to go to work tomorrow, mother," Heather said quietly. While the trolley hooked to the warming plate should be fine overnight, she was not sure about a whole day, and was very concerned about a whole week. Trolley was a lot like an open flame; you never wanted to leave it going unattended for a long time.

"No, dear. He'll understand. Your father is going to see him right now."

Heather swallowed her fear hard. "Um, I don't think he'll be in his lab this late..."

"Oh, you know the Professor. He works late. Just because you leave for the day doesn't mean his work day ends, Heather."

"I suppose..." Heather said. She thought about what the lab might look like. Of course, it would be easy to say the Professor did not come to the door because it was very late in the evening. But what if her father asked around? What if they said they hadn't seen anyone in the lab for days? What if a neighbor overheard the Professor leave? Her heart started to beat furiously as her mind, and while she was dizzy from a sedative the doctor had given her, Heather tried to think of elaborate lies.

Rose January felt that she understood the concern her daughter had. But her health was a priority, and a man of science would understand that. "Since he doesn't pay you, or us, he'll be fine without a girl to wash his dishes and bottles for the time being."

Heather scowled. "Is that all you think I do, mother?"

Her mother smiled. "Of course not..."

"You think I am just his washerwoman?"

"Nothing wrong with that, dearie," her mother scowled back.

Heather bristled in embarrassment. She had momentarily forgotten that her mother was, indeed, a washerwoman. She spent 12 hours a day, six days a week at the local cleaners, doing mostly large linens like tablecloths and hospital sheets. But Heather couldn't help but ask, "Is that... what you always wanted?"

Rose wasn't offended by the comment, but she felt that a formal reply was best given because she sensed this was more than a normal question. Her daughter's attempt to disable the social fabric which bound the rules of society was a common problem, and why she felt her father was sometimes better at handling her odd questions. "Well, when I was your age, I fancied men as all girls do. Of course, my father was a tram operator, and didn't make a large salary. But I settled for love instead of a man who could afford to keep me as a caged bird. Even though I work hard, I think I made the right choice."

"No, I mean... did you dream you'd grow up and be a washer-woman? Don't you ever want something else?"

Rose January sat back in her small stool and tried to think of something encouraging to say. She didn't quite understand her daughter's questions. Morgana's questions about boy crushes and decorative ribbons were more her cup of tea, and deeper questions by her twin sister always seems like something a man might ask to dominate a conversation with other men. Probably the Professor's doings. "I never thought about it, really. It's simply not a question that occurs to women. I don't mind having a steady job. I rather enjoy the satisfaction one gets when making the perfect crease. My boss is very nice. He gives us all bonuses for the holidays."

"You never question your — "

"Enough questions," Rose said as she tucked her daughter in with a warm smile. "I never knew such a chatty little monkey. You have had a hard day and you need your rest. I will tell Morgana to sleep on the sofa downstairs so you aren't disturbed. Your brother will be told not to disturb you either.

"He's five. He will remember that for.... maybe an hour. Then he'll wake me up to tell me that he's not allowed to disturb me."

Rose chuckled. "I will have your sister keep him occupied. Good night, Heather. Get some sleep."

"I will, mother," Heather said. But for a long time, Heather stared at the ceiling in the dark before her eyes finally closed.

Heather didn't know exactly when she awoke, but something troubled her and roused her from her medicinal slumber. She kept thinking about the trolley sitting in the lab. She had left it connected thinking she'd be back the next day, but now it looked like she would be bedridden for a week, and at some point her parents were going to find it odd that the Professor didn't seem to notice. Not only that, but she had to make sure the education passport was sent out, but she could only do that with the fake wax stamp. She tossed and turned, alone in her room, feeling like the empty space was somehow both suffocating her and leaving her exposed. With each throb of her heartbeat, she could feel her wound echo a small twinge against the bandage.

Then she realized she had left the gas lights on. With that disquieting thought concerning exposed trolley, she had enough. Her room had a window to the fire escape. She slowly crawled through it, and escaped the police via a set of steam pipes and cat-walks above the public square. And as she let herself in, she realized she had come in the nick of time.

The green glow of the trolley was far too harsh. It had somehow increased, and the metal in the stamps had heated so much, they cracked the plaster, and melted drops of copper had splattered all over the workplace. As she tried to assess the damage, her ankles itched severely. She attributed it to the fact she had thrown on a pair of old boots, but as she reached down to give them a good scratch, she felt her fingertips burn. As she looked down, she realized the trolley had cracked and was leaking gas all over the floor. The acidity of the gas was eating into her skin.

"Shit!" she cried. "That must have been the leaker!" Or one of them. She had to put the battery away quickly. She set up the tongs on the winch, rushed to the storage locker, and threw open the lid. In the blinding glow that exploded from the locker, she saw green gas erupt forth and spill tentacles over the edge that slithered down to the floor. She gasped in horror, which forced some into her lungs. The burning poison made her gag and stumble as her now melting lungs desperately searched for air. She stumbled backwards and fell onto the floor. Eyes stinging from the fumes, she desperately tried to grab a table leg or a bookshelf within reach top pull herself above the poison fog that was rising by the second. She had to get above the gas. If that trolley was to make contact with the gas lamps...

She found a handhold at the work table and pulled herself up with her severely weakened arm muscles. Then her breasts slammed into the underside of the table. She tried to get higher, but her breasts were suddenly ridiculously huge and heavy. They had never been this big before! The gas was swelling in her chest, pushing the precious air out. She growled in rage, coughing from her trolley-soaked lungs, trying desperately to haul herself up onto the table and out of harm's way. Her skin stung as if on fire, and she looked down to see flesh peeling away from her legs.

As Heather raised her eyes to table level, she saw that the leaking battery had moved. Through the small glass window, she could see that the trolley's mineral oil had leaked out of a crack. The trolley, now exposed to air, was glowing brightly. In the swirling mist in the glass chamber, she saw a large fish eye roll back and stare directly at her. Small tentacles slithered out of the cracked window and the battery started to creep closer to her.

"What is this??" she tried to call out, but her voice was nothing but a hoarse croak as she saw stars. "What are you??" The wound in her head throbbed and she felt it burst open, pouring her exposed brain into the rising green and yellow fog. She grappled with the table, but her hands slid down and she felt like she was falling... falling...

She wasn't aware that she was screaming as her mother rocked her, trying to keep her bandages from coming undone.

"It's okay!" her mother said. "We've called the doctor, sweetie. It's okay, shhh shhh shhh..."

"More blood," said the doctor an hour later. They were outside her door now, thinking that she had fallen back asleep from another sedative the doctor had given her, but Heather wasn't tired or sleepy at all. It was difficult to pretend to be completely still, but she managed to position her head over a cupped hand under her ear so she could hear them in the hallway. "And you say she is still having these nightmares?"

Rose nodded. "They have been happening for the last few months or so, before... you know... the change. To womanhood."

The doctor nodded. "This is not uncommon. The change to womanhood is often traumatic for certain... girls with tomboy qualities. Luckily, they grow out of it."

"Is she going to be all right?" asked her father.

"I am unsure, and am concerned about the amount of blood she has lost. This is not some ordinary bump on the head, you know. She has definitely sustained a concussion, but the crack in the skull may have alleviated the pressure. I have repacked the wound, but unless we get that blood loss under control, we're going to have to hospitalize her."

"I... don't know if we can afford hospitalization," he mother said. Rose was particularly hurt by this statement escaping her lips, as she had lost a child during a difficult birth for the same reason. A long stay in the hospital could financially ruin them.

"I understand," said the doctor. "Perhaps her employer could foot some of the bill? She's an assistant of Professor Gaylord. He is a man of wealth and stature."

"It's worth a try," said her father. "I shall ask him tomorrow."

"Oh no," thought Heather. "No no no..."

"Mr. January, I wish you good luck. Let me know if ambulatory services are required. I will add my examination fee to my earlier bill, but I will not charge you extra for the after-hours visit."

"I will let you know," Bruce said. "Thank you for seeing us on such short notice."

Heather's mind, even with a sedative, was on fire with panic. "They'll find out," she said to herself. "Dear sweet trolley, they will find out, and I'll be in trouble, and my parents will be fined by the school board and..."

Her mind raced as she thought about her family. As annoying as they were at times, and as little as they understood her mechanical mindset, she loved them. She knew that a fine from the school board would make them lose their house at least. One of her parents might be jailed in debtors' prison, perhaps both! Leaving her and her family as street urchins in the lower levels of the city. They didn't have much money to begin with, but her father's job as a difference engine accountant was a steady job. Her mother worked hard as a washerwoman, which filled in the gaps. And when her older brother left to go to Upper Palachian College, they had one less mouth to feed, and another possible income source when he graduated. Heather realized that her actions could cause the entire family to become undone.

"No," she said determinedly. "I have to make things right."

The nightmare of the trolley gas was still fresh in her mind, and fear clutched within her chest. She had to think of something, and fast. She knew she had to get back to the lab, get that education paperwork sent off, the trolley put back in storage, and somehow make it look like the Professor was still working there.

Her first problem was the time of night. Like most of civilization, she lived deep underground where the solar cycles of the surface were but a mere curiosity that didn't match the orderly 32 hours a day below. The hours were divided into 16 for work, 16 for non-work, and of the non-work, 8 of those hours were for emergency or maintenance people only with 4 hour bumpers to allow for travel, shopping, and social life. To be out during that 8 hour window was expressly forbidden, and difficult to violate because the constabulary patrolled the catwalks, piers, and gangplanks that provided a good vantage point for the city below. While she could sneak among the steam pipes between city levels, some of them were so hot that touching them with bare skin would cause second degree burns. It was the same with ventilation and cooling shafts which had metal bars at various points to prevent people escaping from the law from traveling that way. Normally, she might have been able to do it if she had all her faculties, but she had a head injury, and was under two doses of a sedative.

This meant she had to travel in plain sight. She considered pretending to be a policeman or maintenance worker, but even if she posessed a custom-made uniform from a costumer's shop, her height and youthful face would be a dead giveaway. They would demand papers. And since she didn't have a costume, that point was moot anyway.

Heather passed her sister's empty bed, poked at the fire escape panel, and looked outside. When she and her sister were very little, they would often go out to the fire escape and look at the street below them. Their small row house was one of many dirty brick houses on their street. Across the way was a small sweets shop. She and Morgana would drool in envy at the wealthier kids coming and going as they pleased. Almost as if on cue, a policeman came into view and waved his nightstick at Heather until she closed the panel.

She exhaled nosily through her nose in frustration, then stared down at her dirty toes, wiggling them in thought as she usually did when she had a very tough puzzle. Her mother hated that she didn't take care of her nails like Morgana did. Her sister actually painted her toenails robin egg's blue and kept them clean and washed which seemed pointless because she wore spats and boots like everyone else in her school. Heather wore work boots most of the time, which scuffed and split her nails like a common laborer. She was proud of that.

Through the crack in the panel, she heard shouting. It sounded like the typical banter of maintenance people, but after she listened to a few words, she figured out it was the ice men. It was ice delivery day which meant a huge block of ice would be dropped into a small box near their kitchen, cooling meats and certain vegetables while delaying mold and flies for a while. Unlike the wealthier folk who could afford to buy their food daily, for the January's semi-working class, they often bought food when it was cheap and discounted from age. The icebox kept it from rotting for another few days, sometimes longer.

A few years ago, Heather and Morgana went on a class trip that had explained the origin of the ice. Morgana was bored out of her mind, but Heather was, as always, fascinated by the process. Huge sheets of ice were brought in from the north where they were then cut and packed into cubes. The cubes were then sent to city centers, where the ice men could distribute them to the places that needed them. Even the Professor's lab had an ice box for various experiments.

Suddenly, Heather's brain clicked. Ice men often wore uniforms what were nothing more than a standard canvas jumpsuit. In storage above her room, she had such a jumpsuit from a school play she had been in where she played a plumber. It was baggy on her back then, because they'd gotten it second hand from a friend of her father's. Would it still fit?

Quickly, she moved a chair next to her bed, and slid aside a small door in her ceiling. With great difficulty, she heaved herself up into the small crawlspace and looked for a box with some of her old school clothes in it. The jumpsuit was right on top, and a few minutes later, she was overjoyed to find that not only did it fit, it fit well. She decided from then on that she'd keep it because it further removed the girlish look more than just a work shirt and britches.

Quietly, Heather tip-toed down squeaky stairs barefoot, her work boots dangling from her fingers. She passed her sister, snoring softly on the couch, her bare legs and robin-egg blue toes awkwardly poking out from under the quilt. Heather had to suppress the urge to tickle her feet as she usually did when she caught her sister in this way. She then went back to the rear service door, and waited for the ice men. She didn't have to wait long. Heather heard them open the panel and slide the huge block down a chute where it banged noisily into its slot. She waited a few moments, then opened the back service door into the forbidden period air.

The ice truck was right in front of her. Several men were hauling ice around in big tongs, cackling away in their northern Palachian tongue. Heather knew some of the words they used, and without missing a step, she joined the work force and followed the ice cart to the market square; slowly carrying ice on her back, working like a man.

Northern Palachian men were usually pretty small and stocky. While Heather might have appeared slender, she imitated their mannerisms and slump with such precision, even the men themselves would make raunchy jokes at her. She would punch them in the shoulder in response, repeating phrases without missing a beat. By the time she reached the market square, she felt invigorated and strangely satisfied at the heavy work and the fact that she fit in so well.

When a moment presented itself, Heather took her tongs and an ice chunk, and headed over to the lab. Using her keys, she opened up the servant's entrance and entered the lab from the rear. Relieved to see the trolley was as she left it, she slowly turned the dials of the battery down. The warming plate was hot, but still cool enough to touch. With a gentle tap against the store tape, she broke the plaster and dunked the copper stamps in water. Quickly, she assembled the school paperwork, double checked her work, signed a false signature, and sealed it with the new stamps. Then put it in a pneumatic tube, and sent it on with a satisfactory clucking and hissing sound.

Next, Heather then gathered a few choice books and tied them together. Then she wrapped the books with shipping paper and put her address on them. Using a small package pickup form, she filled the request in her professor's style of messy script, and when she was done, she put the slip in a tube and sent it along its way. When she saw the tube get sucked away, she slowly opened the main door, checked for anyone strolling by, and placed the package of books by the door.

Quickly, she placed the battery back in the storage locker, and closed the lid. She turned out all the gas lamps, and after checking a few things, she darted back out the service exit and headed back to her ice wagon.

It was gone.

Heather stopped. "Oh, no," she said in horror. Then a huge hole in her plan seemed very obvious. How was she going to get back? Even if the cart was still there, it wouldn't have gone back the same way. Panic and embarrassment at this flaw spread across her chest like hot syrup and she almost peed where she stood in fright. There she was, right in the middle of market square, in a jumpsuit, with no way to get back home without being seen during maintenance period. Her mind started to spiral out of control with dumb panic but she took a few deep breaths and tried to think things through.

She could always go back to the lab and wait for the maintenance period to be over, but then her father would be awake. How would she sneak back in? Could she wander the streets, claiming to be delirious from the head wound? She didn't want to try that because she was already being thought of to be sent to the hospital, and if her father asked the Professor for help, he'd find he wasn't there and... then everything would unravel. But she knew she couldn't just stand here, so she just walked back towards her home in a nonchalant manner, hoping she would not be stopped.

Then Heather remember she once read in a book that all successful thieves operated under the principle that "hidden in plain sight" was always the best if one could manage it. Trying to appear suspicious and hiding would invite trouble, so, with nothing else going for her, she boldly walked down the main avenue with her ice tongs, shouting various phrases she had just picked up. It seemed to work; she passed by maintenance men and police alike who never even looked her way. Just another common laborer delivering ice on its standard delivery day. It seemed too easy.

In fact, she was doing well until she got to her street, less than a minute's walk from her home. There was one lone man who stopped her. He said something in northern Palachian that seemed oddly forced, like he was trying to appear nonchalant. There was something off about the man, but she couldn't quite place it. The look in his eyes as he scanned her dirty face wasn't quite normal, and Heather had a creepy feeling that something was very wrong. He wasn't a policeman, and he wasn't an ice man. Just... a man wearing a work shirt and britches. Why was he out during a maintenance cycle?

Heather quickly said a few random things as she passed by him, but the man grabbed her shoulder with his meaty hand and said in the Queen's common tongue, "You're not northern Palachian, are you?"

"Wot?" Heather tried to ask in her best Northern Palachian accent.

"What's a young lad like you doing out this late at night?"

"Oo are yoo?" she asked. "Get ye 'ands off may."

"You want me to call the cops? You want me to tell on you?"

Heather said nothing. An odor of wickedness seemed to ooze from the man's crooked yellow teeth. His grip on her shoulder was firm.

"I see a copper right now, lad. I can call him over here. You want that? You want?"

Heather shook her head, buying time. She was so close to home, but she was still a block away. She didn't know what to do. "What do you want?" she asked, her voice heavy with defeat.

"I want you to come with me. Quiet. Say no word."

Years earlier, Heather remembered a poem told to the girls in her class about strange men like this. "Don't go with them, no matter what they say," she was told. "Call for help, and find an adult right away." Of course, that wasn't going to be easy, a fact this man probably relied on. Heather had but one option.

"Alright," she said, thinking quickly. "Don't tell mum I came to the upper levels."

The man snickered. "Your lie is safe with me if you — " But he was cut short as Heather's ice tongs smashed into his face. He screamed in pain, calling for the police. Heather dropped the tongs and bolted down the street as the man called out, "**Police!! I've been mugged!! He went down there!!**"

Even with her head throbbing horribly and the sedative still fighting to keep her calm, Heather bolted down the main corridor. She heard police whistles as she ducked down the alley and darted into the service entrance to her house. She ripped off her boots, and quickly passed her snoring sister as quietly as she could. Without making a sound Heather ran up ran up the stairs, the fear and adrenaline ringing in her ears.

She heard knocking of their front door. Then pounding.

"This is the police, open up in there I say!"

Raw fear pushed Heather past her parent's bedroom and just as she dashed into her own room, she heard her father shouting, "I am coming down!!" Heather quickly pulled off the work suit, and tossed it under the bed. She tossed on her nightgown, and then looked down realized her skin was filthy.

"Shit!" she said. She looked around, and found that the washbasin was still thankfully full of water and the washcloth was right beside it. Rapidly, she took the washcloth and wiped herself down, scrubbing away at the grime a honest night's work gave her. She tossed the rag under her bed and quickly crawled into bed just as her mother came in.

"Heather, are you okay?"

Heather rubbed her eyes and acted as if her neck was too weak to support her head. "What's that noise?" she whimpered.

"Honey, the police are here. They say someone has come into our house. Come with me."

Heather acted disoriented. "What...?"

"Honey, I know I know... but just to be safe."

"But the sed... daded.. ative makes it hard to... walk..." she whined.

Rose quickly picked up her daughter and carried her down the hallway. "I'll carry you, sweetie — " she was interrupted when two gun-wielding policemen ran up the stairs. "Ex-*cuse* me!"

"Madam, we didn't find him downstairs, we think he's up here."

"What?" Heather asked sleepily.

"My daughter is very sick, you know!"

"I found something!" screamed one of the policemen from her bedroom. "I found his work suit!"

Heather cringed. What now?

"Oh dear," her mother said, running down the stairs with her. "Bruce? Bruce? What's going on?"

"It's okay," Bruce said. Morgana was sitting upright on the sofa looking dead to the world.

After a few minutes, the policemen were done searching the house, and the entire family was assembled in the living room with a sergeant was pacing back and forth. The smell of freshly brewed tea was drifting in from the kitchen.

So let me get this straight," he said. "The assailant came into your room, but you don't remember what he looked like?"

"She said she was asleep!" Rose said for the fourth time.

"Yet he had the time to disrobe in the minute he had inside your house. Are you harboring a fugitive?"

"I would *never* — !" started her father.

"Calm down, Mr. January. Standard procedure. I needed to ask..." The sergeant looked at Heather's father with stern interest before continuing. "...I need to ask everyone. Now, we found a pair of boots in the service area where the young man entered. Do these belong to anyone in the family?"

"Those look like Heather's work shoes," Rose said.

Heather wanted to disappear. Everything was falling apart around her. Work suit on the floor, boots in the kitchen.

"Are these your shoes?" the sergeant asked Heather.

"I guess. I don't know."

"You don't know your own shoes?"

"They are the same shoes as everyone else's. Just work shoes," she said sleepily.

"How come a little girl like you would wear work shoes?"

"I work for the Professor..." Heather started to say, but trailed off because what if they called him to verify? Before Heather could finish her sentence, however, the front door opened, and the yellow-toothed man stepped in with an officer.

"Ah, Mr. Bushington," said the sergeant. "I just have to have you answer a few questions. This won't take long."

Heather froze where she sat. Even though the man was not looking at her, she could feel his presence like some kind of cat looking for rats in the pipes. It felt like her world was narrowing in on her, squeezing a confession of all sorts of things, but she was so deep into the lie there was no getting out. Her mother, out of parental instinct, held Heather closer to her.

"Who is that?" Rose asked.

"This is the man who claimed assault. He says that the assailant who tried to mug him went inside your service door. He claims that — "

"I don't *claim*, I *report* that he did!" Mr. Bushington picked a few stray hairs from his work shirt, and looked around the room like a hunter about to strike down prey.

"Mr. Bushington *reports* that the assailant, a young boy, went into your house. Now, we think the boy ran into your daughter's room and ran out the fire escape, but Mr. Bushington was watching the fire escape and said he saw no one leave." The sergeant grabbed Heather's little brother Neil and pushed him in front of Mr. Bushington.

Neil was only five, and he wasn't technically Heather's brother, although he was related. He had been with the family since birth when his Heather's aunt, Neil's biological mother, had died in a factory accident. Both Heather and Morgana were very protective of him, even though they teased him mercilessly. As he was presented before the sinister Mr. Bushington, Neil started to shake and sob as Mr. Bushington tilted his head up to get a good look at him in the light of the doorway lamp.

"This lad is guilty of something..." the sergeant said with a smirk and raised eyebrow.

"**The child is five years old, and not a criminal!**" Mr. January said, yanking the child from Mr. Bushington's grip. "And if you are *so* interested in investigating these sorts of things, perhaps you'd like to solve the case of who hit my daughter on the back of her head a few days ago!"

"Bruce..." Heather's mother said. "Please... we know he's not guilty. I doubt that Neil had the strength to mug anyone even if he could get out. Plus, he doesn't have a worker's jumpsuit."

Mr. Bushington focused on Heather, his eyes pushing into her like the ice pushed into an ice box: cold and stiff. Heather retracted into her mother's bosom but Mr. Bushington grabbed her head and yanked it forward.

"Ooowww!" Heather cried out, making sure to punctuate the air with a believable pain.

"This girl *was in bed under a sedative* while you came barging in!" exclaimed Rose, as she pushed Mr. Bushington away. "Someone struck her head from behind two days ago, and no one seems to care about this, but oh wow, an assailant on a town drunk, well, that *is* important — "

"I want to see her in better light, drag her to the lamp!" Mr. Bushington commanded.

"Now see here, by *what authority* — " Bruce January grabbed Mr. Bushington's arm, but it was twisted out of his grip as Mr. Bushington whipped out a folded leather wallet and flashed a blue badge.

"By *this* authority," Mr. Bushington said with a satiated grin. "I am a truant officer!"

There was a long pause in the room. Heather started wishing deeply in her head that she could vanish. This was the end.

"Well," said Bruce with a hidden smirk. "If that's the case, then you know the difference between a boy and a girl?"

"What?"

"The difference. Between a boy and a girl. You said the assailant was a boy. You can *plainly* see this is our daughter."

"That is what you said," the sergeant agreed, looking at his small notepad. "You said that a boy hit you with a pair of ice tongs. A northern Palachian boy five feet in height. The only boy registered at this address is this small lad here, and he does not fit the height description. And this is a girl, and nobody in this address is of northern Palachian stock or build."

"I am well aware of what I said!" Mr. Bushington. "I'd like to see if those boots and that that jumpsuit fits this child..."

"Then perhaps you are trying to soothe a damaged ego," Bruce suggested. "I am not sure why a truant officer is working in plain clothes during maintenance time, since I believe if you are flashing a badge as a true official, you would be working in your given uniform. Tell me, Mr. Bushington, who *else* saw this assailant?"

Mr. Bushington gritted his teeth as the policemen looked at him.

"Any of the constabulary here? Did any of you see this boy thug hit him with a pair of ice tongs?" Bruce looked smugly around the room. "That must have been some strong boy, Mr. Bushington."

Heather felt she should have felt relieved the pressure was being lifted from her impending confession, but instead she felt deeply ashamed that her father was carrying her lie on his own shoulders.

"I suggest that it was not a boy, but a man, who ran into my daughter's room. But why did he take off the jumpsuit? So we have a naked ice vendor running loose, do we?"

Some of the policemen snickered.

"Can I see this... grievous injury the ice tongs did to you?"

Mr. Bushington aggressively poked at the huge red welt across his face. "This wound does not lie, Mr. January!"

"Oh, that is a *big* wound, Mr. Bushington. Does it hurt? Hurt badly?"

"Damn right it does!"

"And you are saying that a strike by one of two twelve year old girls or a five year old boy could do that damage to your face? Not a fall perhaps? Or a fight with a northern Palachian ice worker who was sick of your sass and dander?"

Mr. Bushington said nothing, but gave Bruce a stare of death.

"Have you been... drinking? Mr. Bushington? Where were you right before this happened?"

"I have *not* been drinking, and I was under assignment by the city to find truant children who — "

"Oh, you were under *assignment!*" Bruce said. "By the city! And I assume incognito? Is that why you're not in your blue truant uniform?"

Mr. Bushington glared in response.

"This is part of the new policy to crack down on wayward children, I assume. Part of why my children have to have valid identification and papers showing where they need to be at all times?"

"That's right..." Mr. Bushington said cautiously.

"So, I can simply go to the city records and find your assignments as public records."

Mr. Bushington remained silent.

"Oh, but I am sure the police will take care of things. They saw your badge. They'll just verify your presence and license to be out and not bother you on your ... secret rounds..." Bruce looked at the sergeant.

"Right, we can... we can do that..." the sergeant said. He looked like he'd prefer to drop this whole embarrassing incident, if possible.

"Good, then I think we have this cleared. You find the man who fits that jumpsuit, and Mr. Bushington will show you his papers. Maybe you can help one another catch this..." Bruce looked at Mr. Bushington's welt, "violent and strong apprehender."

When the police left, the house went quiet. Heather pretended to be asleep.

"Well, that was exciting," Bruce said. "Just to be safe, I want to have a good look at the house, and make sure that all the doors are locked. While four policemen searching the entire place yielded nothing, I know all the nooks and crannies one could hide. Rose? Stay with the children. I will report back every few minutes. If I don't report back or respond to your calls, get help."

Heather didn't remember anything after that, as she didn't have to pretend to be asleep anymore.

𝔉our
Hitting the Books

"Wake *up!*" Morgana shouted, shaking Heather.

"What...?" Heather said noisily into her pillow.

"You have a package," Her mother replied as Heather turned to face the day. "It arrived this morning by express."

Heather looked at the huge stack of books wrapped in paper and twine and pretended to look surprised. "What is it, mother?" she asked dumbly.

"It's a stack of books from the Professor," Rose replied. "And there's a note, but I can't make out his handwriting."

"Why would he send me books?" Heather opened the letter and looked at her own imitation of the Professor's scratch handwriting looking back at her. "Dear Heather," she read. "I heard about your injury. Just as well, I have to leave town for a week. Please study and memorize the following books in my absence, and you will be tested upon my return." Heather balked convincingly. "*Books?* I have to *study* with a *head injury??* Un-*fair!*"

Morgana laughed. "Ha ha! My dear sister has to work after all."

"That was rather cold of him," Rose said.

Heather pretended to sulk. "My god, there must be 7 or 8 books! How am I expected to memorize them in a week?"

"I thought you liked reading?" Rose asked.

"I do... but that's just... *boring!* It's all about language and things."

Morgana laughed again. "I bet you wished you'd be in my school. I am learning how to make hats!"

Heather stuck her tongue out. "Good for *you*. Now you can cover that ugly head."

"Mother!" Morgana whined.

"Morgana, your head looks fine. Heather, don't tease your sister just because she started it."

"But she — oh." Heather realized her mother had preemptively cut her off at the argument. Her mother was wise in the ways of sibling rivalry.

"I guess that's why he didn't answer when your father went round to his office this morning. It's so hard to tell with that man. I wonder why he didn't deliver them in person?"

"I don't think he can carry them..." Heather said with wide eyes. She moved the books around on her bed. It seemed so out of place to see some of these ancient tomes resting on the banal and familiar bed quilt she had known since she was little.

"They were only 80 pounds, really..." Rose said. She was proud that her strong arms and back also made her an excellent washerwoman.

Heather was subtle in the art of parental manipulation. While Morgana had made clumsy attempts at flattering their parents, usually their father, Heather had a good sense of people's underlying needs for approval, and she keyed on it. In fact, Heather's talent in finding the underlying truth is what helped her become a good mechanic. People were not so different, she discovered, from the machinery that surrounded their life. They had repeating patterns, one process always influenced another like gears, and everyone needed to let out a little steam once in a while.

Still, in the last month, Heather saw her options closing in on her. While her parents agreed two years ago she could become the

Professor's assistant, it was becoming apparent they had thought this was a temporary thing and it would pass. When Heather's mother looked at her daughter spreading huge books across the bed, she sighed a little in frustration. Heather knew that sigh. It was the sigh of someone who felt like good times would not last, like when little Neil would make some statement that the Market Square was an amazing and wonderful place. Neil was not aware of the pickpockets, thieves, and danger of being run over by a horse-drawn cart. Heather tried not to think about the future. She had tried not to notice there were no girl mechanics. She tried not to think about the moment when society would insist she wore a dress in public, and not work pants. And as her budding chest became sore, she tried not to think about her body betraying her with the trappings of a woman.

"I will leave you alone here as I go to work, but make sure to rest yourself frequently. I am sure the Professor can deal with you studying less and recovering more." As Rose stood up, her ankles popped gently. She grunted and sighed. "Come on, Morgana. Time for school."

For the rest of the day, Heather set upon learning Korisan and the branched language, Rokasian. She quickly learned that it was not a language with an alphabet like the Queen's Language. There was no 'A = squiggle with a hat' simplicity. It was more like 'squiggle with a hat means one this in the front of a sentence, but a different thing in the back, except when paired with two lines in a triangle, then it means something else entirely.' The books were terrible at translations, and she found the Professor's own hand-written scrawl to be more helpful than the actual book itself. Most of Korisan was a pictograph language, except when it wasn't, and it was driving her mad. She was having so many problems finding the underlying pattern.

Before she knew it, her father had came home. He had picked Neil up from his primary school. "Is it Hour 26 already?" Heather thought. She looked at her bedside table and realized that she hadn't eaten any of the food her had mother left behind.

"I knew it," her father said, coming in her room. "That man was a truant officer, but he was not on any assignment!"

"What man?" Heather faked innocence, as she had planned earlier. She felt the best way to avoid questions was to play stupid, which made her wonder, briefly, if her sister's entire life was a giant act.

"The man last — oh, you probably barely remember."

"I remember a lot of noise and police, but I thought it was a dream."

"**There was this bad man who grabbed me!**" Neil said several octaves above polite.

Her father chuckled and shook his head. "I bet you can't remember because of the sedative the doctor gave you. How's your head?"

"Better, I put another dressing on it. And the headaches are subsiding..."

"Let me have a look..." her father gently peered beneath the bandages, and it made Heather feel a little ill from the pain it caused. "Not a lot of blood. Good good..."

"Is she still bloody and gross?" Neil asked as he ran across Heather's books holding a model airship aloft.

"Yeah... like really gross with chunks of brain and skull!" Heather said with a cruel giggle.

"Ewwww! ...I wanna see!" Neil pined.

"There will be no skull viewing this evening. Let your sister rest." Neil obliged and ran out of the room, stomping off to his own bedroom. Bruce looked down at the bed, looking at the collection of books. "Dear me," he said. "Is all this your homework?"

"Language studies, yes sir..."

"That looks like Rokasian..." Bruce said, looking at a few loose papers. "You studying in Rokasian?"

"Trying to."

"Your older brother had to study a year of that before he went to the University. He hated it. But if he wants to be an engineer working on transcontinental rail, he had to learn basic Rokasian."

"Each letter... well, symbol, is its own word," Heather said. "And the context changes depending on where it is. But I think I have an idea as to why. I bet it has something to do with grammatical structure. Like where verbs and nouns are placed, you know?"

Bruce chuckled. "That's my daughter. The mind of an engineer. I can't believe I have a little girl as smart as a young man twice her age. You'll make a formidable wife to a lucky man someday."

Heather bristled. She knew it was meant as a complement, but still. "What if I chose not to get married?"

Bruce smirked. "Oh, boys seem icky now but... wait until you find a charmer in a vest coat... you'll soon change your tune."

"If I am to marry, I'd rather marry books and machinery. They are more predictable."

Bruce shook his head. "You sound like how a man describes a woman. A lonely, single man." He smiled to himself and continued, "Well, you're 12 years of age. In two years, you'll be right alongside your sister, doing your hair and — "

Heather made a face. "Father? If you please...!"

"Okay, okay. Boys are icky." Her father patted her knee and stood up from the edge of her bed. "Don't grow up too fast but... don't forget to grow up at all..."

The door slammed. Morgana was home from school. She thundered up the stairs and burst into their bedroom, carrying a large scroll.

"You'll never guess who's coming to town oh dear oh dear!!"

There could only be one thing that made her sister act like that.

"Worthingheart *and the League of the Brave!*" she screamed.

"That's not fair, you didn't give me time to guess," Heather replied with heavy sarcasm. Heather could not stand Morgana's obsession with the League of the Brave and its crown jewel of a darling, Lance Worthingheart. "Besides, they come every year. And every year you act as if it's the first time you... you're not even listening, are you?"

Morgana unrolled the poster on their wall. The huge hand-colored woodcut print showed the entire League in some kind of stilted, stylized action pose. Even though Heather despised them, the constant saturation of advertising throughout the years had not skipped past her altogether. She looked at Chip LaCroi, the small but cocky boy sidekick grinning like a damn fool, and wondered for a moment what kind of life he must lead. She then shook the idea from her head and focused back on her books.

"Lookit Goggles and Anna! Oh how I wish I could be beautiful like them!!"

Lynn "Goggles" Stellard was the second in command to Lance, and a female hero to all. A kind of mother figure to the group, she kept everyone in line with a spoon in one hand and a wrench in the other. Heather often wondered how anyone could accomplish what she could do wearing a corset and bustle; her only weapon a parasol and some kind of gun she could barely fit into her feminine hands. Anna Demure, on the other hand, was an annoyingly passive brainy girl, who seemed to lose all sense of loyalty and wit the second a man wooed her. Heather thought her a slut who would be completely lost without her books, and she despised the treacherous cow.

The rest of the League were stereotypes that were just as bad. There was Chang Daggerton, a dark and handsome Roka-sian assassin from the mysterious western lands. For those who preferred darker men, Massood Swarth was the mysterious dark-skinned mentalist from mysterious eastern lands of Yurpa. There was also Stone "Rocky" Pillar: the League's blond-haired brute, a strong and capable mechanic whom Chip adored; the two of them were inseparable. In fact, Chip and Rocky had their own comic series which Heather used to read when she was very little. She'd given it up, however, when she realized she was being pandered to fall in love with Rocky and see Chip as some kind of fantasy child they had together.

Overall, Heather really hated the entire League because she saw them as an unrealistic comic series that happened to have live actor counterparts who would do plays, shows, lectures, and other public appearances. The entire city would go crazy when they showed up every year, and the main parade they had was simply the worst, in her opinion. There would be a main float with the entire cast on it, waving to everyone lined up on the street. The Queen would have her mock knighting ceremony, flanked by an impressive number of soldiers. Guns with blanks would be fired. Calliopes would play. It gave Heather a headache just thinking about it.

"You're not going to put that poster up in — "

"*Our* room? Yes. Yes I am."

"Oh, no you — "

"Heather?" their father said. "Relax. Let her have her fun. You used to like — "

"*Used* to, father. Until I realized how fake they are."

"They are not fake!" Morgana said, looking at Lance with half-closed eyes. "I have seen them for myself when he brought me on his float — "

"Oh, for the love of... Morgana, I do not want to hear that story for the hundredth time about how you got taken onboard Lance's float in the parade! I am *so sick of that!*"

"Heather, Heather? Honey, don't be like that to your sister. That was a happy memory of hers, and we must respect that."

"I used to have a pin and everything. Lance gave it to me! That was until Sandra Plovers stole it from me!"

Her father gave her a stern look. "Now now, Morgana, we don't know that for sure. You still could have lost it."

"I didn't lose it! She stole it from me in the bathroom!"

Heather sighed aggressively and blocked her view of her sister's poster appreciation ceremony with a book. "Can you at least be quiet so I can get some of this studying done?"

Bruce patted Heather's knee again while looking at dreamy-eyed Morgana sighing in the presence of a woodcut of an actor. She had spread the poster upon her bed and weighted it down with dolls and pillows. Her father went to her, and snapped her out of her trance with a grin. "I'll get some poster glue and we can put that up near your bed, okay sweetie?"

"Oh thank you father I will go to bed with Lance and wake up to him oh dear oh dear oh dear!!" Morgana crooned as if she had just been promised cake for every meal for the rest of her life. As she stomped down the stairs after her father, Heather once again noticed the ringing in her ears that always seemed to be present when Morgana finished talking. How come she had to be so loud? Once Heather had put in ear protection from work, showing the small cotton earplugs as a form of protest at the dinner table. Her parents had not been amused.

Heather decided to eat some food so her mother wouldn't complain. She wasn't at all hungry. The sedative seemed to have affected her appetite. She tried to wolf down slices of bread and cheese, before tackling a small tuber, until she felt like she was going to throw up. It was during this calm pause to prevent vomiting that Morgana came up with the poster glue. The smell was pungent and fetid like a corpse.

"Help me put this up!" she demanded.

"Father said he would help you with that — "

"I can't wait! He started talking to the doctor at the door and he'll take forever!" Morgana started pulling hard at her sister's arm.

"She's gone mental," Heather thought. "Morgana, stop! I am going to be sick, please do not — "

"Help me put this up!" Morgana commanded, yanking her sister off the bed.

Heather had nothing more to say, as the contents of her stomach poured out over Morgana's arm and shoulder.

"AAAAUUUHGGGHHHH EWWWWWWWWWW!!! Father father, Heather threw up on me AAAAUGHHHH!!" Her sister ran away like she had been set ablaze.

"That was almost worth it," Heather said to herself after she sat back down, wincing at the taste of sickness in her mouth. "At least none of the vomit got on the books." She looked down at the League of the Brave poster rolling in the spreading puddle. "Okay... that was *definitely* worth it."

Later, the doctor assured her parents that head injuries sometimes resulted in nausea, but he told her parents stop giving her the sedative. As for Morgana's hysteria over the loss of her poster, there was really no medicine for that except time and patience. He was also amazed at the police investigation the night before, as Mr. Bushington had actually stopped by his office to demand proof that Heather was on a sedative. And when the doctor verified this claim, Mr. Bushington did not seem happy about it.

Heather pretended to leave to wash up after the examination, but instead she stayed behind the stairs to listen to adult conversation. "Why in all the Palachian continent would he think Heather was to blame?" The doctor asked. "A weak little girl, on a sedative... who was *bedridden*... is not the kind of assailant that leaves a welt like that. That's a man's strength right there, and I think he was in a fight of some kind. So he claimed to be on some kind of assignment, eh? Doesn't surprise me. Truant officers are the worst breed, if you ask me. It's what happens to school bullies when they are too stupid to take even menial labor jobs, join the army, or even the police force. He was probably using his badge to do some illegal after-hours drinking when he got in a fight. Mark my words, though, his kind is not so easily dismissed. He's on a mission of some kind. I'd keep your children close, if you know what I mean."

Heather felt vindicated, but terrified at the same time. The lie was still holding fast. But for how long? Was Mr. Bushington really out to get her? And what would happen next week? The passport should be waiting for her when she arrived at the lab, but she had to get there first.

Heather went to the washroom, and cleaned up. Her hair was starting to get greasy with all the bandages, and she wasn't allowed to get her wound wet for another few days. She wished she could just cut all her hair off. As she looked at herself in the mirror, she wondered if her face could carry being a boy for very much longer. With her hair short, yes. But she already had a girl's lips and eyelashes. She washed her face, under her pits, and back of her neck below the bandage, then decided to spend the rest of the night with her books.

When she went to her bed, she recoiled in horror. "Mother...? **Motherr???**" she screamed.

Rose ran up the stairs. "What is it, dear? What?"

Heather pointed her shaking hand at the bed, where all her books lay in soaked ruin.

"Oh my... oh dear, what happened?"

"I... I don't know. Those are the *Professor's* books!" Every single book had been soaked with water. A tipped over washbasin lay on the floor. Morgana was nowhere in sight.

"How did they get wet?"

Heather could think of only one reason. She gritted her teeth in rage until her vision went maroon. "Morgana. That little... *bitch!*"

"Morgana? Morgana?" her mother called out. It was not a voice anyone wanted to come to. It was the voice of a very disappointed mother. It was the roaring voice of a punishment coming one's way.

"That little shit-face... whore! I'll fucking *kill her!*"

"Heather!" Rose said in shock. "We do not use that language in this — "

"Those books are worth thousands!! She ruined.. priceless antiques... the Professor is going to kill me! I want Morgana dead! *Dead!!!!*"

Rose held Heather to her chest. "Honey, nobody is going to kill anybody. Let's give her a chance to explain — "

"The Professor is going to change me for those books, and we don't have any money, and we're going to lose the house and — " and for the first time in ages, Heather sobbed and wailed in despair. How was she going to get out of this now? Why did her sister have to be such a little bitch?

"Shhh shhhh.... Heather, sweetie, we'll find a way ... to... something... Morgana??"

When Morgana was found in the downstairs pantry, she denied she had poured water on the books and blamed Neil. But she was at a loss to explain how she knew water has been poured on them and why she was hiding terrified in the pantry with the bags of rice, crackers, and tubers. Heather was not immune to irony. The moment she wondered why her sister continued to lie despite the evidence, she thought about her own situation. Morgana was sticking to her story with the tenacity Heather recently understood all too well.

Wisely, her parents separated the two. Heather was down in the living room with her father while her mother spoke with Morgana in their bedroom. Heather was lost in thought with severe panic at every turn. Nothing seemed to be going right, and her lies were just making things worse and worse. Should she confess the whole ruse?

None of this would have happened if she had gone to public school and been a good little girl. But the thought of that seemed just as bad.

"How... um... how much do you think those books will cost to replace?" her father asked. She could smell he'd been drinking a little.

"I don't know," Heather said. She sat on the floor, up against the wall, where the warmth of a steam pipe behind the plaster and lathe soothed her back. She had never seen her father drink out of nervousness before. She couldn't stop making the entire situation seem dire. "They are pretty rare and priceless. I could see the ink had been ruined and there were irreplaceable notes in the margins. The Professor really trusted me with those books, and no matter who pays for what, when he gets back, I will not have a job anymore." Heather pulled her knees up and buried her head in them. "I guess that's what you wanted all along."

"Well..." her father said, trying to avoid the obvious agreement he had under his tongue. "I wouldn't say this was a plan of any sort..."

"I won't be a woman," Heather said. "I refuse. I will run away or kill myself. I don't want a life of servitude or not working with machinery."

"Your Aunt Gwendolyn died that way," her father said.

"What?"

"My sister Gwen. She didn't want to be married off, either. Wanted to be an accountant like her big brother. Me."

"I didn't know I had an auntie Gwen."

"You did. Well, she died years before you were born. That's why your middle name is Gwennie."

"That's Morgana's middle name, father..." Heather sighed. "Mine is Rebbecca. You don't know me at all!"

"That's what Gwennie said when she hung herself. Left a note the night before her wedding. Mother... grandmother Marion...

found her with the note. We don't speak of her anymore because of the way she chose to die. But she was still my little sister. You want Kye to go through the same thing?"

"My older brother is a man; he can do what he likes. Because I am becoming a woman, I can't do shit."

"Heather...?" her father said in an astonished gasp that tried to sound authoritative, but the brandy was softening his world quicker than he could cope. "We do not speak in guttural terms in this house."

"I don't care anymore. Ground me. Punish me. You can't change me."

Bruce January sighed. "I did not raise you to be a gutter snipe, Heather. Your mother told me you used a lot of very coarse words upon the discovery of those ruined books."

Heather shook her head. "I just can't believe Morgana would do this. I just can't believe the... depths of her petty behavior! She's my twin sister and she's more different than we are alike! I hated that poster. But would I pour water on it? No. I threw up on it because she yanked me around when I told her I was sick to my stomach!"

"Remember, you're not identical twins. Morgana has her ... peccadilloes."

"She's dumber than a slag of lead, father."

"Now now. She just chooses a ... different approach to — "

"**Slag**. Of lead!"

Bruce January sighed and took another drink of brandy. "Here's my plan. We'll take the books to my workplace. We have blotters that specialize in water-ruined paperwork. The finest and best workers will be put to work restoring the books. They'll be cleaner, brighter, and better than — "

Heather's lack of faith accented her bitter retort. "Father, really? Is this... realistic?"

Her father sighed. "I can't pay for them, you know that."

"I'd say sell Morgana to the workhouses."

"Heather! Be reasonable. She is your sister."

"I am not sure why you think that matters. This 'sister' cost the family more than... more than I ever have."

"The workhouses don't exactly pay for their servants. Besides, can you imagine Morgana complaining? They'd fine us for dropping her off as a public nuisance."

Heather snickered at her father's unexpected attempt at humor.

"See, there's a smile. Look, I'll take you to work tomorrow. I know you have always wanted to see the difference engine I work with. I'll show you around, give you some pins and gears to play with, and we'll do what we can to fix those books."

Heather sighed. What other option did she have? But the lure of seeing a real difference engine intrigued her. A machine dedicated to solving complex math! Up until now, she had only seen drawings and woodcuts of one. There was a small one back at the Professor's lab, but it was broken and mainly used for spare gears, screws, and assorted parts for other projects.

"All I ask is that you wear a dress and a large hat to cover that bandage."

"I will wear a dress," Heather conceded. "And the hat. But... I get to see and touch the engine."

"I will make it happen. Deal?"

"Deal."

Five
The Difference Engine

It occurred to Heather that she hadn't seen Market Square while in a dress since she was a little girl. Once she realized she could wear overalls to work, she enjoyed the secure feeling of cloth around her legs without having to worry about boys obsessing to see her undergarments. She forgot how proper ladies undergarments were very restricting, even if her sister was essentially her same size. And while the feeling of lace and pretty frilly things around her was very awkward, Heather was soothed by the fact that this dress was not hers; it was her sister's. Her punished, grounded sister's.

Morgana was forced to give up her favorite formal dress as part of her punishment. In addition, she was not allowed to purchase any new League of the Brave comics, nor would she be allowed to see them in person, even in the main street parade later that month. Morgana bawled openly at this restriction, which made her punishment even worse: plain dresses to school for a month. And she had to help do all the cooking for the rest of the year. Heather's parents came down on Morgana like an iron forge hammer, and any illusion that Morgana could get away with anything was wiped out in a single night's scolding and lecture. Despite the raw hatred she had for her sister, even Heather felt sorry for her when the day was over and hugged her in her bed as she wept. Morgana's life had been destroyed.

The damage to the books was a lot less than Heather had feared. Due to the page material, only the top few exposed pages were soaked, and a lot of the ink did not run as much as it had looked at first. Her father had gotten some advice from a neighbor on how to dry them, and they were shipped right away to his office where they would be waiting for them when they arrived.

The day improved even more as Heather got to ride the tram. She gaped like a surface yokel at the huge sections of trains suspended in the air by a series of pinions attached to linear actuator tracks that scooted the trams along. She craned her neck to see the racks of trolley batteries that powered the steam engines. She could feel the roar of the engines in her chest as they started and stopped at various points, loading and unloading passengers. Even the conductor's brake handle and various control dials and gauges made her eyes bug with excitement. She felt like a kid in a candy store.

"I forget that this is exciting to you," Bruce said. "I travel this daily, and all it is now is just a part of the journey where things are mundane at their best."

They changed trams twice, because there was no single tram line that went from their part of the city to the central financial square. Each time, Heather wanted to know how everything worked. She asked the conductor questions until her father dragged her away. It was odd enough a fancily dressed little girl was traveling to the financial district during a school day, but a chatty one who seemed to have more of a gasp of mechanics than almost anyone she asked was raising a few eyebrows.

"Your father's bank is right ahead," Bruce said loudly into her ear. The noisy tram engine and passengers shouting morning greetings to one another made it difficult to hear anything unless it was screaming in one's ear. Heather turned to face the direction in which her father was pointing, and she became very glad he showed her this vantage point. The usual layers of their vast underground city parted away in a huge drop-off to a massive circular chamber lit by countless lamps and the glow of trolley batteries from hundreds of machines moving about.

Their tram was very high in the air, several levels above the main financial plaza, connected by thin racks and cables strewn in many directions like a tangled spiderweb. People were dwarfed in this distance to the size of small pebbles. In the center of the huge complex sat the main building itself, which housed one of the largest difference engines in the entire world. The effect unnerved people not used to the open space. Living almost a mile underground, almost every southern Palachian was used to being surrounded on all six sides. Agoraphobia was very common, and the rare places like this were often avoided by common citizens that did not have to work in the financial industry.

"Financial One," her father shouted with pride as the building loomed into view. "This is where all the money of southern and lower Palachia eventually must pass!"

But Heather was not concerned about money. Undaunted by any sense of agoraphobia that most of her age would be suffering, she strained at the edge of the tram railing fascinated by the huge array glass tubes shooting dozens of capsules that zipped by every second. From a distance, it looked like bubbles of liquid in small glass pipettes. They snaked and clustered in all directions like arteries and veins, turning the mechanized landscape into an almost organic breathing creature. Her eyes tracked them to the huge massive gathering near Financial One, then she caught sight and marveled at the huge plaza below them.

The Financial One plaza had an enormous garden in the middle with a circular center meadow. Inside this meadow lay a strange kidney-shaped pattern of purple flowers in the center. Given the greenery around it, she felt a pang of déjà-vu.

"That garden," Heather shouted. "Looks like a huge fish eye!"

"Yes," said her father absently, "I suppose it does!"

Heather looked at the pattern passing below them and for a brief second, the memory of the fish eye in the trolley in one of her dreams sucked at her belly with a days-old scar of fear. While she wasn't frightened, it did silence her, locking her in its gaze, until they were suddenly plunged into the darkness of the building.

"Look sharp, sweetie! This is the end of the line!"

The tram came to a gentle stop at a platform marked "Financial One Main Terminus." The rest of the passengers poured off along with Heather and her father. Heather looked around the platform, entranced by the huge sweeping lines of pipes and catwalks that surrounded them. At one point, as she followed a series of access catwalks to the edge of the tram's entrance tunnel, she saw some strange writing on the wall off the edge of the platform next to a large color-coded display of the building.

"What's that?" she asked.

"It's a listing of the various floors. But I know — "

"No, father. Not the map. I mean that symbol someone painted on the wall over there. It looks... Korisan."

Her father shrugged. "Just some graffiti, I suppose. Those symbols have been showing up around the city now and then. Just a bunch of kids trying to impress themselves with their bravado and daring."

"But why Financial One?" Heather strained to read the symbol and memorize it for later.

"Come on, sweetie! Maybe you can look them up in your books when we get them cleaned."

In all the recent excitement, Heather had forgotten the real reason she was here. Of course! The books! When she was done with the difference engine, she could look up that symbol. But her father's lightly patronizing tone depressed her a little. This was to get worse when they passed down a marble hall and came across some maintenance workers fixing a broken pneumatic tube line.

"Wait, father. I want to see this!"

"Come on, Sweetie," he said. "Those men don't want a little girl pestering them with babbling questions."

"But I want to know what broke! I want to see how they fix it!"

"I am sure it's in capable hands, honey. Don't worry about it, they'll get it all fixed."

She was not *worried* about it; she wanted to know how it *worked*. This was to set the mood for the rest of the day, Heather discovered, and turned what she thought would be an exciting tour into a dreadful parade of her father showing her off in a dress. The crinoline itched even on good days, and now it was positively dreadful on top of everything else. It tangled with her legs and made her sit funny. Her father kept asking her to walk a little more... gentle... and not stomp around the wooden floors of the office.

An hour into her promenade, and Heather was bored and antsy. All she had seen were a few offices her father visited to show her off. This would be followed by dull hours at her father's desk in the middle of a sea of similar desks where men with stacks of papers would check and recheck various rows of numbers. And when she got a chance to be shown off, given that she was in a dress, every single one asked, "Is this little Morgana?"

"No," her father would say proudly, "this... is Heather."

"She looks so... pretty!" every single man would gasp. The fact that Heather was previously described in rather masculine tones had filled some strange images in men's heads. It was almost as if they were saying in dumb shock, "Oh my goodness! She looks like a girl!" And Heather hated it.

Her father had work to do, of course. He had to check on the books he had sent, then had a meeting with his supervisors, and then he had a meeting with other workers about why they weren't working. "Maybe they aren't working because they are in too many meetings," Heather suggested, which only drew shallow laughter from her father. Eventually, Heather was left alone so long at her father's desk, she wondered what would happen if she wandered off. Of course, she knew she'd get in big trouble, but as the hours went by, she felt if she didn't take control of the situation, she'd never see anything of interest.

After what seemed like an endless era of mind-numbing boredom, it was lunchtime. The Financial One building had a very large automat cafeteria where workers placed coins in exchange for food served from small little drawers. No one would answer Heather's question about how those worked, either. How did the coins know which drawers to open? How did the food get there? Who makes the food? Each question was met with a shrug of indifference; no one knew or cared enough to think about it. It just was. And Heather was very annoyed at their nonchalance.

"So my colleagues said that the strange paper these books are made from are proving difficult to clean," Bruce said, sitting across from her daughter in a small cafe booth. "But they did manage to get them dry, mostly because of the way I packed them last night." He beamed with pride at this, even though it had not been his idea. "Most of the margin notes are intact, but those that smeared have stayed smeared. I am afraid no one can do anything to fix that. Maybe the Professor won't mind so much…?" Heather's father seemed to be hinting that the books could be returned without anyone being the wiser if they kept it a secret.

"I think he's going to hit me on the head with each smudge," Heather said. "After all, what is he going to give me an exam from?"

Bruce's face slacked. "I am not sure. I didn't… Heather, look; your sister had no idea of the damage she caused. She is not going to get away with this."

"Isn't she? She's the good daughter, after all."

"Heather, that's not true. Your mother and I both love you equally."

Heather's head wound throbbed. "But she's the feminine one. She's the one who will get married off and produce babies. Me? I am the girl who wants to be a boy. Un-marriageable." Heather pouted and kicked her feet.

"Heather, most of your life is ahead of you. Don't think like that. Soon, you'll feel better and you'll grow up and like boys."

"What if I don't? What if I am 16, and don't get married, and want to fix trams and automats and difference engines... which, by the way, we have **not** seen yet!"

"Honey... look, I know I said we could see the difference engine, but today I forgot it's under repair and — "

"Under repair?? I could see its insides??" Heather was about to explode in her seat at this excellent news. "How could you let me miss that??"

"Heather, be reasonable. They don't want little children — "

" — little *girls* you mean — "

"... anyone not authorized to see it while it is in a state of repair, okay sweetie?"

Heather stewed in her own anger. She crossed her arms and started down at the ruffled pastel blue lace on her impossibly puffy sleeves. Heather didn't know how she could contain such raw anger. If she were younger, she would have exploded in a temper tantrum right on the spot. But now she was older and her social awareness in a crowded place prevented the venting of steam she so desperately needed.

"Oh, Heather..." clucked her father. He was sweating in desperation at his daughter's moods, and wished that she would understand that he was doing the best he could. But he also knew that look. His sister Gwen had that look the night before she killed herself. "Look, would it make any difference if I got some iced cream in dipped chocolate?"

"What I am, 5?" Heather asked. She was amazed this was the same father she looked up to for all these years.

"No, Heather. I suppose not. I forget you're a young lady and need better respect in conversation."

"You broke your promise," she sulked.

"I did not. I didn't know that they were not going to let anyone in. They won't even let me in the viewing chamber. Please. Look, I'll ask tomorrow how the automat runs, and report back to you — "

"No, father. Thanks anyway. Let's just go back to your desk." Heather was trying not to cry through her gritted teeth.

"When did you grow up so fast?" asked Bruce, but that made Heather even angrier and quieter.

The desk was not much more entertaining, and all Heather could do to occupy herself was try and figure out what anything in the large room was for. There were over two dozen desks surrounded by doors to closed offices. Some had lights behind them, some did not. Because of the work on the difference engine, most of the accountants there had little work to do. Some were preening over past work, looking for errors, while Heather's father left frequently to see someone else in the building. Sometimes she'd see a capsule shoot through one of the pneumatic tubes above, and after she figured out the patterns of belts driving the ceiling fans, she felt her brain would explode and bury her with the rubble of sheer boredom.

"Look sharp, **look sharp**!" someone shouted. A series of workmen passed by the main entrance to the room. Heather craned her neck and saw a huge wheeled pallet carrying a large intriguing chunk of machinery. She looked around for her father, but he was nowhere to be seen, and everyone else in the room was too apathetic about maintenance men to look up from their work. Curiosity got the better of her, and she went to follow the cart.

A collection of men, some of them northern Palachian, were moving a very large square-shaped section of gears that all sat in interlocking rows. Heather recognized this as a possible piece of a difference engine. The Professor had a small version of one that could count up to ten thousand, but didn't use it because it was broken and he could do math faster in his head than the engine could even if it did work. The difference engine back at the lab was only about 4 feet square; this huge mass of clockwork was easily larger than several storage chests. Heather almost salivated at the thought of it, and felt a tingle in the pit of her stomach like butterflies.

She followed behind the team of men pushing the huge cart down the hallway, shouting and lumbering past various paper workers, accountants, and meek administrative staff scuttling away like insects.

"Stop ho. HO!! HO!!!" shouted some of the men as they strained to stop the juggernaut under massive inertia. They were in front of a large elevator door.

"Ah, blast it fucking all!" said the largest of the team, a massive man with a barrel chest who stood at least seven feet tall. "They didn't open the freight doors!"

The team groaned in response. Heather guessed that getting a cart this heavy moving was a chore, and now they had to wait until the doors opened.

"I told them, 34th floor, right? Right John?" the large man asked. Another worker grunted in response. "Right! Okay. Plan D: we go down all at once, and threaten that weaselly little lackabout for the last time. He doesn't get that door open, we'll use him as the crowbar!"

The men laughed and cheered in response.

"Right, now instead of me having the pleasure... again, I suggest all of you go this time, and I'll stay back and guard this stupid thing!"

The men roared again, pleased to be doing some beating. They filed down the hallway like pirates on a mission. Heather watched them pass, and the hallways fell silent. She realized that the machinery was relatively unguarded from her side. The large man was staring at the elevator doors, growling at them. He lit up a cigar and started puffing in frustration.

Heather slowly built up courage, and tip-toed to the equipment. It seemed even larger up close. The huge man was now idly looking and the floor, and doing breathing exercises. It seemed as if he was more involved in flexing his muscles than looking out for a small girl touching the gears. Heather reached out in a hesitant, daring manner, and for a second, her fingertips were so close to the gears, she could almost feel the dense collection of metal in the small gap of air.

"Ey!" said a gruff voice behind her.

The sudden bellowing next to her ear made her startle, and she squeaked loudly as her entire hand smashed into the outer spindles.

"What are you doing, miss??"

Somehow, this huge lumbering man had managed to get right behind her without making a sound. Her entire hand, dwarfed by the machinery lay like an intricate spider on top of a pile of gold coins. She could feel the deep, cold metal suck her body heat away in an very intimate way that gave her goose bumps. A giant hand that was the size of a bear's paw gently grabbed her arm and pulled it away.

"I'm sorry, but I can't have you touching that."

Heather looked at the man, who had stooped down on one knee and yet was still towering over her.

"Um... sorry?" Heather squeaked. But she wasn't sorry one bit in her heart. Even though only a thin coating of oil coated her hands, she still felt connected to the difference engine.

"Who are you?" the man asked. For a large, brutish worker, he seemed to have an oddly gentle, educated tone to his voice.

"Heather... Heather January... sir."

"Ah... Heather-Heather-January-Sir," said the man. A wide grin spread across his face. "This equipment is very delicate. Like your lace bodice, here. And like lace, you can't be too rough with it or let strangers touch it." He tilted his head with a kind and firm follow-up question mark.

"I won't..." Heather said.

The man took out a rag from one of his overall pockets and wiped her hand. "We can't get this grease everywhere, now can we? Such a nice dress and hat you have!"

"I am not afraid of a little grease or oil, sir."

The man laughed. "Of course not. You're young, still. Like to play in the mud with frogs and poke sticks at dead things, I imagine."

Heather had not heard of such things as poking mud frogs with sticks, but assumed they were surface terms. The people of the surface were usually very large and muscular like this man. "I play with gears, cogs, and trolley — " Heather started to explain.

"Trolley? That is dangerous stuff, little miss! You haven't touched trolley today, have you?"

"No," she said. She couldn't tell if the man was patronizing her or not. "I haven't touched trolley for over a week."

The man sighed. "Thank goodness for that." He seemed oddly relieved. Then he chuckled to himself as if he realized no *girl* would have touched trolley in any situation.

The elevators doors clicked.

"Aha!" the man said. "Been waiting for that!" He opened the doors like they were nothing but paper in frames. With one massive pull, the man heaved the cart, a cart that took ten men to stop, and dragged it into the huge elevator carriage.

"Tell the men, when they get back, I am already heading to the main chamber."

Heather panicked. She didn't want the machine to leave her sight. She didn't know why, but she felt so drawn to it, so satisfied by its touch, she simply nodded and made up her mind to not let it leave without her.

"Right, see you round, miss!" the man said. He pulled a few levers in the elevator, and Heather heard the cables strain under the weight. Just before the doors slapped shut, Heather leaped in and hid behind the huge machinery opposite the man.

As she wedged herself between the gears and the carriage wall, she stopped for a second and wondered just what in trolley's name she was doing. If the elevator should shift, the huge massive cart could roll into her and crush her like a small grape against the wall. And how was she going to get out? Why had she done this? How was she going to get back? What if someone found her? The moment of clarity scared her badly, but the strange thrill of butterflies in her stomach was oddly addictive.

The carriage shuddered and groaned as it descended the floors. The man was humming some random work tune and laughing at certain parts. Heather ran her fingers along the gears, feeling their tiny bumps and niches. She had never touched such a thing. Most of the mechanical things the lab had were large in scale. The main part of the lab had a series of systems connected directly to the root machine, and therefore the gears were large and thick. This machinery had tiny intricate gears, like it was entirely constructed of watch parts and coated with a strange, greasy substance that also felt like powder.

The elevator carriage stopped suddenly. The doors shuddered, groaned, and made clicking noises. A bell sounded.

"Oh, for fuck's sake, really?" the large man asked. He pushed himself to the front of the cart and pounded on the door. "Hey! **Hey!** Open the damn door!"

The door clicked a few more times and then opened with a grating noise that Heather was certain must be producing metal shavings somewhere. Some workers were there, and started to drag the cart out, exposing Heather's poor choice in hiding places. She made a half-decision to dart out when people weren't looking, but the large man was already in front of her.

"Really? You again? What... what...? Did you get caught in the gears?" he asked, looking at her dress. Heather looked down and saw the dress was pockmarked with lubricant residue.

Heather tried to think of the most innocuous small child lie she could think of. "I have to go to the toilet," she said, crossing her legs.

"The toilet?"

Heather nodded.

The man rolled his eyes. "What made you think you'd find it down here??"

Heather shrugged. "You seemed kind and... I was lost?"

The man sighed. "Look at your dress! May the team of a thousand judges find mercy upon my wretched... well, Miss Heather... November... something something... the only toilets here are in the changing room, but it's men only!"

"Please?"

The man watched his huge cart rolling away from him, down the hall. "Okay, okay. Down the hallway, second large steel door on the right, marked for employees only. Just go in, *do not look* at men disrobing, and the toilet is straight ahead. And... you never saw me. Might be bad if you told someone. Then I'd... I'd be mad! Got that?"

Heather nodded as the man bolted down the hallway after the cart. The hallway went almost silent, but Heather could hear the rumbling or large machinery through the walls. Her heart started beating faster. Where was she? She didn't dare follow, but now that she said she had to go to the toilet, she realized that she really did feel the urge. She followed the instructions and went into the worker's changing room.

She gingerly opened the door, and was relieved to find it unoccupied. Huge rows of lockers lined a path right to a room that illuminated a filthy toilet lit by a small gas lamp. She hurried down the rows, ran into the loo, and slammed the door.

In the room was a full-length mirror. She got a good look at herself, and was both disgusted and amused. She was frilly and girly, alright, but the front of her dress had hatch marks and gear prints in grease from being pressed against the difference engine. Those stains would never come out, as her mother would grumble about Heather's work clothing. She could imagine Morgana screaming in terror at the defilement of her best dress, and a smile of satisfaction spread across her mirror image and leered back at Heather in a proud sense of accomplishment. She wished she could have been with those men like she was with the ice workers. Swearing, belching, laughing, and making dirty jokes in a language she could barely understand.

Heather looked at the grease on her fingertips and licked it gently. She wasn't sure why, but as the strange metallic taste spread across her tongue, it filled her nostrils with an oily smell that one could only get from working with machinery. The mineral lubricant that was greasy, yet somehow dusty at the same time.

Then she had an idea. The thrill of it scared her, but she knew she only had once chance. Her heart pounded and she felt lightheaded and giddy in a way that seemed to violate her innocence in a most satisfactory way. She pushed open the door, and opened the lockers one by one until she found what she was looking for: a work uniform in her size.

She grabbed it and ran back to the toilet room and gasped in huge gulps of air; she had subconsciously forgotten to breathe in the excitement. She stripped out of her clothing, wrestling with the crinoline and straps, and shimmying out of her corset with great difficulty. As she stood looking at herself in her thick undergarments in the mirror, she felt again, that strange violation of innocence that screamed out she was no longer a little girl, but a free spirit taking charge of her desires. She held up the worker's uniform across her front, and looked at her flushed face in the mirror. She then put on the jumpsuit, moving the various straps and pockets into position. She was not used to the complicated buckles and belts, but she knew enough about what the finished outfit was supposed to look like to figure it out. A few minutes later, she was staring back at herself, dressed like a man, but with a girl's face and a head bandage. She frowned, but had another idea. She wadded up her girly things, and stuffed them a locker, memorized the locker number, and then looked for some dust and grease which she correctly surmised was prevalent in this filthy changing area.

She dotted her face, making a believable stubble, then put on a worker's cap to cover her bandages and slid the goggles over to cover her eyes. Even though the scratched and smeared lenses, Heather saw a believable northern Palachian face grin back at her from the mirror.

The door to the room opened, and a small worker came in. Heather froze. Would this ruse work?

"Hey, fella," said the worker. He had a rather high pitched voice for a worker, but since he was of small stature, this was not that unusual.

"Yeah?" Heather said back in a gravel-like voice. She had learned that children often make the mistake of trying to make their voice sound deeper to mimic adults, but it only sounded like a woman trying to make fun of a male voice. Instead, Heather tried to sound like she had been inhaling smoke all her life. She accented this with some casual snorts and throat clearing.

"The boss fella said I'd find more workers here," he said. His voice had a northern Palachian twang, but he spoke her southern Palachian language quite well. "You speak southern Palachian?"

Heather shrugged. "A little," she said with a northern Palachian accent trying to sound southern.

The man chuckled, "I need workers who can speak southern without translating. You speak southern well?"

94

Heather noticed the man had a strong lower Palachian accent, similar to the divers who mine trolley. She shrugged again, keeping the ruse that she was faking her own language, "I get by. What you need?"

"Excellent," the man said sarcastically. "Like a fucking native."

"I am not immune to sarcasm," Heather said, a little proud that she was convincing this man that she was incapable of speaking her own native tongue correctly. She was finding that she liked playing dress-up.

"Ohhh!" the man laughed, slightly impressed at the word. "I see! Tell me, if I tell you I need a 12 inch spanner with a self-locking hitch, you gonna give me a single handle or a double ended joint?"

Heather thought for a moment. A test! She knew what the man was talking about, but what answer did he want? Then she realized that it might be a trick question. Or a trick question looking like a trick question but was a real question. She shook her head to clear the self-double-guessing loop. Then some part of her, from deep inside her gut swaddled in men's clothing, whispered the correct way to answer.

"It depends," she said.

"Depends on ... what?"

"Depends on what you are trying to fix. And what I have. Either way, I'll cram it up your ass." Heather was shocked at her vulgarity, but her belly was filled with energy and spunk. She had seen the ice workers talk this way to one another.

The man laughed. "I am trying to fix a 9-inch bolt at an L-bend on a crank shaft."

"Then a 12 inch would be too big. You sure you do this for a living?"

The man laughed again. "Good, **good**! You have good memory. You'll do well. Come with me...um...?"

Heather started to follow, but the man stopped her with his hand across her chest. Between men, this was not as shocking as it being done to a woman. Heather had to suppress the urge to smack his hand away.

"... your name? You have a name, right?" the man asked.

Heather thought, "A name?" She started to sweat. "Ack," she said before she could stop herself.

"Mack?" the man asked.

"Mack. Yes, that will do. Nobody can pronounce my northern name anyway — "

"No, they wouldn't. Mack is a good name, carries well over noise."

Heather nodded. "I have found that to be the case. Shall we go?"

The man nodded, and for the new few minutes, Heather followed him down several hallways, until they came to another freight lift.

"You... new?"

"Yes," she replied.

"They have a lot of new people for this job today. You know why?"

"I was hoping you'd tell me."

"You didn't go to orientation this morning?"

"I was late. The tram had a... backup of some kind. I wasn't given much, only to show up and..."

The freight doors opened noisily before Heather had a chance to continue her story. She sensed the man was probing for something.

The man nodded. "Good. I can tell from your accent you probably do ice work, mainly. Don't worry, if you're mechanically inclined, you shouldn't run into too much discrimination. We have just this one job, then pay. Hope you ate."

"I have. Nice... automat... down there." Heather was bad at small talk, she feared.

"I haven't eaten there myself, I am not from here. In fact, I have never been in this building before. All I know is I have a lot of work, and I need someone who has a brain. I think you're the best I've found. And you speak southern. I need someone small like me to work in some of the deeper places. You don't get claustrophobia, do you?"

"No sir, I am at my best in tight places."

"Good...good..." the man stared at her a little harder. "Your accent is strange. I have worked with a lot of northerners before, but yours is very southern in the back of the throat."

Heather started to sweat a little. "I... I travel a lot. I have picked up... a lot of different dialects."

The man stopped the elevator with the small control lever. "You don't have any trolley on you, right?"

"No sir — "

" — because you should know that there's a gas in the entry chamber that, when it reacts with trolley, will glow red. And red is dead, my friend. I see red on you, we are gonna halt everything. We only have one day's window to do this, and the entire financial world here has ground to a halt thinking it's a standard repair. You have a speck of that green stuff... in your clothing, hair, and even under your fingernails... we will boot you out of here by express pneumatic tube."

"I understand, sir."

"Don't call me sir... Mack. It's creepy. My name is, er, Terry." Terry started the lift back up and they rode in silence for another minute.

"You a diver? Like a trolley diver?" Heather asked.

"No, but my family was. That's the accent you hear. Very astute, Mack. But look, we're not going to be chums. We do the job, I sign your card, maybe give you a little extra... and it's like we were never here. Stone and I — " Terry was cut off when the lift stopped. " — Good. Follow me."

Terry led Heather into a small room trough and oval door that Terry pushed closed behind them with a solid thump. "Now, stand here for a minute. Don't be afraid, there will be some hissing, a loud wind will blow in your face, and you'll smell something a little acrid. Your ears may pop and crackle a little. Don't freak out; I have had at least two workers panic today and I don't want you to be one of them."

Heather nodded as Terry slapped her shoulder and left the room through another, smaller oval door. There was a solid thump as the door sealed and the small wheel lock in the center spun.

Heather waited, seated at a small metal bench that stuck out from the wall. The room seemed completely quiet, which was unnerving. Living in a Palachian city meant there was always noise around. The distant hissing of steam pipes, the grinding of gears, the roar of ventilation, and the persistent low rumble of some of the larger root machinery from deep below them. In Heather's case, there were also the sounds of voices in their cramped set of living quarters, either from her own family, her neighbors, or someone in the streets outside. Pure, clean silence was almost suffocating. She held firm, trying not to be afraid. She could not be a little girl, she would be a man. Men are not afraid.

There was the sound of a bell, and before Heather could wonder what that meant, she felt very odd and the colors in her vision went into an amber hue. There was a hissing that seemed to come from both inside her and all around her. She gagged and coughed reflexively; it felt like her whole face was going to come off of her skull.

"Just another minute, you'll adjust," said a tinny voice from the vents. "Don't forget to breathe. Breathe deeply and slowly. Fill those lungs, or what's left of them. The gas is not poisonous, but your lungs need to be coated with it to continue. You'll be fine, and feel great in less than a minute."

"Okay!" Heather tried to say, but her voice didn't work. She gasped and felt faint.

"Breathe deeply and slowly!" the voice shouted, but Heather's ears were popping so it sounded like it was coming from behind 20 pillows. She tried to oblige, telling herself panicking would end her promise to see the difference engine. She had to focus on what she did this for. Breathe in... breathe out... breathe in... breathe out...

Then she was aware someone was shaking her. "Wake up, Mack!" said Terry.

"Um... what?" Heather.

"You passed out." Terry chuckled. "Don't worry. Happens to a lot of first-timers. They always forget to breathe. You'll remember next time, right? You're pressurized now, and not a speck of trolley on you!"

Heather nodded dumbly.

"Right, okay. Let's get you started. I want you to follow me to the upper racks. You run a winch before?"

Heather entered the difference engine chamber and realized it was more majestic than she could have ever dreamed. It towered inside its own chamber hundreds of feet above her and dozens of feet below her. They were on a small catwalk where Heather could see almost everything, and still she had to crane her neck in all directions. The gears and pinions were so numerous that they joined into one huge blur of brownish-gray like a conical tower of bees. She realized that the huge set of difference gears she saw on the cart earlier was merely a tiny section of this collection.

"Impressive, huh?" asked Terry. "Over five billion separate parts, last count. And it counted itself. Gets about several hundred new gears a day, and requires a team of 100 men to maintain it during calculation runs."

"How do you keep so many gears from jamming?"

Terry smiled. "Now that's an engineer's question right there! We have a particular form of lubricant made only for machines this size. It's mined and filtered. Spreads like a fine powder, coats like the slickest grease. But it's also secret so... no peeking!"

"The tolerance of such gears must be... beyond anything I have ever — "

"The tolerance is measured in microns, Mack. Even a speck of dust can jam something, which is why we put everyone in that chamber. That gas burns off anything not organic, and the air blows all the dirt off ya. It also glows in the presence of trolley."

"Why is trolley not allowed? I can imagine a machine this size uses a lot of — "

"Normally, it does. It uses so much trolley that it actually burns through two of the largest batteries a year, not to mention dozens of smaller ones that have to be replaced weekly."

"Burns out?"

"Nothing left but a dim green gas in the chambers. Yes, it's true; most trolley will last for years, if not decades. But this is a machine that needs its fuel. It is greedy and unpredictable. But today, we are trying some different. We have taken advantage of the normal replacement cycle and decided to run a test using... well, you'll see."

"How can this machine... any machine... run without trolley? Surely not coal or wood."

Terry laughed. "You'll be surprised what you'll see. Now, hook up a tool belt from over there, at maintenance deck B, and winch yourself up to the top. I'll be waiting with Stone near the top."

"Stone?" Heather asked.

"Yeah, you can't miss him. He's *huge*! Don't forget to bring some smaller spanners and socket bars; I have some detail work that needs tuning."

Heather watched as Terry hooked up a harness and winched himself up in the air, aided by other workers steadying the ropes. She walked down to the maintenance deck terry pointed to and looked for the tool belt. While she was searching, she shifted uncomfortably; something was wrong with her undergarments. They had gotten loose or something. They were probably not designed to be worn in a jumpsuit with buckled overalls. Then she remembered she forgot to use the toilet back in the locker room. But she decided she could hold it, and tried to think of things other than having to use the bathroom and focused on the tools.

"Wot chew looking faw?" said a northern Palachian worker.

"Yew gowt smaw spannehs?" she asked. Blank stare. "N'moid spankah."

The man roared with laughter, said some more words, and shouted to his fellow men. Again, like she was one of their own. She didn't even know what a "n'moid spankeh" was, but figured it was a really foul and male thing to say. But just as she was about to give up, one of the workers surprised her with a tool belt with detail tools.

"Roit sah," she said, hoping it meant "thanks."

"Shays roit sah," he said back. "Op yoo gah."

Before Heather could say anything, she was attached to a harness and kicked off the platform where she dangled in mid-air. The shock was so great that she didn't have to worry about the bathroom break anymore as her bladder was forced to evacuate. She hoped the smell of the machinery would conceal her accident, and she was so worried about it, she didn't have time to be afraid of heights even though she was nearly 50 feet above the base level.

Heather slowly winched herself up, pausing every now and then to adjust the huge shoulder strap that held the tool bag to her frame. She had never traveled like this before, and while the idea was simple, she appreciated the block and tackle system used to make lifting herself up far easier, even if it did take twice as long as hoisting a simple rope up. She was held steady by workers on the sides of the chamber, standing on various platforms and holding her line steady with hooks and ropes so she didn't swing wildly from one side to the other.. Sometimes Heather paused not because her arms were tired or her harness was pinching her, but to see the intricate levels of the machine. Most of the gears were not operational, but a few were being tested. Entire blocks of gears the size of small buildings were spinning, clicking, and shifting.

"Oy. OY!" shouted a voice. Heather looked up. "Oy, Mack! Come up here!"

It was the huge man from the freight elevator.

"Oh, no..." Heather said. Would he know who she was? Heather waved in a nonchalant manner as if bored and simply waiting to get there. She didn't want to look too cautious, but not too casual. Luckily, her ascent was interrupted.

"Mack!" shouted Terry from a platform within the engine. "I'm going to pull you to this platform, and we'll walk the rest of the way. You got the — **yes**, you got the tools! Excellent, excellent!

Terry hooked Heather's rope and dragged her to him. As Heather climbed over the railing, she got a good look down for the first time, and realized how high up she was. She looked away, queasy.

"Don't look down, my friend. Therein only lay madness." Terry said with a wink.

Heather soon understood why he needed someone small like her. Some of the openings in the access shaft were barely big enough for either one of them. Someone like Stone would have barely been able to get his head in them.

"Okay, as we go up here, when I tap my foot on your head, turn 15 degrees to the right," she heard him say above her in the darkness. "It's the only way anyone can slide through here. Cozy?"

"Just," Heather responded.

"Glad you're not claustrophobic. I was when I started, but got over it quickly. Must have been because I was practically born in a diving suit," he said.

Heather felt a hard knock on her wound. "Ahhh... **fuck!**" she screamed as she saw stars.

"Whoa, you alright?"

"Not so hard!" she shouted.

"That was barely a tap — "

"I got hit on the head right there," said Heather, then she added quickly, "in a pub brawl."

"Your northerners like it rough!"

"Let's just get on with this."

Heather followed Terry up until they were both pressed into a small area of gears less than a few feet wide. She prayed that he wouldn't be able to see her girlish face more clearly in the dim lantern light.

"I need a point-two-five self-seating cross," Terry said. He sniffed and said, "what smells like piss?"

Heather blushed a deep red and searched through the bag. "I smelled it, too. I think it's the tool bag. I have a quarter inch seater cross," she said. "But it's poorly tempered. You might strip the tip... as I see someone has already done." Heather looked annoyed as she stared at the broken tip.

"Hah, that was me," Terry said. "I know that tool's problems like I know the dirt my fingernails, just hand it to me, will yah, bub?"

Heather handed him the tools he requested, and spent a lot of time listening to Terry's small talk. She was enthralled working side by side to this strange man. It gave her hope that someone of her stature might someday do the same work.

"So, how come you are dragging your pry bar with each pass? Are you doing secondary checks to make sure you have the right gears?"

Terry nodded. "Right. I find it's best to measure twice, fix once. Sometimes these gear boxes get out of alignment, and I work on the wrong cross connecting pinion, and then the worm gear jams if it doesn't have much clearance at the end of a cycle."

"It would also push down on another gear, and make that block go bad, I guess. Start a kind of chain reaction," Heather said, picturing it in her mind. It boggled her mind that the difference engine was comprised of thousands of different blocks, but it made complete sense: you could remove and repair things in sections rather than take the entire engine apart.

"Yeah, and that's always bad. It's so hard to trace, because when a worm gear resets, it won't replicate until it reached the end of the cycle and when you have to repeat the cycles hoping it does it again... it's a bloody mess. Almost impossible to trace. You have to tear the machine apart chunk by chunk."

"Do you have any sort of error-checking protocol, like a kind of flag that can be set if the gears in a particular block aren't working right. Like a polynomial code checksum?"

"Yes, in fact. We call them cyclic redundancy checks. All boxes can be taken out, reset, and then a simple test will determine if the gears might be off by as much as one tooth. But one section may have over a thousand gears, so even that isn't always a quick fix." Terry slid out of the small space he had been working on, and smirked. "You ah... gonna do this kind of work in the future?" he asked.

"I'd like to. Not much up in northern Palachia, which is why I came down here." Heather felt more confident in her newly constructed false identity.

"You could pass for a southern Palachian, your accent is almost gone."

Heather felt a pang of nerves. Oops. "Um, well, I am picking it up from you. No offense."

"None taken, buddy. You also really know the tempering of tools, how a system self-corrects. You're a natural. You haven't handed me one wrong thing. Your family do toolwork?"

"I, uh... well, I grew up in that sort of... area."

"What area?"

Heather thought quickly. "We moved a lot, and my father knew toolmakers. As a little...g-, er, boy, I'd hang around... um, listen, I am not for talking about my past. I do work, I do good work, and I don't fuck around. I like small talk to focus on technical things." Heather cringed at her slip-up, she almost said she grew up as a little girl.

"Right, sorry, Mack. It's just that your accent... and your knowledge... you're pretty unique. Forgive my intrusion, I know you northerners like it private. So, given what you know so far, you must have worked on a difference engine before."

"Not this size. Mostly smaller ones that fit on workbenches and the like."

"Oh! This must be quite a thrill for you, then."

"I will remember this day for the rest of my life," Heather said truthfully.

"Well, if you ever need work, just — "

"Terry!" screamed a voice from above.

"Yeah, boss?"

"**Make it quick.** Stop your yapping with the workers, we have a window!"

"You got it, Stone!" Terry winked at Heather. "Mack, you met Stone? He's in charge of this project. Come on up top, I want him to meet you."

"Um... I'd rather not... um..." Heather tried to think of a good reason.

"Yes, he's scary and all, but he's alright. It would be a great opportunity to prove to his blowhard attitude towards the northern Palachians that you're not all a bunch of tin monkeys. You can be educated."

"We kind of... don't like him..." Heather sensed this might be a way out. "I am not sure if the other lads would appreciate me being seen shaking hands with — "

"Oh... right. I get it. Fraternizing with the enemy. Still. I'd hate for you to lose an opportunity to — "

"*Terry!* Stop yapping and get on up here!"

"Right, right, boss!" Terry scrambled up top. "Just clean up and let yourself out the side where you came in. The harness should still be there. Meet me down at the lowest deck next to the lectromag generator."

"L-lectromag?" Heather asked. She didn't' think she heard him right.

Terry grinned broadly. "It's alright, it's alright! It's a portable. That's why you couldn't have trolley on you, right?" Terry scrambled out of sight.

Heather was left alone in the chamber where she sat, bathed in the adrenaline rush of what she was doing. How long could she keep this up? She wondered. She was going to see a real lectromag generator! This was an uncommon rarity under the surface. What were they doing? She was so excited, that her hands shook as she gathered up the tools and cleaned up the workspace.

"Lower me down, bottom floor, right?!" she cried out to the staff as she got back in the harness. This time, she made sure she adjusted the harness more to her body's dips and curves, and her jerky ride to the bottom floor was far more comfortable.

Although Heather had never seen a lectromag generator before, she had a strong feeling that the huge device in front of her must be it. The gigantic structure as big as her house redefined the concept of "portable," as it was bolted to the floor with steel rods that, she could tell by their cap, were at least a yard deep into the ground. The strange simplicity of the device is what surprised her; it only seemed to be made of a large flywheel that must be at least several tons, held firmly by a thick titanium axle. At the edge of the flywheel were several dozen lodestones, a kind of dark rock that attracted certain types of metal. It was very rare, and she realized that the machine in front of her was probably the only one of its kind. One could not mass-produce this kind of item.

Heather was not the only one at the generator, however. Several people were milling about, and in one area marked "DANGER" were a set of odd hoses that seemed to be filled with hundreds of wires packed like bristles. The hoses were bolted down on the walls, snaking up and out of sight past the top of the difference engine. What purpose this had, she had no idea. Lectromag, she had once been told, was more like a super-volatile liquid that evaporated instantly with air. Perhaps these hoses contained it in some way.

"Coming dowwwwn!" screamed Stone, as he descended. Heather quickly pulled her hat down over her brow, and looked away.

Stone dropped to the floor with a huge thump, landing on his feet as he disengaged the harness. "We have a window of only a few hours, gentlemen, and every second counts. I hooked it up top, now we need to hook it down here. **Terry, are we all clear??**"

"Allll cleeear...!!" Terry shouted through a megaphone. People scrambled out of the machine onto the catwalks. **"Count your men**

at their marks!!" he shouted at the supervisors as he descended from the harness. **"Hup two hup two!! Quickly now!!"**

The air was tense with excitement as Terry jumped on top of Stone's shoulders, slipping off his harness. All loose harnesses, including Heather's, were drawn up and back into the levels above them like curtains before a grand play. The sound of clamps being locked, doors being shut, and the declining rumble of workmen's talk further added to the solemnity of the anticipation. Heather's heart could barely stand the joy and concept that she was being an active part of whatever was going to happen.

"All clear!!" shouted several decks above them.

"We good up top??" shouted Stone through Terry's megaphone. "We good up top??" shouted a relay voice. They heard a voice far away answer. **"We are good up top! All machines are go!!"** shouted the relay voice back.

"Gentlemen?" Stone said, clasping his hands. "This is the moment. Nothing like this has ever been done before. Hook up the temporary crankshaft assembly, and drag the swing arm to the generator. Now, as you all know, lectromag is extremely dangerous. All of you are in harm's way. While the experiment is running, I do not want *anyone* touching the equipment. Especially **metal**. Got that?"

The surrounding workers nodded.

"Good! Now I am going to hook up the cables. While I do that, swing that arm to the main gears here. You!" Stone pointed at Heather, which caused her to jump. "Terry tells me you're good with tools and delicate work. You make sure all the gears are aligned. You should be able to figure out which ones go where. Give me a thumb up when you are ready."

Heather nervously went to the large swing arm that came from the side of the difference engine. It was a huge collection of chains and gears being moved by a set of "fellow" workers. As she carefully had them place it, she saw immediately where they were to match up. There was a differential, and she assumed that when the swing arm was locked in place, two levers would lock the assembly, while another would actually connect a large worm gear gently to the spinning gears of the generator like a spring clutch. Without even thinking about the complex task she was asked to do, she gently slid everything into place, and locked the swing arm solidly to the generator. She checked her work, and gave a thumb up.

"Good!" Stone shouted. He was smoking a large cigar and grinning like a cat. "Now, everyone hands off! I will connect these two cables to a coupling here..." It was evident why Stone was chosen for the job, as each cable must have weighed dozens of pounds as they dragged behind him. He plugged one in, and twisted the locking ring.

"Ready everyone?" he said with a childlike grin that lit up his face. **"Engaging lectromag!"** Stone removed a locking pin and threw down a large lever.

There was a strange snapping noise, and the air became acrid. A spark of blue light shot into the air, and the entire generator began to hum. Stone grabbed a large crankshaft at one end, and spun the flywheel. Faster and faster the wheel spun. It hummed deeply as it gained speed, rising in tone like a musical wind instrument. Heather was so hypnotized by the whole thing, she didn't see Stone come up from behind her. "Now, Mack, engage the difference engine now!"

Heather jumped, and grabbed the wooden handle of the differential level before she even had time to think of what she was doing. Putting her entire back in it, she pushed the worm gears into the generator gears. They slid into one another with a high pitched scraping noise. Heather had never heard something so loud and alien before.

"Ear protection, lads! Put on your ear mufflers!" Stone shouted.

Heather felt her hearing go numb as Terry slid a pair around her head. It was an amazing set of mufflers, as they almost completely drowned out all but the loudest of sounds. She heard the screeching gain pitch to the point that her teeth hurt, but Terry and Stone looked far from worried. Both seemed absolutely delighted as Heather locked the lever in place. Terry gave her a thumb up, and Heather leaned on the lever to rest her aching muscles. She had never felt so exhilarated and tired at the same time. The chugging vibrations of the machine seemed to thump in her chest and rattle her bones. The gears in the difference engine next to her spun and clicked. The entire machine, and all its moving parts, came alive like a swarm of bees. Terry ran to a console of some sort, and read some of the flags that clicked up and down.

Heather quickly became lost in the deep hum that lifted her and trilled her deep inside. This was a new feeling she had never experienced before. She was exhilarated and scared, but felt alive and hungered for more machinery. It was like the machine had taken over her body and was forcing it to act as an extension of itself.

"This must be lectromag," she said to herself.

Her hair stood on end, and she thought she saw small sparks dance between gears here and there. The air seemed to sing with a strange ambient vibration. While fellow workers seemed highly agitated, Heather felt the most marvelous feeling in the pit of her stomach. She could float like this forever, she thought. Then a sense of embarrassment came over her as her cheeks flushed. Was she the only one this thrilled? She tried to compose herself, and look more manly and unaffected. Heather absently ran her hand over the generator and watched, entranced, by the huge spinning flywheel inches from her face. She closed her eyes and felt the thick and gentle wash of air that touched her cheeks.

Then something felt not quite right. Her left hand was on a one of the support braces of the flywheel and seemed to be vibrating in a way that didn't seem in the same rhythm. She looked down and saw one of the support rods was vibrating, and sand seemed to be oozing from beneath the base.

She walked to Terry, and made some hand signals. But he was focused on the flags, writing down things with grease pencil in a book. Terry waved her off in a very agitated way. Stone dragged her back, but she grabbed Stone's arm, and pulled to show him. At first, he didn't even seem to notice, but eventually he looked down at her and she pointed urgently. Stone followed her to the site, and he seemed to mouth, "What is it?"

She yelled, **"The support rod is coming loose! This could imbalance the machine!!"**

Stone shrugged in confusion. "What??"

Heather did her best to pantomime what she wanted to say, but Stone seemed more interested in Terry. She kept having to remind him to try and figure out what she said. Eventually, she stepped on his foot, met him face to face, and screamed **"The flywheel is breaking!!"** She jumped down, grabbed his huge, meaty hand, and placed it on the support housing. Then she pointed at the loosening bolt and the pile of sand. But he didn't look at the sand, he was looking back at Terry, who was motioning for him to come and look at something. He nodded absently at Heather, and shouted some command she didn't understand, but it seemed to be something like, "Just stand out of our way, okay??"

Heather knew this would end badly. So without thinking, she unlocked the differential engaging lever, and pulled hard. The worm gears popped out from the generator, and the whining sounds immediately stopped. For an extra measure, she started to unlock the swing arm, and gave it a hearty push away for the generator before something tore off her headphones.

"What do you think you're doing???" screamed Stone in a voice so angry, it seemed to burn her organs.

"Theflywheelisgoingtofalloff!! Thehousingiscomingundone, the base is unstable!! Look at what I was trying to point to you!!"

Stone ran to the generator, and at that moment, there was a shuddering sound. The flywheel was losing balance and scraping metal shaving in all directions. The air turned thick with smoke.

Immediately Stone jumped to action.

"Everyone evacuate!!" Stone screamed. **"No no, don't — !!"** Stone screamed to some workers, their eyes wide with terror, disengaging the lectromag cables. But it was too late.

A huge arc of light too bright to look at leaped from the generator and snaked across one worker, singeing his flesh like it had been hit with a hot poker rod through a soft dessert. One part of the lectromag slithered across the generator, and tried to gap right where Heather stood near the swing arm, but then stopped as it changed direction and hit the other worker in his face mask. The force blew his head back, and singed chunks of bone and flesh splattered across the opposite stone wall. Spider webs of blue white light clutched the generator, and started to envelop it.

But then, suddenly, it stopped. The light was gone faster than the flame of a candle in a blink of an eye. Heather had never seen a light disappear that fast. Stone was holding onto the other cable with his enormous arms. His clothes were smoldering and the buttons on his overalls had turned to slag.

The only sound in the room was the grating spin of the flywheel, slowing down. Just when Heather was about to ask what happened, the flywheel cracked and one wedge slammed into the stone ground with a force so massive, the entire chamber vibrated and everyone was tossed to the floor. Chunks of stone floor rattled around the room like ballistic gravel. Then, it was silent.

"Is everyone alright??" Stone shouted. Heather saw that her, Stone, and Terry were the only ones left in the chamber.

Terry ran to the fallen workers. Heather followed, but soon wish she hadn't. "Oh no... " Terry said. "They... oh bottomless darkness and haunted despair. What a gory mess..." The lectromag had nearly cut the one worker in half, and the other was missing most of his head.

Stone shrugged. "They're northern Palachians, Terry. They knew what they were in for. I told them not to touch anything, and they did anyway. No great loss. There are more of those tin monkeys where ... oh..." Stone stopped himself as Terry made "shut up" signs with his hands, pointing to Heather.

"Mack... I am sorry... did you... um, know them?" Stone asked awkwardly.

"Mack," Terry said, hugging her. "I am so sorry. I will arrange for a proper burial. I... can't imagine... Mack. Mack? You saved everyone else! *And you saved the difference engine!!*"

"I... did?" Heather asked. She felt very sick, and her head throbbed incessantly.

"Yes. *Yes!*" Stone said in realization. "You warned me. I didn't listen at first, but you warned me! And you pulled away the differential swing arm, and saved the entire machine from being cooked! Had that lectromag bridged to it..." both Stone and Terry looked up at the towering machinery in front of them in a horrific "what if" daydream. "...there would be untold chaos and damage!"

"Mack, you're a ... savior!" Terry said.

"Not to them," Heather said. She felt a lump rise in her throat, and before she could stop herself, she turned and vomited all over the floor. "Oh darkness... oh horrible things..." she said. Heather felt so scared... what just happened?

Terry patted her back. "Easy, buddy. No need to act like a girl. I am sure you've seen death before."

Heather shook her head as she twitched from dry heaves. "I have never seen... anyone die so..."

Terry slapped her back and gripped her shoulder. "Don't focus on them. Focus on you. I am giving you a *huge* pay bonus! Buy everyone a round! Even the guy who hit your head! Come on, we'll find your supervisor and I'll — "

"No!" Heather said. She backed away. "I just... just need to get away... for a moment."

Stone nodded. "Right. Well, see you... later?"

Heather ran up the metal stairs until she got to her level. As she fled the room, she heard someone winch down. "What in exploding trolley's name happened?" asked a voice. A female voice.

But Heather did not notice the voice as she went into the compression chamber. She closed the door behind her, locked it, and threw herself on the floor and cried. She cried in a curled position for a short while, and then when she felt she could stand, she got up, and opened the other door. Her ears popped, and her head wound throbbed so hard, she nearly passed out. She managed to run out into the hallway and find her way back to the lockers. She quickly dressed herself back in her sister's dressy clothing, and without stopping to adjust herself properly, she fled to the elevator lift. Heather didn't know where she was going, but she was driven by panic trying to escape the repugnant vision of those two workers in her head.

"Hey!" said a voice. Heather had somehow found herself in a corner. She didn't remember how she had gotten there, or how long she had been gone. "Hey, you're Heather! I found Heather!" A random employee swam into her vision. "You alright? Oh dear oh dear, you look a frightful mess. You got lost, didn't you?"

Heather nodded. That man had no idea.

"I bet you're scared. Don't be scared. You caused your father quite a fright! I have two daughters of my own, you know. One is about your age."

"I was... trying to find the toilet..." Heather found herself saying.

"Oh, tsk tsk. Poor dearie." The man helped her up. "We'll take you right to your father. He'll be so happy to see you."

Heather would be happy to see him, too. She felt hollow and empty. Her dress was stained with grease, and the only thing she could think of was the corpses of the workmen on the floor.

She barely remembered the reunion with her father. There was talk about the messy dress, and apologies he left her without a bathroom break. Heather only nodded, her mind burning with numb shock. The books had been cleaned "better than new," but she could only look over the side of the tram with disinterested horror.

As she passed over the gardens, she thought she saw the kidney-shaped eye look at her and blink, which sent chills down her spine. She looked at the graffiti as their tram passed, and realized she knew what it meant. It was a very basic sentence, but she had never seen it phrased in that way before.

It simply said, "he who watches while dreaming."

Six

A Visitor from the Past

Heather did her best to bury the incident. For the next few days she allowed the medical sedative to keep her asleep, giving the entire memory an ethereal, surreal quality. For a while, it also washed away the horrible nightmares. Her whole family was aware that something had happened to her. Rose especially noticed that Heather's cheerful demeanor had been reduced to that of a distracted and dulled daughter who rarely complained and stopped talking altogether. Heather simply replied to repeated questions about her well being by saying the headaches were making it difficult to concentrate, that she would be fine, and not to worry.

Morgana took it the hardest. She assumed it was all because Heather was still mad at her for the books. Morgana had never seen her sister this angry at her, and after days of silent nights with Heather staring at the ceiling, Morgana started to feel anxious and irritable all the time. She tried her best to make up with Heather, but her sister only seemed to ignore her or look back at her face like it was made of a transparent glass.

"I appreciate and understand your apology," she said one day, breaking her self imposed silence. "But you must understand that some things cannot be undone, or unseen."

Heather's reaction scared her so deeply that Morgana started losing sleep. Her grades started to slip, and in class she ended up having a very bad accident with a hat pin that left a nasty scar. Then, for the first time since she was 4, Morgana began wetting her bed. Heather didn't even make fun of her the night she called her mother, crying in hysterics. Heather didn't even seem to notice, and when their mother tried to soothe Morgana's underlying anxiety, Heather simply lay on her back in bed, unmoving.

At one point, Heather actually questioned pursuing her current line of deception, but she felt that she was now in too deep to back out. She felt alone and scared with her thoughts, and try as she might, the horror of those two corpses clutched at her belly, mixing with guilt and fear. When her week of rest was up, Heather knew she must "go back and work with the Professor."

Continuing the deception was fairly easy. The Professor rarely had visitors as it was, usually due to his nasty and dour tone that was dismissive of the pride or ego of others. Heather could enter and leave without anyone noticing, as the building was near the end of a long and dirty cobblestone street. This part of the city was mostly vacant except for various storage companies who seemed to have forgotten they had anything here. She could make as little or as much noise as she liked, and when the man who read the gas meter came round, she found out that the bill was still being paid. After the first week, she had cleaned and set up the lab to her entire satisfaction, and started working in earnest translating Korisan. Studying was even more difficult because unlike other language books, Korisan assumed you already knew Rokasian, and it was the same problem in reverse. So she ended "thinking out loud" by talking to herself, writing in chalk all over the floor, and when she finally discovered something useful, she would write it in a blank notebook she found in a drawer. She prided herself on having her own "set of notes" like a real student.

Her biggest breakthrough was understanding that the language was a symbolic lexicon built in steps that built upon previous symbols. A character in the beginning of a sentence meant something different if it was at the end, or if it was behind a certain character rather than after it. There was a slight logarithmic pentameter to it; longer strings of symbols had more meaning and emphasis than short strings. Some symbols acted as multipliers, while others acted as dividers. She knew the language was the one of the ancient ancestors; the ones who had built the mechanical underpinnings of the world, the first who discovered trolley, and the ones who built the Sky Ring. Those first Builders had a very advanced knowledge that left behind huge structural legends. These legends, the machines that ran deep in the ground where nobody would go, had run flawlessly since that time, and their mysteries were only revealed when something went wrong, and a part needed replaced. Thus, understanding math and gear ratios made it easier for Heather to grasp some of these language concepts, and eventually, she felt she could understand some basic sentences. However, much seemed to be heavily metaphorical, suggesting an entire culture Heather was unaware of.

Of course, there was still the occasional visitor, and they always seemed to show up right when she was in the middle of mapping out something very complicated. While the Professor inadvertently made things easier by not telling anyone he was leaving, it became harder and harder for Heather to push people away as time went by. In the past, the most insistent of visitors would eventually manage to have a word with her master, even if those words ended up being short, angry, and dismissive. Now she didn't have that to fall back upon.

"We are very **busy**," she would say. "Never mind with what, it's none of your business. I have instructions he must not be disturbed, and I am not about to get punished for *your* impatience!" Eventually, she stopped answering the door and left a note that said, "Experiment in progress: Do Not Disturb in the Interests of Safety." She had no idea what would happen if someone official came by, like a police officer or worse, a truancy officer.

And recently, truancy officers were getting to be an annoying distraction outside of the lab. Heather had only had her new approved papers for a week before she got stopped for the first time in a while. And unlike the friendly, "Hello, lad. Shouldn't you be in school?" she had gotten in the past, she was now stopped by a pair of truant officers who would gruffly demand her reason to be in the street when she should be in school. It happened almost every other day, it seemed. Each week there were different people, too, making it difficult for Heather to say, "No, you remember, you asked me last week!" Sometimes, they inspected her papers for a very, very long time. If one of them was to follow her back to the lab...

Her father said it was a new ruling from the government, who felt that crime was getting out of hand. Of course, while Heather had seen the occasional theft or arrest in her life, she hadn't noticed any more than usual. Her father had said that money had been recently poured into the police program, and truant officers seemed to benefit just as much as anyone else. They all got new uniforms, and their numbers doubled. The logic of the uniforms and increased truant officers was explained as children were more likely to commit crime than adults, and that children listened more to military uniforms because all little boys wanted to be soldiers. Her father disagreed with this, stating it was a waste of tax money caused by special interest groups formed by companies who made uniforms for truant officers. Besides, there hadn't been a war between Palachia and anyone else in centuries. The Queens Military was really nothing more than a huge social club. Heather wasn't sure if her father was joking or not, but thought he might only be half-kidding.

Truant officers, unlike the regular constabulary, did not have as rigorous training as their higher paid and more prestigious brethren. Thus they were less disciplined, and consisted of a number of drunks and former thugs trying to make "an honest living" as part of a royal work program. More frequently, there were stories in the local newspapers that stated, "The assailant, a former truant officer..." or "When the truant officer's bed was searched, the missing money turned up..." or "The suspect thief at large was last seen working his shift as a truant officer." Nobody trusted them, and even parents would scare their misbehaving their children with phrases like, "behave yourself, or the truant officer will kidnap you in your *sleep*!"

Because of the high turnover in the job there was always a new weekly batch of fresh faces in starched uniforms dotting to common areas with roving eyes focused on children. Even though Heather had her papers, and even when she wasn't doing anything remotely suspicious, she felt ashamed and scrutinized by the truancy glare, and would often take alternate routes to avoid the more common areas.

Of course, she knew she was doing something illegal, which made it worse. Given the nature of the lie, she wasn't sure exactly how much trouble she'd get in if she was discovered. She had papers and passports, all created by forged signatures of a man who was in another continent and nobody knew when he'd return. She was working alone at her age, which was illegal, and if caught, her professor could also be accused of corrupting a minor for purposes of employment. There were an awful lot of ifs, but Heather could not shake the primary motivation of her deception: to avoid regular school where she would be treated like a second class citizen. She knew she had to do this and when she was caught... well, she hoped something would happen to save her from an eternity of lessons on frocks, shoes, and hats.

Her sister was learning about hats. Specifically, how to make them, and to find out what approved styles were released for that year. Heather thought this was suspiciously like last year's class on hats, but Morgana always treated it like it was the newest and most modern thing simply because of a change in style. The fashions were dictated by the Queen's Fashion Office, who released "staple sheets" every year that showed the acceptable manner of dress that was "scientifically proven to be most pleasing to the eye." Heather made pantomime vomit gestures every time Morgana spoke about the "scientific method" under which these fashions were supposedly designed.

"Do they have a statistical control group?" Heather asked at the dinner table one evening. "Do they have trend analysis that shows success and failure rates of their predictions versus actual results? How do they hire a new person? Do they have to pass a test?" Morgana simply ignored her, chattering away about how she was going to save up for new yellow and green-tipped stay pins.

Soon enough, the day Heather had been fearing and putting out of her mind came. Too soon. Not six weeks into her charade, Heather turned the key to enter the lab muttering to herself things she *would* have liked to say at the dinner table in the response to hat research methods, but would have been sent to bed with soap in her mouth had she actually verbalized them.

"I'll stuff hat pins in your red bottom..." she said aloud deep in a daydream.

"I'm sorry?" said a strange voice. "What did you say?"

Heather froze. She realized quickly that the door lock had little give, indicating it had already been unlocked. Standing in the center of the lab was a very well-dressed woman with eyes wide in shock at Heather's sharp tongue. A thin wasted woman, the stranger was wearing a bustle skirt, velvet red gloves, and one hand perched on a decorative parasol.

"Who are you?" Heather asked. "How did you get in here?" Her stomach tightened in panic. If this was a thief, she would not be able to call the police.

The woman smiled stiffly and nodded. "You must be Heather," she stated as if she was labeling things in jars. "My name is Anna. I am a former assistant to the Professor."

"And how did you get in here?" Heather asked, looking at her set of keys in betrayal.

"I see the darling professor hasn't changed his locks in years," Anna said, looking at her own keys.

"Yes," Heather remembered. "I have seen your... notes." She wanted to say, "The Professor uses you as proof I will become a girly poof, and I have come to despise your name." But she felt that a cool head may evade further trouble.

"I am surprised you don't recognize me," Anna scoffed. "I am one of the smartest women in the world."

Heather was taken aback by the boldness of that statement. "Well, that's good to know. It must make you smarter than me because I have never seen or heard of you."

Anna tilted her head back and laughed in a strangely rehearsed way. "Ah... yes. You definitely are one of the Professor's assistants. Unimpressed with pomp and title." Anna walked up to Heather, stroking Heather's chin with her red glove. "I understand. Of course, what I don't understand is what happened to the Professor. Where has he gone?"

"I don't know," Heather said, keeping her face expressionless and resisting the temptation to bite that hand, "I just got here."

Anna pursed an annoyed frown. "No, I mean, he left weeks ago. Where did he go?"

"He returned, and — "

"No, he is still gone, Heather. Let me save us both some time. Many weeks ago, he left rather abruptly. No word, no notice, and certainly under the shield of haste. Since that time, he has not returned. I am not sure why you are still here. Care to explain *that*? Do you have papers?"

Heather sensed a bluff. "I have papers signed by the Professor himself that explain why I still work here. But I don't see any papers that explain why *you* are here — "

Anne laughed haughtily. "I don't need papers. I am an adult. I can come and go as I please. You are but a small child, and a rather bold one at that. I don't like playing games, but I suppose little girls are still — "

"You call me 'Little Girl' one more time, madam, and I will call the police and have you escorted — "

"You will do no such thing," Anna dismissed. "So the Professor didn't tell you where he was going?"

"He did, but not that it's any business of yours — "

"Oh, so you know where he is?"

"You can ask him yourself when he returns, madam. Now, please leave. I have work to do, and when he finally comes in this morning, I don't think he will let my work lax just because I spent time entertaining someone — "

Anna stamped her parasol, blocking Heather from walking past her. "You are really thick-headed, do you know that?" Anna stooped down and stared Heather in the eyes with an intimidating glare. "Heather? With one stroke of the pen, I could have you shoved into the seat of the most girlish, fashion-drooling class where you'll be making poofy sleeves until you're married off to some upper-class dunce! Oh... yes, I am well aware of your charade here, Heather. Nothing has escaped my research. But to the point: tell me everything you know about the Professor's whereabouts and I won't report you or your family or the Professor for falsifying documents, child labor violations, and — "

"If you leave now, I will not report you for trespassing. It is with great regret that I inform you that your research, however much you paid for it, is flawed." Heather said, trying to maintain her cool.

"You are in no position to bargain, Heather Rebbecca January. If these threats don't worry you, I can have you and your whole family executed for government espionage."

Heather opened the door, and pointed to the hallway. "Out, madam. And don't come back. It is obvious that your threats are empty because they defy reason. You may dress like you have money, but you speak like the insanity of the people on lower levels."

"I see," Anna said, smirking. "Let me explain it another way. Your father violated financial law by sending you, an espionage agent, to a closed maintenance session, posing as a northern

Palachian employee to spy on a secret government project using lectromag on a difference engine. Oh, yes, 'Mack,' I am well aware of your jaunts. Stone and Terry were onto you from the very start. Your innocent lies won't seem so innocent if I stick the Queen's nose in your direction."

Heather was caught off guard; she didn't know how to respond. Up until now, things had been going so well, and she didn't know anyone was the wiser. She had almost convinced herself that the death of the two workers would keep both sides silent.

"Your silence speaks in my favor, Heather. Now, I grow tired of these childish games, and if you want to speak and act like a young lady — "

"Don't call me that, either" Heather said quietly, closing the door. "I don't want to be a lady anything. But I will tell you all that I know."

Anna stiffened her lips. "Fine. Where has he gone?"

"He took the Iron Horse to the — "

"I seem to have arrived at a rather awkward moment," said a familiar voice by the doorway, pushing the door back open. "I could hear you arguing down the hallway."

"Professor!" Heather said in shock. She was all at once gladdened and terrified at his arrival.

"Yes, I am aware of who I am. And I am aware of who you two are as well. Hello Anna. Heather? How come you are not in school?"

"I didn't want to go. You approved me working here, and — "

"I certainly did not! I told you to sign up for a public school. What are you doing here, Anna?"

Anna smiled. "Welcome back. I came to find out where you were. This little squeaky wheel of yours here was just about to show the inner clockwork on your whereabouts."

"Sounds like you were forcing this squeaking," the Professor's lips thinned as he placed his work satchel on a workbench. "What does your band of troublemakers want with me?"

"We think it's awfully suspicious, given your sudden departure, and the recent events. I hardly expected you to come back at all. And when Heather here started snooping around, I — "

"I sent Heather to a public school, not to sniff around the difference engine at Financial One. But now it seems that you are using lectromag to power the calculations. I trust this was a success?"

Anna stayed quiet.

"Your silence also speaks volumes. Fine. Tell your team I wish to meet them at once in their usual incognito style. I will send a tube with the location by tonight. Now go. There will be no more interrogating my former assistant."

"Former...?" Heather mouthed silently.

Anna left in a straight line out the door, her bustle and skirts rustling. If Heather didn't know better, she would have sworn Anna was embarrassed.

The pause after Anna left hung in the air like a collection of sandbags on fragile threads. The Professor closed the door, staring at Heather with scorn and anger.

"Let me see those papers, Heather."

Heather handed the Professor her education papers. She stared at the floor while she heard the crinkling of the documents as he scrutinized them thoroughly.

"These are quite good. How did you get my wax seal so precise?"

"They were your seals, remember? You stamped them while you were busy and ... er — "

"I admit I am very absent minded when working. Forgetful to a fault, I have often put my own spectacles in a teapot more than once. I came to work in a work apron but no pants, and there was that time I was certain you had stolen my best work goggles when they were backwards around my neck the whole time. But despite all that, it is with *great prejudice* that *I do not recall approving your education permits!*"

"But I have proo — "

The Professor threw the documents at Heather's feet. "I didn't just sign you up for public school so you could learn how to make frilly waistcoats, you know. *I did it for your safety* and — just, just what gave you the *bold and arrogant right* to refuse my direct orders — "

Heather would not give up. "Do you even have proof you signed me up for another school?"

The Professor paused and gritted his teeth. "This was a detail I left for **you**."

"And where are *those* papers?" She was unsure of her boldness, but she let the shock of his arrival evaporate any fear at the moment.

The Professor's face grew a deep red. He balled his fist and punched the work bench. Then he paused, and the anger drained out of him in sudden thought. Then he laughed and shook his head. "Okay, Heather... **okay**. You have no compelling arguments, but you do have me backed into a corner." He looked around the lab. "Well, you have certainly kept this place clean."

"I also kept up with lessons."

"What lessons? Oh, right. Snooping difference engines. Now I have to hear all about that — "

"No, I taught myself Korisan and some Rokasian. I'm not quite fluent, but I can decode most of the simpler terms and phrases — "

The Professor's face change expression dramatically. "What did you say? Did you say you taught yourself one of the ancient tongues...?"

"Yes," Heather beamed proudly. "I did it all by myself. It took a while. The structure of the language is much different than the Queen's tongue, but — "

The Professor sat down in shock. "I can't believe it."

"It's true. I can draw it on the walls if you like. Look at these chalk lines on the floor. Look at this: here I discovered that math and language were one in the same. The difference seems to be a series of cultural references. I was going to look them up, but I hadn't gotten past another issue dealing with — " Heather stopped, as the Professor seemed badly upset as if he had received disturbing news about the death of a dear friend. "I am not some silly little girl, Professor."

The Professor looked hard at Heather and quietly replied, "Oh yes you are... yes, yes you are... you have no idea what you have unleashed, teaching yourself these things."

Heather paused. She sensed something foreboding and dismayed in his words. "What... do you mean by that? That I have learned something only males could learn — "

"*Should* learn, Heather. My dear, sweet assistant... why didn't you go to a public school like I asked you to? Why?" The Professor looked like he wanted to grab and shake her, but was afraid to touch her.

Heather shook her head. She was confused. She had expected pride, or at the very least some kind of knowing smirk, but the Professor looked like he'd been punched in the lower gut. He looked less angry and more despondent. It was not a becoming look for him. "I... I didn't want to live my life obsessing over hats or making dresses or marrying a man who — "

"You... you really know how to read... Rokasian, Korisan? Any of those?"

"Yes..." Heather said with decreased confidence. "M-most of the basics. The advanced stuff is — "

The Professor interrupted her with a stressful exhale. "That will come to you when it's ready." He stood up and started to pace the lab, looking disoriented and erratic as he stared at the symbols drawn in chalk on the floor. He paused when he came to Heather's notebook. He opened it up, and quickly closed it after a few moments of flipping through only a few pages. "Blasphemy..." he said, a word Heather did not recognize.

"When what's ready?"

"When the dreams start. When the madness takes over. When your mechanical little brain gives up to the... oh dear god, a woman, *a girl* has learned Korisan. Not even a woman this time, *a girl!*"

"What dreams? The dreams of being crushed? The dreams of death and destruction? The dreams where trolley has huge green fish eyes and tentacles like — "

The Professor wiped his face. "Yes. Yes, those dreams."

"Pfft. I had them *before* I learned Korisan."

"Have you?" the Professor asked, staring blankly at the ceiling. "Well then, maybe it is fate. So now you have crossed over, passed childhood, skipped over adulthood into something altogether different... let me ask you something. What did you think of lectromag?"

Heather's eyes widened. "It was simply the *most!* It arced like snakes, spinning through the air and... oh, well, it killed a man. Or two." Heather quieted briefly at the memory she had been trying so hard to suppress. "That... that was unpleasant. But he didn't follow Stone's orders. Stone said — "

"Stone. Rocky Column? The big blond man?"

"Stone. What's Rocky Column have to do with anything? Isn't he that guy in the League of the Brave?"

"One in the same."

Heather shook her head. "No, he's not. Stone was real... he was a real person. Rocky is just some comic book character!"

The Professor laughed and shook his head. "Still so innocent. Knows how to translate the tongues of the Builders, yet thinks the League is make-believe."

Heather wondered if this was a trick. "Are we talking about the same League? The one run by Worthingheart?"

"That is what he wishes. But that's the fictional part. I take it you do not read League of the Brave."

She frowned with a sour expression and replied, "My sister does. Blecch."

"Tell me, who was Stone's companion?"

Heather thought back. "Chip. I think some southern Palachian... no, wait... *Terry*?"

"Terry 'Chip' LaCroi. Deep southern Palachian-raised, northern Palachian bred."

Heather went numb with shock. "I... I met the real Chip?"

"Apparently so. Short man, high voice?"

Heather still couldn't believe it. "Chip... Chip is a boy!"

"Once he was. Not for a long, long while, Heather. You know, you may be the only youth in all of Palachia who has never read all the League's comics."

Heather shrugged, wondering why it mattered. "I did when I was little. But when people started calling me Chip, it got annoying."

The Professor sighed and relaxed his shoulders. "Well, we have a problem to fix. The first is, I can't let you learn Korisan and then set you loose upon the populace. Knowing that language is not like learning some obscure Yurpan dialect. No, Heather. To know the... path to reading Korisan is not a path you can leave once you choose it. In other parts of the world, I would have had the right to execute you."

"Kill me?"

"Right where you stand. No court in any land would jail me for it, either. All I would have to do is tell them a woman learned the Language of the Builders. They would hail me as a savior. Even here, in the more civilized levels of southern Palachia, I could slit your throat from ear to ear and your parents couldn't harm a hair on my head. In fact, your father would thank me. But you see, I think that this lesson cannot be severed so easily. There would be repercussions of my neglect. Accusations of senility at my age are hard to shake as well. Once people think you are forgetful, well, it's a rapid slide down to your death bed. And I have much to do before then. I cannot risk a trial."

"Why... why can a woman not learn — "

"Because women... can give birth. And once that happens, Heather... once a woman who knows Korisan gives birth... her infant will have the same knowledge."

Heather shook her head. "If a woman in a blue dress gave birth, she would not give birth to a baby wearing a blue dress, would she?"

"No. She would not. Nor can a rat have the puppies of a hound. And a well-bred woman will not give birth to a literate son without the same lessons she received as a child. These are lessons on experience and logic. But as you saw, Korisan is not logical. The parts you that you currently cannot surmise, well... you have not learned their hidden meaning. Once you have that, only madness will remain. Even I confess, I do not know a quarter of what I read. I have met men who have professed 50% fluency. Every one of them met an end that drove them insane. Those that could not end their own lives begged for death or simply were unable to communicate what madness had rendered them comatose." He looked at Heather. "But a child! A child who can read Korisan? Once in a rare while, one is born. And it always means things that never turn out for anyone's best interests."

"I don't understand," said Heather. "I was not born knowing — "

"But you had the dreams, Heather. You had the dreams of the green eye, the death by machinery. A woman who wants to be a man, or a man who wants to be a woman. The signs are there. Like the last time."

"What last time?"

"Centuries ago, Palachia was at war with Rokasia. As you know, armies on both sides had taken heavy casualties. All because of demands on trolley. At the time, Rokasia had very little. And what little they had was not supported by a huge mining structure like they have today. They traded metals, however. So in exchange for metals and metalwork, Palachians gave them trolley and machinery. It worked out very well. But then a child from Yurpa was born. It was a man who desired to be a woman. Yurpa is much more relaxed when it comes to gender roles. It is one of the many reasons they are so distrusted. This child learned Korisan to speak with Rokasians. With this knowledge, he made a deal, and exchanged secrets. There was much intrigue, and this man who traveled as a woman was unable to be captured due to his shifting ways. This lead to trade imbalances, tariffs, boycotts, then finally war. When his ruse was discovered, it was too late. And the only thing that saved civilization from their destruction was... "

"Was what?"

The Professor shook his head. "Too terrible to explain. Sometimes the only thing that can unite enemies is an even stronger enemy. That man had summoned a thing so terrible. So... horrifying... it could only be described as the summons of a twisted and tortured mind. Nobody knows what he did, or how it was done. But to banish this thing required the strength of three nations to defeat it. When it was over... there were barely any souls left. We had to rebuild."

"I was told that the Rokasians tried to invade us, but we held them back and eventually defeated them."

"The lies told in schools are what keeps this civilization prosperous and industrious. But enough of your history lessons. We have a greater concern. What to do with you."

Heather smirked. "You can't send me to public school now, can y — "

The Professor slapped his hand on the work table, scaring Heather into silence. "No. We can't. Keep in mind, *insubordination* can make your sister no longer a twin to anything. The fact you still think this is a way to get out of school is just short of... a complete lack of understanding of the seriousness of this situation. Do not speak that way again. You want adulthood? You must speak as if you are already one."

"Yes, sir," Heather said quietly.

"Now. I have a plan. It will be ugly, and neither one of us will like it. But it's the only choice I see."

Heather's next few hours were the ones that would change her life forever. Moreso than the speech with her mother. And when she walked home that evening, she knew that nothing would ever be the same.

Seven
The Professor's Plan

Heather did not know how she had gotten here, but she knew that in order to proceed, she had to face what she had done. Dressed in the very same outfit she had worn as Mack, she found herself standing on the wooden deck of an airship, facing Anna and the Professor. Thick puffy clouds drifted by like leviathans of the sky, dwarfing the setting like Heather had seen in picture books. In the distance, the Sky Ring would occasionally peer down at them before being obscured once more. The leather straps and buckles of the work clothing seemed heavy and stiff. Between them was a simple trestle-style stone table: two slabs of solid granite supporting a large slab on top. There were small wooden cabin houses and everything had a strange pine and tar smell.

"Heather January?" asked Anna. In her hand was a large golden blade with Korisan symbols, which the Professor had handed her. Sunlight from the scattered clouds flashed reflected amber light across the table. Heather noticed that both of them were wearing small stone stars around their necks. "Get on the table."

Heather backed away. She shook her head and winced. Her head injury was still healing, and it ached when she moved her head too suddenly. "N-no..." she said. "What are you going to do?"

"She doesn't want to," said Terry from behind her.

"She has to. She has read Korisan," the Professor said, his frown puckering low on his long face with a solemn determination.

Terry turned Heather around. "Mack... you didn't tell me you... read Korisan." Terry looked hurt. He backed up and hid behind Stone. "And... you're a girl!"

"I didn't know," she said. "I just thought it was just another language. How was I supposed to know it was forbidden?"

"What other lies have you told to us?" Stone asked. "You were a liar when we first met. You claimed to be looking for the toilet."

"Then you tried to *fool* me!" Terry hissed. "Making me think you were a *man*! You *touched* the difference engine!"

"I didn't mean to! I was just seduced by the machinery — " Heather paused, as somehow that line seemed both cheesy and a lie at the same time. But it was all she could think of to say. "I... please don't kill me. Please!"

"Enough!" the Professor said. "Discussing the truth will not help us. What is done is done. Get on the table, Heather January."

"If anyone finds out that she can read and write Korisan, no price will be too high for her murder, Professor," Terry said. "I might even be tempted to turn her in."

"Please don't, I'm sorry!" Heather said.

The wind picked up. The deck of an airship was a cold place, and the moist wind filled Heather's nostrils. It was a strange smell thick with lectromag. Wind was whipping from the clouds, billowing the sails as they stretched from the surface of the huge balloon that kept them aloft in the sky.

"We are safe from Trolley here, Heather. Up in the air. You must fulfill your destiny."

Heather turned back to the Professor. "My destiny?" There was a deep rumble and the sky turned dark.

Anna handed Heather the knife from across the table. "You must kill us all."

Heather shuddered and recoiled from the blade. Men and women, dressed in tattered clothing, materialized from behind the cabin houses, crates, and barrels. At once, she was surrounded. In place of their eyes and mouths were dark holes where trolley gas poured in wispy ropes.

"I won't!" Heather screamed defiantly.

"If you don't," Anna said, "then the world ends."

A huge, jagged arc of lectromag tore from a cloud, jittering its way across the deck of the ship, evaporating the trolley-eyed zombies with tentacles of blue-white light.

"You have watched lectromag kill," Anna said. "And now you must do its bidding. Or it will kill all of humanity. It will find us in the holes where we live."

The sky turned a dark green. The large balloon rotated downwards and became an enormous eye.

"Heather!" Morgana screamed from the table. "Heather! Save me!"

"Morgana??" Heather screamed back, unable to move.

"Trolley has your sister," Anna said. "And will absorb her. You must kill us to save us!" Anna slit her own throat with the huge knife and fell at an awkward angle on the table, her voice gurgling. Morgana screamed as the blood pooled into her dress, wicking into the cloth and slithering up her taffeta undercoat, staining it like a carnation.

"*You killed Anna!*" the Professor screamed. "You were always so jealous of her!"

"No! I didn't kill her! Morgana! Morgana!"

Threads of lectromag danced across the floor and walls, slithering and crawling across everything. Where it touched the green eyed people, it cut into their skin, tearing off pieces of decaying meat like strings scissoring through butter.

"He who watches while dreaming.... shall awaken!" the Professor said, pointing to huge green tentacles that now reached down from the sky. "You are killing your sister!"

"Heather... I am so tired..." Morgana's voice said. The tendrils of blood were now sliding up her face and wrinkling her skin. Only this time, it was not Morgana, but Heather herself. "I am now your twin," said the angry voice of the second Heather.

"Morgana!" Heather sobbed. Somehow, the knife was in the second Heather's throat, sticking at an awkward angle. The air turned green, and the balloon-eye split open like a gutted corpse, spilling tangled green organs all over the deck. "Morgana!!"

"I am right here, silly! Wake up!"

Heather rolled out of her bed into her sister.

"There there there... " Morgana said calmly, petting her shaking sister's head. "It's okay," she said with a smile. "You must have fallen asleep while cleaning."

"Oh Morgana..." Heather sobbed, burying her head into her sister's cleaning apron and weeping.

Morgana awkwardly patted her sister's back. "It was just a dream, you dunce. Luckily I woke you before the real screaming started." She noted to herself this was the first time Heather ever screamed her name from a nightmare.

Heather felt sick, but she stood up to try and clear her head, even if she was a bit wobbly.

"I wish I could take naps when I had to clean for visitors!" Morgana said sarcastically. "You get all the breaks, you know that?"

"How do you figure?" Heather asked. Sweat covered her pale face.

Morgana shrugged. "Anyway, the Professor will be here any minute. Mother says to get dressed in something nice. *Something feminine!* I have another dress you can borrow. *If you promise not to get gear prints on it!*"

"I'll wear overalls if you don't mind. The Professor has never seen me in a dress — "

"That's not true," Morgana said. "He met you in one. Remember? When we were ten? When you played with him at one of father's parties? You had the old green dress — "

Heather shuddered at the word "green."

"What? You don't fit in that one. The fashion is way old, anyway. That color green is being replaced by a lighter green with yellow accents." Morgana said. "Just let me help you. Mother insists."

The dress her sister picked out was lavender and maroon, and Morgana got a sick thrill from seeing how ugly it was on Heather. "She will never be as pretty as me," she thought to herself, "and everyone knows it."

The Professor's arrival was rather banal and pedestrian, as if he regularly arrived for dinner on a weekday. He was usually jovial and social, and much of the evening was spent with the Professor and her father having long conversations about the recent military spending and fiscal responsibility in trade. The Professor ignored Heather as if she were a stranger's child. He didn't even make eye contact. Eventually, the kids were sent to bed. But after their mother was gone, Heather and Morgana had no plans to sleep. They tiptoed out of their room in their nightclothes, using their bare feet to be as quiet as possible.

As Heather and Morgana sat at the top of the stairs, they both strained to listen at the conversation taking place in the living room until they were pressed together. Heather thought that it had been so long since her and her sister were this physically close for a long time, that it seemed like she was next to a stranger. She could hear her breathe softly and the warmth of her smooth skin was comforting. She missed those times when they had shared a bed at such a young age.

"What did he say?" asked Morgana in the barest of whispers. Normally, where they were at the top of the stairs as small children, they would have been listening to their parents fight or their older brother Kye when he was entertaining a lady friend. Often, their giggling gave them away, and when it didn't come naturally, Heather would try and tickle Morgana to torture her.

"Shh..." replied Heather. "They are talking about stupid boring things like financial futures."

"Ugh, it's been like this for hours," Morgana grumbled. "When are they going to talk about your surprise? Can't you tell me what it is so I can go to bed?"

"Just give it time. I don't know exactly how he is going to present it to them. It depends on what mom and dad says," Heather said.

The memory of the day's heavy conversation with the Professor still weighed upon her thoughts. The fact was that she knew Korisan; there was a possibility of execution if others found out, and her whole family could be in serious jeopardy because of her actions. This secret seemed to fortell certain doom when held in the hands of Anna and the group to which she belonged. Whoever they were, the Professor despised them. While her parents knew nothing of Korisan and it being forbidden to women, there was the minor point that Heather had neglected to tell the Professor; the cleaning of the books at Financial One. What if someone made the connection? She didn't recall if her father had told anyone about how the books gotten wet in the first place, but more importantly, had he mentioned that his young daughter was studying the language? She was terrified that the Professor would be forced to kill her if she had spilled that particular tidbit. Given the fact that Anna had been aware of her ruse, posing as Mack, the northern Palachian worker, maybe they knew as well. That little secret thought burned her more than anything else, because with the anger and disappointment the Professor already had towards her, she could not bear to add more confessions.

"Ugh," said Morgana. "More grown up talk."

Heather listened. Her parents were still discussing politics. Most of it was the same kinds of things both the Professor and her father could talk about for hours into the night. Both had a mutual admiration of one another, which was enhanced by the fact that the Professor was trying to put them both in an agreeable mood. Finally, after a few contented pauses, the Professor started to get to the point of his visit.

"So, Mr. January, your younger daughter has worked very hard for me these last two years," the Professor said. Heather could hear him put down his teacup. This was it.

"I am going to bed," Morgana said, standing up while yawning.

Heather pulled her back down. "Wait... shhh. Here it comes."

"Yes," her father said. "She is quite attached to the work."

"This causes you some concern," the Professor stated. Heather knew his approach would be to appeal more to the concerns of her parents, as if this was the best solution for them. It was the same way the Professor had gotten some of his grant money.

"It does, Professor," said her mother. "We're worried about her future."

"Yes," said her father. "We are concerned greatly. She is not taking to her new roles as a young woman very well. But we think with time — "

"This is understandable," the Professor said quickly. Heather could feel his negotiator's voice warming up. "Your concern is about the future of a young girl not fitting in to the usual roles of a woman. I will be frank; she will be miserable and unhappy as a woman with her skills and penchant for mechanical problem solving. She is one of the best assistants I have ever had. Losing her to the wiles of feminine framework would be a wasteful end. So how do we achieve a compromise?"

There was silence.

"I see by your exchanged glances you have discussed this." Heather could just see in her mind's eye the Professor fingering his cane as he addressed her father. He didn't need it to walk, but in most formal settings, it was a subtle reminder of power. It was a strange cane, old and worn near the handle, with a small star at the top of a worn brass ball and Korisan marking on the ferrule.

Her father inhaled in an attempt to bolster his own confidence. "We have. We think that when the semester starts next year, she should join a public school with her sister. We have already discussed this with the headmaster at Morgana's school. They have a special... class for difficult cases."

Both Morgana and Heather gasped. This part was news to the both of them. Heather had known that her parents wanted to return to school, but those "special cases" were often nothing more than bully pens where they simply whipped errant children at will. The only way to survive was to turn against your classmates, so those small buildings outside the school grounds were often punctuated with the sounds of fighting and jeering. It was rumored that kids died in these fights, their bodies carried away at night when no one was around.

"I don't want you to go with those kids," Morgana said. "They are rough and mean. You'll get hurt."

Heather was touched by her sister's concern. "Not likely, but I don't think that's going to happen, either," Heather whispered back. While the seriousness of her own future was weighing heavily on her mind, the thought that she would avoid special classes lifted them somewhat. No, she thought, this is not my future. What is coming is far more serious.

The Professor snorted. "I have a better option. And this will ease your fears greatly."

"Here it comes," Heather whispered. She wished deeply.

"I would like to hire her as an apprentice."

"An apprentice?" he mother asked with shock.

"An official... *paid*... apprentice?" asked her father.

The Professor acted as if the decision had already been made. Only Heather knew the precariousness of this. If her parents said no, and stayed firm... Heather would have to cut off all ties with them and disappear. If they agreed, she would not have to change her identity. "Paid with room and board," the Professor continued. "You realize, of course, that there will be a change in her lodging and contact time with you."

"What does 'lodging' mean?" Morgana asked. Heather realized they had been unconsciously holding hands throughout. What did her sister sense?

"It means that I would live in the space upstairs from the lab, next to the Professor's apartment," Heather explained. She did not see the look of sadness on her sister's face as she strained to hear her parents' response.

"This is a very serious change in her future," her father finally replied with a cautious tone. "A full apprenticeship means that... she would become a professor like you?"

"Of sorts. The choice is up to her, of course. I cannot grantee that — "

"But... women cannot be professors. Or mechanics!" her mother protested. "This is absurd. Did you tell her this? She can't get her hopes up only to face the stern facts that her childish dreams are simply impossible — "

"Mrs. January? If you please. I know you are a woman of practical nature. This trait comes through in Heather. And Mr. January, your sense of detail and mathematical skills are part of why she does so well, too. But true skill and ability know no sex or age difference. Your daughter is highly skilled, and right now, we are a little short in the prodigy department."

"A prodigy?" her mother gasped. "A prodigy *girl?*"

"Given time, madam, yes. Heather is more than likely a prodigy. Which means she could get a full scholarship."

"But they don't give scholarships to girls!" her father said. "There's no female student body in any university — "

"Mr. January, please. It is true that universities in Palachia do not allow women as students, however, there are other universities in Yurpa that do."

"Yurpa?" exclaimed everyone in shock. Including Morgana as she looked at Heather.

Heather knew very little about Yurpa that wasn't already scant common knowledge. Yurpa was the continent to the East; a mysterious land of people who could only be reached by boat and by airship. Unlike Rokasia to the West, Yurpa was so distant that mail often took weeks or months, and travel was often one way due to the sheer complexity of it. Only the very wealthy could afford to go there, and many times they didn't return because the journey was so taxing. It was usually a complement of airship and steamer through treacherous skies and waters.

"I... I don't want you to go to Yurpa..." Morgana said.

The discussion they had at the lab before she left mentioned she'd become an apprentice, travel with him, and eventually replace him when he grew too old. The Professor had no children of his own, and had said that the same would happen to her once she learned just how much of an outcast she had made herself be. There had been no discussion on where they would travel to; Heather assumed it would have been Rokasia. But her future master did say that he might have to use deception to persuade her parents. The very admittance that she knew any Builder tongue would be suicide. She had been thrilled, despite the Professor stating, repeatedly, that this was not as great as her grin made it seem.

Now she started to understand why.

"So, what you're saying is... we may never see her again," her father said. Heather couldn't see his face, but she sensed he was about to tell the Professor to get the hell out of his house.

"No, certainly not," the Professor said. But Heather knew that could mean, "No, you'll get to see her again, don't be silly," or "No, it is certain you won't see her again." The Professor had a habit of using words distinctly to suit future changes. "I cannot say when you'll see her again, because it depends on my schedule. As I said, I will provide all her food and lodging. Her education would continue and I dare say, the world would be a better place because of it."

"I don't want you to go to Yurpa..." Morgana repeated, holding back a few tears.

"Shhh..." Heather said. "Don't be a moron. I'll come back for you."

"You promise?" Morgana's voice was so tight; it barely came out as a squeak.

Heather did not look at her sister when she answered, "I promise." Her heart grew cold at what could be a lie, and for the first time, she had serious doubts about her future. She would have to leave her entire family forever. The Professor had said this, of course, but the word "apprentice" distracted her like a pile a jewels. She might have agreed to anything, she realized. "But then again," she thought, "did I have a choice?"

"This is Heather's choice? To leave us for the apprenticeship?" her mother asked. Heather could hear that she had started to cry. Morgana echoed her mother's sadness beside to her with silent sobs.

"What would you have her do? What about your son, studying in the university in northern Palachia? What do you think he will do? You must have paid dearly for him to study there."

"We did," her father said, "but he has a future with my company. They subsidized part of the — "

"How would you like the other half subsidized?" the Professor asked.

"By whom?"

The Professor must have smiled at this part, Heather thought. "By me, of course."

"What?"

"I realize that this comes at a great sacrifice. To be blunt, Heather is simply not a woman you can marry off successfully. She will never be an asset to you financially. Her future, as it lies without my assistance, is to attend public school, make dresses, cook, and eventually marry a man who can tolerate her questions. The educational world would be at a severe disadvantage, as would her husband. A woman like her would try to improve things, think practically, and frankly, be so stunted socially that she would be an embarrassment. I understand you doubt my confidence in her apprenticeship, which is why I am putting forth a proposal to subsidize your two sons in university positions."

"*Both* our sons?"

"Yes. Even your little one. The funds would be put in an account that would only be allowed to send them to Northern Palachian University. I do this because my standing there is exemplary, and their sponsorship by me would guarantee them a spot, even if I am not alive to see your youngest graduate. I assume that your other daughter... Morgana, is it? She would be exempt because I assume she would make someone a fine wife."

"He... said I would make someone a fine wife..." Morgana said in awed joy, as if someone had just validated her entire existence and handed her the key to immortality.

"This is where our lives differ," Heather said quietly. Her stomach was heaving in indecision and she had difficulty letting go of Morgana's hand when she pulled it away to wipe tears from her face. "This is where we drift apart for good," she whispered to herself.

"This is quite an... honor!" her father said. And Heather knew that from that point on, it was a done deal.

Heather stood up and went back to her room, and Morgana followed. She sat in her bed, and thought about what she needed to pack. The Professor had said only to bring her work clothes, her sanitary needs, and a few items from home. "But it must be able to fit in a small satchel. No dolls, no stuffed toys, no... unnecessary childhood novelties. Just tools, a few personal effects, the less you bring, the better. Oh, and my books, please..." he added with a stern face. Just how she would explain the state of them was tying her belly in knots. Could she sneak it by him?

"When will you leave?" Morgana asked, sitting beside her on her bed.

"Tomorrow. I   am   going   to   pack,   and   then... ....tomorrow..." Heather couldn't finish her thought.

"When will I see you again?"

"I don't know, Morgana. We're not leaving right away. In fact, I will be living in an unused room above the lab. But when we travel, we travel. I will let you know when I leave here."

"You promise?"

Heather nodded. "By tube."

"You'll send it *by tube*?" Heather mused at her sister's naive impressions. She worked with tube mail daily, but it was a positive luxury back home.

"Yes. I promise," she said with a snicker. "At least twice."

Morgana's eye grew wide.

Rose January came into their bedroom. Her eyes were red, but she was forcing a smile. "Heather?"

"Yes, mother?"

"I'll... get a satchel."

Heather nodded. She felt she should feel very happy, but instead, she felt the first sign of things to come. She ran to her mother and hugged her tightly. "I will visit. A lot. And when I am away, I will send mail by tube."

"By **tube!**" Morgana punctuated.

"You leave tomorrow morning," her mother said. "I am thinking maybe... we should have one final meal together."

Heather nodded. "I would like that very much."

Rose hiccuped, which was something she did when she was trying very hard not to cry. "We'll eat what the Professor didn't eat, and I'll scare up some more things to round out the dishes... oh, baby? I will miss you!" she said, and squeezed Heather tightly.

This was the last time that Heather felt she would be embraced the warm bosom of her mother. She squeezed the last drop of love from the hug, and forced herself to remember the smells and fabric of her apron.

Eight
The Signs of Things to Come

"I trust that the goodbyes were bittersweet?" the Professor asked as Heather walked into the lab. She noticed the room was already slightly askew.

"They were a little painful... but I have made my decision," Heather said as she put down her satchel and stack of books. "And it's not like I won't ever see them again — "

"*That...* is actually very likely, young lady," the Professor warned.

" — see them again," Heather continued stubbornly. "When I become a grown up."

"*If* you live to see that. I believe I did mention the dangers involved, or were you listening — ?"

"I was listening. I'd rather not be pessimistic. It gives me no strategic advantage over my destiny."

The Professor scoffed. "Your destiny... What fool told you that?"

"You did. Sir." Heather said quietly.

She was still hurting and hadn't slept a wink all night. She had just left her home earlier than normal so she wouldn't have to face a second final goodbye. The dinner the night before was so painful, nobody could eat anything in front of them. There was a lot of talking and promising to write, but Heather couldn't even remember one thing that had been said. When her older brother, Kye, left for the University, Heather remembered it being far more jovial and a planned affair. But now the dinner table was a mashed assortment of leftovers. The entire time she was thinking about trying not to think about goodbye. Although she was now no further from them than a 20 minute walk, it felt like they were already somewhere in the deep heart of Yurpa.

"Let me see those books," the Professor commanded, pointing to the heavy, string-wrapped collection Heather tried very hard to conceal.

Heather handed the Professor the stack. He cut the string with a pocket knife and pulled the first copy from the top. "*Korisan Symbology and Marks*," he read from the title as he flipped it open. "A pedestrian approach, but I knew the author of this ... Heather? Has this book been... altered?"

"I cleaned it, Professor."

"You cleaned — "

"It was very dusty and dirty," Heather interrupted. "I thought I would repay your loan by... cleaning the dirt from it."

The Professor flipped through the book, turning to the most affected pages. Heather had to fight the instinct to flee. Where would she go, anyway?

"That sounds like something your mother would say," the Professor said in disgust. "My notes... my margin notes have been smudged!"

Heather was glad that she chose to stack the books in order of ruination. "You should see the last title," she wanted to say in a moment of suicidal thought. But instead, she quipped, "That's why I stopped. I tried to be careful, but once I saw the notes were smudging I stopped — "

The Professor cut her off by slamming the book shut. He picked up a second book. "*A Study in Korisan Sentence and Paragraph Structure: Gears and Axles.* Well, I am sure this was a fun read."

"I particularly focused on verse and pentameter. It helped speed the reading when — "

The Professor cut her off again with a book slam. He picked up a third book. Heather looked at the fourth with growing worry. If he saw just how bad it got, he might read the fifth book and see the worst of the damage.

"*Korisan Philosophy?* Tell me, did you just pick up any book that had the word Korisan in it and read it?"

"No, I selected books I thought would be most useful for private study at home. You took a lot of the basic books with you, so I had to learn from what I could find. And that book is not actually about Korisan Philosophy; that's the title in the Queen's Tongue. The real title is *Korisan Meter and Structure*, as indicated in the cover plate."

The Professor flipped open the book, and read the cover plate.

Heather tried to continue. "You can tell it's a Korisan title; the pentameter of the syllables are in a 3/4 meter, which the text is usually 4/4 for easy reading. This comes from how they used math and gear ratios. If you — "

The Professor slammed the book and simply pushed aside the last two titles. "'*Korisan Cultural Roots.*' '*Archeology and History: Korisan Influences Throughout the Eras.*' You know, that last book was the least of my favorites." Heather cringed as he reached for it, but then the Professor stopped and looked at her. "I have never taught anyone fluent Korisan, only enough basics to decode various mechanical diagrams, and even those students knew these books were mere gibberish. The fact you learned on your own and used these works both astounds and saddens me. But given what I have learned in the last few months, I should not be even the least bit surprised. I only wish that you hadn't have taken this path, because the curse you placed on yourself in self-righteous arrogance may have doomed us all."

Heather screwed up her face, trying recover what was left of her pride. "You never told me of your trip. What did you learn about the substandard gears in the last few — "

"**Enough**! Put these books back, you won't need them anymore. As that language seeps your brain in its own stew of insanity, it will rip your psyche in twain without needing the help of a bunch of scholars who paid for these works with their very lives. I watched grown men go from educated boors to unkempt gutter rats drawing crazed formulas with their own excrement on any available surface." The Professor's eyes lowered to the floor, looking at Heather's scuffed drawings in chalk. "You apartment is upstairs. It's the one we were thinking about using as trolley storage. It's got a large window in it that faces the market square; I suggest you smear lubricant on it so people are unable to peek in. I have sent off paperwork for you to be my apprentice. Later, I will have suitable clothes sized for you."

"Clothing?" Heather looked down at her work clothes.

"Yes. I have a tailor who specializes in... discreet fittings."

Heather gave her professor a puzzled expression.

"Last night I spoke with some of the people who have met your alternate personality, and I felt it was best to continue that line. From now on, you will not be Heather January. You will be Mack Van Horne. You are a northern Palachian apprentice. Work on your accent some more, and learn their actual language, not just the accent."

Heather smiled. "Okay, I see what you're doing. I will — "

"Wipe that smirk off your face. Just because you can speak basic Northie doesn't mean you can pass as a native. A few curse words and foul phrases do not make polite company where we will be going. It is important that you stick close to me. No jaunts back to your old house, and you will no longer be addressed as Miss January. We're going to cut that hair short and dye it. Then we're going to — "

Heather's chest grew tight. "I can't go back to my old house?"

"Ever. You are my apprentice. You agreed to this. How far has your memory — "

"No, no... that's fine." She felt there were other ways to get what she wanted. "It's just that going that way is more convenient to — "

"It is convenient to nothing. Now, I want you to put your things in your new room. I have a list you must carry to this address. From the lockbox, take some money for some tram fare. I trust you can find the place on your own, Heather?"

Heather looked at the address. "Yes, I think — "

"What??" the Professor screamed. His scowl was crushing his eyes into small dark slits.

"What what?" Heather asked in shock. "I said yes, I think I can — "

"You answered to *Heather*! I tricked you on purpose! For the next few weeks, if you answer to Heather, Miss January, ma'am, or any other feminine term I *will* punish you!"

Mack swallowed. Punish her? He had never spoken like this before. "Y-Yes, sir."

"Good. Normally I despise the term 'Sir,' as I work for a living, and I am far too educated enough to fall prey to the temptation of soft titles royalty gives as party favors. But it is the accepted apprentice address to their master. Now that I have made myself clear, do you know how to take care of your feminine sanitary needs, or shall I send for those as well?"

Mack stared. "What would I need with feminine sanitary things," she asked tentatively, "as a boy?"

The Professor nodded and released his scowl. "Good."

Mack paused for a moment in thought, and then asked, "But... as a boy, may I have to purchase some for a girl I kn — "

"*That* will be dealt with in another lesson. Now go put your things away; they clutter the lab. Here is a key for the apartment, and since I have not seen it, you may find it needs cleaned. I don't know what's up there; living or dead. When you are done, return here quickly for your first list of errands."

Mack grabbed her satchel and the key, and ran to the apartment above the lab.

Unlike the heavy metal door to the lab, the door to the apartment was a standard plank door with a metal rim. As Mack turned the key into the lock, she noted the flimsy connection that would have made kicking in the door to be trivial; even for her sister. The apartment was very small and rather cold. Barely the width of her outstretched arms, it had a small bed with no bed linens, a dresser with a dirty mirror, a wobbly chair, and a washbasin. The "window" was a filthy glass slanted roof that overlooked a small portion of the market below, but mostly faced the back alley of a vegetable cannery storage warehouse. High above her were the harsh gas lights of the ceiling of her city level which she knew would never turn off, even during maintenance time. Mack decided to properly arrange the room later, so she put her satchel on the dresser, and put the key in her pocket.

As she looked at her face in the mirror, it looked back at her rather sadly. "Heather," she said to the reflection, "I don't know what our future holds, but this is what we wanted."

"What *you* wanted," said the reflection back.

Mack paused. Did the reflection just speak back to her? She shook her head, let the pain wash away, and the reflection in the mirror spoke no more. But it did seem very discontented. Mack shoved her satchel in one of the dresser drawers, closed the door behind her, and ran back down to the lab.

Mack found the Professor making a list on a small sheet of scrap paper. "Professor, I require some bed linens, as the bed does — "

"You will not be there long enough to need bed linens. You will sleep in your work clothes."

Mack titled her head a little. "I'm sorry, but — "

"When we travel, we may not be able to afford luxuries like bed linens or night clothes. I never use them."

"The room is rather cold — "

"So curl up. The rooms closer to the upper levels are always colder. That's there some of the ventilation shafts exit, knowing cold air sinks. Sadly, our sleeping rooms are in the way. But we will often find our journeys up north cold. A Northie does not shun the cold, he embraces it. I suggest you do the same."

"Do I even get a blanket?"

The Professor shrugged. "You tell me."

Mack nodded. "Yes. I think I do."

"Don't get anything you can't carry. You will travel light enough to carry all your belongings in one trip from now on."

Mack took the list with the address. It was in Korisan, but she guessed it was a list of clothing measurements from the context, although a few of the items were a little confusing.

"Don't let *anyone* know you can read that," The Professor reminded her. "The second someone finds out, they could execute you for a reward and that simply will not do, Mack."

"Yes sir," Mack said, looking for some tram coins in the lockbox.

"And Miss January?" Mack almost turned, but stopped herself. "Miss January?"

Mack took the money and pocketed it. "I will see you later."

"Miss January you will not dismiss me!! Say you are sorry at once!!"

Mack stammered, but held firm. "M-Miss January was your f-former assistant, I think?"

The Professor smiled, but it was more of a leer. "It doesn't get easier with time. I will slip you up, and you will have to repay me with hard labor."

Mack nodded as though she understood, but given the labor that she'd already done, she was not sure what harder labor might be. She took her things and left the lab, still shaking in her chest. "I am Mack. I am northern Palachian." She repeated this to herself over and over as she took the tram.

From time to time, Mack noticed strange Korisan markings. She had lived in the city her entire life, but never noticed them before. They were just random lines and squiggles, perhaps even just ornamental designs to break up monotonous walls. Most of them were faded symbols made in old paint or chalk, but the thought of former students of the language driven so mad that they used their own excrement made Mack shudder. And one symbol seemed to dominate above all others, "He who watches while dreaming."

The address listed on the notes the Professor gave her was near Financial One. In fact, it was on one of the balconies that overlooked the large plaza and garden overlooking Financial One. As she tried to find the building numbers, people slammed into her in an unforgiving, impatient manner. Quickly, she realized that if one did not go with the flow of traffic, it was like being a loose screw in clockwork. It took her a while to find the pattern, but eventually she got the hang of it. Sadly the address was confusing as the building numbers on the balconies were obscured by ornate artwork and the order of the addresses seemed to be aggravatingly random.

"6925 Credit Row... 6924... 6923... 6922... 7001...? Where is 6921?"

"Can I help you, sir?" asked a man at a cafe table.

"Y-Yes," Mack said, trying to keep the northern Palachian accent. She decided to make it sound stilted like southern Palachian was learned phonetically. "I need... find... 6921 Credit Row."

The man grabbed the paper from her before she could stop. "Ere! What kind of script is this?"

"I... can't read so... good," Mack said. "Please to give back..."

The man handed her the paper back. "There's no 6921, lad. You might want to try 6912."

But 6912 was a coffee shop. Eventually, Mack sat down at an empty cafe table, and tried to figure it out. It was not like the Professor to get an address wrong. And it was supposed to be discreet. So maybe it was a code. Mack thought about it for a small while, and noticed that there was a subtle gap between the 69 and 21. They both had common factors of 3. That left 23 and 7. So she decided to go to 723 Credit Row, but that didn't exist. Neither did 237. So she tried 3-7-23. And behold, there was a small tailor shop! She was to get clothing, so she assumed this was the right address.

Cautiously, Mack entered the tailoring shop. The outside rush of sounds was silenced the moment the door closed behind her. The faint ringing of a bell above the door announced her arrival, but nobody came out from the back.

The tailor shop was for men, and men only. The mannequins were dressed in the latest fashion in men's suits. Vests poked out from single breasted coats, and faceless heads adorned the latest in headgear. Various handmade signs stated in elegant fonts the latest approved styles as per the Queen's Fashion Office, including what cloth went with what style. Men's fashions had not shifted much since she was little. In fact, her father still had the same suit that he'd worn to work every day for years. Racks of cloth were displayed in slanted shelves, along with selections of buttons, and posters of what a well-dressed gentleman should wear. Other men's products were also sold, from colognes to hair cream. Mack went to one corner of the shop and looked at the worker's selection.

"Well, what might I do for a young man such as yourself?" asked a voice.

Mack looked around, but saw no one. "Hello?" she asked.

"Hello. I can see you, but you cannot see me," said the voice. It had a strange, mellow quality to it, and yet it seemed impish in its statement.

Mack slowly panned the room, looking for any sign of movement. It was difficult because the subtle ventilation coming from the ceiling was moving all the loose fabric. But she knew how to scope a pattern when she needed to, especially when working on machinery. She looked for movement that was out of place, and saw what looked like a curtain that moved like something large was behind it.

"I think you are behind that red curtain," she said.

"Very *good!*" the man said, stepping out from behind the fabric. "You must be Heather — "

" — Mack," she corrected.

"Right. Right, Mack...the newest northern Palachian. The Professor sent notice that you would be here today for a fitting." The man speaking was of slim build with a curled mustache and wearing a tailor's apron. He had very handsome looks for someone who had what was essentially a lower labor job. Mack guessed he was the owner.

"Yes, I have come for a fitting. I have a list for you, but I can't read it."

The tailor took the paper and studied it. "Are you literate?"

"I am. But not in that funny script."

"I see you solved the numeric puzzle we gave you. Sorry, but we didn't want anyone else to find us."

Mack looked at the man quizzically. "Then why do you have a shop front?"

"Because no one would suspect we're at a tailor's," said the man with a straight face.

That made even less sense. "But your sign says you are. Right on the glass," Mack said, pointing to the lettering.

"It does. But you know, we are not actually tailors. Well, okay, we are. We do it all the time. But not officially."

Mack felt she was being tested, and tried to break apart the conversation logically. "So you're tailor, but not officially, hiding out in a tailor shop that no one will come to because...?"

The man put the note in his vest pocket. "...they will be looking for someone else."

Mack paused. "I'm sorry, I am confused."

"And that is why it works for us so well."

Mack simply said nothing for a while, letting the silence speak for itself, but she thought for a moment that she heard a woman snicker from the back room. Finally, she felt she should proceed in the conversation. "Well, I am here because I need a tailor, so should I look for something else and find you, or..."

The man nodded. "Right, well, let us begin. I know you have a rather... unique issue. I will state, however, that in order to make this issue less noticeable at your age, you will require constant tending. It will also require a certain... change in behavior when with ... other men."

"Right," Mack said. She was unsure what he meant.

"Let me ask you, have you... had... um... a certain... change... um..."

Mack was unsure. "Change of what?"

The man sighed. "Are you... are you... menstruating?"

Mack blushed. "What, now?"

"No! No no... I mean... in general..."

"Yes," Mack said. She felt incredibly ashamed and embarrassed, and wondered if this was also part of the Professor's test.

A boisterous female laugh came from the back. "I find this *most* humorous!"

The tailor stood up straight and shouted into the air, "Lynn, I do not — "

"Oh, hush! Mack, please come to the back fitting room. Lance? Put the closed sign out front."

Lance led Mack to the fitting room behind the curtain where the style and display of the storefront gave way to the stacks of shipping crates, loose bolts of fabric, and general trash lying around in hastily pushed piles.

"Forgive the mess," said a woman whose appearance shocked Mack to the pit of her stomach. Instead of the usual styles of crinoline and skirts, this woman was wearing a men's shirt, vest, and slacks. On top of her head was a small leather cap topped with goggles. The entire effect was completely confusing, as instead of the usual straight shape of a man, the men's clothing on this woman was rounded at the hips and topped with a bust that didn't seem to complement that vest very well.

Mack was speechless.

"Never seen a woman dress like this before, have you?" Lynn said with a smirk.

Mack shook her head. A nervous laughter was starting to crack her face.

"Laugh if you must, everyone does when they see it for the first time," Lynn said with a bored expression. "Get it all out now..."

Mack let a snicker escape, but she quickly composed herself.

158

"Good. Because this is the kind of stuff *you* are going to wear from now on."

Mack blushed in shock. She didn't know why, either, and she rapidly tried to act like it was no big deal, but there... right in front of her... was a woman dressed as ... man.

"Oh, don't give me that look, Mack. In fact, we're going to work on your posture and disposition. You are going to work with men, you are going to act like them. No hands on hips, no feminine swagger, and when a gentleman swears in your company, there will be no blushing. You will guffaw, you will smoke, you will drink, and you will never, ever, ever support women in any way."

Mack nodded. It was all coming too fast. She had always wanted to be a man, but this was such a jarring change. Her father was always a gentleman, as was the Professor, but it seemed like she was among the kind of company that might be much like the Northern Palachians. But before she could recover, Mack heard something even more horrifying.

"Now, strip down to your bare skin, I want to see what I am working with."

Mack blushed and stammered, "Er, ah... okay, ah — "

"What's the matter... lad? You have problems being naked?"

"Well, ah..." Mack had never been naked in front of anyone but her own mother before. "I guess ah — "

"You have until the count of ten to be completely undressed and on my fitting platform. None of this sand in my gears, you hear me? Men love being naked. They do it all day."

"Oh, were that to be true..." Lance said from somewhere in the shop, but Lynn rolled her eyes and snorted.

Mack decided to suck up the courage and do as she was told before she lost the nerve. She quickly disrobed while Lynn watched. She paused when all she had on was her bloomers and work shirt. "Can you at least turn around while I do this?"

"What? Why? I am going to be measuring you naked, lad." She looked at Mack's shaking fingers. "This is the last time you'll be wearing those bloomers. Look at you; you look like a girl or something. Have some pride in your looks, boy!"

Mack stripped down to the very skin she was born in and quickly stood on the measuring platform.

"Will you stand up straight and remove your hands? You think I have never seen a naked person before? Please, I have a mirror in my dressing room."

Mack did what she was told with great embarrassed difficulty. The air in the shop was cold as the ventilation seemed to blow right on top of her.

"And stop shivering!"

"But I am cold!"

"Then be cold without shivering. For trolley's sake, lad. I can't measure a flapping fish, now, can I?"

Mack shook her head.

"I can see that you're still quite young. That's going to make measuring you difficult, as you will change quickly. But it can also make things easier. I am going to get you an adjustable soft corset. I am also going to have you use a binding wrap for now, and possible padding in your midsection for later. We have to hide that shape as it develops. Now, what do you have as far as clothing now?"

"I have a — "

"Burn them. I don't care if they look boyish or not. People have seen you in those clothes, and they are not exactly northern Palachian in style. I will send you home with new clothes, but I need you to scuff them up with some hard work. Have the Professor send you to do some gear work or something."

"Yes ma'am — "

"Do *not* call me *anything* feminine! I look it now, but when we work together in the future, you address me as *sir*, do you understand?"

Mack swallowed. This was becoming very confusing. "Yes... sir."

"She's having your leg," said Lance as he entered. Lynn was laughing despite herself, indicating that she was a bit of a prankster as well. "You think with that chest, she could be called anything but? I call her ma'am all the time. People expect her to be a lady." Mack immediately put her hands across her vulnerable parts and gasped in horror.

"*Don't do that!*" Lynn said angrily, prying her hands back. "I could have stabbed you with scissors or something!"

"*Must* he be here?" Mack gasped in embarrassed horror.

"Who, Lance? Hah. He's not interested in *your* nudity, *believe* me..."

Lance laughed to himself as he passed them.

"What do you mean?"

"Lance is ... oh, dear boy. Lance is someone who does not prefer the company of ladies."

"Not true, not true!" Lance said from somewhere behind some crates.

"Right, correction, Lance loves the fairer sex. Adores them. To the point he wishes he was one, and that makes him popular with the ladies but not for romantic purposes."

"What does that mean?" Mack asked.

Both Lynn and Lance laughed. "What does that *mean*, Mr. Worthingheart?"

Mack's jaw dropped. "Wait, that's Lance Worthingheart of the League of the Brave?"

"Sorry to burst your boiler, Mack. Yes. *That...* is *the* Lance Worthingheart."

"Guilty as changed, m'lud!" Lance shouted from somewhere else.

"Then... you're... Goggles?" Mack nearly fell off the platform in shock. In the comic series, Lynn was a bit aggressive, but always portrayed as a motherly figure. The woman in front of Mack looked like a bar maid... in men's clothing. "The woman who hits people with a frying pan?"

Lynn slapped Mack's shoulders. "Honey, you are all sorts of naive. This will be fixed sooner rather than later. While I am handy with any type of metal in this hand, a frying pan to the head is a last resort. I have fired a gun with my eyes blindfolded. I have strangled wild beasts with nothing more than a rope and a pair of boots. I am more man than my boy Lance, here — please tell me you didn't have a crush on him."

"What? No! I mean, I am a boy..." she tried to lie, despite the fact Lynn was measuring her inseam at that very moment.

Both Lynn and Lance laughed hearty guffaws.

"If *only* you were a boy!" Lance said, coming back with bolts of cloth and sighing. "Any boy I'd like within the confines of my alone time would have... something more worthy between his legs.

"Look, I am confused..." Mack said. She was completely disoriented, and started to feel dizzy from the sheer mental complications of her surroundings while Lynn's calloused hands scratched across her cold skin. Here was Lynn "Goggles" Stellard, the main heroine in the League of the Brave comics, dressed as a man. Then there was Lance Worthingheart, the very heartthrob of all women everywhere, who acted like a girl. And the entire time, she had thought neither one of them actually existed in real life.

"I bet you are," Lynn said. "No," she said to Lance, pushing back a bold of cloth. "I don't want wool now. I will do the overcoat last. Get me a selection of trousers, and I will hem them up. I have to send her back with some temporary clothing today, according to this list."

"You can read that?" Mack asked. She felt that stating how illiterate she was to Korisan might prevent some questions in the future. But she was alarmed when Lance and Lynn both looked at one another and looked at her. What did they know? "Looks like chicken scratch..." she said.

Lynn looked down at her. "Look, it's Rokasian. You know, people from Rokasia?"

Mack frowned. "I am aware of what Rokasian *is*, I just can't *read* it."

Lynn and Lance looked at one another. "You have the biggest mouth," Lance said, and with that line, he slipped away behind crates again.

"Fine, fine," Lynn said. "It's true, I can't read it. But I have a machine that does it for me."

Mack gasped. "There's a machine that does that?"

"It's a secret. Do not tell *anyone*. The Professor will be told Lance read it, understood?"

Mack nodded. "How does it work — "

"Apparently, the word 'secret' is not in your vocabulary," Lynn snapped. "Now stand still. I have to measure your hat size... why... you're wearing bandages. What for?"

"I hurt my head."

Lance came from the back. "I was wondering when we were going to talk about the elephant in the room. What happened to your head? Did you try and cut your hair short like that and stabbed yourself with the shears?" Lance started to pull back the bandages.

Mack swatted his hand away. "No, I fell on some granite and split it open."

"You what?" Lynn asked in shock.

"I split my head. It's healing though..." she said, but they were not listening and pulling back the bandages.

"Goodness, that's quite a split," Lynn said. "Hand me some sterile alcohol."

"I think we need Massood to have a look at that," Lance said, handing Lynn the bottle.

"This will sting a bit, dear — " Lynn said as she pressed something very cold on the large, fragile scab.

"OOWWW!!" Mack shouted, nearly falling off the platform.

"I am surprised that the Professor did not mention this," Lance mused with a voice tinted with deeper concerns.

Lynn sighed, "The Professor will tell you only what he wants you to know."

"So nothing has changed, has it?"

"My hope is that Anna will be able to get through to him and find out what's going on."

Mack held her tongue. She felt they were fishing for information, but she felt that until the stinging in her head wound stopped, she wouldn't tell them anything. There was a long silence while Lynn took all the measurements, writing them down on a sheet of paper. Finally, Mack could no longer stand it. "When can I get dressed again?"

"I am not sure, **Lance**?"

"That's my name!" Lance called from somewhere within the shop.

"Why are you *so slow*? This g... boy is *freezing!*""

Lance appeared from behind a collection of crates with a small tray with folded clothing. "Here is a union suit, and I shall have a work shirt in a moment. Somebody... did not put them back properly, and now I can't find a — "

"Just get Mack a shirt!" Lynn growled.

"My sister rode on a parade float with him," Mack said after Lance left.

Lynn clucked. "Lucky her. Safest man to be with in all of Palachia if you're a woman, let me tell you. Even the loosest of..." Lynn started into Mack's eyes, still wide from all the changes. Even though earlier that day she had punched a man in the jaw, and nearly drowned him in a rain barrel, there was still some mother hen left in her. A pang of regret shot down her spine. "...never mind."

"Does he really do all those acrobatics like the comics?"

Lynn shook her head. "That's just the comics, lad. Put these on. The longer I stare at you, the less of a boy you look."

Mack unrolled the pair of long underwear. She had seen her father wearing them before, but something seemed rather... out of place... for her to wear them.

"Men don't wear baggy or heavy bloomers. Just linen union suits like this one. We will give you three, because I know they become soiled rather quickly. These are special ones with a... gap... in the unmentionables. Men only need the rear flap, but yours will have a flap that goes from the front and snaps in the rear. At a casual glance it looks like a men's undergarment, but when you unsnap this part... see? Full access for lavatory functions."

"That's... handy..." Mack said, as she stepped into them. The entire suit fit her from ankle to wrist, and snapped down the front. As stated, the small flap snapped down near her hips, between her legs, and to the small of her back. "Now I won't have to pull down several sets of undergarments to take care of things."

"Men have it good, don't they? Now. Before you snap up, I want you to wrap this around your chest. It's a binding cloth. It will keep you... well, it will flatten things. When you get older, it's purpose will become more apparent." Lynn pulled the cloth around Mack, and as her face became close, Mack could smell cigars and cologne. "I daresay you don't even need a soft corset but one has been ordered for you, so I shall make it easily alterable for when you come back for modifications. It will save me a lot of time."

"My goodness, that is tight — " Mack gasped as Lynn wrapped the cloth around her.

"Just wrap it from the back to the front, twice, like this... and cinch it tight here. Your chest will be sore, but... well, you'll get used to it."

"I never thought I'd be getting a clothes fitting from the members of the — "

Lynn cut her short. "Mack, listen. We're not like the comics or the stage shows, is that understood? I don't want to explain that I cannot leap between girders with grace and poise."

"Don't worry," Mack said. "I didn't even think you existed until yesterday. I mean, I never really read your stories, but my sister did. Spoke endlessly about — "

Lynn gasped. "You never read our stories? The books? Anything?"

"No. Not really. I didn't... care for the... um..." Mack suddenly wished she had said nothing. "Well, it's not important."

Lynn laughed out loud. "Ha ha ha! No wonder you weren't upset about Lance. You have no idea who our characters are. Lance? Guess what?"

"I heard everything!" Lance said, bringing in a satchel wrapped in paper. "One of the few people who have rarely heard of us in these parts; the Professor was right! Oh, my boy, you'll make an excellent northern Palachian!"

Lynn sighed and buttoned Mack up. "Well, then Mack, I feel a *lot* better. You will know us as who we actually are. But how people treat us may confuse you, I suppose."

"How come you own a tailor shop?"

"We own many things in Palachia. We mainly stay in blue collar districts with the working class. While we wine and dine with the queen, we find the knowledge and information among the lower bowels of the cities to be more... helpful. You have already met Rocky and Chip."

"Stone and Terry?" Mack asked.

Lance held a work shirt up to Mack's frame. "Yes! Good, good. You will be very easy to be around. No star-struck nonsense, no retraining you real names."

Lynn nodded. "I think we should have toast. Bring out some of the Yurpan brandy. Just us lads!"

"Brandy?" Mack asked.

"Better get used to it, lad. There's going to be a lot of drinking when you're with us."

The hours passed quickly. Soon, Mack started feeling like the room was spinning. She'd had only had a few drinks of the sweet, burning fluid and was feeling a combination of sleepy pleasure and a rolling stomach. As a child, she had a taste of some of the "spirits," as her parents called them, but she had never experienced this kind of drinking with adults. It seemed very social, and Mack now found herself extremely happy with the world. She was now certain that she'd made the right choice, and that Lance and Lynn were utterly charming. She couldn't wait to tell her sister how she was hanging out with the League of the Brave like they were friends. It also occurred to Mack that she'd never really had friends before.

Until that night, she had never even considered it, having always found herself the outsider. Both Lynn and Lance had said they would gladly be her friend, and that they were glad to have her working for them.

Eventually, all good things had to come to an end, so a slightly tipsy Mack, dressed in newer work clothing, retrieved her package of other clothing and strolled out of the shop. Lynn had told her that the rest of the tailors items that had to be crafted by hand would arrive in their shop in a week. At least that's what Mack thought they'd said. It was all very foggy, and as she got on the tram back to the lab, she didn't keep an eye on the time. As the tram ran on its tracks, it felt like she was flying; everything was amazing and just so... wonderful. Her life was amazing.

She became acutely aware of the time, however, when she was stopped by a truant officer as she got off the tram.

"Just where do you think you're going, lad?" he asked gruffly. The man was wearing one of the new crisp blue uniforms that Mack would normally have been able to spot from a mile away, but her head was still swimming in Yurpan brandy.

"Hey... I'm a boy..." Mack said. Her eyes had trouble keeping focus as she crowed. "I'm gonna be with the League of the Brave, you know!"

The officer dragged her out of public view, his expression empty. "You have papers to be out in your... condition?"

"League..." she said. "It's like it's not even a real word... you know? Leeeeeaagueee..." she snickered.

"*Papers?*" asked the truant officer strongly. His grip on her shoulder tightened until the pain crossed the alcohol's defenses.

Suddenly, Mack felt her head clearing. She was in trouble. Fumbling for her papers, she realized that she hadn't gotten them back since the Professor realized they were forged. She had no identification on her whatsoever! She sobered up almost completely at this realization.

"I'm sorry," she said in a gravelly voice. "My papers are with my master. But he's a block down this way, we can — "

"*No papers?*" The truant officer looked Mack in the eyes. "You can't be more than 12, lad. Long way from home, are you?"

"I am sure we can work this out, you see — "

The officer tapped at the bundle she was carrying. "What's in that package?"

"My work clothes, sir."

"That's a package from a royal tailor. You haven't nicked it, have you? Do you have a sales invoice to prove you paid for it?"

"What? No." Mack was glad she was out of the public view, because this would prove to be embarrassing.

"How did you pay for it, then?"

"My master, Professor Gaylord, sent me to pick them up — "

"You said they were *your* work clothing!"

Mack suddenly didn't feel comfortable being alone with this man. The alley they were in seemed confining. "They are, I was being fitted. Please, if we can just go to the — "

The officer grabbed Mack by the shoulders. "No, lad. We are going somewhere else. We need to check you in with a constable, but I don't see one. Do you?"

"No!" Mack said, looking around. "I don't."

"You mean to say I have trapped a thief and there is no police officer to turn you into?"

Mack realized that this might be a problem. "No. And I am sure if there was one, he'd know I was working with the prof — "

"Nobody at all?"

"No."

The truant officer looked Mack dead in the eyes. She realized too late, in horror, it was the same man that she had hit with ice tongs. Did he know? Yurpan brandy started to dribble into her new union suit as she shook, very scared now.

"Good," he growled in a low tone, grabbing Mack by the neck and dragging her deeper into the dark alley.

That night, what was left of Heather in Mack met an untimely end with a gruesome death of innocence.

Nine
The Results of Lost Innocence

Professor Gaylord paced his office. As much as the events of the past few months should have prepared him for the rapid changes, he was not prepared for his assistant being the one of the possible chosen. His trip to Rokasia had certainly been eye-opening, and the things he'd feared most seemed to be coming true. And though he thought he had severed all connections back in southern Palachia, when he received word that his former assistant was not only still working in his lab, but had also drawn Korisan symbols all over the floor in chalk, he had to return. He could not let that girl get into the hands of the Queen's League of the Brave, but he could not let them know that by being so obvious as to hide her. No, Anna had made sure of that.

His choice to make her an apprentice was very, very risky. He wasn't even sure what he was doing, but he felt if he taught her everything he knew, that maybe, just maybe, his life's work would not be in vain after all. This would be an excellent feather in his cap; a chance to advance into a new era. But his new apprentice was late, and it was very uncharacteristic of her. His fear and paranoia grew as the evening pressed on. Had she left him? Did the rest of the League know? Would they now turn him in?

How much could he trust Anna? He hadn't so much as heard a peep from her until she sent him that smug letter via the express tubes. Who was she working for now? What part did she have in all of this? Drake looked over at one of Anna's old notebooks, remembering a simpler time. A time when she trusted him, and not the Queen. He felt that he had given her the intelligence she needed to succeed. But then she became one with the League, and their contact ceased.

"I shall await, dreaming," she had written ages ago, in that annoying script she seemed so fond of. She knew about The Builders. She had asked him questions, and stupidly, he had provided her with answers. He had heard that Chang Daggerton, also with the League, was one of the people who knew about the Builders Project. Chang was more than likely the one who had lured Anna away. Or was he? Was Anna working for Chang, the League, or the Queen? It had been such a long time, he had neglected to keep track.

The Professor took another swig of brandy from his sniffer. He was not usually a man of drink, but he was finding that recent events required a strong nerve tonic. In his mind, he was half prepared to flee the lab in the event that the Queen's guard came for him. He only had a few choices; either let Anna and her group have Heather without him, or gain their trust once more as the old days had been. He could have kidnapped Heather and run off on his own, but they would have easily found him. The signs were all there; the large golden blade, the discovery in the mines near The Spike, and now a girl who could speak and read Korisan. The Professor stood to gain much from this, but he knew that the Rokasians would hunt him down, and he was too old to put up a substantial fight. The Professor was no servant to the Queen of Palachia, but felt that his interests did not lie with the Rokasian emperor, either.

The Professor nervously fingered the stone star around his neck. "You have paid a terrible price for your quest for knowledge," he said to himself. "Was this really worth your life's trip?" He remembered back to a simpler time at the university. He recalled Anna back then, young and pretty, studying privately in his quarters, seducing him with her intoxicating scented hair. So young and bright a pupil, she was. She had to be the one, even though she was nearly 25 years younger. The League was but a plan then, formed from a former group that had gotten old and tired. The newly appointed Queen decided that it was time to start a new League, but this time, she wanted to make it more public. The Professor personally appointed Anna, using all his might and muster to push her to the front of the endeavor.

In the end, Anna's knowledge and wit were reduced to little more than a beautiful face and seductive prowess. She no longer retrieved information with quick thinking, but by batting her eyes, waving her fan and showing a little bare ankle. The truth behind the League would know the difference, and the Professor had always known who was really in charge. His disgust with their popularity grew, until one day in a drunken rage, he called them out at a Queen's Investiture for the League's work in preventing a large uprising at a trolley mine. Since then, the Professor had the stomach for neither drink or social events. He much preferred being an outcast.

And truth was, he missed Anna. Heather was but a reminder of the loss of innocence.

"Speaking of that brat, where is she?" he asked aloud to the clock. "Have they stolen her from me already?"

Minutes before maintenance time was to start, he heard his lab door open. He exited from his office, looking down at the balcony. He breathed a sigh of relief when he spotted Mack, but regained his composure.

"Just *where* have you been??" the Professor shouted, scaring Mack quite badly. He descended the metal stairs to the lab floor, making very precise and controlled steps, his displeasure evident. "You are not starting your first day off in a decent manner."

"I was... mugged," Mack said.

"You were what?" the Professor asked, very irritated. He looked at Mack and was aghast as he finally took in her appearance. She seemed to be walking with an odd gait, her new work clothes disheveled.

"I was mugged," said Mack through a split lip. Both eyes were nearly swollen shut and her face was purple and red.

"As in attacked by a street thug? I thought you'd have more common sense than that. Where were you walking, why didn't you stick to the main streets?"

"He was a truant officer," Mack said. "I had no papers, so he attacked me and left me for dead."

"Oh," the Professor said. "You didn't... call the constabulary, did you? All of our work must remain secret, and I wont have you dragging them into this like you did when you — "

"They wouldn't help because they thought I was a Northie," Mack was crying but the Professor was unable to tell due to the cuts on her face.

"Well, that was lucky. I don't have your paperwork yet, so I doubt it would have done us any good. In fact, it could have ruined everything. For now, we're on our own, so don't you forget that! Now...clean yourself up. You're late and there's work to be done."

Mack dropped to her knees and sobbed. She collapsed like a wad of cloth, lying softly on the lab floor. This stunned the Professor, who was normally a compassionate man socially, but he felt that showing compassion in private would be the same kind of weakness that led to Anna's betrayal.

"Get up! For trolley's sake, lad, people get beaten up all the time! If you want to really be a Northie, you have to take a beating like a man. Not like a girl! There is nothing anyone can do to a man that a girl can't survive! I know, I'm a professor!"

But Mack just rolled on the floor, holding her stomach and crying.

"If you don't get your sorry self up, I will personally beat you with a stick! I see you still have your clothes in a package. What did he take from you? Your tram money?"

Mack shook her head, her head full of confusion and misery.

"What, did he take food? What? What did he mug you for??"

Mack shook her head and started sobbing out loud. "I don't know!" she cried, curing up into an even tighter ball. "He just... I don't know!"

"Well, truant officers are bullies. Get use to that, and do better avoiding them next time — " the Professor sniffed the air as he picked up the package Mack had dropped. "Is that... its that the smell of *Yurpan brandy?*"

Mack ignored his question and kept weeping, clutching at her stomach.

"You're... not hurt. You're just *drunk*! And there's only one person I know that has Yurpan Brandy. That Lance had his way with you?"

"No!" Mack shouted in protest. Didn't the Professor care that she was beaten up? Then she realized what she'd said. "I mean, yes! Sort of. They gave me brandy but I was mugged by a truant officer on my way back — "

"Well, that's just great. They got you drunk. Well, no time like the present to empower your knowledge with the evils of distilled spirits. No wonder you're clutching your stomach and hate my shouting. *Think about this the next time you decide to have a drink!!* Now, go work it off. Mop this floor of all your chalk marks and tomorrow, you're getting up *early* for your first lesson! Shake that mugging off; it won't be the last time you find yourself roughed up. I have been mugged plenty of times, but I fought them off when I learned how to defend myself! There will be *plenty* of other times in our work where we'll have to fight our way out of a scuffle. Maybe Lance or Stone can teach you... " He paused in thought for a moment, then said, "No, I don't want to leave them alone with you anymore. Bloody Queen's servants! I should have guessed they'd do this. Tried to get information out of you, did they?"

Mack shook her head, but honestly, she didn't remember. She only remembered that they were nice to her and so funny. But that seemed like a lifetime ago. Her entire insides hurt, and she was

175

bleeding into her new clothes. She sniffed her last tear away, and sat up. The room spun and her headache came back in sharp pains.

"Get up, all the way up. Mop the lab! I am going to be in the office. Take your clothes up where you are done, and put them away. Be here down in the lab, ready to work by the first minute of the new day. You have 8 hours!" the Professor stomped up the stairs, went back into his office, and slammed the door.

Mack's insides went numb. The pain in her nether regions and legs became the only sensation she could feel. Slowly, she pushed herself upright, grabbed the mop and bucket, and headed off towards the sink. There was no mirror over the lab sink, though she found herself looking up to see her face as if there were. She found only a shelf with cleaning items and some rusting lab tools. Mack filled the bucket, then mopped the floors as best she could. After she was done, she left the lab, went up the stairs to her apartment, and tossed her clothes on the dresser.

Mack carefully undressed and took a look at herself in the dresser mirror. A bashed and bruised face squinted back at her like a tight knot. Her new union suit was torn and bloody. The damage the truant officer did to her focused on her face and neck, and then between her legs. She was bleeding pretty badly there, and her bruised skin was sensitive as she tried to wash the area up with some of her sanitary garments. The water in the washbasin became red with blood. She decided that even though this wasn't her usual time, she would wear the towels with the belt. The union suit was hopelessly unmendable, so she tore the fabric into strips and used them as bandages. She decided that when she had a moment the next day, she would properly dress her wounds and put on an astringent.

After she was done, she carefully lay down on her bare bed and looked up at the dirty slanted window. The harsh gas lights from the ceiling of her level shone down like several sets of yellow eyes. Even though they were maybe a hundred feet above her window, Mack could almost feel the heat from the glare of the lamps baking her skin. She didn't want to get her new clothes bloody, so she used the paper they were wrapped in as a crude blanket. Her entire body hurt, and she wanted to cry, but feared that the pain needed to cry would be unbearable. The worst part of it all was how incredibly ashamed and vulnerable she felt. She had let the Professor down. She had gotten drunk like a common pub crawler, gotten herself beaten up and nearly killed. She had no idea what the truant officer had done to her but for some reason, it just added to the hatred and shame she felt for herself. She felt completely insecure and terrified, and there was no mother's bosom to comfort her. She considered running home, but she knew that she couldn't go back. How could she explain what had happened? The Professor would reject her, her parents wouldn't have education paid for, and the part of her that used to be Heather would have to get married off. She would have killed herself like her aunt did.

She knew that drinking brandy gets you drunk. Why had she done it? Why hadn't she stopped? Mack cried a little, despite trying hard not to. Eventually, she began shivering and couldn't stop. Her mind couldn't handle the strain. She stood up and paced the floor. She redid her bandages. She looked out the window at the maintenance workers outside. Hours passed and nothing seemed to make her feel better. She knew she had to go to sleep, but she simply hurt too much.

Mack tried to remember what she used to do to fall asleep as a little girl. She remembered her mother soothing her, rocking her back and forth, and singing to her. But memories of her mother's embrace were so far away and untouchable, they felt like they were behind layers of thick glass. Even memories of her voice seemed muted. Mack gingerly sat down, clutching one of her work shirts in a rumpled ball, and sang to it. She laid down on her side, and hugged the wad of cloth, and told herself it would be okay. Eventually, exhaustion cast a heavy spell, and put her into a deep unconsciousness.

She suddenly woke to a banging on the door. The ambient light in her room alerted her that maintenance time had ended. She had overslept.

"I will be there in a minute!" she shouted.

"I am not your mother, Mack!" the Professor shouted through the door. "You should have been down in the lab two hours ago."

Mack got dressed. She knew her clothes might get stained, but she figured she could wash them at some point later in the day. The bleeding had stopped, and when she used the water closet and looked herself over, the bleeding was not as bad. She could almost walk normally. She tossed the blood-filled washbasin out the window into the alley, smoothed her hair as best she could, and headed out the door.

"I take it you're hung over," the Professor said when she entered the lab.

"I have lost a lot of blood, but I am fine," Mack said.

"I... I want to apologize. We got off our apprenticeship on the wrong foot. The last apprentice didn't leave on good terms. She was ungrateful, late, and a braggart. Eventually, she just packed up and left. I haven't had another until you. I might have... projected her sins unfairly."

Mack nodded. "I am sorry I got drunk. I had never been in that sort of situation before, and it won't happen again."

"No, actually, I think in the end, that turned out for the best. Lynn and Lance trust you. They said you were very charming and funny. I need them to trust you if I am to find out what they are up to."

"What they are up to?"

"Sit down, Mack. We have a lot to discuss. But first, maybe we should have breakfast."

Mack nodded and yawned.

The Professor looked at Mack's wounds. "You haven't slept, have you?"

Mack shook her head.

The Professor sighed. "Okay, to make up for last night, I'll call today's lessons off. I didn't get much sleep, either. Get yourself cleaned up; you're a complete mess. There's a private bath and shower at the end of the hall. You'll find the key in the large desk somewhere. Make sure you lock the door behind you. Take some bandages and astringent with you. I know you know how to dress wounds. I can't have a doctor coming round and snooping, but if you need serious medical attention, I might be able to scare one up who knows how to keep quiet."

Mack cracked a smile. "Thank you, professor."

"You're welcome. But this isn't being soft on you, it's being practical. In fact, I think I will call my doctor friend. You'll meet him soon enough anyway, why not have it an official call. But get cleaned up for him. Key's in the desk... I said that already."

Mack grabbed the key, a few rags, and collected her medical needs. She went down the end of a long hallway to the bathing room; the only one in the building. Originally, it had been used by some of the wealthier people who used to work there, but those people had long since moved on. This was the only part of the building that still hinted at the splendor it once contained. The washroom had granite sinks with greenish bronze shells as accents. The tub was deep and recessed into the floor slightly. Mack turned on the water and began to carefully disrobe.

As the hot water filled the room with steam, she started feeling a little better. When she stepped into the tub, the water was extremely hot, but she knew that the stone tub would not keep it hot for long. The water became pink with blood as she used soap, pumice, and a sea sponge to clean out the wounds. There was great deal of blood in her hair as well. When she was done, the remaining water was a reddish brown, like a weak tea. With the gore washed away, it was easier to assess her cuts, and using a hand mirror, she was able to finally tell how bad the damage was. It didn't seem as bad as she once thought once her face was cleaned up. The swelling had gone down, and the face of a survivor gave her a shy grin back.

There was a knock at the door.

"This room is occupied!" she called out. There was no response. She wondered if she remembered to lock the door, but then reassured herself she had as she saw the key in the lock turned the proper way. After a few minutes, satisfied there was no one there anymore, Mack slid down into the water to relax her sore muscles. As she was starting to slip away into unconsciousness, she heard the rattle of the key in the lock fall to the floor and heard the door creak.

"Occupied!" she shouted.

"I know," said a voice. It was the truant officer.

Mack gasped in horror, sucking in some bath water. Get out **get out!**" she cried between coughs.

The huge form of the officer in regular workman's clothing loomed over the tub.

"You can't be in here! Leave me alone!" she screamed. She splashed water at him, but it did little to deter his approach. She threw the soap at him, but it just bounced off him like it was a ball of paper. It only seemed to encourage him.

"Just do as I say, and don't make any noise, and I won't tell the Professor what happened..." he said, stepping into the water. The water around his legs rustled and spread across the surface like brown, greasy paper.

"Get out of here, leave me alone!" she screamed. She tried to scramble out of the tub, but the surface had become like some kind of paper she couldn't get a steady grip on to pull herself out.

The truant officer grabbed her by the neck and forced her under the water. Mack struggled and screamed but his large hands were too heavy. Mack tried everything to slip away, but she kept sliding towards him, just like in the alley. The water changed from brown to green as she felt her consciousness slip away. Just before her lungs burst, the water turned a bright green and she found a huge fish eye staring back at her.

"Let me penetrate you or you'll kill us all!!" the officer screamed. The eye slid into her chest , impaling her like an enormous stamp cutter.

Mack suddenly found herself on the apartment floor, partially covered in brown paper. Her throat was sore from screaming. Mack tried to get out from under the paper, but her clumsy kicks couldn't quite get it to come off her body cleanly, until she finally managed to get up and run back to the bed. She quickly came to her senses, realizing that it was another night terror. It was still maintenance time. The paper was still the paper the clothes had been wrapped in and she had been using it as a blanket. There was no truant officer or green fish eye. There was no ornate bathtub in their building. She was alone in the apartment, and her bed was stained with streaks of blood.

The feeling of being alone crushed her like an insect under a boot, and as she wept, she called out for her mother several times. She couldn't stop shaking, and she wasn't sure if it was because she was cold, or lost so much blood. Finally, she decided to just get dressed and clean up in the lab sink downstairs. As she cleaned her wounds and washed her makeshift bandages, she slowly succumbed to the mixed feeling of relief and disappointment that it had all been a dream. The professor hadn't been nice to her, and no doctor friend was coming to assess her condition. Her feelings were so damaged; she couldn't stop shivering even though she was no longer cold.

Looking in a hand mirror, she tried to calm down. Mack's face was pretty badly bruised. She knew the swelling would go down, the cuts would heal, and the physical pain would go away. The face that stared back at her was no longer Heather. Heather was dead. Mack was a survivor by necessity, just like the Professor said. Mack was a man. A man could handle the pain.

Mack Van Horn would save her.

The gas lamps outside turned back up. Maintenance period was over, and the streets would be fully lit in anticipation for the new day. And she was down in the lab right on time. A determined Mack dressed her wounds, straightened her clothing, and set to work.

 **Ten**

The Dinner Party

"This is your first test at how well you take direction," Professor Gaylord said as they approached the restaurant. Mack was sitting next to him quietly, dressed in a vest and overcoat. The fact that she was wearing pants in public was unnerving, but she tried not to bring attention to herself. Lynn had told her how to swagger like a young boy, and yet the Professor was not impressed. "I will ask you to not speak unless someone asks you a question, is that understood?"

Mack nodded. Even though nobody was staring at her or even paying attention to the "young man next to the Professor," Mack felt incredibly self conscious and exposed. She tried to tell herself that she wore workman's pants all the time, like overalls and things, but it seemed somehow different in a social environment. Until recently, there had always been her generic child's figure. This time, she had to pretend to be a man at all costs wearing thin slacks. Her waistcoat would hide her figure, which was still rather boyish, but she knew with time, her hips and chest would expand and make things difficult.

The northern Palachian lessons were surprisingly quite complicated. To Mack and her fellow citizens, "Northies," were considered a labor class of whom people barely paid attention to. Their mannerisms and culture were considered separate, even though they both had similar pasts. Mostly they came from northern Palachia, which included part of upper Palachia, but there were quite a few living scattered about all of Palachia, wherever the work took them. Like most surface dwellers, they were considered backwards and uncultured by the southern Palachian people, fit only for menial labor and simple directions. It was perceived that their only useful native lifestyle was farming and agriculture. Their language, while similar in structure to Queens Language, had different vowel sounds, and even words spelled the same could be pronounced differently than one would expect. Mack assumed it would be easy, but after a few weeks, she realized that speaking northern Palachian was not as simple and swapping pronunciation.

Northern Palachians, as surface dwellers, had entirely different concepts of scale and reference. While Mack might say something was "scraping the ceiling," if it was tall, a northern Palachian would say, "brushes the clouds." "As wide as a central plaza" was "miles across." In fact, a a great number of idioms used words Mack had heard, but had never actually used in daily language. Concepts like sky, moon, tree, sunlight, rainbows, mountains, and so on were mere scientific trivia until now. Part of the northern Palachian humility was due to being dwarfed by their unpredictable natural surroundings. Mack had never seen anything bigger than Financial One, and had never experienced weather. Now she needed to act like she had grown up under the glow of the great Sky Ring, running for miles across hills and valleys, and ducking for shelter when lectromag slammed the ground with its bright fist amid pouring water called "rain." She had to learn over a hundred animals by sight, manner, sounds, and smell. And since trolley was too dangerous to keep above ground, Mack had to learn how a lot of mechanical labor was processed on the surface: wind, waterwheel, animal, and burning things like wood, coal, and even manure. While her kitchen stove was heated by trolley-fed gas and the home heated by radiant steam heat pipes, it was only used when needed. Northern Palachian people always had a wood fire burning, and it was usually in one central area where people gathered for cooking and warmth. Whereas pipes, steam, and air ducts were Mack's life, water, fire, and dirt were the lifeblood of northern Palachians.

"Isn't having an open flame in a small stone alcove dangerous?" she asked the Professor.

"Yes," he replied. "Sometimes their houses burn down. Fire has consumed entire towns, burning them to the ground."

Mack was astounded, unable to imagine the horror of an uncontrolled fire. In fact, in one of her readings, sometimes it didn't stop at houses. She read an account where lectromag set an entire forest on fire, and uncounted numbers of surface dwellers were killed as it spread across the continent.

The most difficult was trying to get a normally quiet northern Palachian to divulge some of their personal memories. There were many books on them, to be sure, but they often contradicted one another, especially when it came to customs. Did they dress in red clothes with blue stripes on the shortest day of the year, or did they dress in gold clothes with green stripes? Why were some of their infants wrapped so tightly until they could crawl?

One thing she had to learn fast: they despised being called "Northies." They didn't have a word in their language for themselves, and they had no real central leader to speak of. They didn't mind being called, "northern Palachians" much, but when they spoke of themselves, they simply called themselves, "us" or "we," in an almost subtle reminder they only worked with the more civilized folk out of convenience. Their attitude towards life in general was called, "Demedlewah," or "The Middle Way," a phrase meaning not too extreme on one side or another, don't make a fuss, think in the long term, and steady work and steady rest are the key to a happy and productive life.

Their carriage stopped in front of a large restaurant in the finer part of the city, near the Queen's parliamentary building. The restaurant was simply called, "The Royal Plate," and was made of sparkling white granite. Gold accents lined various architectural features and large glass windows stretched across multiple floors.

A very well-dressed and proper man greeted them at the large glass doors. "Welcome Professor Gaylord," he exclaimed with a dramatically gracious gesture. "I have been expecting you. I am the manager of the Royal Plate, Herbert Swallington. Your party waits in the Queen's Room!"

"Good day, Herbert. This is my new apprentice. As he is northern Palachian, please do not address him directly." This was a subtle ruse to avoid detection until Mack perfected her accent and vocabulary.

Herbert clucked his tongue in nervousness. "Professor... I am sorry, but we... don't allow..."

"... allow?" asked the Professor.

The manager whispered into the Professor's ear.

"I see," said the Professor. "Let me ask you something: considering I am about to meet a group of people who have a lower Palachian, a Rokasian, and a Yurpan in their company, what makes you wish to ban a northern Palachian? Were you aware that the world's largest University is in Upper Palachia, part of northern Palachia?"

Herbert looked down at Mack and stuttered in embarrassment. He had apparently not expected the Professor to break the discreet nature of the comment he had whispered into his ear. "I um... well, it's not that... I have clientèle..."

"Do they not work in your kitchens? Do they not clean the droppings of your finest elite as they droop their stretched waistcoats across your sturdy chairs? Are they not numerous and bold in your establishment? Why would one more be a threat?"

The manager stood up stiffly. "Yes, but — "

"*Drake*, my good man!" shouted Lance from the entrance. Just like in all public events, Lance was dressed in the grandest of finery. His suit was expertly tailored, and his foppish top sat crooked on his well-groomed hair. A slightly drunken smile cracked across a waxed goatee in all its blissful charm. "I see you have brought your new apprentice! Most excellent, I will order some Yurpan brandy."

Mack cringed at the memory and did not look up to see the Professor's expression.

"This *will* be a pleasant evening," the Professor growled.

"Right this way..." the manager said, regrettably relenting to what was an obvious exception to his rule about foreigners when the League was dining there. As he led them to the private rooms in the back, the tension in his walk was almost a light sprint. The floor was a very slick and polished marble, with alternating carpeting, making Mack's new shoes slip and skid randomly with the changing terrain. They passed by tables of some of the wealthiest of southern Palachian's elite, wearing clothing that was the height of fashion, which Mack only knew because of Morgana's insipid obsession speaking about it at the dinner table. The color for this season was apparently a light green on a darker green with yellow accents that made them look a little like trolley gas. Their dulled cow eyes followed her with only momentary interest as a few whispers about Worthington by the ladies ended in giggles.   Every table had its own gas lamp hanging on a hose from the tall ceilings, infusing a warm glow over everyone's meals through crystal lenses. As bloated guests leaned back on padded chairs, dabbing their lips with fine linens, they remarked on things like financial futures, trade agreements, politics, and how the poor got in their way. It was everything the Professor had spoken about, and Mack felt a pang of sorrow at humanity that was interrupted by a sudden stop at a rather ordinary wooden door.

"Welcome to the Queen's Room," the manager said, avoiding all eye contact with them.

The Queen's Room, the largest room in the entire establishment, was hidden behind this mundane entrance. Mack stepped inside the large private room; quite possibly one of the most extravagant rooms she had ever seen in person. The quilted walls were a deep maroon, framed with fine rosewood, and gilded leather buttons shone at the crosses of perfect pleats. Displayed on the shelves were some of the finest pieces of sculpture and artwork the Palachian Empire had to offer. The crystal chandelier in the center of the room was lit with tallow candles while a fireplace roared in one corner, fueled by real wood. Flicker-less gas lamps gave the entire room a cozy glow, and small mirrors reflected the accents of the room giving a strange rosy color that, when mixed with the rows of gauze that hung from the ceiling, gave a strange dreamlike quality.

Seated around a thick tigerwood table sat the entire League. There was Lance, Lynn, Stone, Terry, Chang, and Massood. They all turned to the doorway and posed for a moment in greeting like the cover of one of their books. Mack couldn't believe her eyes, and thought if her sister were here, she would have fainted dead away from the excitement. Even she had to admit to herself that when the League was together, they made an impressive window display of social grace and perfection.

"Welcome, Mack!" said Lynn, who rose from her seat. She was wearing a small waistcoat with a large bustled skirt, looking feminine, but tough. Lance was already seating himself, returning to a conversation with Chang as if he was picking up where he'd left off. Massood nodded quietly, but stared at Mack with uncomfortable intensity. Anna smiled politely, but returned her gaze to her wine glass. Stone and Terry beamed wide smiles. Terry hopped off his chair and shook Mack's hand roughly.

"Welcome back, Mack!" he shouted with percussive enthusiasm. "I always hoped I'd meet the face that saved a difference engine again!" Then he laughed at some private joke as he waved at Stone. Stone smiled and nodded.

"Have a seat, why don't you, Professor. It *has* been a long time..." Lynn seemed very happy to see the Professor, who returned her smile.

"I has been a long time," the Professor agreed. "Perhaps I have stayed away too long."

"Have some food," Lynn offered. "There are some tea and scones left, and I dare say it was quite a spread before you arrived. But not to worry, a new course is about to be served, and we have a variety of pickled meats; some of them we had prepared from our own stores in our recent travels. This has been the first group meal we have had since our return. We have all been..." Lynn darted a glance at Anna," ... busy with our own preoccupations for the last few weeks."

"I bet you have," the Professor said. "Good to see you again, Anna." He inclined his head in her direction.

Mack noticed that Chang had stopped listening to what Stone was talking about, something that sounded very technical, and was now looking with narrowed eyes at the Professor.

"Come have a seat next to me," Terry said. "Us short people have to stick together!" He thumbed towards Chang as he said this, but Chang took no notice.

"That sounds lovely..." Mack said, before she gritted her teeth at how feminine that sounded.

"Er, yeah. So," Terry said. "Have you ever been to the surface, Mack?"

Mack nodded.

"I mean, *really* been to the surface?" Anne followed up, silencing the rest of the chit chat in the room. "I know we're all pretending you're some northern Palachian goon, but this is a very important question. Was Heather January someone who ever came close to the surface?"

Mack bristled at the old name as the entire table looked at her. "I am told she was," Mack said carefully. "Twice. School outings to the surface."

"School outings," the Professor said with a scoff. "Such as they are."

"Why is that not acceptable, dear Professor?" asked Lynn.

"Tell me, Mack," the Professor said with an airy swallow, "what was that trip like?"

"I went... er, I was told Heather went to the surface. There they had huge glass windows and small zoological park where we saw cows and sheep, as well as a history of — "

Lynn sighed, "So you really never went outside on the surface?"

"Well, we were on the surface — "

"In a visitor's dome," Lynn said with a sigh. "But never really out in the open, exposed to the sky and sun and Sky Ring... all that?"

Mack hesitated. "Well... no. They said that the sky was bad for us. Lectromag and everything."

The table uttered a few hidden snickers.

Lynn sighed. "Allow me to explain what is in store for you. How much do you know about the surface?"

Mack paused. "It doesn't have a ceiling or roof of any kind."

"And how is that possible?"

Mack shook her head. She had never thought of that before. All her life she had a ceiling she could see above her. The concept of no ceiling at all seemed... impossible. Everything has to end, right? Where does the sun or Sky Ring attach? A strange nervousness crept into her chest.

Terry continued, "Many people who have spent their lives under the surface never get to experience what the surface is all about. There is a word for what many experience: agoraphobia. Fear of open spaces."

"I know what agoraphobia is, I just never — "

"You have no fear of small, cramped spaces," Terry said. "I noticed that when we worked together. Some people have a sense of spatial perception that compares themselves to their surroundings. Heather January grew up in a small house surrounded by stone walls and metal balconies. Heather knew nothing of wide open spaces that had horizons."

"Horizons?"

"Yes, Mack. Can you imagine where there is no wall, but the ground and sky just meet up at an arbitrary point in the distance?"

"Like a pitched roof in an attic room?"

Some of the table snickered again. Mack was becoming annoyed, and the Professor tapped the side of her boot with his walking cane. She knew what the surface was like: she had read books, it was taught in school, and it wasn't like the concept of being on the surface was a completely alien and terrifying thought. She also knew a few of the people at the table were drunk, and this annoyed her even more.

"Not.... exactly." Terry fumbled for the right words. "Imagine this... attic room, where the roof meets the floor so far off in the distance, you could walk for days and days, and it never got any closer."

Mack thought about this. Just one huge room. Ceiling was... somewhere, just really, really far away.

"See, as Heather sits there thinking, Mack would already know this as a northern Palachian. As you know, they are mostly farming folk, and while they do have cities like southern Palachia, most of them do not live very far away from their roots. As a matter of fact, many spend their whole lives without going below the ground at all. They rarely come across modern conveniences like trolley. Most of their steam comes from wood or even coal."

"But they have lectromag?" Mack asked.

"No, because lectromag comes from the sky randomly. It seeks out metal and tall things, and worst of all, it seeks trolley. You know what lectromag does to trolley, right?"

Mack nodded. "Bad things."

"Bad things indeed," Anna said in a patronizing manner. "However, in recent years, there have been people who have built lectromag generators. You saw one a few weeks ago. And you saw how terrible the consequences were."

"What powers the generators?" Mack asked. She was trying hard to deflect Anna's obvious attempts to anger her. Her sister had pulled tricks like this, and Mack had a feeling that if Anna got the upper hand, she'd never give it back.

Terry laughed. "These kinds of questions are why we invited the Professor here."

The Professor bowed and smiled politely, "I am afraid I do not travel by surface much to learn about the mysteries of lectromag — "

"But you were on the surface just last week, via the Iron Horse and Rokasia," Anna said.

The silence lingered in the air with anticipation, but the Professor kept his clam. "My affairs are my affairs, but since you are so insistent on knowing why I was in Rokasia, I will tell you. Recently, their gear making has taken a solid downturn in quality, so I went to investigate for the local merchant's guild. That's why I didn't know when I would be back or — "

"They are saving their manufacturing skill for something else," Anna said. "What is that something else?"

"I don't know..." the Professor said. "They took me on a tour, and sent me back with some samples of what they are working on. They are experimenting with a titanium alloy that — "

"The tour was staged..." Anna said.

The Professor tensed. "I am well aware of that. I am not stupid, Anna. Of course it was staged. I wanted to know the reason for the facade, and who was behind it. You do realize that it is possible to tell what someone is up to without resorting to coquettish flirting — "

"Now now," Lynn said, noting Anna's furrowed brow ready for a fight. "No fighting at my table. We are all aware that Anna has far more skills that simply batting her eyes. She did not fire a volley at you, so I would ask that you respect her and not preemptively retaliate. Let us not derail the purpose of this meeting, and why we requested Mack's presence."

"We want to add her, er... him to our crew," Terry said proudly. "Newest member of the League!" This announcement was followed by a muttering of approval, some stronger than others.

Mack gasped. She would be in the League of the Brave? This shocked her to the point of being almost dizzy. A million thoughts flashed through her head, all a mix of good and bad. The assumed honor, the fact that she had openly stated they were insipid, the Professor's disdain, and a way to impress Morgana and maybe show her up a little. She would have never thought of wanting something like this. She didn't know what to think. Lynn stood up and shook her hand in congratulations before giving her a subtle wink and picking a piece of lint off Mack's shoulder.

The Professor's laughter was polite, but dismissive, "No, no. That's not going to happen, Terry."

"Oh, but I disagree, dear Professor," Anna said sweetly. "See, we are directly under the Queen's employ. What we ask for, we get."

At this, the Professor grew angry. "That is preposterous, Mack is my apprent — "

Lynn placed her hand on the Professor's arm and gave it a gentle squeeze. "You filed for her apprenticeship, and that will be granted. However, the conditions are that your apprentice travels with us."

"But you will come with us, of course," Terry said, "to maintain the apprenticeship. And you and Anna here were once partners, so it will be like a reunion — "

"I will do **nothing** of the sort!" the Professor shouted, and stood from his chair. "I am not property that can be called on a whim, and neither is my apprentice! This is outrageous!"

"But it is already done, dear Professor," Lynn said, returning to her seat. "Please sit back down, and have some tea and scones."

"I have a job, you know!" the Professor continued. "I have valuable services that **cannot** be interrupted to jaunt around the continent with foppish dandies under the guise of scientific research — "

Chang spoke for the first time. His Rokasian accent was light, but noticeable, and flowed like a fine cloth. "And yet you still went to Rokasia, half a globe away, rather suddenly just a month and a half ago, and despite our reasonable questions, you won't fill us in on the real reasoning behind this? Surely not just for a tour of their false gear factories. Perhaps you'd like to explain about some of the people you met with who are neither in manufacturing or production?"

"That is my *own* business!"

"It is the Queen's business, professor. You are one of her subjects."

The Professor pursed his lips. "Then I will tell it to her in person!"

Lance stood, facing the Professor, his charming swagger replaced with a firm stare and stance. "We are the Queen's lips and ears in these matters. Sit down and tell us what we request, or we will regrettably forced to handle this with guards and imprisonment." The stare that a few of the members directed at him were not ones of support, but of slight astonishment and embarrassment.

"Guards and imprisonment? Under what charges?"

"Suspicion of treason," Lynn said, as if apologetic of the ungracious term she was forced to explain prematurely.

"Suspicion of treason? We are not at *war*, gentlemen and ladies!"

"Are we not?" Lynn asked.

"It would seem we are starting to wonder," Lance said. "There has been some curious embargoes and tariffs lately. The borders of Rokasia are not as open as in previous years."

The Professor frowned as he sat back down. "I was just there, and I don't recall any sort of unfriendly — "

Stone looked across the table. His huge size and gaze were predatory, like a bear. "That may be so, Professor, but we need these details. It is very important to know exactly why you went there. If it was a social call, we understand. You have old friends on Rokasia, and you have nothing to hide. So please... explain your journey in detail."

The Professor looked over at Mack, then sighed. "Very well. As I said, we were curious about a shipment of — "

"We?" Lynn asked.

"Yes... my assistant, now apprentice, and I."

"Go on," Stone said. His deep voice was soft but powerful, and it demanded the attention of all in the room without using excessive volume.

"... as I was saying, we had been getting more and more substandard gears. Usually badly mixed alloys and poorly cast molding. It seemed the quality of manufactured parts from Rokasia was substandard. So I went there to find out why."

"And what did you find?"

"I found nothing. I found no explanation other than a possible accident in the manufacturing process. They gave me fake tours in staged factories that were hardly fooling anybody. I watched the factory work an entire day like clockwork, and yet did not witness any shipments leaving the factory. Not one horse carried anyone but myself and my escorts, and even my escorts were embarrassed by the poorly-designed ruse — "

"Did you tour just the facilities?" Lynn asked.

"I did. I toured two factories as a matter of diplomatic courtesy — "

"Did you notice anything unusual, such as a strange lack of workers to space, like cities with empty streets?" Stone's eyes seemed to be searching the Professor's face for any hint of lying. "Or perhaps a lot of furnaces were not lit, or maybe something else that indicated that the tours you took were fronts to disguise their real factories? Is there a fuel shortage? Are they using more coal? Were there trolley shortages?"

Mack could feel the Professor trembling with anger next to her. He sniffed and answered, "Well, I am not as obsessed with finding pointless clues where there are none as you seem to be as I stated before it was obvious the tour was just for show. I associated with old fellows at the university, sure, but only for social calls. I am not sure why you sent spies after me, if that's even what you did. I really don't see why you care, but I understand that you must do what you can to feel valuable and employable as you traipse around the world on citizens tax money."

Chang narrowed his eyes. "You object to our line of questioning — "

"I object to your line of reasoning!" the Professor shouted. Hearing his own volume, he lowered his voice, but not his intensity. "When I helped create this group almost two decades ago, I had high hopes that it would serve the Queen as a scientific flagship of intellectual prowess built on logic, mechanics, and reason. But I see in my absence, it's become a foppish shadow made of fine linens and expensive holidays that use scientific words to wine and dine other scientists for no other purpose than to further the politics of war." The Professor waved his hands around to use the opulence of their surroundings as the prime example.

Anna smirked as Chang replied, "Your patronizing comments fail to conceal your flawed and intentionally vague recount of your activities. Our Rokasian intelligence has informed us of some strange inconsistencies in your visit, professor. Most notable during your visit were the lack of contacts you would have normally made, the abruptness of your departure, the strange people you associated with, and the lack of a return travel date until the very last minute when it would appear that your true intent would be discovered."

"My true intent," the Professor scoffed. "You mean the story you want to be true. I am afraid that my boring journey leaves little to the imagination, as evidenced by your creative, yet impotent attempt to fabricate espionage. I am sure your vague interrogation techniques work on the weak minded, but against the truth they fall flat."

"This conversation is growing unnecessarily unpleasant," Lynn said. "Tension is poor for the digestion and the next course is about to be served. I suggest no more travel talk until we have eaten."

"I prefer not to dine with pigs," the Professor said, straightening his gloves. "Come on, Mack. We are — "

"You ask us to help you conceal Mack from the prying eyes of the public, and now you just take your leave?"

"You will be paid for your services, don't worry. I had no intention of pulling favors."

"But we do," Lance said. "And the favor is that we will allow you to travel with us, at the Queen's expense, to Yurpa with Mack. That way, you do not have to pay."

"I travel alone, I have no intent on giving Mack up to you. Mack is far more valuable to me than — "

"If Mack has value, then why did you not speak of the real purpose of your travels? Why did you just leave Mack to fend for herself?"

"*Himself*, if you don't mind!"

"Yes, true," Lance said. "Mack is a boy to the eyes of the public. And currently, the Queen knows nothing of Mack and Heather being one in the same. I cannot imagine why you took Mack on as an apprentice. Did you think you could conceal her gender forever? No, we know how to keep things from the Queen. We were aware that Heather was spying on us the moment we saw her sneak around Stone and the difference engine. Dressed as a boy, she was allowed to work on our project. We wanted to see what she was up to, and more importantly, why you sent her."

"I did *not* send her, she went under her own volition!"

"The Professor did *not* send me," Mack said. "My father took me to work — "

"So the story is written," Anna sniffed. "And why did your father take you to work?"

Mack opened her mouth, and then shut it. The Professor still did not know about the books. And even if he did, she did not want anyone to know she was learning Korisan. "I wanted to go to see the difference engine. I begged and pleaded, and he said he'd show me it. But then it was closed off. So I spied around until I could get in."

"Then why the guise about the books? The books you were attempting to fix were only in Korisan. Perhaps the Professor was trying to send messages to someone inside Financial One?"

"What books?" Mack lied, but her flushed face gave her away, and she knew it. She did not look back at the Professor. This was probably why he told her not to speak, she thought, and hated herself for letting her guard down and breaking her promise to the Professor.

"I find the entire affair very strange," Chang said. "On the very day of the secret project, one of the Professor's assistants shows up with Korisan works, which she has already admitted to Lynn she can't read, to get the books 'cleaned.' Then, while she is there, she slips away, dressed in disguise as a man, and works on the difference engine. It's also apparent that this assistant, despite being female, is a very accomplished mechanic. This speaks of deliberate distraction techniques; a female child would not have been attracted to such skills without a great deal of external influence. I can't tell how many layers of deception lay between you two, or what your motivations are. There are too many loose ends and unexplained coincidental events."

The Professor stamped his cane to the floor. "Your pathetic attempts to get me to confess to whatever crazed espionage you have dreamed of is exposed with completely made up clues. No books were ever sent to Financial One. No messages were sent, and I had no idea about the experiments with the difference engine until Anna accidentally spilled the news in my very lab."

Chang pulled out a large book labeled, "*Korisan Symbology and Marks*" from a leather satchel next to his chair. "Does this book tug a memory, Professor?"

The Professor looked at the tile, and Mack looked at the floor, her face red with shame. "Yes. I have a copy."

"You do. A copy," Chang said with a wide grin. "I have the original."

The Professor scoffed. "Then sell it for a pretty penny at an auction. The fact that you have the first printing doesn't impress me in the slightest. I have wiped my bottom with many first editions."

"You misunderstand me, Professor Drake Gaylord. I have *your* original copy. With your notes in the margin." He tossed the book at the Professor. "We swapped your books when your assistant here brought them for the so-called, 'cleaning.'"

Mack felt her entire body grow cold and she wobbled slightly trying not to faint. She didn't dare look in the Professor's eyes, only straight down, expressionless. She instantly regretted any lies she had ever told.

"Then you failed," the Professor said calmly, looking at the copy. He flipped through the book casually. "My notes are missing." He tossed the book back at Chang, where it landed with a thump and clatter of dinnerware in front of him.

Chang raised his eyebrows, and took the book back. He flipped through it as calmly as a casual reader mildly interested in purchasing it for his drawing room.

"I grow weary of your sad interrogation techniques," the Professor said with a lilt of disappointment. "Anna should have taught you better. So what is this really about? Payment of services rendered?"

"The choice is yours," Chang said, tossing the book aside. "You keep your apprentice, travel with us, and we all work as a close team or we take Mack, and leave you in prison until the Queen makes a decision as to what to do with you."

The servant's door opened abruptly, and servants wheeled carts stacked with food into the room.

"Ah," said Lynn. "The fresh feast is about to begin. Sit down, professor. The tension of this agreement will be soothed with some of the best food southern Palachia has to offer. We will become friends."

"To close friends," Lance said, rising his brandy glass in a toast.

"Keep your friends close," said the Professor sitting down at the table, "...and your enemies closer," he whispered to Mack with a dangerous and scolding tone.

Mack was not hungry and did not eat the rest of the evening.

‚ÄúEleven

Mack Finds a New Family

"Dear Morgana," Mack wrote. "I am sorry I have not visited you since I left. It was my attempt to do so, but being an apprentice is hard work."

Mack looked at her travel chest at the edge of her bed. Even though she could have left the chest on the floor, she always put something in that spot to cover the dark stains on the bed. Every time she looked at them, she was briefly reminded of her awful encounter with the truant officer. That memory still haunted her every time she spotted one of their blue uniforms. Even though she now had travel papers and proper identification as Mack Van Horn, she was very careful to avoid anywhere the truant officers went. She would even take hidden back routes and illegal short-cuts to avoid the pubs and street corners where they usually pa-trolled. The truth was that, there were times that Mack could have visited the old neighborhood, but had no desire to risk running into one of them. There was also something else intangible.

The incident with the officer had shamed her so deeply that she no longer wished to visit her family anymore. She didn't want to face her parents, didn't want them to fuss over her, and she couldn't quite figure out why. Being Mack, a young northern Palachian man about to become part of the League of the Brave, was a separate life that didn't have to face what had really happened to Heather. In fact, it was taking great courage to write to Morgana. Whatever the truant officer had done to her had left her feeling so violated and exposed, she felt infected like a diseased wound that, unlike her head wound, would never really heal properly. That deeper wound had killed Heather January, and from the remains of her psyche Mack Van Horn had risen like a walled fortress she could stay safe behind.

She knew that this letter might be the last she could send for a very long time, and she missed her family terribly, even if she didn't want to see them. She even missed Morgana as much as her parents. Sleeping alone in her apartment had made her realize how Morgana had always been with her, even if they couldn't stand one another as they grew older. She found herself wondering if Morgana missed her, or if she had already forgotten that she'd once had a sister. Part of her hoped that she did, but the very thought of her sister just going on without made her heart ache.

Mack continued, dipping her drying quill in an ink well. "Please do not think my lack of contact over the last month means I do not think about you every day. I have a small apartment over the lab, but my work day is waking up, working, and then going to bed. I get only about six hours of sleep a night, and no days off. When I am out doing errands, I don't have time to detour back to our neighb..."

The ink kept running dry, which was the problem with quills. She wished that she had one of those fancy fountain pens, like some of the League members had. The Professor was very strict about receiving gifts of any kind from the League. "We must remain our own separate team," he'd said, "like Stone and Terry. They know how to keep their identity and purpose on track." This didn't prevent the League from attempting to bribe Mack behind the Professor's back, however. Angrily, she dipped the quill back into the ink with such ferocity, it dotted her knuckles.

"... neighborhood." Mack continued. " I have something for you. Inside this tube, there is a small wadding of cloth disguised as a scarf. Inside this scarf are some pins from the League of the Brave; one representing each member. I remember how you got a pin from Lance Worthingheart when you were on his float, and how Sandra Plovers stole it from you. But now you won't have just one; you will have *all* of them. I cannot tell you how I got them, but these are this year's pins for the parade. They haven't been sold to anyone yet, so you will have them before anyone else. I know you were banned from going to this year's parade, and I am sorry about that, but I hope to make up for it by giving you these pins. They are very valuable and expensive, so take good care of them."

Mack looked at the wadded up bundle. The dinner a few weeks ago had certainly changed the Professor's mood. He was now furious and frustrated most of the time. The incident with cleaning books was never brought up, and Mack was not stupid enough to do so, despite her intense curiosity with the conversation. The Professor often forgot their lessons, choosing instead to drink alone in his office above the lab. Mack had never seen the Professor drink so much; usually he only drank at social events, and until now, she had never seen him even the slightest bit tipsy. Now he was quickly going through a decade's worth of spirits from a cabinet in his office. He'd accumulated them as gifts throughout the years. The bottles used to lay dusty, only opened for the rarest of visitors, but in the last few weeks Mack kept seeing two empty bottles or more every time she took out the rubbish. When the Professor wasn't drinking or ranting, he would attempt to work before finally giving up in disgust, saying uncharacteristic things like, "What's the damn point?" and "Who can you trust anymore?"

All Mack could figure was the Professor and the League had some kind of rough past. When his assistant Anna left him for the League a decade or so earlier, apparently for the unrequited love of Lance, this had effectively ended any relationship the Professor wished to have with them. Now, a few times a week, a member of the League would drop by, and there would be meetings. After these meetings, the Professor would be in the worst mood of all, even though it seemed that nobody in the League was unfriendly to him in the slightest.

In fact, Mack had to admit her impression of the League was very much mistaken. The popular image of the League's deed and adventures were not that far off from what they had actually accomplished. They were a scientific investigation team which doubled as ambassadors to the Palachian Empire. Their popularity was promoted for well-being among the citizens as upstanding models of heroism, progress, morality, and the results of hard work and skill. But once Mack had a chance to work with them, she found some staggering personality inconsistencies she would never have expected. She saw them now as flawed human beings, no better than anyone else, and they didn't even attempt to disguise it. They were fun, smart, and liked to prank one another. Heather had never had friends, and now Mack did, which she considered a positive boon. The Professor, however, seemed always unimpressed with anything they did. He considered them silly and pointless, and every time he had to spend a long time with them, he would stare angrily into a neutral space on the wall, as if his attention had been permanently fixed there.

First, Lance Worthingheart, who was considered the handsome and dashing leader, was actually a foppish dandy used to the finer things in life. His main skill was his charm, as opposed to his leadership. His love of the ladies was also a little off center because, as Lynn had informed her, he preferred the company of ladies, but not their flesh. Ladies considered him charming, witty, and flirtatious, but Lance was much more interested in the well-groomed males whom he'd invite back to his private quarters for long talks of some sort. When she asked why Lance preferred to be alone with young men, the rest of the League would quickly change the subject. Mack thought that this was because they thought Lance was kind of a blowhard that tried to impress the younger boys with his collection of books and stories of adventure. "He's not always all in his right mind," Lynn would say, "and his private affairs are his own business. But in a rough patch, Lance is loyal and brave!"

Lynn "Goggles" Stellard was only called "Goggles" in the comics and fictional literature. Her masculine nature seemed a perfect complement to Lance, and many assumed they were secretly lovers, perhaps because of the romantic tension depicted in the fiction. However, Lynn stood alone most of the time, and didn't seem to have any obvious love interest within the group, except perhaps Terry whom she would have long talks with. The oddest thing of all was Lynn constantly telling Mack how to act more like a man. "When you sit comfortably, spread your legs apart and slouch. Don't be ashamed to scratch what itches, and jokes about flatulence and naughty acts are always popular when the evening winds down." Lynn said she studied men like a zoologist, and would often practice repeating their gestures. "I know more about men than they do," she said once, "and in a pinch, I can act as rough, brisk, and coarse as a drunken northern Palachian without anyone being the wiser."

Anna Demure was somewhat of a mystery, as she stayed away from the Professor, and thus, Mack as well. As far as Mack could tell, she was not the libidinous deceiver she was written to be, but a very quiet and private person who spoke little unless she was angry, and then people had difficulty keeping her silent. She was also considered very smart and learned; like a walking library. Anna was the one they would send places to discover things, where her wile and feminine wit often charmed men and women alike. She was obviously the most feminine of the group, which annoyed the Professor greatly.

Stone "Rocky" Pillar was the anchor, as well as secretly being the silent leader of the group, which was quite the opposite way he was portrayed in all the fiction. Despite his large, brutish appearance, he was very sharp and impressively skilled in all forms of work. In person he did not speak much, and when he did it was often direct if not tactless. The entire group respected him for his words and suggestions, even Lance. Mack asked Stone why he was portrayed as a dumb brute in the fiction, and he cracked a wide smile and explained, "Because I listen before I act. I let Lance do the opposite to deceive my opponents. People tend to forget me because I am like the stone walls around them; quiet and ever present, privy to everything. Let them think Lance is the leader so I can get work done."

Terry "Chip" LaCroi was the most skilled technical mechanic Mack had ever seen. His small stature made him nimble and able to fit into small and tight places. Often sent ahead as a scout, he was not the hapless boy who so often got into trouble as he was written in the comics. Mack was surprised to find that she respected him most of all for his quick-thinking and timing. Terry and Stone were inseparable, and preferred to room alone with one another like big and little brothers looking out for each other. In a way, Terry and Stone were almost their own team, separate within the League.

Chang Daggerton, the Rokasian, was quiet and brooding, as Rokasians are assumed to be. Chang seemed to only be useful when doing Rokasian work, which was often, but he rarely interacted with anyone else otherwise. He was supposedly born in northern Palachia of Rokasian parents who were working as ambassadors when they were killed. Chang was very small when he was adopted by a northern Palachian couple, and his knowledge of their culture was relied upon greatly. Mack suspected that Chang and Anna had some kind of private fling between them, even if no one else did. Terry said, "They appreciate each other's intellectual company, and no more."

Massood Swarth, the southern Yurpan, was the most difficult to figure out. He was usually quiet, and when he spoke, he had a velvet voice of reason that calmed the nerves of most people. His skin was dark, like ebony, and his main skill seemed to be medicinal remedies. He quoted things from his tribe, and compared the human body to machinery quite often during his treatments of Mack's head wound, which was healing nicely under Massood's expert care. He was also useful as someone who could fabricate anything out of anything else, and often found creative ways to accomplish something when Terry's mechanical skill was not helpful in a given situation. Massood was the one who the League would go to if they wanted to find the big picture in a series of strange and underlying clues that didn't seem to match.

Mack looked at the small pocket watch hanging from her dresser mirror; a gift from Lynn that she kept hidden from the Professor. Soon it would be the end of maintenance time, and time for her to begin her work. She needed to finish the letter to her sister, so she could send it off before the Professor woke.

"I am working closely with some other associates of the Professor, but I cannot say who." Mack desperately wanted to share her secret, but she knew it would be a very bad idea. Not only would it jeopardize the secrecy of the League, but Morgana would probably either explode with jealous glee, or simply not believe her at all. "After the League of the Brave parade in a few days, I will be taking leave of southern Palachia for northern Palachia, and possibly Yurpa by airship. I will be on the surface, the real surface, for the first time. Not the domes like they have on school trips. I will experience wind and rain, sun and possibly even snow. I do not know how long I will be gone, but it may be a year or more."

In the last weeks since the dinner, Mack had been getting additional northern Palachian lessons from the various members of the League. They wanted to pass her off as such to other northern Palachians who had the experience of their own culture through their many travels. This involved knowing the casual conversation and subtle customs of the northern Palachian people by heart. She was given lessons on the style of clothing by region, their various forms of dance, and various stories. She also learned that even though most of them lived in rural huts and cabins above ground, a lot of them lived in northern Palachian cities that were almost as modern as her own. This greatly eased the pressure on Mack, as she felt that she didn't have to dumb down anything when she spoke to them. She often had to do this with Morgana, and it never came off as anything other than arrogant. Northern Palachians hated arrogance in all its forms, and she was strictly warned about using a superior attitude around them.

They prepared her for the trip to northern Yurpa, where they had a goodwill mission as well as a side investigation into some of the geothermal steam utilities that allowed the Yurpans to have huge cities above ground without the use of trolley. The Professor seemed more displeased about this more than anything else, stating that they were forcing them to leave as far away from his lab as possible to dally with royalty in foreign countries which he despised as social flattery and nonsense. In fact, since he became part of the League, he had received more invitations to balls, parties, formal events, and was distressed as he became "uncomfortably important." The big event coming up was the parade; the League would have three days of solid events and parties, all of which the Professor declined, and stated Mack was not allowed to attend, either. It would end with the parade before the League would be officially "sent off" by the Queen herself to Yurpa.

Mack finished the letter, which ended up being convenient, as her inkwell was running dry. "I will not be at the parade, although I have been invited, because I don't think it would be fair to you. Besides, I still don't think they are all that great. Please keep me in your thoughts. I hope you get this before you leave for school. Give mother and father a kiss from me, and I will write to you again as soon as I can. Cordially..."

Mack paused. She almost signed it "Mack." A terrible shudder went through her body; a pang of homesickness and disconnected loneliness grabbed at her sore gut with a cold claw. But she found she could not sign it "Heather," either. Her hands trembled, leaving two small dots neat the end of the paper.

"... your twin sister," she finished. Mack packed the letter and scarf in a tube, and brought it to her lips. "Please don't forget me..." she whispered, and kissed the tube. Tears welled in her eyes as she put it down and started dressing for her daily chores.

The first thing Mack did when she went down to the lab was to send the mail tube up into the pipe. As she watched the tube get sucked up and sent away, she noticed that a tube had arrived over the night, lying still in the padded basket like an orphan at a doorstep. Night mail was rare, since much of the pneumatic tube system was tuned and repaired during the maintenance period. It must have been sent with haste. She opened the tube and found that the letter was similar to the one the Professor received before he left. She felt she wasn't allowed to open it, even though her duties were to open all mail. Carefully, she opened the wax seal in a way that would disguise it breaking, and looked at the Korisan lettering. While she already knew many of the words and the basic structure, the lettering was in a different set form, and it was difficult to decipher the syntax in the order of arrangement by the writer. For the first time since she started reading in Korisan, she realized that not everyone followed the complex Korisan rules, and often made sloppy symbols and used incorrect order, just like deciphering grammar school scrawls in the Queen's language.

"We receive your [comment/message?] regarding the [group/team?] of strong hearts. [Something] [shows/points] [something] is in southern Palachia. You stay in southern Palachia. We come to southern Palachia and find [something] together. We have the trolley. — He who watches while dreaming shall awaken."

There was something foreboding about the letter. It seemed to stink of bad things, and Mack felt dirty from having read it. Instinct told her that she had inadvertantly stumbled upon some private taboo that may have explained the Professor's recent travels. She carefully resealed the letter, put it back in the tube, and placed it in the basket, just like she'd found it.

Later in the day, when the Professor asked if she had checked the mail, Mack looked in the basket and took the small tubes that lay there.

"There's a bill from the gas company," she said.

"Pay it," the Professor said, rubbing his temples as he sat over the work table.

Mack decided to be nonchalant. "There's a letter from... looks like Rokasia — "

"Let me see that," the Professor snapped as he reached for the tube.

Mack handed it to him, and opened the third one as if she didn't suspect anything. "... and I think an invitation to a ball being held after the Palachian symposium..." she trailed off as she saw the Professor read the letter. His expression was blank. "I assume you're not going?"

The Professor said nothing in response, but Mack could almost feel the tension in the room build.

Mack acted casual. "I guess will take that as a no, you are not going."

The Professor quickly folded the message, and looked at Mack. His expression was complex and impossible to decipher. Did he know she'd read it?

"I am sorry, what did you say?" he asked. He seemed angry. The Professor's paranoia with his recent drinking had been unpredictable. Mack did her best to avoid him when he seemed "complicated," but there were many times that he just threw things and stomped to his office without another word.

Mack chuckled nervously with attempted good cheer. "I said, I assume you're not going to the... um... Palachian symposium ball...?"

"No. I am *not* going to that insipid function." The Professor's expression turned dark, and it faced Mack like the edge of a rusty sword.

Mack nodded. "Okay, that's what I figured — "

"Figured? *Figured??* You think you have it all *figured* out, don't you?"

Mack didn't know what that meant. "Um, no?"

The Professor swept his arm across the work table, knocking the tubes and letters to the floor. Mack backed away, alarmed as the tubes clattered and rolled on the floor around her.

"You're *not going to make it easy, are you?*" the Professor screamed. He stood up and leaned over her.

"I'm I'm sorry... professor. Whatever it is, I'm sorry — "

"No. No. You're *not* sorry. You're just this impudent little... nosy *brat*! What fucking gave you the *right* to get yourself involved with the League of the Brave like some little hero-worshiping... shit?"

The Professor rarely swore. He considered it guttural and undignified. So the curses seemed far more dangerous. "B-but you sent me to get fitted with Lynn and Lance. I-I didn't know that — "

The Professor slapped her hard across her face. "Did I send you to see the difference engine? Did I? *Did I??*"

Mack held her stinging face and started to cry. "I'm sorry, I didn't... know!"

"You didn't know? Oh, so you had no idea! Thinking I'd just drop the whole taking the books — no... *my books* and sending them to be cleaned at... *Financial One?? What was that about??* If Anna hadn't swapped back the books... are you even on my side? Huh? Or are you working for the *Fucking league??*"

"I w-work for you and only f-for you — " Mack stuttered as she backed into a shelf.

"Then why do you constantly do things to sabotage my life?? Did I give you that permission??"

Mack sniffled as tears went down her cheeks. "I don't know..."

"No. I did not! And don't give me that rhetoric that you didn't know. Like you were some sort of... innocent!" The Professor swung his hands into the bookshelf next to them, bursting clouds of dust. "You knew that it was wrong. Yet you forged my signature, disobeyed my direct orders to go to public school, read and learned a forbidden language, sent books from my private collections, with *my notes* to a huge, greedy, selfish, money-grubbing institution that doesn't know what — and then — **stop crying!**" The Professor hit her again, this time hard enough to knock her to the floor.

Mack's head wound, which had been healing fairly well under Massood's care, stung with sharp pains as she landed. She was terrified. She didn't know what to do. She wanted to run away, but feared she wouldn't make it to the door and open it in time.

"You secretly *love* the League of the Brave, *don't you??*"

Mack shook her head. "No, I like you more than — "

"Don't lie to me!! This whole time..." the Professor grabbed his head and laughed with hysteria. "This *whole time* you were using *me* to get to that stupid, useless, Queen's harem of knowledge harlots like... you were *playing me* like some *father figure!* Like *your* stupid father! Bruce January. Oh, he thinks he's so smart..."

Nothing the Professor was saying made any sense, and it was more than obvious that he had been drinking. Mack had forgotten about the letter. Her head now hurt and her ears were ringing. As the Professor paced back and forth in small circles, Mack got up and tried to put as much distance between her and the Professor as possible.

"No matter what I do, Heather January is going to fuck it up! Just stumbling around like a fucking court jester and doesn't care a tinker's cuss about my work or my life!!"

Mack stung at hearing her old name as she wiped the tears from her face. "Please, I don't understand — "

"You don't understand is the whole problem with you!! Why couldn't you have been a normal girl and left me the hell alone?? *Why do you scream so loud at night??"* The Professor grabbed some books from the shelf next to him and started tossing them at her. *"Why do you scream at night???"*

"I don't know!" Mack sobbed, trying to curl up into a lower shelf as books tumbled all around her.

The Professor grabbed her by the arm, yanked her out of the book case, and flipped her over a work bench.

"Just go away and get out of here!! *Never* **come back!! I wish you had never come into my life!! I will never pay for your**

brothers, and I will tell your parents what a ... miserable failure you are!!"

Mack's entire universe narrowed down to a small pinhole in front of her. Her ego shattered at these words, and she stood numbly before him in shock. "Where... where do you want me to go??" she sobbed.

"I don't care! Grab your stuff and never return!!" he shouted and grabbed a large glass beaker and hurled it at her. Mack ducked, and the beaker shattered on the wall behind her, raining her with glass. "Go live with the League and be their stupid... Northie mascot!! Let them deal with hearing you scream and whimper all night!!"

Mack ran out the door, feeling bits of glass fall off her clothes. She ran up to her apartment, grabbed her trunk, packed what small things she had, and heaved it on her back. She went down the stairs, ran out of the building, and took the next set of trams to the tailor's shop near Financial One.

A hour later, she found herself in the familiar tailor's shop, barely remembering the journey. She was sitting on top of her travel trunk, in a daze of shock and pain. Massood had redone her bandages and given her some mild sedatives. After a while, she was able to explain what had happened, and Lance, Massood, and Lynn listened with sage nods.

"I see," said Lynn calmly. "Then he just threw you out?"

Mack drank another glass of brandy and nodded. She held out her glass for another.

"I am not giving you any more to drink. There's calming your nerves in a soothing warm brandy and then there's drowning them."

"I just received a very interesting message via tube," Lance said coming from the back. "It appears that the Professor has canceled his application for apprenticeship on behalf of Mack, and is handing her over to us as per our request."

Mack coughed out a few sobs.

"There there, dearie. You'll always have a home with us. This may be an unusual turn of events, but not wholly unexpected. And there was nothing that triggered this, you say? He just started shouting at you?"

"There was the letter from Rokasia," Mack said. She blew her nose into the handkerchief Lynn had given her earlier. "But as I said, I don't know what it contained. It was sealed." She neglected to tell them she had read the letter, perhaps out of shame and fear of rejection, but also because she didn't want to confess she could read Korisan.

Lynn nodded. "Well, we have a spare room above the hotel suite Massood stays at. It's not much, it's windowless, but it has its own private bath and a feather bed. That should be enough until we disembark to northern Palachia in a few days. You can eat with us, and we will continue your lessons."

Mack managed to crack a smile. A feather bed! "Thank you, Lynn. You are very kind."

"You are welcome, Mack. You're our family, now. Now, go wash up. When I finish this dress for the parade, we will meet at the hotel ballroom where we're being received by some archduke something or another. I'd like you to meet him, he's very... well, it will explain some of the private jokes we have at his expense."

Mack nodded and went to the water closet. As she sat on the toilet, she could hear Lynn and Lance through the keyhole.

"Take her to Yurpa and dump her there, eh? He must have really been furious at something," Lynn said.

"I wonder what was in that Rokasian letter?" Lance wondered. "I bet he's been told to stay here. He might be one of their essential operatives and they need him to work on the inside."

"Or... they think we'll find out what he's up to if he travels with us. Now we know he's an essential axle in their gears of espionage. I bet a lot pivots on him. The Queen was right."

"Should we send... Terry? Or Chang to find out?"

Lynn hummed in thought. "No, send Anna on this one. Have her find out through the routing office who sent that letter, and we'll work our way back. I think Chang can help when it comes to where it came from in Rokasia. This might be helpful if we can expedite this via priority code through the Sky Ring."

"Why not start from the Iron Horse mail office?"

"You are assuming that it actually came from outside Palachia, Lance. I have two thoughts: either it did, or it was meant to look like it did to the casual observer. No, I want this traced at each hop."

"I'll get right on this," Lance said.

"Meanwhile, I'll get this stupid dress done. Ugh, Lance, I can't wait for this stupid parade to be over with, and leave this city as quickly as we can. This whole Rokasian pre-war nonsense is dragging me down."

"It's because we're the only ones outside the royal cabinet who know we're at war, Lynn."

"Don't remind me, Lance. Soon everyone will wake up and see what's going on."

Mack gasped. "We're at war with Rokasia?" she wondered to herself. Then she remembered. "He who watches while dreaming," she thought. "... shall awaken."

Twelve
The Parade

Mack had attended dozens of parades in her life, but she had never actually been *in* one. Disguised as a northern Palachian float worker, she stayed close the League for the entire mind-numbing journey. The costumes they wore seemed surreal. Like parodies of the League she knew, her new friends waved and played their parts. Lance looked handsome as he caught the flowers that screaming women along the route threw to him. Lynn stood stoutly by his side, looking disapprovingly down at them. Stone stood silently behind them with Terry on his shoulder like a pet monkey. Chang sat on one side, looking brooding and dignified, and Anna sat on the opposite, reading a book with a coy smile. Massood simply had no expression, as he sat on his padded tuffet, holding onto his staff and staring blankly off in the far distance, as if to say, "I miss running naked in the fields of my homeland."

Massood and Mack had become quite close over the last week. As he tended to Mack's wounds, he also attempted to mend her hurt feelings as well. With a combination of quiet humor and distractions, he continued her northern Palachian lessons, correcting her accent, and building a wonderful story that Mack Van Horn would be able to use among "her kind." He also began teaching her how to fight, showing her Yurpan techniques that utilized an opponent's balance against them. Mack tried to foster an inner calm to help balance the damaged little girl inside as best she could using these techniques. Massood had warned her that burying a thing was not the same as making peace with it, but Mack could not find it within her to balance the 12 years of Heather, especially when it came to addressing the death of Heather at the hands of a truant officer.

The night terrors did not cease, either. In fact, they now came more frequently than ever. Mack often woke up hoarse from screaming after experiencing visceral, nauseating visions of being torn apart by strange green arms, the the arms of the truant officer that had assaulted her, or the Professor himself. Visions of being sucked into gears and crushed with machinery mixed with the all-knowing, all searching predatory eye dominated her resting hours. Slowly, she began to see that kidney-shaped pattern everywhere, and it was unnerving her. It would be there in the gaps of the drawing on an advertising poster, a shadow cast before her, or a pattern in the brick. Sometimes it was in the shape of a cam. Massood did what he could to calm her, providing a mothering role to calm her as she curled up against the headboard in terror. Still, she did not tell him of her visions because she was ashamed and embarrassed of the remnants of Heather screaming to be let out. She always lied, instead saying that she couldn't really remember what she had seen, or that she was unaware that she had been screaming. The lack of sleep was getting to her as well, and she started self-medicating herself before bed, taking sips of the warm Yurpan brandy; the only thing that seemed to guarantee a good night's sleep.

The days leading up the parade were harried and chaotic. In between all the social events the League was expected to attend, they also had to make fashionable wear that was different for each social event. The secret quarters in the tailor's shop made perfect sense to her now. Mack often had to help them haul fabric around or search for various buttons and broaches, but this was often mixed with other errands, like collecting messages or sending along information. They had gotten her a Queen's pass, which meant Mack could now go anywhere and everywhere she pleased; even during maintenance times, which delighted her. She was also pleased to find that she no longer had to pay a cent on any public transit system. Most of those times, however, she was busy running from one area of the city to the other, and didn't have time to stop and enjoy anything. Just as her father had said about his daily rides on the tram, "soon, you forget about the miracle of it all, and it becomes as dull and full of drudgery as walking up and down the hallway stairs." Mack realized that this was now happening to her as well. It had been the fourth tram ride that day, and she had barely even looked at anything mechanical.

"Our lives are not always about sewing and tailoring," Lynn offered as a form of apology. "Just while we're in town. Things will calm down a bit and we will have a much more relaxed and dare I say, boring lifestyle on the rails."

Mack looked down the parade route, steadying herself on the huge framework of the backsplash that showed the League in all their glory. While she was claiming to be the personal northern Palachian aide of the League, it was difficult to get the other workers to take their jobs seriously. She found several structural design flaws, as well as evidences of fatigue and stress. The float itself was older than anyone could recall. She found tool markings in the trolley-powered motorized assembly that were at least 80 years old. She was amazed it still worked. While metal lasted forever with minimal care, wood was a strange beast that needed constant attention, and this float did not seem to be getting that attention. Every parade, they just slapped on more paint, colored paper, and fabric. Mack knew as they started down the cobblestone streets that this ride was going to be very bumpy indeed, so she tried to anticipate it by keeping her eye on the roads and turns ahead.

It was during one of these moments, her head adrift with lack of sleep and boredom, that she noticed her father, and before she could stop herself, she looked for the rest of the family. Morgana was banned from the parade, and her mother would be working, because even though it was a Queen's holiday, the working class rarely got those days off. The thought of her family living without her punched her heart with the pangs of nostalgia and regret. She had only been gone a short while, and all she had learned in the many weeks distanced her from the jovial faces shared by her family. She pulled her worker's cap over her brow tighter, and tucked herself closer to the float to conceal her presence. She looked away, but found herself looking back as they drew closer to the corner. That's when she saw Morgana. Her parents let her go after all.

Morgana seemed older now; more like a woman. She was wearing a new pink dress with lots of frills, just the way she liked it. Through all the shopping she had done for the League, Mack had discovered that pink had just replaced green and yellow as part of the celebration of the League of the Brave. Mack was glad to see Morgana wearing the pins on her dress. She was waving desperately at Lance, screaming out his name along with every other young woman in the crowd. Mack shook her head, distracted for a moment by her inner amusement, when she saw something else that changed her mood instantly.

The truant officer.

Truant officer Bushington was standing in front of Morgana, dressed in blue buttons finery, holding her jumping and eager frame back away from the road with his huge, beefy hands. But his hands were pressed against the oblivious Morgana's chest, fingers spread wide to touch every single corner of the forbidden private area of a young lady. His eyes were expressionless, but his face had the subtle hint of a leer.

The noise from the crowd dimmed in her ears as Mack's entire perception focused on the face that attached itself to the name "Mr. Bushington." Memories of the night Heather January wandered the streets alone during maintenance time and those dark hours of destroyed innocence tore into Mack's senses like a spreading cloud of flammable gas wafting towards a lit candle. Time seemed to slow, and before Mack knew what she was doing, the Heather side of her was taking action. She pushed back an access flap and dove into the inner workings of the float looking about in the dim light that shone behind the fabric. The other workers were all outside the float, focusing their attention on the crowds. The person driving the float was far above her on a platform, looking with glazed eyes at the road ahead, focusing on the brake system rather than the steering as they were on a slight decline. Next to the rack and pinion steering assembly of the forward wheels, she saw what she needed: a pry-bar. She grabbed it, disengaged the clutch, and reset the rack off center. Then she let the clutch drop with a huge **BANG**.

The float lurched to the left at an alarming speed, as the momentary loss connection with the wheels disengaged the poorly-constructed brakes. Mack used this momentum to swing back outside the access flap in the float, and saw the crowd attempt to flee from the huge float suddenly barreling towards them. With nowhere to escape, the crowd pressed thick against the walls of the surrounding buildings, causing confusion and panic. She saw Officer Bushington push people to the ground as he tried to crawl on top of them, including her sister, who was still pretty clueless as to what had just happened. The driver screamed some kind of warning as he suddenly regained steering and brake control. This overcompensation pitched the edge where Mack was right next to the truant officer. In one fell swoop, she leaned out from the float, swinging the pry-bar straight into the truant officer's skull where it hit his helmet with a satisfying crack before the distance between the crowd and the float dipped away sharply.

Mack, still unsure what had just happened, dove back into the float, and screamed up at the driver, **"The clutch is slipping!"** The lie just came from her mouth as if she was completely unaware what she had just done, even though the pry bar was still in her hand.

"I know I know!!" the driver screamed in panic. Now the float was steering to the other side of the street, wobbling dangerously. The driver was unaware that his steering was badly out of alignment, and the years of predicable behavior of the float had dulled his reflexes. Mack realized that the main priority now was to stop the float entirely.

"What's going on??" screamed Terry, who had cut his own access hole in the fabric up top, and was trying to make his way past the driver down into the mechanics.

"Stop the float!!" Mack screamed, and when that didn't produce an immediate response, she climbed to the back, and pulled a steam release valve. The pressure in the boiler dropped, and the forward momentum of the float drifted on sheer inertia, which was increasing because the brakes were not working properly on the downhill slope. Mack then realized the front brakes were the only working breaks on the float, and both of them were pushing against nothing but air due to the misaligned front wheels.

Terry made his way down to the steering assembly platform and immediately looked around for what Mack assumed was a piece of metal.

"Here!" she screamed, but before she could hand the pry-bar off, the float steered sharply to the left again, and with the sounds of screaming coming from all around, the float tilted on its side. The steam in the boiler hit the trolley assembly, and the sudden heat change blew out an entire feed pipe with a loud **BANG**, forcing the entire float to tip over. The wooden framework, only built against stress from the top down, splintered and cracked under the new weight shift, and the entire float buckled inwards. Huge wooden planks and a few metal pipes fell towards Terry and Mack as the float started to crush them across the steering rack. The pinion and clutch assembly, free from its brackets, shifted towards them and inches before the jagged metal teeth struck them, Mack's pry-bar stopped it in mid fall.

For a few moments, there was a sudden calm inside the float. Mack was facing the prybar, which was now holding a huge pinion gear in place where Terry's head was pressed against the toothed rack. The muffled sounds of crowds fleeing and shouting, combined with the creaking of the float frame, were all that they could hear.

"You okay?" Terry asked in an incredulous tone.

"I think I hurt something in my leg," Mack said.

"That gear would have crushed my head like an egg," he said. "You saved my life!"

"I did?" Mack tried hard not to think about what had caused the incident in the first place.

"Don't move!" screamed Stone from the outside. **"The entire bloody frame is unstable!"**

"I guess that means us, too?" Terry said. He even winked and gave a smile.

Mack did not return the smile. What had she done?

"I guess you were right about this float, Mack. I mean... wow..." Terry shifted delicately. "I have been in dozens of these parades, and never thought the float would — "

"We have cracked trolley!" Stone cried out. It was the worst thing anyone could say, and the tempo of the crowd shifted into panicked cacophony like an incoming wave.

"That's not good..." Terry said, echoing Mack's feelings. The images from her dreams filled her thoughts as she looked around the frame to see if creeping tentacles of green gas were coming for her.

"It's bad... It's bad... where's Terry?" she heard people cry.

"We're down here, inside the float!" Terry screamed. His voice had risen in pitch, and almost sounded feminine, Mack thought. She had never seen Terry look so frightened.

Seconds later, Massood was beside them. He'd crawled in through a hole and was looking down at Mack's leg. "We must leave quickly," he said. "The situation is very volatile."

"Turn off those gas lamps!" Stone screamed outside. **"Everyone run up the street. Don't be downhill of us! If you are going downhill have people get uphill away from this street as quickly as possible!"**

"The entire clutch assembly became disengaged somehow," Terry said. "Mack was down here trying to fix it, alerting the driver. He even shut off the main boiler pressure!"

Massood nodded. "I am going to hold this plank up and you're going to have to crawl out from under me, okay Mack?"

Mack nodded. As he lifted the plank, Mack cried out in pain.

"Is Mack down there?" Stone shouted.

"Yes, Mack, Massood, and myself! We're down in the inner workings," Terry replied. **"We're trying to get out as fast as we can!"**

"Mack has a serious laceration, I am going to need bandages when she gets out!" Massood shouted.

"There won't be time! You, there! Put out that pipe! There's trolley gas spreading!"

Massood said into Mack's ear, "I have assessed the situation, and I apologize ahead of time for the pain that you will endure."

Mack nodded. "How am I going to get free — " the rest of her response was interrupted by Massood yanking her leg from the splintered wood. "G-**trolley fuck** OWWWW!!!" Within moments, she was under the dim lights of the street. The gas lights had all been extinguished, and the entire main square had turned as dark as a vacant alley.

"I have the broken trolley sealed off," Lance said. "I was able to fetch some emergency mineral oil." He looked at Mack, and then at her leg. "Oh, no..." he said.

Mack tried to look down at her leg, but Massood tilted her head away. "It can be repaired," he said.

"He saved my life," said Terry.

"The back of your head is bleeding!" Stone shouted in grave concern.

"I'll be fine, I'll be fine. Mack, how's... oh. Massood, is that even salvageable?"

Massood smiled. "I have repaired worse."

"We travel tomorrow," Lance said with concern. "Mack can't travel like... that."

"We will leave on time as scheduled. Get me some bandages, hurry. Mack is losing a lot of blood."

Massood released her forehead as he started to wrap the bandages, and Mack looked down at her leg. Her foot was at a right angle, and most of her shin seemed to be missing. Before the horror of the shock consumed her, Mack passed out.

hirteen
The Train Ride

Mack stood in front of the locker in her work clothes. This room was similar to the one at Financial One. Northern Palachian workers milled about, making bawdy jokes, as the work day began winding down. Mack had to wait for them to leave before she changed. She could have changed out of her work clothes in the loo, but it had been occupied for the last hour. She would have to wait.

Mack limped around to kill time, trying to look busy as men changed around her. At least her leg injury wasn't as bad as it had looked, initially. She was able to put steady weight on it, and apart from slowing down her stride, she was able to do a full day's work. She wasn't the only worker limping, many had various injuries that had accumulated over the years. Some were simply old. One by one, the workers left, and soon, she found herself alone. She took her street clothes, closed the small toilet door behind her, and looked at herself in the full-length mirror. She hadn't changed much since she had left southern Palachia: same short dirty blond hair and same dirty face. She was glad that she didn't look quite so feminine yet, and all the chest binding and clothes shaping seemed to be working well for now.

She peered curiously at her face in the dirty mirror. Her features were slowly growing softer, but she was able to pass this off as being "baby-faced," a condition that a lot of workers had due to various bloodlines in their family.

"Not bad, Mack, not bad," she said.

"It's not good," said her reflection.

"What?" Startled, Mack took a step back. Standing in the mirror before her was her old reflection. It was wearing the dress that she had worn back at her first day at Financial One.

"Surprised to see me?" asked Heather.

"I don't look like that now," Mack said. She shook her head.

"Oh, but you can't hide from me, Mack. You can bury me, ignore me, and pretend I never existed. But I am still here."

"Go away!" Mack said, turning away from the mirror.

"I'm still here, Mack," said the reflection. "You can't look at me, but you will always hear from me."

"Go away!" Mack shouted.

"I won't!" Heather said stubbornly. "Just how far do you think you can run?"

"Isn't this what you wanted?" Mack asked.

"I didn't want to lose my family. I didn't want to be hurt by that truant officer! I didn't want to be rejected by the Professor!"

"But it was the only way we could live as a man, and not a woman —"

"I *am* a woman, Mack! I am *not* you!"

Mack shuddered. "No, you're *not*. You didn't *want* to be a woman! You didn't *want* to serve a husband in some banal, hat-making —"

"Stop ignoring me!"

Mack turned back to face the reflection, her face strained with tears. She realized that this Heather looked a lot like her sister.

"Morgana *needs* me!"

Mack shook her head. "Morgana is fine without us, Heather — "

"I *miss my mother!*" Heather screamed. Tears were running down her face now, streaking her eye makeup.

"Are you wearing makeup?" Mack asked in shock. "Heather *never* wore — "

"Well she does now!"

Mack shook her head. "No. No, Heather. You made your choice. You decided to see the difference engine. You disobeyed the rules. You read Korisan. You are gone, Heather. You are a part of me that died."

"*I am not!*" Heather stamped her foot in defiance. *"You're trying to kill me!"*

"You died when you made those choices. This is our life now. With the League of the Brave."

"I did *not* make those choices, they were made *for* me! I didn't *ask* to be here!"

"What do you want me to do?" Mack asked.

"Go home. Go to mother and father!"

Mack sighed. "We can't do that, you know we can't — "

"Nooooooo!!" Heather screamed in a high pitched tantrum. The mirror cracked.

"Is everyone alright in there?" asked a voice in northern Palachian tongue.

"Yeah, sorry," Mack replied back, quickly changing into her street clothes.

"What's going on in there? Is there a girl in there?"

"No girl here," Mack replied. She straightened her street clothes, and without looking at the mirror, looked down and checked her buttons. "I'll be out in a second." That's when she saw the stain.

A dark stain of blood was soaking between her legs down her trouser legs. She shrieked in horror.

"What's all the screaming?" asked a voice. The door to the loo then opened.

"Hey! I'm not — " Mack looked up into the face of the truant officer; but in the place where two human eyes should have been, rested one big green fish eye.

"I'm not dead, I can hear the screaming..." he said, moving into the room and pressing her into the cracked mirror with his large body. "I can smell your blood, Heather January!" He pushed an enormous hand into her mouth, then penetrated her abdomen with clawed tentacles. Mack screamed and screamed, trying to force him to go away. She felt her organs being crushed by razor-sharp claws that tore into her like splintered float wood.

"Take your hand off his mouth!" Massood shouted. "Can't you see he can't breathe?"

"She *has* to stop screaming!" Anna said.

"Mack has nightmares she cannot control — "

"That doesn't help me when I am trying to sleep! What if other passengers heard this??"

"Anna, you must be patient. Mack and I are trying to work through her night terrors. She's been through a lot. She's nearly lost her leg, almost died in a float accident, and has to spend the rest of her life under an alter ego."

"This is a very important trip, you realize. Now we have to babysit a 12 year old brat. How long do we have to put up with this... screaming?" Anna asked, pulling her hand away.

"I don't mean to..." Mack said groggily, tears running down her face.

"She does not mean to," Massood said with a quiet smile.

"Were we any different when we joined the League?" asked Terry by the doorway.

"You're up?" Anna asked in surprise.

"I couldn't sleep," Terry said.

"Wonder why...?" Anna said with deep sarcasm and rolled eyes.

"Can you get your knee off my arm?" Mack asked, looking at Anna through closed eyes.

"You tried to hit me with it!" Anna scoffed, but released her.

"You are lucky he didn't claw your eyes out with them," Massood said. "You have not been through some of his deeper terrors."

Mack rolled to her side and laid still, breathing peacefully.

"She should sleep now," Massood said. "She doesn't have more than one a night."

"I couldn't sleep for other reasons," Terry said with a smirk. "I just wanted to check on Mack."

"You must have wanted to strangle her, too," Anna said.

"No, no. I just wanted to make sure you didn't strangle her. Relax, Massood's right. Mack has been through a lot."

"And *I* haven't?" Anna snapped.

"I didn't say *you* haven't," Terry said. "Stone told me about what you said when you joined us today. About the Professor and some of his visitors."

"Chang said he knew some of them from some of the Rokasian business meetings. He thinks the Professor's pivotal role is his root machine access and something about building a large war machine within the Palachian borders."

"I know, Stone told me. So why do you think the Professor wants to build a war machine, and defect to the other side?"

Anna stretched and cracked her back. "I am unsure. The Professor is an odd bird. But he won't succeed. I suspect that he's being used by the Rokasian Empire as a double agent, only he's not really an agent for the Queen. They just think he is, and he lets them think that. In reality, he cannot get away with building a large war machine inside the borders. No matter how many things you hook to the root machine, you can't just make an instrument of terror."

"You think he's ferrying them trolley?" Terry asked.

"No, not without detection. I think he's the classic case of an educated man dallying in political affairs blindly. He's not as smart as you think he is, Terry. I know; I worked with the man for nearly four years."

"But that was decades ago. People change in their old age, especially after a broken heart."

"Not my problem anymore," Anna shrugged.

"I can't believe you're that cold, Anna. In fact, I think a little bit of your heart is still back in that dusty lab. I think enough of it that when you saw Mack here was going to be his next apprentice, you decided to make this more of a priority than was necessary."

"What my heart did back then was that of a foolish young woman. I am far more sensible — "

"I didn't say you were less sensible, I am just saying that a heart wants what it wants, and even though you two parted ways decades ago, there's still a part of you back there."

"And why would *that* be?" Anna asked.

"Unresolved problems of the past trap a soul so that it cannot grow," Massood explained.

"There's no such thing as a soul, Massood," Anna replied quietly.

"Maybe not to you, but where I lay, I can see a troubled and jealous young woman who wanted to silence a rival with physical strangling."

"I did *not* strangle her — "

Terry laughed. "No, but you said you wanted to. Even suggested I wanted to. Why is this plainly obvious to all but the most educated and learned person in our team?"

"I don't have to stand here and take this," Anna said.

"So, sit down," Terry joked, slapping her behind as she passed by him.

There was a long period of silence as Massood lay back in his bed and Terry stood in the doorway. The train rocked occasionally in its journey. "Why do you think Mack has those terrors, Massood?"

Massood did not open his eyes. "Mack does not want to tell me the truth. She cannot handle what is presented to her, so she makes up stories about what she sees in her dream world to match what she thinks would make sense. Once she is ready to tell me what she truly sees, then the healing will begin."

Terry shook his head. "How do you know?"

Massood smiled. "I have my ways."

Terry grunted a response, and then left to go back to his cabin.

Mack snored quietly, until she heard Massood doing the same. She then slowly got up and curled against her small bed, taking a look out of the window at the rolling countryside around her.

"So the Professor really was romantically involved with Anna," she thought. She wondered about the visitors. That must have been what that letter was about. A spy? For Rokasia? It didn't seem real. Although, the Professor had never been intimidated by Rokasians, and he despised people who were racist. Maybe the entire time Heather worked for him, she was unaware that she was working for someone who was attacking their own country. This possibly explained why he hated the Queen's pomp so much. As Mack watched the trees and houses go by, she realized the Professor that Heather knew was no more real than the stories about the League.

The last few weeks had been more life altering than her entire life in southern Palachia. It started with the float accident, which was something everyone thankfully blamed on the clutch and poor maintenance. Mack's silent guilt over the event was buried under praise for saving lives. Not one casualty was reported by anyone struck by the float, and the Queen herself praised Mack for his deeds.

Because of this, she had gotten to meet the Queen. Never in her life had she assumed that this would be even a remote possibility. It all seemed so unreal, even when Mack found herself dressed in exquisite male tailoring, and on one knee before Her Majesty. She had been honored with the golden star, one of the highest awards of bravery and sacrifice. Mack was then publicly inducted into the League of the Brave as a permanent member, and for the following week, everyone wanted to know about Mack, the heroic northern Palachian who saved the day. She would be in next year's fiction! This cemented the formerly uneasy labor relations with the northern Palachian people, and boosted their image in the public eyes as hard workers, toiling silently for the good of all. Mack was now seen as a both a role model for young men and northern Palachia, which was almost ludicrous because she was neither.

She remembered Lance's tilted smile as he'd looked down at her and said, "Welcome to the League." The rest of the members had found themselves laughing at their own similarly ridiculous situations. "Wait for the books to come out; then you'll really see what the public wants in a hero."

Lynn had explained that this was a good thing for the upcoming war. The strength of labor would seal the bond between northern and southern Palachia from the frozen north to the Palachian divers in the deep south. In her opinion, this couldn't have come at a better time. It was almost like it had been planned.

Of course, it was all bittersweet because as Mack leaned on one knee in front of the queen, she was in terrible pain from her injury. Massood had saved the leg from amputation, but the pain limited her movement. The trouble was not just from the threat of gangrene, but the wounds had shown that she had been exposed to trolley gas, and the leg had been horribly burned. In fact, trolley gas had entered her bloodstream, and for a week afterward, Mack was down with fever and shaking before she fully recovered.

They had to delay their trip due to her illness, which also worked in their favor due to complications in discovering the Professor's source of correspondence. Even though they had to leave without Chang or Anna, they were able to meet up with the rest of the League before departing for Yurpa.

The train travel was much like the Iron Horse one takes to Rokasia, but it was much smaller, partially underground, and partially on the surface. The League traveled in their own private cars at considerable expense, but it did make things easier. Being a member of the League was socially taxing because if you were recognized in public, it could quickly escalate into madness.

"Women won't leave me alone, even when I demand it," Lance said.

"Men want to court me," Lynn said. "Often men try and make up for their looks by being wealthy. They are very persistent and are unused to being told no by anyone, much less a woman."

"People always want to prove how much stronger they are than me," Stone said. "I am attacked without mercy by men who think they have something to prove. And I have to defeat them, to keep up appearances. One day I fear I will lose just enough strength to be felled."

"Young boys look up to me," Terry said. "It's not so bad. I am hoping this works out for you as well."

"Men want to court me as well," Anna said. "But unlike Lynn, I have to appear flattered. I can get great information like this, but as I age... my looks are not what they once were. Many men are... disappointed... that I do not look as alluring as the posters and woodcuts make me look. There is nothing more jarring when people think you don't look as good as you did in their dreams..."

"I am often ignored, even by my own Rokasian brethren," Chang said, and this was all he had to say about it.

"I do not care for the opinions of others," Massood said. "I live my life, and when it is done, I can only hope I that I have made things better for those left behind."

The trip to the surface was made tense by the League's fear of how Mack would react. The first stop above the ground involved a change of train cars and a new shipment that arrived with Anna and Chang. All trolley was quickly hidden, and there were more notices about lectromag coming from the skies than anything else. Signs upon signs warned of lectromag being attracted to trolley, metal, and even "people of a salacious nature;" something Mack could not figure out. Lectromag was so mysterious and violent, it was almost used as a general warning sign to do as you were told. "Perhaps this is why Northern Palachians are so docile," Mack pondered to herself. "It must be humbling to live in a world where a jagged light from the sky could simply burn you where you stood." With everyone surrounding her, Mack stepped out of the car and onto the train platform, above the surface for the first time. There was no visitors dome, there were no teachers, and nothing but the Sky Ring above her.

Mack had been nervous. She had discussed the common symptoms repeatedly with the League, and each one of them had explained what it had been like for them the first time. Both Anna and Lynn had panicked badly. Anna had to be sedated heavily, and Lynn had to be kept in a small box with no windows for a week. Stone was shaken for weeks, but got over it. Lance said he didn't care, although nobody seemed to believe him. Terry had spent part of his life above ground in an open sea, so he didn't really care, either. Massood shared this sentiment, stating that he had a definite place in the universe as a whole, so he was happy where he was. Mack decided that she wanted to be like Massood and tried to remember to balance herself, that she was not changing, that just her perceptions of her surroundings were. Mack also had enough self perception to be aware of "the unexpected." Her night terrors seemed to be her own worst enemy, so as long as she survived those, she thought that being on the surface wouldn't be so bad. But she had prepared for anything, just to be safe.

As she looked up at the clouds in the sky, she did get a sense of severe vertigo, and stumbled in spite of her cane. The entire League nearly jumped in unison to grab her. As some of the northern Palachian workers passed back and forth, hauling luggage and cargo, Mack simply tried to look confident. But she was shaking visibly as she did what she had been taught: stare at the ground until you get comfortable again.

"You okay?" Terry asked.

Mack nodded. "It's the leg," she said, tapping the wound with her cane, trying to look robust. There were a lot of subtle changes in the air surrounding her. The air seemed cold and damp, and had a lot of strange smells. Sometimes a damp wind would waft by, carrying more unfamiliar smells. It smelled like rot and decay, with a hint of flowers, fruits, and a leathery heavy odor that pushed deep into Mack's sinuses. Everything sounded different. There was a distinct lack of echo, as if the air around her was stealing sound away. Given the strange smells, lack of echo, and no ceiling, Mack could easily see why people had panic attacks. It was if you had suddenly become so insignificantly small, you shrank down to the size of a mote of dust.

With great care and sense of determination, Mack looked up and faced the horizon. Just like the books had said, the sky met the ground in a distance so far away, it defied all common sense. Mack lost her balance again.

"Easy, Mack," Terry said.

Mack looked up at the clouds. How far away was the end of the sky? The books said it went on forever. That didn't seem possible, and the very impossibility of a reality without a ceiling above her made her queasy. What were the clouds attached to? She knew the sun was behind her, and not to look into it. How can you live in a world where there was a bright light in the sky half the time that could blind you if you looked at it? The sun was very hot, too. It lightly burned the back of her neck like she was close to a hot steam pipe.

"This is..." Mack paused to find the right words. "Amazing. Disorienting, but amazing."

"Wait until you get in an *airship*!" Terry said with enthusiasm.

"One step at a time, Terry," Stone said with concern. "Mack is in a delicate frame of mind right now."

"If you turn around, and don't stare at the sun, you can see the Sky Ring," Anna said.

Mack turned around, and even though the train was in the way, she could see the giant brownish-green band arch from horizon to horizon.

"Whoa..." she said, dazzled. No amount of images or color plates depicted in books could prepare her for a structure so large, it surrounded their world. She all but forgot about the sky, and focused on the gigantic ring that painted its presence with a great sweep of a mechanical brush.

"The Builders made that," Lynn explained. "Nobody knows why for sure, but it's been there since we first went underground. Very few people live there. It is a very harsh and inhospitable place, but it looks even more beautiful at night."

Mack closed her eyes, and focused on how she felt. Apart from the lack of echoes and the smells, she didn't feel smaller anymore.

"Come," Lance said. "We have a connecting train to catch."

Mack didn't feel like she was going to panic, but when she changed trains, she did feel a lot safer inside six walls.

Now as she watched the night countryside zip by her window, she felt a kind of thrill. The skies had their own light show. There were huge dots of light, and the Sky Ring shone as a glowing light green band that launched from the East and disappeared where her window stopped. She was proud that she was adjusting to the surface so well. In fact, when the train stopped to refuel and exchange cargo, she always made an excuse to get out and stare at the sky; day or night. When she wasn't doing lessons or attending League meetings, she would look out of the window marveling at the vast open plains of farmland dotted with small rural Palachian towns and small barns. She even saw living things like squirrels, birds, and a deer.

But when she relaxed her body, trying to live the thrill of new and exciting adventures, it would be replaced by a pang of anxiety. Once she passed the southern border of northern Palachia, the last large city on their tour, she would be further north than anyone in her family had ever been. And she would go further north still. And then on to Yurpa.

"What do you dream about, Mack?" Massood asked.

Mack jumped a little at his voice. "Bad things, Massood. Murder. Death. Broken machines I cannot fix."

"Why do you call out your sister's name?" Massood asked.

"What?" This was news to Mack. "I do?"

"Is she a machine you cannot fix?"

Mack shook her head and shrugged. She did not believe she remembered dreaming about her sister. "My sister... Heather's sister... is a little broken. Very girly. Which is fine, she's supposed to be."

"Is she? She is your twin — "

"Fraternal! Twin."

Massood hummed. "I see. You shared the womb, but you are separate?"

"Yeah. That is what they tell me. She doesn't even look much like me. She's completely different than I am."

"But you share a common bond." Massood rose from his sleeping spot on a huge pillow on the floor, and moved to sit on the edge of Mack's bed. "I have a brother, and we are separated by half a globe. Yet I still feel as connected to him as I did the day my mother showed him to me for the first time. Among my people, we learn to hunt as a group. So communication between brothers always leads to a successful hunt."

Mack shook her head. "I am not sure it's the same with me at all. I don't really remember any dreams with my sister. She's so different from me."

"Then what are your dreams about?" Massood asked. He stared at Mack's reflection in the night window, looking distantly at the Sky Ring in the southern horizon.

Mack remained silent.

"There is a saying among my people. It is an old story, but it was about a man who dreams he was a butterfly."

Mack smirked. "A butterfly?"

"When he awoke, he wondered if he had just dreamed he was a butterfly... ... was he a butterfly... dreaming he was a man?"

"That's stupid," Mack said. "Of course he's a man."

"How do you know?"

"Because butterflies do not dream."

"Perhaps that is the dream, being a man who dreams that butterflies cannot."

Mack shook her head. "I listen to you talk a lot about balance, but I don't think I believe about butterflies dreaming they are people like you and I. Anyway, logically, since the story is told by a man, it is a story without a point."

"I disagree, Mack Van Horn," Massood turned Mack around and stared in her eyes. "How do you know you are not dreaming right now, and your nightmares are the reality?"

Mack's skin crawled as goose bumps rose on her flesh. "D-don't say that!"

"Why not?"

Mack twisted away from Massood's gentle grip. "It's not nice. Those nightmares are just... there's something wrong with me, that's all."

"Or maybe you're the only one who is real, and you are trying to awaken."

Mack puffed her cheeks in thought. "He who watches while dreaming shall awaken," she said absently.

"What did you say?" Massood asked. His calm face changed radically, although Mack did not notice it.

"Nothing. Just a phrase I heard once."

Massood grabbed Mack again. "No, no... what did you say?"

"I said, 'He who watches while dreaming shall awaken...' Nothing, really, I just heard — "

"Where did you hear that??"

"Let go of me," Mack protested. Massood's sudden anger was alarming.

"That's an old Korisan saying! Very old. Very... very bad saying. I need to know where you heard that!"

"Let go! I don't know. Somewhere in my studies," she lied. She remembered the symbol on the walls of Financial One and the signature in the Professor's letter. But she couldn't admit she could read Korisan.

"Did Professor Gaylord ever say that to you? Answer me!"

"Let go of me!" Mack screamed.

Massood released his grip. "I'm... I'm sorry. It's just... that's a phrase used by a group of people. Very bad people. Forgive me; you gave me quite a bad scare."

"What does that mean? I mean, why do Korisans say it?"

"They do not say it. There are no more Korisans, Mack. It does not matter."

Mack grabbed Massood. "It matters to me. You just grabbed me in anger, and you have never done that to me before. I can't read Korisan, so you'll have to tell me."

"And that is why women are not allowed to read Korisan. But never say that phrase again."

"Why are women not allowed to read Korisan? I was always told they couldn't."

Massood regained his usual calm demeanor. "I know you wish to be a man, but there are some things that must stay sacred. Like how you must bleed every few weeks by the Palachian clock. That will never change. Reading Korisan by a woman is forbidden, and always has been in any culture."

Mack sat back down dejectedly. "It seems like it wouldn't be hard to learn Korisan, I can't imagine every woman has stuck to that rule."

"They have," Massood said with a dark tone. "Because the women that learn it go insane. There are old things... old things the Builders left behind that cannot be known by women."

"Like what?"

Massood laughed. "No, Mack. In the first place, I do not know. Many men go mad as well. In fact, there are a group of them that have formed a cult. Do you know what a cult is, Mack?"

"It's one of those secret clubs that people have where they all go in a room, get drunk, and teach one another to dance or something. Fraternities, my father used to call them — "

"No. A cult is far more dangerous. I take it that you, being of sound mechanical mind, do not speak of spirits and gods, as if they were real, and controlled our daily affairs."

Mack laughed. "No! That is silly."

"Some men not only speak of them, but speak as if they were real. There is one cult in particular, a Rokasian cult that worships an old Builder. Very old. It was said, as some believe, he was cast out and imprisoned deep below the surface of the sea. The name of the Builder is never to be spoken, for it is said among their kind that to speak his name is so summon him."

"So... what does this have to do with women learning Korisan?"

"Korisan, and you may have heard, is the language of the builders. The last time the Cult of the Unnamed Horror rose to significant power, thousands of years ago, a Korisan-speaking woman was at its helm. She brought terrible pain and despair to millions. Large creatures erupted from the depths of the earth, attracted by the cult's power, and in the end... slaughtered all but a few, leaving the surface in ruins, forcing many underground for centuries. Those that survived altered Korisan to the languages you know as Rokasian, the Queen's Language, and Yurpan. Each took a part of the structure, but altered it so it was nearly unrecognizable from the root. Rokasian took the symbology, Queen's language took the grammatical structure, and Yurpan took the phonics. The only thing that remained was the taboo of women speaking the root language, Korisan, which had to be preserved with men so we could continue to maintain the Root Machine. Many small cults have sprung from this; the last one was a few hundred years ago under the guise of the last Rokasian war. They summoned forth one of the Unnamed Horrors... but it was defeated. Ended the war over a common enemy."

"So... women are only forbidden, not unable, to learn Korisan."

Massood looked at Mack darkly. "If you so much as learn one word or utter one more ancient phrase... I will be forced to slit your throat where you stand."

Mack shivered. "All...all right."

"Listen closely. That cult is very, very dangerous. Small splinter groups are still alive today, but in insignificant numbers powered by rich people who are bored and have nothing better to do. It is currently little more than a secret social club. But there are some who wish to seek the power of the old cult, and those people are very dangerous. They never speak the name of the cult, or refer to the ancient builder they purport to worship. They simply say..." Massood swallowed, "he who watches while dreaming."

"... shall awaken," Mack finished in her mind. It was becoming a reflex at this point.

"To say the entire phrase is such a dark curse on all who utter it, I fear anyone will go mad at the thought. A few decades ago, a small section of this cult attempted to kidnap women and force them to read Korisan. Each woman went mad, of course, and eventually they were captured and executed. It terrified the city for months after the scandal was exposed. The League was part of the capture, but that was before I joined. From what I have heard, I am glad I was not part of the heroics."

Mack nodded. The concept that groups of people worshiped some invisible force of darkness seemed completely absurd, but she kept those thoughts to herself. She didn't believe in curses, spirits, or old Builder cults but she knew anything that made Massood act in this way was worthy of respect.

"Now, we must sleep. Close those window shades and rest. I will do the same, and will not bother you again tonight."

Mack nodded, and pulled down the shade. But she could still see some of the stars through the gap by her bed. As she watched the winking of the stars, she let the rhythm of the tracks lull her back to sleep.

Mack awoke to the sound of noise outside her car. They must have stopped for a refueling. But there was another sound she had never heard before; a hissing clicking sound that came from all around her like someone was pouring lead bearings all over the train roof. As she peeked through the gaps of the window, she saw that the light was gray and the window was streaked with what looked like water.

"Ever been in a rainstorm before?" Lance asked, entering the cabin.

Mack shook her head. "That's where water falls from the sky, right?"

"That's right. You might also see the flashes of lectromag dart between the clouds. Shouldn't affect us, though. We had to stop for a refuel and cargo exchange. We're a little behind schedule, and I just spoke with some of the porters to get the local gossip. Once we're back moving again, the League will be meeting in the private dining car. I have some rather usual news from the Upper Palachian front."

Mack stretched and scratched her head. "Is there breakfast?"

"Not until the meeting. But we have other things to discuss. Take a shower and get dressed in your northern Palachian finery. There's going to be a public appearance by request of the mayor of the city."

"So why do I have to come?"

"Have you forgotten already? You're one of our newest stars!"

"But they don't know that... not yet."

Lance laughed. "Mack, news travels fast. Gossip travels faster. The entire continent knows by now. You are the talk of all of northern and upper Palachia. You are their hero. There has never been a northern Palachian League member before. We need to put on some darkening makeup and test out your accent."

Mack's chest tightened. "I have to be presented to a crowd of northern Palachians?"

"Yeah, so don't miss a single loosened bolt, or the engine of your deception will break down and the Queen will have your head."

Mack felt the pangs of panic grip her chest.

"But don't worry, Mack. We'll back you up."

As Mack dressed, Terry sat behind her. "Remember," Terry said, "you don't have to answer any questions you don't like. Stay in chaotic crowds, and avoid one-on-one conversations with anybody. You have it easy, you're northern Palachian, and are naturally shy and not attention-seeking."

"That's just it," Mack said, adjusting her cravat. "I am not northern Palachian. I barely speak the language beyond basic conversation, and while I have dye on my hands and face, my nose and ... my whole face does not look it."

"That's why you wear the hat. In addition, we will be at the end of the covered caboose. No rain there. Act shy and humble, state some patriotic stuff about northern Palachia and we'll cut it off there. It's a standard 5 minute speech while we refuel."

Mack heard her name. Being chanted by thousands. "Are they... ?"

"They are all shouting Mack Van Horn, yes! We better get out there before the crowd tears the train apart looking for you."

Mack laughed.

"That's not funny, that really does happen," Terry said with a straight face.

When Mack exited the caboose, she was stunned by what she saw. Mack had never seen so many people on her life. They flooded the entire valley behind the train. They were on top of every fence post, pitched roof; some were even perched on top of one another. There were so many wet heads packed together that it washed out all the ground features and Mack thought it looked like her train had just pulled out of a giant sea of human faces. The entire crowded roared at the sight of her, pushing hard against the train until it rocked. They didn't seem to mind the rain and gray skies.

"There must be hundreds of thousands of people here..." Lynn said in amazement.

"This is smashing," Lance said with enthusiasm. "We really needed this boost up here," and as he said that he raised Mack's arm up. The crowd cheered again, drowning out every other noise from miles around.

"Speak into the megaphone," Lynn shouted in Mack's ear, handing the huge conical tube to her. "Just talk in the small end and slowly pan the crowd so everyone gets a chance to hear."

"How can they hear with all this noise?" Mack shouted back.

"You'll see."

Mack had thought hard about what she wanted to say, and had run a few tests through Terry. "My people... of Palachia..." she said in her proudest voice.

The crowd went quiet almost immediately, and all that could be heard were a few coughs and mutterings.

"My people of Palachia, I am glad to be home..."

The crowd roared approval; cheering and clapping like this was the best thing that had ever happened to them. Mack let them cheer for about a minute before she calmed them down with her hands.

"I am... at a loss for words. I am not used to speaking. I am not a proud man, but like you, a hard worker. But in my heart, I am proud to do my job, knowing my people are the backbone of all of Palachia."

The crowd roared again, congratulating each other as if each one of them had been personally recognized at long last. The mood of the crowd washed over Mack as she felt their joy and camaraderie.

"Well played, Mack," Lynn said.

"We're ready to go..." said a voice behind them.

"I have to leave you now," Mack said. Then she froze. She didn't know what to say next. Her mind seized up and she looked to Lynn for guidance, but she was too enthralled by the crowd. Lance was also looking away, blowing kisses at ladies. The crowd went quiet, looking at Mack. Seconds turned into eons. Whatever she had memorized had been hijacked the moment the train operator said they were ready to go, and she couldn't think in northern Palachian. She tried desperately to think of something, when the phrase she learned at the difference engine bubbled forth to her lips.

"Ah... n'moid, spankah!"

The crowd roared again, this time with laughter, and the train shook violently as the League darted back into the caboose. The cheering was deafening, and even inside the shaking caboose, Mack had difficulty making sense of it all.

"What did you just say?" Lynn asked in shock.

"I am not sure. I used it when we were working on the difference engine — "

"Oh, my," Lance said, his eyes red with laughter. "I can't believe you *said* that!"

"What does that mean?" Mack asked.

Lynn widened her eyes and rolled them away. "We'd better go," she said.

Anna looked at Mack with narrowed eyes, as Chang passed behind her. Massood gently shook Mack's shoulder and said, "I am not sure what you said in the end, but the men loved it."

"It's a colorful metaphor in the Northie tongue," Terry said, patting Mack on the back. "I owe you a strong drink. That took some serious backbone. Where in the world did you learn such a filthy word?"

"It's a curse word?" Mack asked in disbelief.

Stone and Terry howled with laughter. "You didn't know?"

"No!" Mack shouted. "I just... I didn't... what's it mean?"

But Stone and Terry shook their heads and kept laughing. "See you at the meeting, potty mouth!"

Everyone left, leaving Lynn and Mack alone in the car. She could hear the shouting of the train staff and cargo porters shooing the crowd away. The train jerked forward, and Lynn just stood there, glaring at Mack. Her eyes were red.

Mack felt panic break down into complete misery and embarrassment. "I'm... I'm sorry... I didn't know it was..."

Lynn interrupted her with the most bawdy, hearty laugh she had ever heard. "In the name of trolley and lectromag, *you!*" Lynn dropped to her knees and had trouble breathing. "You... you... I can't believe... that was the *best*... oh dear dear dear me... I need to get a hold.... of myself."

Mack stood there, confused and scared. Lynn caught her expression.

"My dear... boy!" she said. "If anyone ever doubts you are a man, that was eradicated in one small phrase. There is no need to be sorry. You did... *great!* What a northern Palachian thing to do, to utter the most foul... guttural... in the presence of royalty. In the presence of *children!* Ha ha ha..." and with that, Lynn patted Mack on the shoulder hard, and said, "Come on. We have a breakfast meeting!"

The breakfast meeting was held in their private dining car.

"I have heard some disturbing news from the north passage," Lance said.

"I heard disturbing news from Mack's mouth," Terry said, snickering.

"Never mind that, it was a good move. If anything was more Northie than Northie, it's a good, putrid swear," Lynn said. "It will further cement our relations with them, and we will be considered more working class. Information will be even easier to come by. Please continue, Lance."

"Thank you, Lynn. As I was saying, disturbing news from the north passage alerted me that airships have started turning back passengers because of lack of coal. Further investigation showed that coal had thinned out and I have been able to trace some paperwork that details the coal shipments nearly cut in half from the Iron Horse passage."

Anne continued. "A Rokasian company owns the sole rights of that coal line since the dissolution of the Queen's Royal Coal. They are now the only suppliers of coal to Palachia. They stood to make a tidy profit over a three decade term, so the cessation of that coal means that they have either run out, or they are using it for something else."

"Thanks to Anna's hard work," Lance continued, patting Anna's back, "we have been able to trace some of the purchase orders over the last few months. We found that half the orders have gone unfulfilled. The coal line that goes from the neck of upper Palachia has thinned so badly, the suppliers have not been able to get even half the coal needed."

"Then... where did it all go? Do you think the Rokasians have decreased coal because of the embargo we put on their trolley trade?" Stone asked.

Chang shook his head. "Perhaps it is symbolic, but it would have shot themselves in the foot. No, I think they are not selling us coal because they stand to gain from it in other ways. I think they are using the coal themselves for some reason."

"Yes, what is this reason?" Stone asked. "And is it, again, because of decreased trolley?"

Lance shook his head. "That is not what we think. Rokasia as you know, has their own trolley mines. It's not perfect, but even if we ceased all trolley shipment, they could continue for months, if not years, on their existing supply."

Lynn waved her hand. "Before we continue, Mack?"

Mack looked up, her mouth clogged with a dense and sweet scone. "Yff?"

"Do you understand what's going on?"

"Perhaps we should give her a primer, and we all could use a refresher," Lance said. He pushed aside some of the food and started drawing with a charcoal stick directly on the table linen. "Mack, out of the three continents, we continue to exist in modern comforts because of a mutual trade agreement on natural resources. Palachia has labor, agriculture, wood, and trolley. Rokasian has metal, labor, and coal. Yurpa has agriculture, wood, and manufacturing. Palachia is in the unique position of cornering over 80% of all mined trolley. Trolley, as you may know, is mined underwater, near the spokes that hold up and power the Sky Ring. But unlike the trolley deposits in Rokasia and Yurpa, ours is in a relatively shallow sea, and very rich and abundant. The other continents, well... not as lucky.

"But Rokasia trades metal and metal manufacturing with us. They mine titanium, steel, gold, silver, and almost 90% of mined materials including coal. Sadly, they have very little arable land. So they trade agriculture and wood with us and Yurpa. Yurpa has no real resources other than flat, abundant land. They are the agricultural powerhouse of the world. They also supply forests with timber and wood, which is used for raw building as well as fuel.

"And thus, we are in balance. The financial experts work out who owes what whom, and depending on the growth of the continent, debts are assumed and stored in good faith. Sadly, in recent times, Rokasia has accumulated a great deal of debt, putting their continent at a disadvantage."

"How did they accumulate this... debt?" Mack asked.

"Intelligent question. And one that has been speculated for the last decade or so. But in recent years, the more negative speculations have proven more and more alarming. We think they may be preparing for war."

"We haven't had a war with Rokasia in a long time," Lynn said. "In fact, our military has been reduced to little more than a silly little social club for men. All uniform and show with very little training for real combat. And why should they? The police see more combat dealing with lower levels in a day than the army or navy sees in a lifetime of service."

Lance tapped the table and pointed towards the drawing of southern Rokasia. "That aside, to answer your question, we think they have been using resources more and more to build up war machines and their own army."

"At first," Stone said, "there seemed to be no real way they could make it to our shores. They would have to make a real effort beyond their resources to attack. But for the last few years, we have discovered that they could focus more and smaller direct attacks on certain key points, like our trolley mines near the Southern Spoke. If they gain control of that, Palachia will be squeezed to a standstill within a few years."

"And that's why they would send us substandard gears..." Mack realized. "Things will break or become unusable."

Lynn nodded. "Exactly, we still depend on them for metal and metal manufacturing. And coal. We have realized that coal was thinning out below our noses. While coal only represents 10% of our energy needs, that 10% is wholly above ground transport."

"That would cut off agriculture and our airship connections with Yurpa," Chang said.

"We used to own half the coal transport operations until about 10 years ago, when there was a series of failures along the Iron Horse line that forced the Queen's hand to give the remaining stake to Rokasia," Anna added. "And at the time, it was a great deal. Of course, it could have all been an elaborate plan."

Lance frowned. "We think this is the beginning of the actual war. We have dallied with tariffs and custom excise tax and all manner of export and import fees."

"Normally, this would have caused a lot of warning flags on the financial exchange markets, but they have been oddly silent," Anna said. "So that's why we were at Financial One."

"But we didn't find what we were looking for. The financial exchange market was oddly calm and stable for such rapid changes. You'd think with the export of substandard gears, and then the dwindling of coal, there would be some kind of... rattling in the system that would be impossible to ignore. But it seems that something has been correcting the imbalances that should naturally occur.

Mack thought for a moment about the Korisan symbol she saw at Financial One, but decided to stay silent until she could think of a good reason to bring it up. "But what about the lectromag experiment?"

"Ah..." Lance said with a wide grin. "Now we come to the second, more secretive part of this discussion. Fellow member of the League of the Brave? The Queen has approved our plan, and we are traveling with credit, bonds, and vouchers to match the Yurpan alliance with the lectromag ocean line, which we simply call the String."

Mack furrowed her brow, asking, "What is that?"

"Part of our problem with the Yurpan alliance is the vast distance they are from us," Anna explained, tracing her finger along the route of the table linen, which by now was becoming quite smudged. "Communication takes weeks, if not months. Even by airship, the trip from the major cities of Yurpa to southern Palachia is measured in months. Communication is no better. The fastest and most direct letter still takes at least a week to reach northern Yurpan cities. Then a response must be made, and then a week to go back."

"And most cities are in southern Yurpa," Lynn said with a sigh.

"Which takes even longer," Lance said. "But a few years ago, one of their more skilled scientists came up with a way to use lectromag to cross vast distances in a very short period of time. Faster than a train or any pneumatic tube system ever made, communication via cities is now measured in minutes rather than days or weeks."

"Minutes?" Mack asked. "What, do they shoot it into the air by cannon?"

"That was once tried, but it was too unreliable," Lance answered with a chuckle. "No, it seems that if they generate lectromag on one side of a long unbroken metal cable, it will swing a magnet on the other side. If they stop sending lectromag, the magnet rests. If they keep doing this, they can send coded messages to one another."

"We use the same technology now with the Sky Ring," Stone said. "It's used by sailors on the open seas to communicate weather to those at the ring and vice versa. But it requires huge amounts of light, a large telescope, and it's not very practical for anything more than a few crude, daily messages."

"What's a telescope?" asked Mack.

Anna sighed in frustration. "We're really going to have to teach this little one some uncommon basics."

"It's a good thing she asked that," Stone said, "because while the strobe lamp and telescope is used for weather, we also have one of our League agents in the Sky Ring reporting on Rokasian activity. Telescopes are made of polished glass lenses like a magnifying glass. Only a telescope makes something very, very far away seem really close. So if you know where in the sky to point the telescope, you can see someone shining a bright light from the Sky Ring. They send a series of flashes which can then be written down and then decoded. So far, we have been able to keep an eye on some of the larger operations of Rokasia by doing the reverse: pointing a telescope down and looking at the lights of their furnaces and some of their surface cities lit at night."

Lance nodded. "We haven't seen much, but we have noticed a flurry of activity at one of their port cities. It would seem they are building a large quantity of strange ships. We think they may be steam-powered battleships."

"This could be where the coal is going," Lynn realized.

"Precisely. They can't use trolley on the surface, especially in the open ocean. That's suicide."

"So why does Rokasia want to attack us?" Mack asked.

"Easy: material goods. If they take over Palachia, taking over Yurpa would be easy since they would control 2/3rd of all the world's resources."

"Why don't they take over Yurpa first, then?"

"Because Yurpa is the weaker of the two, and easiest to conquer last. Also, it has the largest land mass and would be difficult to conquer all their cities, which lie on the eastern coast far away from them. They would have to sail west, go around Yurpa, and attack that way. In our case, 90% of our cities are on our eastern coast, closest to them. Plus we're only separated by one shallow sea, and the Iron Horse."

"We also think they may be sneaking inside troops. That's why we were interested in the Professor's visitors. They would attack from inside as well as our eastern coast. But as you can see, Chang's people are very easily identified on sight with their dark, brown eyes and black hair. The Professor, on the other hand, would blend in with southern Palachians without any thought. Thus, the empire rots from within, so the incoming troops can just finish the job."

"This is where we stand currently," Stone said. "To make allies certain with Yurpa, we have agreed to finance half of the String. The String will be a metal cable that will cross the ocean that divides Yurpa from Northern Palachia. If this succeeds, we could have communication with Yurpa from northern Palachia in about a few minutes. And unlike the strobes from the Sky Ring, communication could be done in very large volumes. They have developed ways in Yurpa to transmit entire images as well as letters. Somehow... they break down images into some kind of code. And we could do the same."

"If this succeeds," Lance said excitedly, "we can run these lectromag strings from all of upper Palachia to southern Palachia. Communication will be revolutionized."

"But how will we prevent the lectromag from destroying trolley?"

"The strings will be above ground. There will be stations with strings and pneumatic tubes. These will be translated and sent underground by the tubes. We can have several of these stations above ground. We can lay as many strings as we want!"

Mack grew excited with the thought. But then she remembered the workers at the difference engine. "How will we keep people from being killed by lectromag?"

"Ah..." Terry said. "That is the question, now, isn't it? That's why we're being sent. If the deal goes sour, we plan to simply use what we learned to build our own."

Lance leaned forwards and spoke softly. "Contained on this train is the money we will be using to finance the deal. We have cars filled with titanium and gold ingots disguised as crates of lead bearings. We also have three airships at our disposal to carry them to Yurpa."

"That is, if we have enough coal when we get there," Anna said.

"Hence my concern," Lance said. "I hope we have enough coal to make the journey to the airship ports. The conductor had to make some exceptions in our case, as travel has been severely restricted. The Queen's passports we have are good for many things, but they will not make coal appear out of thin air. That's something we may have to do."

Lance rubbed the charcoal on the linen into a gray smudge. "Here is a proposed plan. Anna and Chang are going to stay behind at our stop in the city of Kaybeck, and work on some of the communication lines to get more coal. The rest of us will go on ahead to the airship ports. Stone and Terry will work on setting up the cargo transfer, and we'll use whatever coal is left on the train to power the ships. We will wait for Anna and Chang. Lynn and I will work with the townsfolk to get more gossip, and Massood will continue with Mack's language lessons. I think if we can get Mack to buy a few rounds at the local pub — "

Lynn sighed and shook her head. "Bad idea, Lance. She's only 12..."

"But she's already been drinking brandy on a regular basis."

"Only to get sleep," Mack said.

"How come she gets sleep and we don't?" Anna snapped. "I'd like my own jug of that brandy as long as we're all self-medicating! And nobody will think highly of a drunken girl — "

Lance slapped the table. "You need to refer to Mack as man, Anna, we've been over this. If we make mistakes in private, they will slip out in public. Mack is a young northern Palachian man, and there's no — "

"No, Mack is Heather, a young southern Palachian girl! You assume she's a man, and then act all surprised when she's having nightmares like a little girl — "

"Anna, take the grit of your personal problems outside the machinery that runs the League!" Lance shouted. "Mack is not the love interest of your former fiancée, and that's the end of it!"

"Lance, *please!*" Lynn yelled in disgust. "We're not going to squabble like petty classmates in grammar school. We have been cramped together for months, it's true, but we can't turn on one another. Lance, ease the boiler pressure in your words. Anna, stop grinding Mack's gears. Just like all of us, Mack is a hard worker under the Queen's employ with a past written by skilled artisans who assure the public we're all just like them. Mack is a full League member. Heather is a southern Palachian. We left her behind, why can't you?"

Anna said nothing, but narrowed her eyes at Lynn in response.

"How will I know what the fiction writers wrote for me," Mack asked. "If I am to be among my... my people... I have to have a story that — "

"Mack is correct, we cannot leave her to her own devices. Mack will be traveling with either from Massood, Lance, and myself, and never be left alone."

"They will be suspicious," Chang said, "that Mack is not a bawdy and loose-lipped fellow, but always guarded by the League."

"This is because Mack is wanted by the cult that tried to sabotage our float," Lance said. "We think it was a Rokasian traitor, according to the preliminary draft of the fiction that was relayed to me at our last stop."

"Which they will think is me," Chang said bitterly.

"They always think it's you, and in the end, it's never you. I think all those years of plots ending with, 'it's not Chang after all' will take the edge off. Besides, you were on that float. You would have been killed as well. I think a Rokasian might have realized your alliance to us and tried to kill — "

"We are off topic," Stone said. "I like Lance's plan, which was my plan, and I vote we leave Anna and Chang to do what they do best. I will also request they find out as much about possible movements around Rokasian ports and the whereabouts of some of our targets. There is something very odd about this. I suspect Rokasia is holding back a trigger. They are waiting for something, some event. I want to find out what that event is. Anna? Try looking for any sort of... cult activity that might be out of place."

Anna snorted. "Cult activity? Please. I don't see Rokasia having any sort of masterful plan. No offense to Chang, but I don't think Rokasia has the history or past to support any sort of grand master strategy. I think it's the typical case of multiple groups within Rokasia fighting with one another and while an invasion may be attempted, I doubt most of the country is even aware of it. And cult work would be like investigating an individual fly off a rotting corpse to find the murderer."

Chang put his hand gently on Anna's shoulder. "Stone has hunches that always expose hidden gears. I agree; I think we should look to cult activity."

Anna shrugged. "I guess I get paid either way."

Lance smiled, "Now that's the spirit! When you two return, we'll ship off right away. I will inform the train staff of their extended stay at the airship ports, and make sure they are generously compensated. Meanwhile, I want Mack's head to be deep in northern Palachian custom and culture. Nobody speak any other language to her than Northie, got it?"

"Got it," said everyone in northern tongue. They all turned and smiled at Mack.

"Got it," she replied back in northern tongue, and gave a thumb up.

But Anna looked troubled. She avoided eye contact with Mack and as she packed for her trip back south and Mack tried to make the best of it. At the advice of Lynn, Mack visited Anna to say goodbye to maybe soothe relations.

"Anna?" she asked, knocking on her doorway.

"What?" Ann asked angrily. She was brushing her hair to prepare to put on a large hat.

Mack expected this response, but since Anna was leaving, it helped her not care as much. "I just wanted to say goodbye. I am sorry we got off on the wrong foot — "

"Save it, girl. I don't think you could say anything useful to make me like you," she said. "I bet Lynn sent you to kiss and make up. Didn't she? Tell me the truth."

Mack avoided the question. "Look, before you go... I have a question. Do you think that Korisan symbol at Financial One has anything to do with their silence in the exchange markets?"

"What?" Anna asked, pausing in her hair brushing.

"I can't read Korisan and all, but I noticed when I was at Financial One there was a lot of graffiti that looked like the same symbol, and I was — "

Anna stared at Mack through the reflection in the mirror and shook her head. "The fact that you read Korisan is just the worst part of this."

"What?" Mack bristled. "No, I just noticed that — "

"Relax. And keep your damn mouth shut. I saw those chalk markings on the lab floor. I know what you were doing, Heather January."

Mack tensed. Did she know? "Uhm..."

"Those night terrors are just the first part of the madness that will consume you," Anna said. "I've seen it happen to men with far greater minds than you will ever know. If any one of those other League members finds out about your ability to read Korisan, they will slit your throat where you stand. Even motherly Lynn."

"I can't — I mean, what..." Mack sighed in frustration.

Anna smiled with a dark leer. "Before you consider me an enemy, consider I have you by the throat with what I know. Your time on this planet is limited, Heather January — "

"Stop *calling* me that!"

"It is your real name, is it not?"

"It was, but no longer — "

"Shut your childish tongue, Heather. You have no idea what you're doing. You don't see the levels of complexity of the adult world. You're just a pawn for everyone, and the fact you're only twelve makes it so much easier for everyone to pull the wool over your eyes. You may be Mack to a bunch of dumb laborers, but you'll always be Heather January to me. You have done a fine mess, and you will pay the price. My favor to you is brutal honesty. Trust no one. Not even me. Mention nothing about the markings, don't even say the word Korisan or admit you even know what it is to anyone. When I get back, I might have a way to delay your inevitable grinding death. At least stop those night terrors. But I don't do you any favors for your own well being, I will do them for mine. Got that?"

Mack was too stunned to say anything.

"Good! Now go play with your dollies and try to sleep with your face down into your pillows so the rest of the League can get some damn shut-eye! Pray that you suffocate; it will be far more merciful than what's to come."

Later, when Anna and Chang said their formal goodbyes, Mack only went because she didn't want to disappoint Lynn. But Anna made sure to repeatedly stare at Mack in the eyes until the train pulled away into the dark and rainy night.

Fourteen
The Airship Port

"It's been far too long," Terry said. His brow was deep in concern as he tightened the roller chain on the main sprocket gear of one of the propeller assemblies. "I don't know where they are, and we haven't heard from them in weeks."

Mack tapped the tension of the chain, and slowly worked up to the propeller to make sure there were no kinks. "I don't know how many times you want to go over these air propellers, but I don't think they will run any more smoothly than they already do."

"I have three airships to manage, and I can only be on one of them at a time. So I want to make sure the other two work flawlessly. Now let's fire up this array again, and see if we can get a smoother thrust."

"I still think the last two runs were no different, but okay..." Mack said as she hooked up the test pipe to the multi-tube feeder. She twisted it in place with a large locking nut and released the boiler pressure. Nine propellers roared to life, blasting Terry's hair back in a huge stream and filling the hangar with a deep roar. Mack watched Terry slowly move his open palms around, testing the strength of the whole array. She had seen this test too many times today to count, and she slipped into a daydream.

"Dear sister," she'd written in her recent letter. "By the time you read this, I will probably be in Yurpa." This was an optimistic hope, as they had been at the northern Palachian airship ports for over a month. They were only supposed to be there for two weeks at most, but Anna and Chang had still not returned. Every day, there were countless meetings going over plans of what to do when they did return, but it became plainly obvious that nothing more could be said after the second week.

"I have been subject to dull lessons, but even worse, I have been subject to even duller meetings. While I would never admit it to anyone else but you, I'd rather sit through a dozen lessons on making hats than another meeting on what to do the next time there's a meeting discussing what we did in the last meeting. The surface has not been as scary as I had been led to believe. I have seen all kinds of people , animals, and cultures. Oh, how I wish you were here to see some of the wonders around me. However, the dry and bitter cold can become tiresome."

Boredom had been their worst enemy. Due to the bitter cold, not much outdoor activity could be planned, and the only places to collect were the local hotels and pubs meant more for travelers who were only staying a few days at most. The local townsfolk had mostly moved back to where their families lived because the lack of coal had kept people away. People couldn't get to town, because the trains had all but stopped. Airships didn't have enough fuel for the long flight, and much of the coal left had been used for heating what few buildings remained open.

Mack had never faced cold before, but the worst part was the dryness of the cold northern air. The League had explained that all of Mack's life she had lived near or around steam, so her skin was used to constant humidity and heat a little above her own body temperature. The airship port was bone dry and seemed to suck the moisture out of Mack's body. Her skin became chapped and red, and her lips and nose always seemed to be bleeding or scabbed, no matter how much ointment she used. The nights were miserable as she huddled under blankets and furs, always choosing between heat and humidity with her radiator. If she wanted humidity, she had to release the steam valve, which reduced the heat. Even the teapots the hotel staff had placed on top to the radiators did little to comfort her, and a thick layer of frost had built up on all her windows. At least under all those blankets, her night terrors were muffled. She had also been placed on the top floor where there were no other guests at the request of the League. Massood visited her as she went to bed and woke up, so at least she had company.

Sleep was very difficult for other reasons than nightmares. Apart from the cold, the surface had an entirely different time system that was roughly 25 hours a day instead of 32. This changed constantly the further east they went because the stations measured all their times from the zenith of the sun in the sky, and given that they lived on a globe, this was different in each longitude. Living by southern Palachian city time was hopeless. Mack didn't know when to eat, when to sleep, and as they traveled further and further up north, the winter had only a few hours of daylight. There was no dark "maintenance" time to judge by. People were up, down, asleep, drunk, eating, or running around whenever they pleased, and it was affecting the entire League. But it wasn't all bad.

"There are many times when I think back to the lessons we were taught in school, and how pathetic and understated some of them were. The Sky Ring is very low on the horizon here, and is partially obscured by the huge mountains, but the diminished glow shows more stars than I ever thought possible. There are simply no words to adequately describe the lights I have seen. Like millions of small gas lights, they flicker in the never-ending darkness. Sometimes, there will be huge bands of color that will ripple behind the clouds making me feel like a very small cog in a vast natural machine."

From time to time, between lessons, Mack would wander outside, bundled up to the point of feeling like a balloon herself. She would watch the strange northern lights, staring at the stars in the clear night air. In the far distance south, she'd see the tip of the Sky Ring poke above the mountains on horizon. This strange land was dark most of the time, with the sun only peeking above the horizon for a few hours before setting down, and most of that was behind the mountains, too. Much of the night sky was magical, and she was proud that she did not feel agoraphobic. Even though the League members were supposedly over it, only Massood, Terry, and Stone seemed to really be unaffected. Lynn and Lance stayed inside almost exclusively, trying to find grains of gossip in the cracks of the floors that made a drying social setting.

"It is my hope that by the time you get this, the meetings will be over, everyone will be ready, and I will have been high up in the air. They expect the journey shall be less than a week, weather permitting, which is a small fraction of the time it would have taken by boat."

Nobody wanted to state the dense fog of the question permeating the room: when do we just say we leave without Chang and Anna? It was a difficult question that seemed to be on the tip of everyone's tongue, as the League had always operated on staying together during these larger journeys. Going to Yurpa without them would have left them blind in one eye, as Chang and Anna were the roving eyes and encyclopedias of the team. Where Lance and Lynn were the King and Queens of gossip, Chang and Anna were the royalty of worldly and obscure knowledge. There was talk about doubling back to see if they had been unable to travel the two day journey north. Perhaps the coal supply had halted altogether, which would explain why no mail had come from them as well. The last message received had been a week into their stay, and it came by empty train only sent north to fetch remaining travelers stuck in the small airship port town.

"Normally I am not a fan of oscillating cylinder engines," Terry shouted, snapping Mack out of her daydream. "But sometimes simplicity is easier to fix. That's why they are used on airships and boats. Cut off the pressure, I think we're done for the day..."

Mack pulled the valve back, and the propellers died quickly to a stall.

"See? Easier to shut down. Drops pressure like a stone, and you need that when dealing with precise steerage. Not like a triple expansion compound monstrosity. But they are temperamental. I would have had some kind of differential gear assembly. Get more power behind the inertia of a flywheel, you know. I'd get those propellers to blow the feathers off a goose from yards away. Although, they are always obsessing over weight, so I guess a huge iron flywheel isn't going to make the cargo list."

"I bet they could have a larger hull if they have more nacelles," Mack said. "Given the lift ratio, I bet a ship twice this size could be multi-chambered into six different sections, instead of two. That would increase the pitch control to a finer point, add more lift, and carry more cargo."

Terry chuckled. "There are a lot of designers who think like you do, but no one has ever invested in this. It's a shame; I think that's a good idea. Most are concerned with making one big balloon, not having a nacelle made of six or more independent chambers."

Mack and Terry had become quite close. Terry always valued her input, and Mack always liked his company. Sometimes Terry would talk endlessly about his real life and how it differed from his fictional one, and Mack would just sit and listen. And while Terry sometimes became very obsessive about engine and mechanical maintenance, Mack had never had a friend who shared common interests. Mack had all but forgotten how she admired the fictional "Chip," then considered him a sham, and then felt somewhat validated in her assumption when she realized he was an adult and not the child plagued with seemingly infinite youth. In fact, it was very hard to see any of the fictional "Chip" in him.

"I think Mack has a crush on you," Lynn said one day during a meeting. Mack was horrified at this accusation, but all she could do was blush and stammer in protest. She denied this, of course, but late at night, she started to understand what her sister must have felt with her crush on Lance Worthingheart. Terry laughed it off, and made some bawdy statements about Lance and Lynn behind closed doors, which derailed the entire meeting into nostalgia about previous missions.

Mack was learning a lot about the League, as well. At first, she had to get over what little she knew about their fictional identities. Since she never read their popular fiction, this was easier for her than most, but popular discussion had bled into Mack throughout the years. Then she had get over their daily surface banter into some of the more late evening talk when deeper personal characteristics and flaws started to appear. There seemed to be a lot of drinking in the League, which led to hushed giggles and private jokes. Mack often felt left out, even though no one seemed to intentionally exclude her. But with no one else to hang around except some uncomfortably lascivious laborers, she would sit and endure.

In time, Mack learned about the history of Anna and Professor Gaylord. After Anna had been his assistant for many years, they were engaged to be married. But the engagement always seemed to be delayed by the Professor's work and this eventually led to it being cut off rather abruptly. Anna started with the League immediately afterward, which made the Professor react as if he had been betrayed. Mack was horrified at this, because many among the League thought Anna was jealous of Heather because they believed Heather was her romantic replacement. Mack didn't think Heather would have ever considered such a romantic arrangement, but the League wasn't so sure of the Professor's hidden intentions, especially because the entire "apprentice who will replace me" was the exact same line he gave to Anna. He had also gone to Anna's parents and promised her family financial gain. This angered Mack, even though she was sure Heather would have never believed it.

While Mack was aware of the concepts behind courting, they had always slipped by unnoticed in her passion for mechanics. But as her own heart started to soften to the idea of spending evenings alone with someone of the opposite sex, she had trouble accepting some of the more lewd statements that flowed freely. To make matters worse, when she spent time with her "northern Palachian brethren," she learned just why she had been raised to call that particular area, "privates." Women rarely discussed their unmentionables, and the men made up for it by describing their own as well as the women's. The northern Palachian men even more so. Mack had to keep up appearances by making these comments herself, because she was supposed to be one of the boys, but the more time she spent with them, the less comfortable they felt with one another. Her chapped skin seemed even less likely an ailment for a Northern Palachian, so as her guise wore thin late into the night, and she often made excuses to leave, citing black lung or some other illness.

Cramped up together as they were in the only hotel remaining open, Mack found herself learning a lot more than just the northern Palachian language and cultural lessons. She spent a lot of time listening to people when they forgot she was there, and eventually she learned the physical aspects of courtship, which seemed even more strange than Morgana's comments on what fashion was. Once in a while, as Mack lay in bed, she'd think of something from home that suddenly made a lot more sense, and how Morgana probably would have laughed at Mack's confusion. Mack's life grew further and further apart from the life Heather knew, and this caused a new complication: the night terrors were slowly being replaced with Heather coming to life. She was no longer just a reflection in the mirror while she was alone or some part of her inner dialog. She was now somewhere outside Mack, taunting, mocking, and hating her in the daylight. Mack started having fights with her like she used to have with Morgana, and Massood assumed this meant her "twin soul" was calling out to her.

"You love Terry," Heather said to her one day from the mirror.

"That's not true — "

"Admit it. You love him. You want to court him. He's nearly 30 years older than you, and you want to dress in lace and feathers and woo him. That's disgusting."

Mack shook her head. Usually this was the part of the dream she could wake up in, but she was already awake. She was in her hotel washroom, and Heather was staring back at her in Morgana's frilly blue dress, lightly stained with gear prints.

"I don't want to 'woo' him or anyone else!" Mack said.

"You disgust me!" Heather said, and was gone.

Mack was a little shaken after that. She didn't know. How did she feel about Terry? He was an older man, after all. But he wasn't attached, either. Lynn certainly seemed affectionate to him, though, but then Lynn had a motherly instinct over everybody.

"Does Terry have a lady friend?" Mack found herself asking one day.

"No, I don't think so," Lynn said. "But you'd better get the idea of trying to find him one out of your head."

"I didn't say I was trying to find him one, I was just curious because he's the only one that doesn't seem to be attracted to bawdy humor and jokes."

Lynn chuckled. "Stone doesn't. Neither does Massood, Chang, or Anna for that matter. In fact, I think only Lance and I find great pleasure in the company of guttural humor. Nice try, Mack. I really don't want to see you get hurt, and a schoolgirl crush on Terry is not going to end well."

"You ask one simple question, and everyone thinks I am looking for a companion to a box social," Mack grumbled.

"Your blushing is giving you away," Lynn laughed. "Trust me; he is not your type."

"And what is that supposed to mean?" Mack demanded.

Lynn simply laughed like Mack had said something adorable and stupid. Mack was furious at her for days afterward and avoided all conversation with her.

"I apologize for anything insensitive I said about you and boys," Mack wrote in her letter to Morgana. "I now understand what you went through, and I was callous and unsympathetic. It was rude of me."

Mack tried not to think of Terry like a male companion of romantic interest, but she found that her dreams were betraying her once more. Her night terrors were subsiding, and visions of Terry saving her repeatedly from her various nightmares left her waking up with a rapidly beating heart and other feelings she was unaccustomed to.

"Why can't I court him?" Mack asked Heather one day.

Heather's angry young face twisted up in rage in the mirror. "If you try and woo Terry, I will hate you."

"You hate me already. I am not the small silly girl who left southern Palachia anymore. I have had adventures and worldly experience — "

"You have *nothing*. You are a *fraud!*" Heather screamed. More and more, her face was taking on a yellowish green cast, like bread in the first stages of decay. "You don't even *exist!*"

"Yet I am not the one in the mirror," Mack said. "*You* are a figment of my imagination. A combination of sleep deprivation, boredom, and regrettable alcohol consumption. Massood said so. Anna says you are nothing more than a... result of reading forbidden tongues."

"Massood is a stupid old man! Anna is a *whore!* You are treading on dangerous catwalks, Mack Van Horn!"

"And Heather January is dead, Heather January."

"We. Will. See...!" Heather spat, and vanished.

"Goodness, no wonder I didn't have any friends back then," Mack chuckled nervously.

The mirror fell off the wall and shattered behind the dresser.

She had spoken more and more with Massood about seeing Heather in the mirror. Massood was troubled by this, but gave Mack the confidence she needed to deal with it. It was just a phase. A minor mental quirk of some sort that would sort itself out. Part of puberty. Menstrual cramps. Drinking. Boredom. Homesickness. None of these things seemed to be connected in the slightest way, and it certainly didn't make Heather go away.

Once in a while, Mack would catch Heather glaring at her in a reflection in the hotel pub, or staring back at her from the flames of a boiler. Even that subtle color blue of Morgana's formal dress seemed to appear in the reflections of the snow around her, slowly circling her, and closing in.

"I miss you," Mack said. "Cordially, your Yurpan-bound sister." She sent the letter on the last transport out two weeks after they arrived. It was now another three weeks later when the motley assembly of the League met for another meeting.

"It has been five weeks since we left Chang and Anna, and we have had no word," Lance said. Mack thought he had really let his appearance relax. No longer interested in fine clothing, he usually wore the same stained work shirt and britches, and his beard was getting longer and more unkempt. He kept his hat and working goggles on like he had forgotten they were even there. "We have decided to make a decision."

"Decided to make a decision," Lynn snorted. "That's parliamentary talk right there." She was reading the newspaper; the first issues that had come in via cargo coach in a week. The trains had all stopped coming in, and all deliveries now were being made by horse-drawn coach in small caravans. Many of them left with more passengers as the town thinned down to a skeleton few. "Are we going to talk about the Professor's disappearance, or has anyone read the paper yet?"

Mack sat upright. "The Professor has disappeared?"

Stone knocked on the table. "We will get to that. First things first. This morning I finally heard from one of our contacts. Mail has backed up, which is why we haven't been getting much word. The news is... puzzling." Stone said "puzzling" with an ominous tone.

"What is it, Stone?" Lynn asked, putting down her paper.

"Chang and Anna are no longer in northern Palachia," Lance said. His voice was unsteady.

"Wait, what does that mean?" Lynn asked. "Are they well?"

"They took the first train back to southern Palachia right after we left," Stone said. "They didn't even unpack their bags, according to the hotel porter."

"Why did they do that?" Mack asked.

Lynn was silent. "Perhaps they knew something that — "

"They would have sent notice if they were going somewhere away from where we assigned them. The Queen's aides in foreign affairs said that no recall was done by them, but they stressed that they were alarmed we were not in Yurpa by now, as things were getting dire."

"Getting dire?" Lynn looked through the paper. "I don't see anything — "

"No, you don't. And neither do we. In fact, it seems Chang and Anna have had other plans for this trip all along. Lance here apparently searched their travel belongings and found them entirely stuffed with packing straw."

"What?" Lynn asked. "Lance, why didn't you say something? What did they say when you saw this?"

Lance stammered. "I didn't think... well, it was their business. Yes, it seemed odd, but..."

Lynn's face twisted up. "Lance, you are an *idiot*!"

Lance tried to regain some kind of composure as a rise of fear filled the room. He tried to stammer something, but only a few mumbles about being in people's private business managed to make it past his unsteady lips.

Stone patted Lance on the back, perhaps for comfort, or perhaps to keep him from saying something even more stupid. "Think about it, Chang and Anna were our eyes for most of this mission. We sent them to Financial One; they said the markets were unaffected. We had the communique with our Sky Ring connections, and there were no troop movements."

"I doubt Chang and Anna would betray us," Lynn said.

"Why would you doubt that?" Massood asked.

"Because... well... what would they have to gain?"

Massood closed his eyes. "There is a saying among my people; a snake in the grass that does not move is still a snake."

"I think we're suffering a little madness being cooped up; we're starting to distrust one another..." Lynn said, nervously pouring a new cup of tea even though she had just poured it a few minutes before. Tea spilled over into the saucer before she stopped herself. "It's easier to blame the people who are gone, but really, do we have any reason to believe that both Lynn and Chang would betray us and what their possible motive would be?"

Stone nodded. "This is what I have been trying to figure out. The only way they stood to gain anything is if they believed betraying us would be in their better interests than staying with the League. If they thought the Rokasians were going to be victorious, perhaps? Now, let's take the second item you mentioned, the Professor's disappearance. That newspaper is dated three weeks ago, talking about the Professor being missing for a week. The entire lab ransacked and set ablaze."

Mack's stomach dropped. Everyone's eyes darted to her and then darted away.

Lance sighed. "This happened a week after we left, and it would have taken about a week for Chang and Anna to return. The timing is too close a coincidence."

Mack heard a scream. She jumped. "What was that?"

"What was what?" Lynn asked.

"That... scream."

"I didn't hear a scream," Lance said with a concerned tone. "Anyone else?"

Stone went outside the private room, and perked his ears. "Maybe it was from the kitchen."

"Someone must have tripped or cut themselves, I didn't hear anything," Lance said.

"Terry, go check it out. I didn't hear it, but Mack's ears are more sensitive than mine, I suspect."

Mack heard it again. "It sounds like a wail," she said. Mack got up and walked outside the door, but she couldn't hear or see anything other than Terry cautiously walking down the hall towards the hotel kitchen.

"Let's all get back inside. We have a plan, and time is getting short," Stone said. "Terry will come back if he hears anything."

Mack felt her insides burning. The Professor was missing? The lab burned. She heard the wailing again, but now it seemed to be coming from inside the private room. "You don't hear that?" Mack shouted over the wailing.

"No. No we don't," Lynn said, a little panicked. "What does the wailing sound like? Do they have words or is it just a long noise?"

Mack looked at one of the mirrors that was above the credenza. The mirror was old, and the silver backing was cracked with brown threads. But in the reflection, she saw Heather, her face puffy and swollen with despair.

"You let him die!!" Heather screamed. **"You killed him!!"**

"No. No!!" Mack screamed.

"I will kill you, Mack Van Horn!!" Heather screamed, and the entire room erupted in flames. **"I will burn you to the ground**

like the Professor's lab! All of you traitors will perish and only I will remain!!"

"Mack, **Mack**!" Lynn shouted. "What *happened*?"

Mack found herself on the floor. She was shaking, and the remaining members of the League were around her, looking down at her like from inside a surgeon's amphitheater. There were no flames, and the room was silent. "I... I don't know."

"What were you screaming?" Lance asked.

"What?" Mack was disoriented, and realized she must have fainted.

"You just started... screaming 'no no no' and then went mad, flipped over a chair, and then passed out." Lynn said.

"Yes. I mean, if you didn't like the scones, try some of the sweetbreads," Lance joked. "I admit, the hotel's concept of what should remain preserved is a little ancient, but — "

"Lance, hush!" Lynn said. "I think I know what this is. I don't think we've been very sensitive about the Professor's disappearance in her presence. I think... Mack had a mourner's episode of some kind."

"I guess you were the source of the screams," Terry said with a warm smile. "That's okay; it gave me an excuse to steal more bacon and marmalade from the kitchen. I'll share it with you."

Mack sat up. Her ribs ached, probably from flipping over the chair.

"Well," Lance said. "No offense to Mack, but this is the most exciting meeting I have been to in weeks with all of you. I think we should have more screaming from now on. I feel a lot more invigorated."

Mack cracked a smile.

"Really, Lance?" Lynn said, helping Mack up.

"I will try to provide more entertainment," Mack said, trying to brush off the incident and cover her embarrassment, "if that's what's required. Anna can go hang herself if she wants. We are still together, after all."

Stone nodded as everyone took their seats. "Mack speaks for me as well, although if we are wrong about Anna, I suspect we'll never hear the end of it from her. Let us continue. Chang and Anna are out of the picture, and we only have enough coal left for one journey on one airship to Yurpa. We will probably have to make that now."

"How will we ship our cargo?" Lynn wondered. "We needed three ships just to get all those ingots and such. We can't just take some of it and leave the rest here. I mean, people are starting to get suspicious why we are guarding crates full of lead bearings as it is. Who guards lead bearings?"

"Indeed, and who ships them to Yurpa by airship?" Mack asked.

"If time was of the essence, that advantage was certainly stripped from us when we waited for Chang and Anna," Lance said. "It is vital that we get this exchange to Yurpa. Already, we are courting disaster. I am surprised the Yurpan consulate hasn't sent us an angry decree of some sort."

"Wait, who was in charge of telling Yurpa we were coming?" Mack realized. "Wasn't that Anna?"

The table went silent.

"You think she told them or not?" Lynn finally wondered aloud.

"She did," Terry said. "I saw her do it, as a matter of fact. The same time she had to calculate the cargo for the ingots. I remember because we had to calculate the weight needed for the airships, and she wanted to know what kind of thrust they used and whether the cargo should be balanced or not."

Mack thought for a moment. "Wait, wouldn't they be suspicious if the cargo balance was off? I mean, lead bearings are heavy. Titanium is not. Paperwork is certainly very light. Those crates must have been about a third of the weight they should have been. We need to alert the airship captains."

"I would imagine they would be weighed before they were loaded," Terry said. "That way, we don't have to worry about explaining their lightness to the airship captains because we'll be on our final leg of the journey."

"Wait, how did we explain the lightness to all the train cargo operators? I recall the northern Palachian workers were all groaning about the weight and why lead bearings were being sent up north where there's not much machinery. I told them what we discussed before the trip, it was ballast. But it's funny none of them mentioned how light they were."

The table went silent as everyone exchanged glances.

"Oh... no..." Lynn said nervously. "You don't think... I mean... did any of you also just get a feeling..."

The entire table emptied, and they ran down the hall to the locked cargo rooms. Terry fumbled with the keys. "Oh dear God, I hope you're wrong."

"Me too," everyone echoed.

They opened the private room where their crates were. "Lead Bearings," each one of them had stamped. "Southern Palachia."

Stone grabbed a crowbar and broke the royal seal. He ripped off the lid and started pulling all the small cloth sleeves. "Here, you all go through the crates. Try and find *anything* that is not a small sack of lead bearings. Open some bags if you have to!"

In only took half an hour before the entire League was standing among broken crate lids, packing straw, torn sacks, and lead bearings.

"Lead bearings. Just like they said," Lance finally admitted. "Not a stitch from the Queen's coffers."

"These are also fake seals," Stone said. "I checked the seals myself with Anna before they were put on the tram to the train station. I checked the seals again once during our journey, but Anna was the primary person responsible. At some point, these seals got switched."

"The crates got switched," Lance realized. "Chang and Anna must have switched them and taken them back to southern Palachia."

"Why? Why?" Lynn shouted. "How could they? How do they think they will get away with this??"

"What do we tell the Yurpan royalty?" Lance asked.

"We tell them in person," Stone said. "Come on. We can't stand around here; we have lost too much time as it is. Let's get the next air ship, load her with coal, and tell them to plan for just us and our luggage. The String must be completed, even if we have to lend our backs and skills into this. We have a mission, and we can't let a pair of traitors succeed. They already have a five week lead on us. We must go now!"

𝔉ifteen
The Airship Flight

The first day into their trip to Yurpa, Mack realized with a chest-swelling thrill that she'd lived her whole life underground, and now she was as high as she could be without being in the Sky Ring itself. Sunlight poked above the horizon for less than an hour now, but it was enough to light the clouds below her like a giant orange and pink featherbed. The air above them was a royal purple, and a few stars were already visible.

"Pretty amazing, isn't it?" Terry sighed next to her. Both were leaning on the railing, looking towards the calm horizon. "I have been on a lot of airships in my life, and I never tire of views like this. You can even see some of the pink on the Sky Ring to the south."

Mack looked behind her and agreed. The journey had a hectic start, but now they were making good time as they sailed above the storms. The ship had to use the fans to move them past the eastern mountain range, but when they had gotten high up enough, a good wind started pushing them east, and the roar of the fans was replaced with the rush of the lofty winds. The main sails were unfurled around the airship and all were taut with the directional pennants billowing. The winds on the deck were brutal and cold, but Mack and Terry had found a cozy spot near the bow where some spare sails and tarp made an effective windbreak. Above them floated the main balloon, looking like a giant pale cigar. They were standing near the bow of the huge wooden gondola, where everyone lived and worked. Mack had made sure she had gotten an entire tour around the ship, asking questions and getting excited answers from the crew and captains. Most were northern Palachian, mixed with a few Yurpans, and apart from the League, there were only two more actual passengers; some southern Yurpan merchants who were very interested to hear about the recent changes in Palachian politics, so they kept Lance and Lynn occupied. The crew even let Mack and Terry work on some of the equipment, glad to get a break, and happy to know someone appreciated their work.

Despite her best efforts, Mack had developed strong feelings for Terry. She was sure he felt the same way, but that he was maybe apprehensive about their age difference. Mack had never met a man who didn't care that she was a girl interested in mechanics and machinery, and Terry was happy he finally had someone to teach, as he'd never married or had children of his own. "I would have liked to," he confessed one day. "But with this life, who can take care of children?"

Mack also worked hard to avoid the creeping fear that Heather was giving her. Heather didn't say much anymore; she would just show up in daydreams with gritted teeth and an angered brow. Mack didn't know what this meant, as it seemed the "Heather" part of her was growing more distant and foreign. There had always been a feeling of "Heather is a part of me I must grow out of," but now it seemed like Heather had taken a whole new life of her own. She had grown angry and dark. Her skin was almost the color of trolley, and the dress she wore got filthier and filthier. It was almost as if she was rotting but not dying.

"Your dreams seem to be better," Terry said. "That's good. Massood says you don't wake up screaming anymore. Maybe some fresh air and a few decent nights' sleep was all you needed."

Mack found that if she worked herself to the point of exhaustion, and drank some alcohol before bed, she would sleep so deeply, the nightmares couldn't rouse her. When she did have dreams, they were more focused on seeing Heather standing before hundreds of people, speaking in tongues, and all the people echoing what she said in blind faith. She didn't wake up screaming as much as she woke up frozen in terror, repulsed by the images. One of the new fears was a strange aversion to fire, which made her avoid the ship's boiler during any tours or work she and Terry did. This would become a hindrance to any steam work she did that didn't involve trolley. Sometimes, Mack would wake up and feel like something was on fire, but it was always the barest tail edge of a dream quickly which dissipated like the wispy clouds that surrounded their airship. All of this added to an uneasy fear of the future that was looming. "How long can I continue like this?" she would wonder. She wondered about what Anna had said, about the madness that Korisan readers eventually succumb to, as this echoed what the Professor had said: knowledge of Korisan drove some of his own, highly-educated, colleagues mad. If a rational mind could not keep away the insanity, what hope did she have? Massood's comments about the cult and why women were forbidden to know Korisan was also part of her concern. Would Anna tell?

"Yeah, I think I have a better handle on the nightmares. But I feel I have someone to comfort me and give me a feeling of hope has more to do with what I feel than fresh air."

Terry laughed. "Who, me?"

Mack's heart raced, and she dared to take Terry's hands in her own. "Yes... maybe a little." She looked into Terry's face and wondered what it would be like to kiss those lips like she had seen others do. She almost smiled at the thought of Heather making a retching face.

But Terry gently pulled his hands away. "Mack, listen..."

"Look, I know what you're going to say. The others have told me to not take things in this way, and I am being very careful, but I care an awful lot about you. We have spent the last week together, and hasn't it been wonderful?" Mack blushed, as she realized all her words sounded impossibly stupid. Now she understood why poetry existed; it gave you something to say when your own words would fumble.

Terry stepped back. "Mack, please don't do this. You have no idea... what you are saying..."

"You want to have a family. We can be that family — "

"Mack, look — "

Mack's words rushed to her lips before she could stop them. "Terry, why? Why don't you want this? We are so perfect for each other! Look, I know I have to conceal I am a girl and play a boy, but I can change that. I mean, I think. Keep the secret from everyone else. Just two boys sharing a cabin, and — "

"Yeah," Terry said chuckling nervously. "A secret. Funny you should mention secrets." He rubbed the back of his neck nervously. "I am going to break a rule here and give you some insight as to why Lynn makes fun of us together."

"She's just jealous — "

"Oh, don't tell her that. No no. She doesn't... want me that way. Mack... oh, this is going to be bad."

Mack sensed something she hadn't felt before. Terry's face was wrinkled in painful concern. "What, you don't like me?"

"Mack, I like you a lot. But as a friend, a fellow... man... " Terry laughed nervously. "Yeah... this is complicated."

"What is?"

Terry took a deep, nervous sigh. Mack tried to hold Terry's hands, but he backed away again, almost pressing against the canvas windbreaker. "Mack, stop. Stop stop."

"Are you afraid to feel the same way?"

"No. I am afraid of how you are going to react to what I am forced to tell you. Your heart is young, and while it is vibrant and powerful, it is also easily broken. On top of that is one of the biggest secrets I have to share with you. See, you and I are alike. Very alike."

"We both love mechanics — "

" — and we are both women!" Terry said.

Mack paused. The roar of the winds around the canvas and the flapping of the distant pennants on the airship masts were the only sounds she would remember of this moment.

"Oh... sorry to be so blunt," Terry said, breaking the tense silence. "I'm sorry, Mack. This is very hard to tell you. I wanted to tell you early on. But you know how hard it is for us, and I have been concealing it for so long, I just... can't ... I have trouble even saying the words, Mack. Everyone knew but you, and they told me not to tell you for a while because we didn't know how far we could trust you. But I trust you."

"No..." Mack said in shock. "No, this can't be true. Tell me it's a joke. It has to be a joke!"

"Oh, boy.... Mack, please — "

"But how can... you told me about all those stories as a boy. Working with divers. Learning mechanics from your father. You room with Stone all the time — "

"Stone is my husband," Terry said. "We have been married for almost 20 years. And all those stories were true, by the way. I just skipped all the parts about being a girl. I had the same problems. I did the same as you did. Our lives are very similar. Being with you reminded me of simpler times as a youth, and I enjoy working with you. But our love can never be. And you have to be... Mack, I know this hurts. I didn't want to hurt you, but either I said something now, or — "

"And everyone... knew." Mack felt she heard Heather laughing in scorn in the distance.

Terry nodded. "And they should have said something. It wasn't fair. But it's such a big deal. I mean, Lance is a homosexual, and Stone is the real leader and fucking Chang and Anna are traitors. Secrets hurt, Mack, and I am sorry. I couldn't hurt you anymore."

Mack squeezed her eyes tight, trying not to cry, but tears of betrayal squirted out despite her efforts.

"Oh, trolley's fire, Mack. I am so sorry. It's not your fault. You're young and — "

"Stop saying that. Stop saying I am young," Mack said through gritted teeth.

"Okay, you are not young. But your lack of experience has... well, just been made more up to speed. You know what we mechanics say, 'experience is what you get when you didn't get what you want.'" Terry paused. "I am not helping. I am trying to make you feel better."

"I'll be fine," Mack said. "It was silly anyway!"

"No, not silly. The heart wants what it wants. You just didn't have the big picture. I don't blame you at all, and you shouldn't either."

Mack had to get away. Terry's kindness was somehow making it worse, and her heart ached like it was structurally failing at the foundation. "I... I need to get some sleep." She lied.

Terry nodded. "I understand. But keep in mind we land in about 5 hours. We are stopping at Reiland off the northern Yurpan coast, as our hydrogen has been running low and the storms have not let up." Terry looked at the western horizon. Large anvil-headed storm clouds were cracking with lectromag in the distance. "This could get bumpy. Make sure your cargo is tied down, and let Massood know. We're going to wait out the storm on the island, and probably take a boat to the mainland."

Mack nodded, "Yes sir... ma'am... sir..."

"See? This what we have to deal with when we speak of you, sir!" Terry cracked a smile. "Just call me Terry like everyone else."

Mack nodded and faked a smile before she headed down to the lower decks, desperately trying to convince herself it was okay. When she settled down in her stateroom, Massood was not there. She busied herself making sure everything was tied down, and she lay on her bed and listened to the constant creaking of the hull.

"Told you," Heather said with sadistic glee. "You're a pervert!"

"Shut... up!" Mack growled. She did not look up, and closed her eyes to avoid seeing Heather in any reflection.

"You will never have love. Never never never and now Terry went back and told them, and they are *all* laughing at you. Mack Van Horn, a girl who wants to be a boy, fell in love with another girl. Stupid!"

"Shut up," Mack warned.

"Laughing at *styuu-pid* Mack Van Horn. Fake boy. Fake accents. Fake language. Fake heritage. *And fake love!!*"

"Stop it, *stop it!*" Mack screamed. She felt the cabin tilt slightly as they started their descent, and as she looked at her feet, she was surprised to see Heather sitting at the end of her bunk.

"Now we're going to do things my way, Mack. You burned your past, turned your back on the only man who ever cared about us, left your family, and all because you wanted adventure. Now it's my turn to take you back."

"Go away! I don't even know you anymore!"

"Why did you read about Korisan, Mack? Why did you disobey the Professor?"

"You disobeyed him!"

"No, *you* did. You disobeyed your father, too! None of this would have happened if we had been good. What happened to you? Why did you do those things? I'll tell you why, Mack. You're a *slut!*"

"I am not!"

"You wanted to see boy's parts! That's why you went into the locker room, isn't it Mack? When you took off my dress and tried on those work clothes, you felt it, didn't you? You felt the urge. You got the vapors, didn't you? Whore. Harlot! You're worse than your sister humping her pillow."

Mack gasped, "That's not true! I wanted to know how mechanics worked — "

"No! And that thrill that you got near the lectromag generator? Huh? Forgotten that, didn't you? I didn't. You're why those people died, Mack! You killed those workers! They died because you had to go off sneaking about where girls don't belong!"

Mack saw the two dead corpses on her stateroom floor. **"No! Stop it!"**

"So you took their identities, didn't you, Mack? You left me and took them! But I want you *back*! I am Heather, and I want my *life back*!"

"Stop it, please! you're just a bad dream! go away!!"

Heather slid on top of Mack's body which was too terrified to move. "No, not this time!!" Heather's body then turned into that of the truant officer, his eyes glowing a hot yellow-green with trolley. "I am going to penetrate you, Mack Van Horn! I am coming back into this body, Mack Van Horn! I am taking wot's *mine*!"

Lectromag flashed outside her stateroom porthole. For a second, she could see Morgana standing beside her, petting the back of the truant officer's head. "How come you don't write to me? I am going to marry this man, Heather. I wanted you to come to the wedding... don't you love me? Don't you miss me?"

"Go away!" Mack closed her eyes as hard as she could. But she could still see everything around her as if her eyes were forced open by spikes.

"You can't escape us," the Officer Bushington said, straddling over Mack and crushing her hips against the thin mattress. "He who watches while dreaming," he shouted, raising both his fists above his head "... shall **awaken!**"

There was a huge flash and a crashing noise. Heather reappeared with a phosphor stick in one hand and a leaking battery in the other. **"I shall burn you all!! Burn you all down and only I shall remain!!"**

Mack was suddenly on a huge stone table. Her wrists and ankles were tied down, and she was completely naked and exposed to the truant officer on top of her. An audience of assorted wealthy and southern Palachian rich people rose from hundreds of benches, all carrying trolley in their hands, casting a yellowish green glow over everything. They were all singing nonsense words in their own different rhythms which rose to a loud crescendo of a huge gibbering choir. The sky opened up, and a huge vortex appeared with the center being a huge, unblinking fish eye.

"**Go away you aren't real!!**" Mack screamed.

"**Rise old one, rise!**" the thousands of people screamed. "**She has broken the seal! The old builder awakens!**"

Mack turned her head and saw Heather with a chisel and hammer, breaking a large red star. On the wall around her was Korisan, written in steals of trolley that was oozing tentacles of gas onto the floor, burning the audience, who were now screaming in horror yet didn't try to escape, like they were trapped by their own primal fears. Some were still shouting praise.

"The root machine has been compromised," someone shouted over the sizzling of bodies in the trolley gas. It was the Professor, but his eyes had been torn out and replaced with chunks of trolley burning into his flesh. "Mankind has infected the root machine that the builders left behind."

"I will purge the world of this human parasite!" Heather shouted, as she pulled away the seal. The wall split in twain, and a dark green light started to pour into the room. "Behold, the First Builder!" she shouted.

Mack had stopped screaming, as she saw the huge clouds spinning around her like a giant flywheel. Something felt different. Her hair twitched and snapped. Her lips started to move. "Trolley is mined from the shallow seas, and gives us the power to do our deeds," she recited. "Trolley must be sealed away from air, or harm will come to those who are unaware."

"Stop her!" the Professor shouted. The truant officer swung down his fists onto Heather's chest, but the moment he made contact, huge arcs of light leapt up his arms and covered his face with a spider web of light. His eye sockets fried and teeth shot out of his jaw like popcorn.

"Trolley must be kept from the Sky Ring's domain, for the light from the clouds will kill and maim!" Mack shouted. The burnt husk of the truant officer clattered to the floor. Heather screamed as a huge set of tentacles slithered from the crack in the wall and swallowed her up.

"No, **no**! **Heather you bitch**! No matter **what I do**, Heather January is going to **fuck** it up!" the Professor shouted in betrayal, and as the acidic gas stripped at his shins, he fell to the floor on his knees, screaming in pain.

Mack found that she could pull free of her chains, and as she sat up on the stone table, she saw a hideous, bloated, giant monstrosity slowly ooze from the crack in the wall like a gelatin dessert slowly collapsing into the room. The oozing beast seemed to be neither alive nor dead, but moving like some kind of hideous machine made only from bursting organ sacks.

Mack held up her hand. Lectromag shot from her palm, and seared into the flesh of the creature, rupturing the skin where impossible waves of knotted and slimy gore poured from the unraveling wound. Where the entrails hit the floor, fire erupted, which spread quickly in the trolley gas, turning the dark green light into flickering orange and red.

"Mack! **Mack**!" she heard. Mack turned around, and saw that her stateroom was on fire. Or rather, there was an orange glow that made it seem that way.

"We're falling!" she heard Stone scream.

The stateroom lurched. Mack's stomach felt light and filled with fear.

"Mack?? *Mack??*" she heard Terry's voice scream, like it was being forced through crying. *"Pleease open the door!"*

Even though furniture was secured, it had broken loose, and was tumbling around the room. Mack tried to get up, but a huge dresser smashed into her side, knocking her against the wall. Her old head wound head rang with light and pain, and she cried out, "Terry! **Terry!**"

"Mack???" she heard for one last time before the room jerked upwards, and a strange cold, wet darkness pushed her into unconsciousness.

ixteen
Reiland

Mack awoke, barely aware of her surroundings. It was dark, but she could make out a few blurry shapes. A window, a headboard. She heard a sound. A high pitched voice said something in a sing-song tongue she could not understand. She heard footsteps, and the figure of a large Yurpan woman filled her view. The woman said something, but Mack didn't know what it meant. She looked down and saw a Yurpan child holding a large washbasin.

"Hello?" she asked. Then she realized that sounded stupid, but she was too groggy to make any sense. Had she been drinking? What had happened? She tried to ask but she didn't know if she was really speaking or only dreaming she was.

The woman said more in her language.

"Do you speak northern Palachian? Southern Palachian?" she asked. The woman paused, and then repeated her language, but none of it made sense. It had a strange, musical quality about it, and Mack somewhere remembered that Yurpan language was very melodic. "I guess not." It seemed odd that she had never been taught Yurpan, she thought to herself. She remembered a few phrases, and tried to speak them, but what she thought she was trying to say and what came from her mouth didn't seem to match.

For the next few days, Mack tried her best to piece together what had happened and how she had gotten into this situation. She remembered a fire, and something about Heather, and a man... a stone table. Terry screaming... Mack figured out that she had been severely burned. She was missing most of her hair and eyebrows. Her ribs had been broken, and she suspected she had a severe laceration on her back near her kidneys, but lacked the strength to turn her head around and get a good look. Her consciousness went in and out, and she didn't try to assess what might have happened to her too deeply because she knew she wouldn't be able to mentally cope with it. Much of her existence seemed to be sleeping.

The family that was taking care of her did what they could do accommodate one another. Mostly it was done by hand gestures, although they started to learn a few words in each other's language. Mack was feverish, and as she shook in her host's only bed, she was wracked with guilt that the entire family was sleeping on the floor with their three small children. The humble abode only had one room with one door and two long and squat horizontal windows on the eastern and western walls. Light came from tallow candles, and the only source of heat was a fire pit in the center of the room, which had to be kept lit to prevent the smoke from drifting down the metal cone above it. Food seemed to be very basic tubers and sea grass with fish being the only meat. Mack tried to eat, but it was difficult to keep any food down.

The eldest woman was the mother, and her name was Wasa. Wasa did her best to heal Mack, and she was very skilled. Almost as skilled as Massood. She even tended to Mack's old head wound and the weakened leg from the parade injury. Wasa spent many nights massaging points in Mack's limbs, trying to keep the jerking muscles from atrophying. She also drew symbols on Mack's belly, chanting in her musical Yurpan tongue for hours while the children and the father would bring her various things. Often Wasa would collapse in exhaustion, and Mack would feel waves of gratitude mixed with guilt at this woman's sacrifice. One day, the eldest child opened the front door when the sun poked above the horizon for a few hours. While the cold air numbed her skin, the light felt good on Mack's face, and afterward, she felt better and a little more able to eat. Her skin was sore and raw where the Yurpan family had placed cloth soaked in some kind of fatty residue. Eventually, the nagging questions started to creep back into Mack's consciousness.

She didn't remember how she had gotten here. She remembered speaking to Terry about her love for her, and then there was something about her stateroom and a fire. Had Terry accepted? What was the fire from? Did the hydrogen in the airship explode? Did anyone else survive? Where was she? But none of the Yurpans could comprehend her questions, and eventually, Mack just accepted silence as part of the healing.

One day, a visitor came to the small house. He was dressed a little more tailored than the bundled firs and felt than her hosts. He was wearing what looked like a large winter coat, and brought with him a modern gas lamp. The bright light filled the small dark room, and a face not unlike Massood's looked down on Mack with a smile.

"How are you feeling?" he asked with a thick accent.

"You speak southern Palachian!" Mack gasped with relief.

"A little. Please do not speak... eh, I speak slowly. You speak slowly, right."

"What happened? Where am I?"

"You are on Reiland Island, just north of Yurpa coast. Yes?"

Mack nodded, "I guess so. I don't know."

"Good, good. I know." The man paused, and when Mack didn't respond, he continued with great discomfort. "You were in airship. It crashed. Big storm."

"Yes, yes, with the League of the Brave! Where are they? Did anyone else survive?"

The man sighed. "Slowly, please. I think you said with League of the Brave, yes?"

"Yes. Did anyone survive?" Mack asked, her voice tightening at the answer she was dreading.

The man shifted uncomfortably at the foot of Mack's bed. He said something in Yurpan to the woman, and the woman said something back, and soothed Mack's bandaged head with motherly care.

"No. You are only... person. We find. Ehm... I am sorry for this... error."

It was as she feared. She went numb with shock, even though she thought this was a likely possibility. Mack nodded and wiped her face as tears traveled down her cheeks while Wasa rocked and comforted her. Mack tried to tell herself that maybe there were more survivors, and they didn't know. The man couldn't even speak her language well, so maybe he meant something else. But Mack felt in her heart that if no one had come for her, they were most likely dead.

The man spoke after a considerable amount self reflection. "You... come with me, when you not sick. We... we find out where your home go."

Mack nodded. After a long conversation with the woman of the house, the man left with his lantern. He left behind some clothing for Mack to wear when she was able to move around.

Days turned to weeks. When Mack was able to get out of bed and walk without hanging onto something, she helped with the daily chores of the house. She also took care of her own wounds when possible, and started doing the exercises that Massood had taught her. She was a little distraught that she was wearing a large Yurpan dress, but given that she was probably found with burned clothing, they would have quickly discovered she was a girl. They did what would have been correct for anyone else.

Sometimes the mother and father left Mack to care for the children. The children were not very calm or well-behaved. They would chatter at her in Yurpan, and even though she couldn't speak but a few words in their tongue, they became upset and yelled at her. There was an older boy who threw things and two young twin girls who seemed to cry if the other one cried, and that was far too often. Mack often thought of Morgana and how much things had changed since they had last parted. Mack wondered if she would ever get off Reiland, and if she did, where could she go? Would she go home? Sometimes Mack would cry in her sleep thinking more of her family than the League.

Mack noticed the days were getting slightly longer when it wasn't raining. She walked around the outside house to build up strength, using the brisk cold island air to get her blood flowing. She didn't have shoes, so she couldn't walk for long, but the snow and slush that surrounded the house soothed her pains somewhat. The house was on the side of a very steep mountain, right in front of a road where people would pass by and gawk at her strangely pale skin. Most of the people she met were very dark-skinned, so she was somewhat of an oddity. The road led down to a small fishing village she could easily see from her vantage point. Sometimes she saw giant chunks of ice float by the harbor, where men with large, bladed pikes would cut it up and prevent them from drifting into the docks and clogging the daily flow of small boats. Behind the house was a steep cliff that ended a few dozen feet up to another road. This pattern repeated itself a few times until the very top where stream poured out from some large factory behind the mountaintop.

One day, the previous visitor from the village came by and said it was time to go with him to town where they would find her a home more to her liking. Mack said goodbye to her host family, thanked and hugged Wasa for her hospitality in what little Yurpan she had picked up. The woman had blushed and seemed grateful. The man had brought her a new dress, which Mack put on, pleased to find it a great deal warmer. There were also a pair of boots, which didn't fit very well, but they were better than nothing. Wasa stuffed straw in the boots to adjust the fit, but it didn't improve matters much.

The long walk down wore Mack out, and she had to rest frequently. Eventually, they found someone who loaned them a horse. With the man leading the horse by foot, Mack rode into a small fishing village where she was introduced to a southern Palachian named

Dirk who had a bit of a diver accent like Terry did. Mack didn't realize how much she had missed Terry until she heard that familiar verbal twang.

The news was grim. Dirk had prepared what he needed to say, and Mack listened to him go over his checklist of things the village wanted Mack to know.

The first was a rather formal welcome. Introductions were made. The Yurpan man was an ambassador for the island, and his name was Loopska. He explained, through Dirk's translation, the airship Mack had been on had landed very low to avoid a large thunder storm crossing the island. The intent was that they would approach the airship port low over the ocean and be towed in by a steamboat specially designed for airship towing over water. However, before the boat could reach the airship, the storm suddenly took a strange turn and pushed a storm surge right across their path. The current pushed the steamboat off course, and before they could correct it and head back they saw the winds had pushed the airship to the side. They had attempted to hold fast by half a dozen anchors, but either the ocean was too deep where they dropped down, or the strong current dragged the anchors across the ocean floor. The airship had lurched to one side, and the boiler exploded in the rear of the ship. To prevent the hydrogen from exploding, the balloon was opened with vents on the top to quickly release the gas. But tragically, a huge arch of lecrtomag dove from the sky, and slammed into the metal frame surrounding the balloon. The hydrogen quickly ignited, and before they could fully vent the gas, the balloon exploded violently, tearing the gondola apart. The flaming remnants of the gondola fell almost a hundred feet to the surface of the ocean, followed by the huge flaming structure of the balloon hull.

"Even with the high winds and rain," Dirk said, "the fire continued for almost an hour. The wreckage broke apart, and scattered in the current quicker than the mooring boat could recover anyone. No survivors were found, until we heard about you, rescued by the fishing people. We have found the ship's registry, but there was no young girl listed. So, without sounding rude... who are you?"

Mack almost said her name, but hesitated. How would she explain Mack was a girl? Then again, did they know about her yet? "I am..." she started. "I am with the League of the Brave," she said. "We were on a mission with the Yurpan royalty to bring over some assistance in their String project."

"What is the String project?" Dirk asked.

"I am not at liberty to tell you if you don't know, which is, sadly, why I can't tell you who I am."

Dirk and Loopska discussed a few things in Yurpan. "Understood, understood. Would the consulate be able to tell us who you are?" Dirk asked.

"I will be honest; I was helping with the project, but not privy to who to meet over it." Her mind raced with a dozen possibilities when an idea came to her. "We brought a fair amount of currency from the Queen of Palachia. Has that been recovered?"

Dirk conferred with Loopska, who seemed to get excited and agitated. "No. In fact, we recovered only a few pieces of luggage, the some of the captain's logs, and several barrels of hard tack. Villagers have brought in random pieces of flotsam from time to time, but to be honest, if they are of any monetary value, they probably kept it for themselves."

Mack looked very displeased. "If any of those titanium ingots turn up in someone else's hands but the Yurpan King, we won't be pleased."

"I'm sorry," Dirk said, "but who is 'we' in this case? If you were with the League of the Brave, unless they became fireproof mermen with gills, I doubt they survived. You might be the only one left."

Mack thought quickly. They may not have known who "Mack" was yet, as the fiction had yet to be written, and gossip wouldn't have made it this far with the airship being the only one that had traveled to Yurpa in recent months. She wondered how much they really knew of the League, and without thinking, she found herself sitting upright in a haughty manner. "Then my name is Anna Demure," she said with a confident stance that amazed even her. The idea came from somewhere deep in her mind. She didn't know if it would work, but if it did, she might have more clout to get to the mainland quickly as the remaining member of the League who was to bring them the money, which she could now claim was at the bottom of the bay of Reiland. Yurpa could have not known Anna was a traitor yet, and when she got there, should could explain everything to the King.

Dirk's eye opened wide. "I have heard your name! We get some of your comics here. You're the... " Dirk looked over Mack carefully. "You seem shorter in person. Less buxom. And I thought you had darker hair..."

"Comics flatter me," Mack said. "I make sure of it." A wide grin crossed her lips.

"Right, right!" Dirk replied, blushing. "Sorry, I forget. I have been reading those comics since I was a wee lad. You must have aged significantly."

Mack's eyes narrowed. Her imitation of Anna was most unflattering, which gave her a great sense of satisfaction.

Dirk caught the glance. "Oh, sorry. I am making an ass of myself. I *mean fool!* Oh, goodness, I am not used to being a celebrity. I mean *with* a celebrity."

"See why I wouldn't tell you?" Mack said, acting annoyed. "Men always become flustered in my presence, and the women hate me with jealous eyes. I'd rather travel incognito, if you don't mind."

Loopska became agitated and started asking Dirk many questions. Mack was sure some of them had to do with his sudden change in behavior. They spoke for a while before Mack interrupted, "What are you saying?"

"I'm sorry, I though you spoke Yurpan."

Mack blushed. Yes, of course Anna spoke Yurpan. Anna spoke dozens of languages. "Um... that's my fictional personality; I do not actually speak more than a few words. I will ask that you refer to me by my traveling name, Mack Van Horn."

"Yes, of course Anna. I mean Mack! Sorry. Wait, why a northern Palachian name?" Mack started to answer, but Dirk interrupted her with his own answer, "Right, sorry. I'm stupid. To throw people off. Right." Dirk leaned over to her, and said in northern Palachian, "You speak Northie?"

Mack leaned back into him. "Fluently," she said back in northern Palachian, "and we hate being called Northies."

"Right, right! Enough! I am so sorry, Anna, I mean Mack!"

"This is going well," Mack said, adopting Anna's jaded posture and personality. "Look, for the rest of our lives, I am Mack Van Horn. You never saw Anna Demure, you never heard of Anna Demure, and as far as you know she's a dark-haired buxom lady who fucks around for knowledge."

"Right," Dirk said, but Mack was certain Dirk was quickly losing his grip on the matter. He seemed shocked at her cursing, and she felt this would give her an edge on diplomacy. A part of her heart took a sharp dip at the memory of Lynn, who taught her this skill.

Mack recovered quickly. "So, can you contact someone on the mainland who knows about the String project? And get them to fetch me and whatever things survived the accident?"

Dirk nodded, and started commanding Loopska many things. The both of them argued for a bit until Loopska left in a huff. "He's going to do all those things right now."

"So where am I going to stay?" Mack asked. "And who will tend to my wounds?"

"There's a hotel that is used to Palachian guests. We have a room for you, but I think I will make sure they put things in better order. We will send a priority mail to the mainland, and contact the Yurpan King's Counsel. Tomorrow we will have a transport ready to deliver you, if you wish."

Mack nodded. "I need to rest. Fetch me a medical specialist, and have them check me in my room."

"Do you wish better clothes, A — Mack?"

"I do. At least better boots, these are killing my feet." Mack smirked as Dirk looked at her feet and reacted with embarrassment to see straw sticking out of them.

"Right away!"

This must be how Anna got men to do what she wanted, Mack thought. It seemed too easy to be real. A flirtatious grin, the batting of the eyes, and a bit of a commanding tone. It gave Mack a comfortable sense of control while she rested her mind to try and find a way to the mainland and then... where? Home? Where would she go after that? After the String project. Could she even handle the String project on her own?

Dirk took Mack by horse to the hotel, and after some rapid exchanges, the staff had a nice room ready for her. Mack was secretly very appreciative of the room, even though the Reiland standards were very low. The room was even smaller and shabbier that her room back at the Palachian airship port. It was almost as bad as her apartment back with the Professor. The doctor they assigned was very thorough, but lacked the care the woman had shown back at the house where Mack had recovered. After he left, Mack lay on her soft bed, and stared up at the ceiling. Her belly was full of Reiland food, which was heavy and oily.

As she lay there, the entire experience on Reiland caught up with her and slammed into her feelings with a sticky fist. For the first time, she allowed herself to fully understand that the League was dead. Lynn, Lance, Massood, Stone, and worst of all, Terry. Chang and Anna were traitors, doing who knows what with money earmarked for Yurpa. Rokasian soldiers might be taking over the trolley mines, and erupting from the lower levels of the Palachian cities, attacking from within. The thought of Heather's family, and her sister Morgana, scared her. She wanted them to be okay, but didn't know how to do it from a cold north sea island thousands of miles away.

"Oh, you'll get back home alright," said a haunting voice.

Mack turned and saw Heather standing over her. She wanted to scream at her, but then didn't want to give Heather the satisfaction, so she swallowed her horror until it formed a knot in her stomach. "What are you doing here? Didn't you die back in the fire on the airship?"

Heather tore aside Mack's bandages, digging her fingernails deep into her burn wounds. Mack squealed in pain. "You like feeling that? You like that, Mack Anna Demure Van Horn? Or whatever name you fucking try to hide under?"

"Just go away," Mack whimpered. But she knew Heather wouldn't. She had all but forgotten Heather, and now was scared. There was no one in her life now to help ease the feelings Heather gave her.

"You're right, I won't go away. I am part of you, Mack. No, I *am* you. Mack is just a figment of *my* imagination!"

"What do you want?" Mack sobbed.

"I want your body, Mack. I need to stay alive."

"You're just a psychosis from Korisan — "

"Don't *give* me that Korisan language *shit*! Korisan is all we have left now, Mack. It made you. It changed me. We owe it a reply."

"A reply?" Mack asked, and she was suddenly surrounded by the strange room with the stone table, but this time, it was vacant and disheveled. Northern Palachian workers were digging in the walls surrounding the large chamber, uncovering what looked like a huge, ancient wall.

"Look familiar?" Heather asked.

"It's that dream I had — "

"No! This place is real, Mack. Oh, so real," Heather looked around and shrugged. "Maybe needs a spot of cleaning, but that will be done with all our followers. We don't clean, remember?"

Mack thought of the cleaning and childcare she had done with the host back in the mountains to be proof against that.

Heather grabbed a broken chair and hurled it against the ground, reducing it to several pieces. "Nooo!" she screamed in a high-pitched tantrum. "Your slavery to a woman's work is a curse against me!"

Mack cringed. She remembered her anger at difficult times. She tried to remember what her mother and father had done in the past to soothe her. "Heather, sweetie..."

"No, Mack. I will not be tamed..." Heather stood up and wiped her face in an agitated manner.

"Just let's... sit and see what you want."

"I want things back the way there were, Mack. Before you came along. Before my life was so fucked up!"

Mack didn't know what to say. "I ... understand things have changed. Believe me when I say I didn't want them to get this bad. I didn't know the Professor would get so angry — "

"You *knew what you did was wrong!* Why did you make me do things, Mack, why?"

Mack shrugged. "I — "

"*Spare* me your fireside chat, Mack! I don't want advice from *you!*"

"What would you have me do? You know we didn't want to go to school — "

Heather kicked at the broken chair pieces, letting them bounce on the walls. "I wanted a *choice*, Mack! I wanted a choice, someone to ask me — "

"Heather, believe me, I know. But we were not given a choice — "

"**I** was not given a choice, Mack Van Horn! You showed up and *fucked* everything up!"

Mack wanted to explain to Heather why they were here in a Reiland hotel room, but the chain of events over the last few months seemed somehow completely alien to explain to her former self.

"Your silence speaks volumes, Mack. But no matter, I had our followers burn that wretched house to the ground."

Mack's heart stopped for a second, before she remembered that Heather was only a dream. "No," Mack said. "You will not fool me. You have no real powers beyond the will to torment me."

"That is true, but I cannot say the same for my followers. Oh, they grow strong, Mack. They have followed your trail from the house to the village to the town and and they will bring your body home to me, and I will be Heather and whole once again!"

Mack sat on one of the long benches. "None of this is real. I am still in my bed at the hotel."

"Do you think?" Heather said sarcastically. "Yet how are you here?"

"I am dreaming," Mack said, closing her eyes and feeling the hotel bed against her back. When she opened them again, she was back at the hotel.

"Very good," Heather said with a slow clap. "But you won't be able to do that for long. Soon, you will lack rest and food, and I will be the more powerful one once again."

"What do you want? What is that place, and what was the creature that came through the cracks in the wall? I have never been to such a place. You may pretend to be the former Heather, but you know nothing of who I am — "

"*You are a fraud!* Look at you. Claiming to be Anna Demure now. Want to be popular? Want to fuck men to give up their knowledge? Is that it?"

"No! I mean, I don't know. I said it because I didn't think... Mack is still new and... I didn't..." Mack started to cry. "Why do you torture me? I am doing the best I can!"

Heather mocked Mack in a tinny voice, "Neh neh tortune meeee? Neh neh neh doing da best I can... bew hew hew... *pathetic!* Weak and fake, you deserve your pain!"

Mack said nothing, but took a deep breath. Suddenly, she understood. "You are not Heather."

"Shut up, Mack — "

"You never were Heather January — "

"I am, Mack — "

"I am the real Heather January, and the Mack van Horn is just a subtle name change..."

"I will *kill you Mack Van Horn!!*"

"You can't because you have no power, which is why you taunt me. It's all you have — "

Heather jumped on the bed and howled. She straddled Mack and started beating her with her fists. Mack just lay there, enduring the pain of the tantrum. Nothing could get to her now. Heather could beat her fists all she wanted, but she was nothing more than a spoiled brat.

"*I will not be ignored!!! You will pay for your lies!!!*" she screamed, but faded away. The beating of her fists faded to rapid knocking at the door.

"Miss Demure?? Miss Demure??" someone was shouting. "Are you okay in there?"

Mack sat up. The room looked like it had been torn apart. "Yes!" she shouted. "I think. What happened?"

"There's been an earthquake. They are common on the island, and this one wasn't very strong, but we heard screaming. Do we need to come in?" She recognized the voice as Dirk's.

"No, no. Let me straighten up and... I'll be fine."

"We understand that an earthquake can be scary if you haven't been through one before. It's okay."

"I know," Mack said, annoyed but a little amused at the tone of compassion.

"We have arranged transport to the mainland Miss Demure — oh, damn, I mean Miss Van Horn! Ergh, I keep forgetting! Sorry! Sorry! Your arrival was expected, as you said. They had a steamship leaving in a few hours, but the docks have been damaged by the quake..."

"Excellent, and may I have more appropriate clothing for when we depart? I am expected to be in the reception of the King — "

"Yes... uh, a team of tailors and seamstresses have been arranged by Loopska. They will make sure you are ready to receive the King's welcome."

"Excellent," Mack said. "You will be rewarded for your work," she added.

"I should hope so!" Dirk replied. There was something sinister in his voice as he opened the door and closed it behind him.

Nothing warned Mack about what was to come. "What are you doing? I said I was fine!"

"I'm sorry," Dirk said. "I can't... can't help myself. I've lost control of this situation, and... I haven't seen a non-Yurpan woman for so long..."

Mack recognized that tone of voice. "Go away..." she said. "I am warning you!"

"I'm... I'm so sorry..." Dirk said, removing his vest. "I have needs. I am so lonely. Please."

Mack backed away from her bed, stumbling over some of the fallen objects in her room. She grabbed part of a broken chair leg and held it in front of her.

"You stay away from me!!" she shouted.

Dirk stopped. "I haven't come unprepared," he said, pulling out a small flintlock handgun. "I can't fight you, Anna, I know that. I have read about how dexterous and strong you are. You could easily defeat me in a test of strength, but as I said, I have come with a backup plan." His face was nervous and glistened with sweat. He took a deep breath. "I am the only person who knows who you are and why you are here, apart from Loopska, who has entrusted me to your care until you leave. I am the only person who speaks both your language and Yurpan fluently. I am the only one who can get you a ship to leave. My needs are simple. My power over you is complete, even if I don't look it. You hurt me, you are stuck here. You will be jailed for assault if not outright hung, as no one believes the word of a woman, even a League woman carries no weight in a swift court that ends at the gallows. These people are simple and want no trouble. If anything happens to me, you die. I am not trying to be difficult. I am a very lonely man, and I am quite reasonable. I won't hurt you. I will get you the ship, I promise. Just... give me a few nights. Please. No one need know. I have dreamed of this since I was a child."

Mack gritted her teeth. "I thought you said you had a ship!" She heard Heather laugh somewhere in the distance. The hand that held the broken chair leg trembled.

Dirk slowly approached her, and gently pushed the chair leg down away from him. Softly, he kissed Mack's eyelid as it closed. "I will get you a ship... just please..." he whispered to her.

303

"I hate you..." Mack hissed through gritted teeth. She dared not open her eyes as Dirk's mustache smelled of sour milk, alcohol, and sweat.

"This isn't about love, dearie — "

"Don't **call** me that!" Mack shouted.

Dirk whispered softly into Mack's ear, lightly flicking his tongue across the rim of her ear while she shuddered in revulsion. "This is about my needs! And your needs..." Dirk pressed his lips across her terse closed mouth. He slid his callused hands across Mack's small breasts; fingers probing for a strap to loosen. "You're shaking... like a delicate flower..."

"Leave me alone!" Mack wept, but she stood frozen in her spot, unable to move. She wanted to get off this island so badly, and Dirk was her only escape. "I swear I'll scream!"

"You have screamed so much since you've been here, everyone has been told to expect that from you. I told them southern Palachian women always scream. They don't know. Most outside the airship port have never even seen one."

Mack's shaking turned into sobs as Dirk wrapped his arms around her and kissed her neck.

"Don't be scared my little rabbit. You will like it. You'll see."

"I highly doubt that," Mack said, but her resistance was wilting. She had no more fight left in her to stand. Once Dirk had put her on the bed, her mind faded into a numb disconnection. She felt her garments being tugged off, item by item, as she stared at the cracks on the ceiling. Her expression became as lifeless as a doll, and Mack's final thought was that at least he wasn't as painful as Officer Bushington had been. That was something. And with that thought, the last bit of fight she had gave way as the contents of her stomach burst from her cheeks before she passed out.

Dirk didn't even seem to notice.

Seventeen
The Journey to Destiny: The Lie Unfolded

"You have a visitor," said the guard.

Mack sat up from her quarters, weak from lack of food and fresh water. "Who, may I ask?"

The guard sneered laughed. "I was told not to tell you. In fact, I was just asked to make sure you were conscious."

Mack sat up. "Fine. I am. Barely." The waves tilted her ship slightly, and she had to steady herself to avoid smacking her head against her bunk. The chains around her ankles and wrist had left worn cuts into her skin, which were still raw from the burns.

The last week had been a series of disasters that tested Mack's resolve. Heather had not appeared again, but she didn't need to; Mack's life was nothing but an example in misfortune. Heather had been right: Mack was paying for her lies.

Dirk lost control, as he put it. He could no longer deal with the Yurpan women who didn't meet his needs. The next few days, Mack was not headed towards the mainland as promised, but instead locked in a room and forced to deal with Dirk's needs. Dirk kept promising Mack a ship would come, but if she still wanted to meet it, she would have to endure giving up her body to Dirk. Mack knew what Dirk was doing to her. She had learned back at the Northern Yurpan airship port what what was happening. She also finally understood what the Officer Bushington had done to her, and she knew that sometime in the future that Dirk would also get a pry-bar to the back of the head. But for now, she had to survive. Mack endured the daily molestations. She didn't even bother to dress properly between visits, as any clothing that required unbuckling or untying would just lengthen the visits. It didn't seem to hurt her anymore, although she drank a lot of alcohol to help numb her feelings, and passed the time by planning various escape scenarios. And eventually, if not surprisingly, Dirk made good with his promise for those many nights, as he actually got a steamship.

The steamship that loomed above the docks was rather large for something to take her to the mainland. This turned out to be because it was not taking her there. As she boarded the vessel, she saw that Dirk was taking what looked like a large amount of money. Before Mack put the pieces together, she was grabbed by some guards, and tossed in a jail cell.

Anna Demure was wanted for treason against the Queen of Palachia. That's when Mack remembered that a message had been sent back to the Queen about Chang and Anna, and it must have reached Yurpa while she was in Reiland, and when she claimed to be Anna...

"Why *did* I claim to be Anna?" she asked herself, angered at her own lack of forethought. Her motives seemed more unclear with each passing day. Her holding cell was a small room at the aft of the ship near the waterline. It was damp, cold, and there were rats. The only thing keeping her from despair was the thought that once she arrived in Palachia, she could explain she was not Anna. They would know who Mack Van Horn was. But she had to survive first. And the ship would take almost a month at sea before it reached the eastern Palachian coast.

The visitor entered, snapping her out of a cloud of memories.

"I am your representative for the Queen's court, Anna," said a tall and thin man that reminded Mack of her father. Then he narrowed his eyes. "You... don't look like Anna."

"I am not Anna," Mack said, relieved. "I am actually Mack Van Horn, one of the only survivors of the airship crash at Reiland."

"Mack is a young boy, not a young girl," the man said.

Mack hissed at her own mistake. "Actually, that's not true, either."

"Then who are you?"

"I am Heather January, daughter of Bruce and Rose January. I was hired by the League to be Mack Van Horn — "

"They hired a girl... to play a boy?"

"Yes. Terry was a girl, too, but — "

The man laughed. "You have to come up with a better story than that, Miss."

Heather seethed. She listened to her own words and wished she had thought out a better explanation. Right now she just sounded like a lying fool. "Look, my parents can identify me — "

"Perhaps that is so. But why were you arrested as Anna?"

"I claimed to be Anna so I could... okay, see — "

The man chuckled and shook his head. "If I am to represent you, I need the entire, truthful story."

"Yes," said a familiar voice in the cell. "Tell us all who you really are..." Heather was looking through the bars. She was also thin and gaunt, and the same chain around Mack's ankle was around hers as well.

Mack cringed. "I am Heather Van — no, Heather January — "

Heather laughed. "You have no idea anymore, you *fraud!* Look at you in this cell. You will rot, there, you know."

Mack ignored the taunting, and tried her best to tell the story to the man while Heather made grunting noises and jeered her. Eventually, the man stopped writing in his notebook and stared blankly into space. Mack realized the man did not believe her one bit, and had stopped listening. Suddenly, without saying anything, he got up and left.

"Wait, where are you going?" Mack shouted.

Heather laughed. "He thinks you're *mad*! That's true, you know. Not a sane bone in your fake little body."

"Go *away*!" Mack hissed.

"Shut up in there!" The guard shouted.

"I won't shut up," Heather said. "Make me! Come do to me what Dirk did for a few pieces of silver you coffee-nosed pugilist!"

The guard came in, and shut the cell door. "You will shut up, and I will make you if I have to."

Heather spit in the guard's face. Mack was impressed by the distance, but alarmed when the guard opened the door and hit her with a cudgel.

"I didn't do that, *she* did!" Mack screamed, but the man kept swinging at her.

"*We are one in the same, Mack Van Horn!*" Heather laughed with glee. She wiped the blood from the corner of her mouth while the guard punched Mack repeatedly.

The next few days, Mack was in silence. Her beating had broken a few teeth, and made what little food she was given difficult to chew and swallow. She knew whatever Heather said, people assumed Mack had said. It didn't seem fair, but her lack of visitors gave her somewhat of a relief. As Mack dealt with the pain in the prison, she tried her best to shut out Heather.

Eventually, Mack withered in her cell. She did not know how many days or how many storms she had gone through. Her frame was reduced to skin and bones, and she no longer rose from her position even to relieve herself. The only movement she gave was to keep rats from gnawing at her sores.

A day came when she felt the ship had changed gears. The distant memories of knowing how engines worked and the excitement it had given her were but shadows of a former life, but parts of her still remained alive as dying sparks in the nighttime embers of an untended fire. These distant glows told her they must have finally reached port. Her instincts were proven right when some people in Palachian guard uniforms came for her. They read charges, but she did not hear them. They hauled her off the boat, where her frame was looked upon by passing citizens with scorn and confusion. Streets flashed by, and she was underground once again.

She was being transported from one train to another, when something happened. There was a commotion. A scuffle. Gunshots were fired. Mack was moved to a small box. More gunshots. The smell of flint and gunpowder. Sounds of fighting. Something cool was brought to her lips.

Mack awoke in a small bed. The familiar green glow of trolley, something she felt she had not seen for a lifetime, shone through her window. There were two women in the room, sitting lazily on a large sofa, reading some magazines. Before Mack decided whether to call out to them or not, she heard the door open. She shut her eyes to listen and realized that the distant hum of underground machinery was present.

"How is she?" asked a voice.

"Fine, mum," said a deep southern Palachian accent.

"She hasn't risen at all. We have been giving her the treatment, plus some food and that nutrient paste. But still no change."

The first voice seemed anxious. "It's been days. My leader will be very angry. She has been questioning our progress daily."

"What more do you want us to do? She came to us on death's door. We have given her water, and tried to give her real food, but she won't chew with broken teeth. She's been burned, cut, had her ribs broken, her head's been injured dozens of times. Scars upon scars. Even the Yurpan doctor said it will be a miracle if she lives."

"She will live," said the voice. "I don't give a damn what that doctor said. I want you to double the treatment."

"That could kill her — "

"No, it won't. Not this girl. If she's the one... and if she's not, she's better off dead anyway. But if we don't fix her up soon, my leader will show up and all of you will be executed!"

"Yes, mum."

Mack felt someone walk up and look over her. "Trolley's flame, she looks a mess. I hope we got to her in time."

Mack opened her eyes slightly. The face over her was southern Palachian, dressed in black, with her hair up in a bun. A green necklace with the Korisan symbol for "He who watches" was dangling between her cleavage along with a small stone star.

"She's barely conscious," the voice said as Mack shut her eyes. "That's good."

The next few days, Mack awoke and passed out randomly. Once in a while, she felt someone pour a bitter liquid into her mouth, or force her to choke down a bitter paste. Eventually, she was able to open her eyes and look around. The day she tried to sit up was a relief to those around her.

"Good, you're up," said a voice. "My name's Martha, and this is my daughter Delilah. We need you to get well. Fast."

"Where am I?" Mack asked. It was hard to speak. Her throat was dry, and her missing teeth felt odd against her tongue.

"You're safe for now. We rescued you from your execution. Thank goodness you're able to speak; our master will be pleased."

"Who is she?"

"In due time, miss, in due time."

That time came soon enough.

"I heard our patient is speaking," said the woman as she entered the room.

"Yes, mum, she is. Wants to know where she is, who brought her here, and so on..."

The woman nodded. "Excellent," she said, but did not sound pleased. "Well, let's have a look at you." The woman's bony and cold fingers forced Mack's eyes open and she looked deep into them. "Hmmm... still not out of the woods. We need to administer the treatment some more, but our time has run out. My supervisor will be here today. I want you to clean her up and make her presentable. I have some dental partials that will fill in some of those missing teeth. She stinks like filth, however. Fix that, and when she's gone, I want this mattress burned."

"Yes, mum."

"Who are you?" Mack asked.

The woman looked over Mack's wounds. "One of many unknown strangers you shall pass in the next few days. I am your head nurse, but not for long. We have to get you out of here, as a moving target is a target less likely to be hit."

"Where are you taking me?" Mack asked, as the nurse propped pillows around her head.

"Someplace safer than this. You're in the lower levels of southern Palachia. But the Queen's guards have been snooping for you — "

"I am not Anna Demure," she said.

The woman laughed. "I know. Just who you are, however, is a bit of a mystery my leader hopes to clarify."

"Who is she?"

The woman chuckled in response. "Rest. You will find out soon enough."

Later that evening, Mack was moved by a handful of men to another place on an open stretcher. Mack could tell by her surroundings that she was now deep under Palachia, in the lower levels where criminals and vagrants lived. Houses were built of scraps or random material, and people in decaying clothing roamed around filthy streets with flies and loose animals. Huge sections of root machinery were exposed, hissing and thumping like a twisted heartbeat of the world. A bunch of men carrying someone wrapped up on a stretcher didn't even register as unusual in this chaotic underground world.

Mack's next place of rest was a rather opulent room that stood in stark contrast to the decay outside. There were no windows, but detailed paintings of surface scenes were placed where windows would usually go. She was attended to by two female Yurpan doctors who worked on her injuries and got her strength up to where Mack could walk a little unassisted. She was given fresh clothing, and the food was very lush and varied. But as she became healthier, no one would tell her who this leader was. Mack only knew that it was a she, and that "she" was very impatient at Mack's slow recovery. Mack was also not allowed to leave the room, and there were no clocks to tell her what time it was or how many days had passed. Her sleep cycle had been heavily altered by her health, surface time, and the lack of any external news and everything kept her in the dark. She felt suspended and hanging by a thread held by an unknown benefactor she neither knew nor trusted.

"Our leader wants to see you in person," said one of the Yurpan doctors. She seemed nervous. "I would advise not looking directly at her. She is very old and very wise, but has a violent temper. You cannot outwit her, or say anything hurtful that will not get you hurt a dozen fold in return."

Mack acted as if she understood, but days went by and no further word was made. Until one night, Mack awoke to a dark room and several guns and blades pointed at her.

"Do not get up," said a powerful female voice.

Mack gasped in recognition. "Anna..."

Anna Demure poked her head out from behind the armed guards. "The late Mack Van Horn..." she replied.

Mack's blood boiled. "How *dare* you — "

"Shut your blabbing little mouth, Heather. Mack Van Horn is dead. You are back to just plain Heather January now."

Mack blinked, but did not reply.

Anna looked around the room. "Like it here? Yes, these are my quarters, usually. Deep in the belly of the world, I have made this place comfortable, don't you agree?"

"You are a traitor to the crown and — "

"The Queen is a fat old lady who hasn't seen her own feet for decades while rats crawl below her. You think I am impressed with your accusation? No, Heather. I am not impressed with her royal opulence, and as you can see, I can create it even in the filthiest of places. But enough about me. What about your adventures? I have to say, when I heard someone was posing as me to the Yurpans, I was quite curious."

Mack remained silent.

"I also heard that it was some babbling little girl who not only spoke to herself, but screamed and yelled at herself. I knew it had to be you. Gone dotty on trolley, finally."

"At least I am crazy and loyal to the Palachian — "

"Oh, there is no Palachia. There is no Rokasia or Yurpa. Just the same miserable little shits that live under the Sky Ring's domain. Pissing in their own territory like it bloody matters."

Mack stayed silent and surveyed the room. The guards were all women, which was unusual. Anna snapped Mack's head back to face her.

"I have to ask you, why the float, Heather? Why did you sabotage the float?"

Mack opened her mouth, but then shut it.

"Yes, I know about you swinging into the crowd. I know you were the one who lifted the gear shift off the clutch. I pretty much know everything; it's my job, remember?" Anna pushed aside some guards and sat on the edge of the bed. Mack decided that no matter what she said, she was trapped here anyway. She pursed her lips and looked away. "Oh, the silent treatment. Well, if I lived months not knowing, I can probably live my whole life that way. What was very curious is that one of the dead from the accident was your own sister, Morgana."

Mack felt a like she had been punched in the heart, but remained calm. Anna was probably lying. "Nice try. Nobody was reported killed in that accident — "

"No, because the Queen suppressed that in the news. If word was to get out that a float with the League of the Pompous had killed spectators, why... no one would attend the parades anymore. And you *have* to have parades!"

"You lie," Mack said, but her voice betrayed her concern.

Anna snapped her fingers and a servant brought in a wrapped bundle. Anna unwrapped it and unfolded a pink dress. Part of the dress was worn away, as if burned, and a huge bloodstain spread across the bodice. "Trolley did this. There was a trolley leak on the float, and it went downhill rather rapidly. Some people were trampled in the panic and didn't get away in time. This little pink frilly number cost your parents a pretty penny," Anna said, and turned it around. On the front were six League of the Brave pins.

Mack tried to remain silent, but Heather started to sob in shock.

"No one is sure if she was trampled to death or died of trolley asphyxiation. She was one of many. I took this dress because I felt it would come in handy some day... oh, look, that's one of my pins. I gave that to you; remember? But don't worry, I don't want

314

it back. You can keep them... and the dress." Anna tossed the dress on the bed. For a second, Mack could still see Morgana's face, but then it was gone.

Mack was only barely aware of her wailing. Her weakened body could not keep Heather away, and Mack's entire persona collapsed and drifted apart as Heather rocked back and forth, clutching the dress and sobbing into it.

"But not all the news is bad, Heather. As you can see, I wanted to keep you alive because you are very, very special to us. And, I can keep Mack and Heather as... one single person."

"I don't want to be Mack anymore," Heather said. "I don't want to be Heather. I don't want to be anything!" she sobbed. The guards shifted uncomfortably, but Anna snapped them to attention with a glare.

"Heather, that's not an option. You are Heather January, and we need you alive — "

"I don't want to live!" Heather screamed, and grabbed a gun from a guard, firing it at herself. Her vision grew dark red and she slumped onto a pillow. Heather could not see, but she heard screaming and scuffling.

"You fool, you *fool*! They weren't supposed to be *loaded*!" Anna screamed. "What if there had been exposed trolley? I want that guard out of here!"

"She's okay, it's just a flesh wound," she heard someone say. "She missed her skull – it's only across her temple! I'll get the doctors!"

"There's blood everywhere! On my pillows and sheets!" Anna said in frustration more than concern. "I want that guard slit apart and his meat given to the pigs! *Heather has to stay alive or we're all going to die, do you understand me??*"

"Yes, mum!" someone said.

"I speak Korisan!" Heather screamed in a last-ditch effort to destroy everything. "I am a girl, and I speak and read and write Korisan!" She struggled against a dozen unseen hands pinning her to the bed.

"I know I *know!*" Anna said before Heather slipped into unconscious. "We all know. And that's *why* you're important!"

Eighteen
The Journey to Destiny: Folding in On One's Self

"I cannot lie to you," Anna said. "When I went to the Professor's lab and saw all the Korisan writing on the floor, I knew then that you were more than just a brat who had crept in like a rat to see the difference engine. The books, which I had to swap back, were a strange ruse I thought was a communication attempt by spies. But no, you were innocent the whole time. Typical. I should have known in the end you were only 12 and incapable of any decent intrigue."

Heather leaned on the air ship's railing, remembering Anna's explanation in a haze of bored ennui. In had been weeks since the incident where Heather had tried to kill herself in despair and Anna hadn't left her side since. She personally oversaw all the operations to get Heather well again, despite all Heather's attempts to the contrary. When she wouldn't eat, they forced pulp down her throat. When she tried to hurt herself, they tied her down. And as Heather screamed and cursed, they simply acted as this was nothing unusual. Anna would do all her work in front of Heather, patiently explaining why things had to be this way. Anna wore a small stone star around her neck which she fingered and dangled absently while she spoke.

"The Professor knew you were special, too," she explained. "We were both shocked. We knew you would descend into madness from reading and writing in the tongues forbidden to female folk. I learned that the night terrors had already started and I made up my mind to have you killed. But the Professor didn't want you dead. No, he wanted you to live. I asked why, and he told me that you were the Chosen One. For days he argued his case. He said Rokasian mystics had told him that the girl would be in his city, but when he returned, he was shocked it was you. But it all made sense. The chances of your life were so remote, so unlikely, that it had to be divine intervention. Thus it was decided he would take you on as an apprentice, and we would travel down to the Southern Spoke to have you waken the builders. Our people are known as The Wakers, and we have been around for quite some time now, awaiting this grand moment."

Heather knew she could jump over the edge of the railing into the sea below, but her despair had even taken over the desire for suicide. Nothing seemed to matter. Even if an impulse was to take hold, Anna was also leaning over the railing next to her, and would have stopped her. Instead, she looked away from Anna and towards the south. They were on their way to the Southern Spoke, and already the gigantic tower was dominating the skyline as it rose from the horizon and thrust through the clouds to the Sky Ring above. They had flown so far south that the Sky Ring was reduced to a thin line directly above them.

"Something went wrong, however. Some of the Rokasians wanted to claim you. The Professor knew they would be sending men, hundreds of them from a splinter group, to kidnap you and force you to the Rokasian Empire and use you as a bargaining chip. Thus, we got the League to take you away. Hide you in plain sight, as it were, with Chang acting as my second. The Professor rejected you for your own safety, Heather. It broke his heart, but he knew the League could protect you when he could not. After you left, the Professor fled south to where we were going, and I went to the League to oversee the last stages of my operation. Yes, it's true, Chang and I stole all the money earmarked for the Yurpans, but some of them were in on it, too. In fact, all countries have members of The Wakers. We have spent almost a decade infiltrating the core of the mechanical and scientific community, waiting for your arrival, Heather. We have been financing the Wakers through various slush transactions and plans within plans."

"One thing we did not foresee was when you went to the surface." Anna confessed to her one night after tucking her in, "The lack of trolley started affecting you. It's known that those who spend their whole life with trolley go through withdrawal, most of which is misdiagnosed as agoraphobia. We think it's the trolley gas used in the street lamps, but you worked with trolley a great deal; far more than most people your age. Quickly, you started to pull apart in a kind of *schizophrenic* dementia. I heard Mack in the washroom, speaking to Heather in the mirror. Both the same voice. Girl forced to be a boy. Wanting to be a boy, but still a girl. I knew you were the Chosen One. You had to be. Not one sex or another, and still an innocent, purely scientific and mechanical virgin. The prophesy states everything that has happened to you and what is yet to come. The problem was I didn't know if anyone else had any idea, and I knew I had to leave before I could fix you. You do a lot of things we can't explain, Heather; you have survived some pretty impossible odds. When I found out about the airship crash, I was dumbstruck. I had to find out if it was true. You cannot believe the level of relief I had when I found you were the only survivor. Of course, then you were jailed and extradited, because you had claimed to be me. That delayed our meeting by almost a month. But this worked out, as we were able to get more people to rally to our cause. Again, a sign you are the Chosen One. That old Professor was not the fool I believed him to be. He was still as spry and quick as he was when we courted."

Heather didn't believe any of it. It was a cult, run by unscientific minds that made illogical excuses to shore up their beliefs. But her protests were pointless. Anna simply did not see where she was wrong, and Heather knew she was trapped in the wayward mind of a woman who was growing old and her fading looks did not gain her the favors she could once bring. Thus, a cult mentality was the only option.

Trolley gas was infused with her food by Anna's orders. The normally poisonous chemical supposedly kept away the night terrors, and the Heather and Mack arguments had faded back into internal dialogue. But Heather believed this was because the reason for the terrors had ceased when her own waking life became the real terror. Anna assured her that it was because the trolley, the Builders blood, was keeping her whole. The face that started back at Heather in the mirror was gaunt and haunted now, with a strange green pallor from the trolley gas. She knew she was being slowly poisoned, possibly for compliance, but she didn't care anymore. All the while, Anna kept repeating the reason Heather was making this journey.

"You are the only who will end this stupid war and make the Builders awaken and fix the root machine. Your bloodline... flowing with trolley, the blood of the Builders... flows within you. You are one of their descendants. The Builders were men and women, equal, side by side."

Anna gave Heather books to read, but she did not read them. So like everything else, Anna forced her to listen to them by reading them aloud as she worked. Anna's voice became hoarse over time, and gained a gravelly quality. The entire time, she ran her section of the cult, moving people, giving commands, arranging transport, and shipping money and cargo. Heather listened in on some of the twisted politics that bent the flow of money in their favor. They manipulated markets, bribed politicians, operated crime syndicates, and were in charge of hundreds of smaller groups that had no knowledge of their ultimate purpose.

Anna tried to be as mothering as possible, but often it came off stilted and frustrated. Anna explained that the original Builders had not died, but gone to sleep, only to be awoken when things started to break down. The root machine had been running for thousands of years, but it was starting to show its age and needed maintenance. When this happens, Anna had explained, the trolley seeks a Chosen One who will awaken the Builders that could then fix the root machine, and get everything in the right order. Wars would end. People would be born into a new era.

"What a waste," Heather said to Anna once, "that a mind as cunning and brilliant as yours should be wasted in such a way."

Anna soothed Heather's hair and clucked in a motherly way. "I know it's a lot to take in, but... when you see where we are going, you will forget all about how you got here. Your pain will subside, and truth shall fill your blood with vigor and purpose."

To Heather, Anna sounded more insane than when Mack was arguing with Heather in mirrors. All Heather knew about where she was going was that they were heading south to the world's equator where the Southern Spoke jutted a few miles off the coast of the deepest of southern Palachia. It was one of the spokes that held aloft the Sky Ring that loomed above them like a curved blade, getting thinner and thinner the farther south they sailed. Beyond the spoke was nothing but uncharted seas. Heather went from train to sailing ship to airship. For the last few days, she had been traveling with a caravan of airships that dotted the sky. There must have been thousands of visitors coming to meet them.

"We should be at the Spoke in less than a day," Anna said, pointing to the huge pillar in the distance. "There we shall complete the set up for you to awaken the Builders. The Professor is already there, along with Chang and some other Rokasian and Yurpan Wakers."

Heather shrugged and shook her head. "Cult nonsense," she said.

Anna rubbed Heather's back. "Oh, you will see. You always wanted to see how trolley was mined. You are about to enter the world's largest trolley mining and refining plant. It is hundreds of feet under the water. Exposure to some of the largest pieces of root machinery anyone had ever witnessed. You will see the very gears and columns that make the Sky Ring function! That should be a treat..."

Heather was so dead inside; she didn't even allow any feeling left. Not even for the thrill of machinery. Her life was over. Nothing mattered. She was nothing but a used tool, broken and scarred by dozens of neglectful and outright abusive owners. There was little use left in her, and she no longer cared. She wished that whatever she ended up getting used for, she would get to sleep forever when it was over.

Anna slapped Heather's bony shoulder. "Well, that's enough fresh air for today. You have enough trolley in you to summon a dozen storms. I see some clouds coming down from the northeast, but we'll be underwater by the time they get to us."

"I am staying outside," Heather said. But she put up such little resistance, that before she could think to do anything obstinate, she was already inside, locked in her little jail room and chained to a bed.

"Is this what you wanted?" Mack asked quietly at the foot of the bed.

Heather said nothing. She had let them believe that their treatment had stopped the schizophrenia, and Mack only spoke to her in whispers when they were alone.

Mack's ghostly image lay down in the bed next to Heather and soothed her hair. "I won't let them kill you, Heather," she whispered. "I'll take care of you," she added as she faded away. "I will show you that I still love you." Heather's tears ran down her face as she stared at the ceiling, believing for a brief moment that Mack was really Morgana, soothing her like they did when they were little.

When the air ship docked at the floating platform, the winds had picked up fiercely. They had been traveling ahead of a major sea storm that Anna said was symbolic. As they were escorted off the ship, Anna was still shouting commands in the thick salt air.

"I want the entire cargo from the rear put in my chambers!" she shouted. "I don't care if you have to stack them around my bed and pile them to the ceiling; I want every crate and every scrap of work in my chambers! Heather, come with me!"

The city at Southern Spoke was little more than thousands of floating platforms tied with bridges and cables that extended for miles in each direction. As the sea rolled underneath them, the entire upper city rose and sank like a slow-moving flag. The rumble of lectromag flashed in the distance.

"Pretty big storm is coming," said a voice who met Anna as they head towards a large tubular entrance. It was Chang.

"You said it, Chang!"

"So here is our girl... finally." Chang said as he looked at her face-to-face. He looked into Heather's eyes with both curiosity and respect.

"Finally!" Anna agreed.

The wind picked up and a salty mist blew across them.

Chang laughed as he rose to sniff the air. "We have been told this storm has been brewing for days. She seems such a ... mundane young girl for the noblest of purposes!"

"She may be a little girl," Anna said. "But a woman all the same. With a man's skills. A virgin who is both sexes. It is as the prophesy states."

Heather did not scoff at the word, "virgin." She did not tell Anna of her tales, and Anna never asked. It just cemented for Heather what a joke the entire thing was.

Chang nodded. "We'd better hurry. When the seas pick up like this, they disconnect the surface tubes. The Professor is waiting by the northern root gears."

Anna, Chang, Heather and a crew of various followers went into a large entrance. It felt odd to go into a large building, Heather thought, which slowly rocks back and forth. The entrance building was larger than any building Heather had seen. The actual tube entrance itself was several stories high, and constructed from a black-accordion-like material that flexed and puckered with the movement of the waves outside. She thought it looked like the gaping maw of a lamprey eel.

"They are going to release the cables, soon," Chang warned. "We had better get her down first, and then the cargo next. The rest of the visitors will be bumped back because the show doesn't start without us anyway." He was oddly jovial, and bubbling with excitement. With a few snaps of his ungloved hand, he directed the cargo into a large waiting area.

Anna escorted Heather onto a tram suspended by cables that ran down the flexing tube. Heather watched the cables go taut and slacken with the rolls of the waves. The cables adapted to the flex through a series of pulleys and belts that were watched over by several workers. They were shouting at one another, as the tension was something that they were quickly losing control over.

"Down we go," Anna said excitedly as the tram was released from its clips. The tram took a serious dip, but then evened its keel with the help of a few operators swinging counterweights on each side of the gondola like large oars. The rolling movement ceased when they came to a bend in the tube where the large black accordion ended and a giant glass tube began. The gondola shuddered, and started to roll smoothly forward with loud clacking noises.

"This is the permanent structure. It's kind of like a giant pneumatic tube, but instead of air pressure, we're on a small track."

"Then it's nothing like a pneumatic tube," Heather said under her breath.

Anna ignored her. "This will lead to the main tube where we'll approach the Cathedral where the Northern Root Gears are."

Heather looked out the glass panels. They were framed into panels with a metal that had turned green in the sea water. Steaks of dirty green water had stained the glass as it ran down into a gutter system under the tracks. Through the filthy glass, Heather could make out large shapes of buildings underwater. She recognized some of the shapes as trolley refineries, but the others were nonsense jagged shapes dotted with lights where she figured portholes were.

They stopped at the main entrance, and everyone got off the tram on a moving wooden platform. Northern Palachian workers spun the platform until the tram was on another track going in the opposite direction. As Heather looked to see the tram driving away, she heard a voice that haunted her from a past that was both distant and unwelcome.

"Hello, Heather..." said Professor Gaylord.

Heather stared at the tram platform, not turning to face him.

"She's tired," Anna said.

The Professor moved in front of Heather and looked at her with the most apologetic face she had ever seen. "Heather, I want to apologize for... all of this..." he said, waving his arms around them. "If I had a choice, I would have never gotten you involved. But it seems fate and destiny made fools of us all."

Heather said nothing, but felt his kindness was worse than his anger. Her heart strained against her rage and despair. "I hate you so much..." she whispered to herself, but couldn't tell if she hated herself more than the Professor.

The Professor and Anna walked down a polished coral floor to a vast space filled with hundreds of tables, all bedecked with fine linens, plates, and silverware. Already half the tables were filled with the elite from all corners of the civilized world. Yurpan in their brown, blue, and red coats dined with the tailored silk suits of the Rokasians. Southern Palachian high society in taffeta and lace mingled among them alike, laughing and chatting as if in a gay garden party. Above the vast hall were huge panes of glass that allowed sunlight to filter in; if there was sunlight to be had. Instead the glow of trolley gas lamps helped fill in the darkness cast from the storm above. Heather could see the waves roll and boil in the wind.

As they passed by tables, people murmured to themselves, pointing to the trio with excited gossip and banter. Heather hated it, but Anna and the Professor walked tall and proud.

"Many more will come," Anna said. "The ships are landing everywhere there is a dock. Some even brought their own ships to get people here."

Light flashed outside the windows, distorted by the water that separated them from the air above the sea.

"The lectromag is becoming more frequent," The Professor said. "I trust that all the cargo will arrive safely?"

"It was coming right after us. Chang will deliver it to my quarters. But we must get Heather ready. She has a grand feat ahead of her very soon."

The Professor nodded. "I hope everyone can get safely here before the storm. The last report was that it was a very large one and may last for days. Hurricane force winds have been reported when it passed over southern Rokasia."

"We will be safe here," Anna said. "Lectromag can go through water, but not this far down. Apart from the Spoke, we are insulated with at least 30 feet of water at our highest point. The spoke is coated with a natural patina that repels lectromag quite well."

"What is my 'Grand Feat?'" Heather asked.

The Professor stopped in front of a very ornate wall. "You mean you did not tell her?"

"I don't have to," Anna said smugly. She pulled down a lever, and with the sound of cranking chains and gears and the hiss of steam-driven hydraulics, a huge crack appeared in the wall. The gigantic doors, nearly 50 feet high, slowly opened. A cool and dry draft poured across Heather's face as she peered into the room beyond.

It was as her dream predicted.

"Welcome to the Cathedral," Anna said with a grand air. "I trust, Heather, you have seen this place before?"

Heather was dumbstruck. How could she...? There was no way... was there? She wondered.

"I take that as a yes," Anna said smugly. "Come; let us show you where you will be performing your duties." Anna led them down a huge nave lined with hundreds of benches. "These pews can contain over twelve thousand followers. I hope to have them all filled, weather permitting."

"We already have six thousand, and hundreds upon hundreds have been arriving every day," the Professor said, his eyes wide with pride. "I expect we shall have many people standing for the ceremony."

Heather felt she had seen every stone, every tile, and every book and cranny of this place in her dreams. The nave had huge vaulted ceilings with enormous stained glass windows. In some places, Heather could see the waves crashing and churning. In others, only rippling shadows cast jagged shadows and light, as if lectromag itself had found a way to the walls and floor.

After nearly five minutes of solemn walking, they stopped at the main altar. Heather shuddered.

Across the raised dais was a giant table made of a dark gray stone. Veins of green and white slid across the surface in thin meandering trails. Behind the stone table was a cross hallway with a transept at either side. The floor had a huge circular groove that was bisected by another groove that led to a giant wall that was featureless but for one item: a reddish coral star.

Heather stopped and backed away.

"You see? She does know what is to come. We found this when we did a survey of the root machine several years ago. We knew by the markings that all we had to find was the huge golden blade to start the process, and the Rokasians found it several months ago. We knew then that you, Heather January, would show yourself. And lo and behold, you did! You will free the builder from his slumbering tomb, and he who watches while dreaming shall awaken!"

Heather backed away some more, but the Professor grabbed her. "Easy, Heather."

"A h-huge monster comes out of that... thing!" she said, pointing a shaking hand at the star. It almost seemed to pucker like a sphincter in a trick of the water shadows.

"No no... not a *monster*... a *builder*..." Anna said.

"No, that was *no builder!*"

"She is tired, professor," Anna said. "I will take her from here."

"I am not summoning that thing!" Heather said.

"You don't have to summon anything you don't want to," Anna said calmly amused. "Don't worry. I will not let anything harm you. Let's get you to your quarters."

"I don't want to do this!" Heather said, surprised she had some fight left in her.

"And you don't have to, nobody will force you. But will you rest on it? Perhaps? Get something to eat? Hmm?"

Heather simply walked away. She didn't care which direction, she just started walking.

"What is she doing?" asked the Professor.

"Let her go," Anna said. "She won't get far, just let her adapt to her surroundings. It wouldn't be much of a prophesy if she got away, would it?"

"What if someone kidnaps h — "

"This place is guarded heavily. She won't get far."

Heather wandered the cathedral as far as she could, but given the fact it wasn't like home with twisting passages, alleys, steam pipes, and ventilation shafts she quickly realized that she was going in circles, and the amused smirk of Anna as she kept passing her and the Professor infuriated her. Eventually, Heather found stairs to the upper level and sat quietly in a small alcove above the pipe organ. It was as her dreams had predicted, down to the dirty and disheveled appearance. Nothing surprised her, and as she looked at the huge blank wall above the altar, she knew that this was the wall where the split occurred.

"You don't have to do this, you know," Mack said from behind her.

"I know," Heather said as she started down at her shoes. "But why not?"

"Because you know it's wrong. They think you're a virgin, and... well... it's apparent they don't know what they are doing."

Heather wrinkled her nose in anger. "*You* may not be a virgin, but — "

"Heather. Please. Neither one of us are free from the ravages of lonely men. You yourself said we were one in the same.."

"You can't control me," Heather said darkly. "Nobody can."

Mack gently touched Heather's shoulders. Heather shrugged free. Mack's touch had been soothing, but she didn't want to admit it. Still, she was a little dismayed how easy it was to shake it off.

Mack stood in front of her, blocking her view of the huge wall. "If no one can control you, how come you are going along with this?"

"Would you rather I fight, Mack? Did that work out for you?"

"Did giving up work for you, Heather?"

"Might as well."

Mack walked in front of Heather and blocked her view of the altar. "Might as well... what?"

"Might as well bring an end to this whole stupid civilization. Might as well... bring on whatever it is that comes through the crack. The people in charge will ruin us one way or another. They are as corrupt as they are incompetent."

"So you know they are not summoning a Builder?"

Heather nodded. "I am aware. He who watches while dreaming..."

"... shall awaken."

Both of them looked at the huge Korisan symbol etched in stained glass in the ceiling. Water rippling through the glass danced lines of light across their faces.

"You know, that looks like lectromag..." Mack said.

"Maybe it is," Heather said, her eyes closed.

"I will... I will stop you, you know. If I have to."

Heather smiled, feeling the light wriggle across her face. "I know."

Nineteen
The Summoning

"The time has come...!" Anna's voice echoed across the pews that lined the great hall and the crowd hushed.

Heather had spent her last few hours on this world looking at rich and poor people, from all nations, as they worked together to clean the cathedral. The normal northern Palachian staff that would have done this were either dealing with the floating platforms and the storm, or were unable to actually get to the main central spoke when the tubes were cut off from the surface. So whoever could be scrounged up, guests and staff alike swept, washed, scrubbed, and hand-buffed every piece of wood, every floor tile, and every column that rose to the vaulted ceilings. There must have been several thousand assembled, and the rows of people became lost in the distance of the narrow vestibule.

"Tonight we shall witness the birth of a new era as we bring forth the great Builders who made this world. They have been sleeping for *millennia*, waiting for us to beckon them from their slumber."

The crowd mumbled a respectful agreement.

"It hasn't been easy. Even now, a great storm rages above us. Many who wished to come by air ship or boat are unable to dock. Many of them had to anchor out in deeper waters. I am told the waves are dozens of feet high. A vast eye of a central storm has arrived — our final guest — to greet the Builders."

The crowd applauded.

Heather chuckled at the entire farcical ceremony; it was just as the Professor would have described: all shallow pomp. But that very same professor stood beside Anna and Chang, along with a few other prominent scientists and philosophers. They were clad in robes that said, "He Who Watches" in Korisan and wearing small stone stars around their neck. All of them had solemn and proud faces as Anna gave her speech, entrancing the crowds in her chosen clothing: a revealing dress that overly accentuated her bosom for everyone's pleasure. Heather's clothing was only a few layers of a fine sheer muslin that didn't leave much to the imagination. Her small and youthful frame, marred by burn scars and poorly healed gashes, stood in the room like a broken piece of furniture that someone had tried to conceal beneath a thin sheet.

"With us is the Chosen One, Heather January, former League of the Brave, as was I. A girl who wishes to be a man. Pure and untouched, her scientific mind thinks only of mechanics and is not complicated by the slovenly and lustful desire of the flesh. She has never known love. She has never felt hate or anger. She only knows mechanics, and despite all odds, she has been brought to us today."

Anna held aloft a large golden blade and continued her speech for nearly half an hour. Heather did not bother to listen; she had heard Anna practice it so often by now that it was nothing but background noise. Instead, Heather found herself distracted by the large sword. It was made from a solid piece of gold, and its dead weight was giving Anna some difficulty keeping it still. She had seen it once before, in the letter that the Professor had received months earlier. Unfortunately, gold made for a poor blade; this heavy knife wouldn't have an edge that could cut, which was one of the more puzzling parts. On the blade were etched strange symbols which spelled out nothing sensible Heather could make out in Korisan. They seemed to be instructions of some kind, marred with deep parallel scratches. As she mumbled the words to try and make sense, a growing understanding of what they were for started to emerge in her head. While the words were a string of nonsense, they didn't have to be. They were words within words, and suddenly, Heather January understood her dreams, her prophesy, and her purpose. She understood why she had been chosen. Her muscles started to twitch as her fingers started to move like they were looking for something; something to hold or something to press.

Heather then had the greatest epiphany of her life, and in this she knew why the ceremony must continue at all costs.

Anna finally finished her grand speech. "Now, we must have her blood to start the Calling of the Builders. Behold the tools of the Wakers! The hammer and chisel! The wrench and axe! And the golden sword! Five tools like five points on our stars! Waken, O Great Builders, *awaken!*"

Heather held up her arm, and winced slightly as Anna slashed the gold knife across Heather's slender arm, but no blood came forth. The knife was far too dull, and as Anna sawed aggressively across her arm, all Heather could feel was something that was similar to a rope burn. Before Heather could crack a smile in amusement, the Professor pulled out his pocket knife and gashed Heathers arm, causing her gasp in shock. A trickle of blood poured down her wrist and started to weave across the wrinkles in her hand.

In the first stone pew, Mack stared at Heather with concerned and frightened eyes. "Please..." she whispered. "Remember who you are. Don't do this..."

Heather pretended not to notice. She allowed herself to be led to the giant stone table where she lay back obediently, as if in a trance. Anna was very pleased how easy everything was going, and squeezed out a "thanks" on Heather's other hand. As Anna let the drops of blood from her wound land in the green stone bowl, she started reciting things to Heather, who then translated them into Korisan as she faced the lectromag flickering through the huge windows above her.

"Oh **great builders!**" Anna started. "Many millennia have passed since we have gazed upon your faces. The root machine needs your help to rebuild civilization in your image! Come to us, as we recite the holy words! Trolley will guide us!" She shouted, and held aloft a battery. The battery was one of the smallest sizes made. It would have barely been enough to heat a pot of water. The end cap was different, Heather saw, and realized it was made to be opened by human hands. She remembered the dream she had with the crowd and the trolley. Mack turned in her pew, and saw the entire crowd rise with their own small, modified batteries. Her eyes were wide with horror.

"Trolley is mined from the shallow seas," Mack started to recite from reflex.

Heather started to translate Mack's voice into Korisan without thinking, and realized the Korisan pentameter sounded like a primal chant. Its rhythms seemed as old as the root machine itself, with the odd exception to the word "trolley" which didn't seem to have a Korisan equivalent. "And gives us the power to do our deeds," she continued. "If... trolley is used in your working day, Remember these rules, and respect their way."

Mack turned to her, and kept reciting the poem in the Queen's language. She saw by Heather's goose bumps that she, too, was beginning to realize there was more to this poem than just a shop safety lesson. This was not to wake the Builders. This was a warning. An old, ancient warning. "Trolley must be sealed away from air," she screamed. "Or harm will come to those who are unaware!"

"Trolley must be kept from the Sky Ring's domain!" Heather shouted in Korisan, looking at the skylights. The waves were crashing and thumping at the glass. Falling drops of water were highlighted by the huge amounts of lectromag ripping through the sky. The drops clicked noisily at everyone's feet. "For the light from the clouds will kill and maim!"

"Why... why is Heather still speaking?" asked the Professor, but he received no answer, as Anna remained concentrating on the wall, waking towards the groove in the floor.

"Trolley must be respected as if it's alive!" Mack shouted, standing up.

"Or misfortune will befall all who survive…" Heather replied. She knew the beast was coming towards the wall. She didn't know how, but she could *feel* it. It felt like a massive juggernaut of something solid and thick. As its blubbery, scaled skin touched the other side of the wall, it vibrated the air like the loudest, but lowest note of a kettle drum. A strange, sickeningly sweet odor drifted into the room like a damp rot.

"Trolley is mined from the shallow seas," Heather and Mack said as one voice. "And gives us the power to do our deeds. If trolley is used in your working day, Remember these rules, and respect their way!"

The room went silent. The nave echoed Heather's last words until they were lost in the fury of the storm above. The dripping of water was picking up pace. Small rivulets were starting to dribble down the walls in steady streams, pooling at people's feet.

Anna poured the contents of the bowl into a groove in the floor. She then exposed a small amount of trolley to the air, and stood back as the thick green smoke mixed with the liquid running down the groove to the altar. As if in a neck-to-neck race, the thin rivulet of trolley gas and liquid traveled with one another until they were sucked underneath a great stone star; the only feature on the wall.

Then, breathlessly… nothing happened.

Mack snickered, cutting the silence as a few other people in the pews coughed nervously. When the same amount of nothing happened, a few people started muttering to one another, until the cathedral was filled with a low buzz of whispers and mumbles. Had something gone wrong?

Heather felt the tension of the creature behind the wall. It, too, was waiting for something.

Anna remained unfazed, focusing on the crack below the altar until the Professor came to her with a mallet and chisel. "I think…

these are more than ceremonial. Perhaps the door needs some help. It's been a while since it has opened, you know."

Anna growled, and snatched the tools from the Professor. "Here," she said, handing them to Heather. "You take a crack at it. Only you can open the door."

"Heather, wait!" Mack shouted. She ran to the stone table. "Don't do this."

"What?" Anna said. She did not see Mack and Heather as two people, but Heather arguing with herself. "No, you *must* do this."

"No!" Mack shouted at Anna. "There's something there that is not supposed to be opened."

"How would *you* know, Heather? Just do as you're told or you'll be made a *fool* of!" Anna sounded desperate, as the talking in the cathedral was getting quite loud. She grabbed Heather's arm, and pulled her towards the wall.

"I will do as commanded," Heather said. "I think I know why this must happen."

"No! It doesn't *have* to happen, Heather! Anna's just controlling you, can't you see that?? If you won't stop this, *I* will stop you!" Mack said, but then found herself suddenly tied to the table. She struggled to free herself, but looked helplessly as Heather approached the star with the mallet and chisel. "Don't do it... *stop*, *Heather*! Morgana would be so upset!"

"Morgana is dead," Heather said, and stopped the entire noise of the audience with a single crack of the chisel on stone. The very air seemed to split.

"Morgana is *not* dead!" Mack said. "Anna lied to you..."

Heather stopped.

"Yes, Heather. Morgana is still alive — "

"Your sister is dead!!" shouted Anna. She didn't know why Heather was arguing with herself. She had given Heather the trolley-infused food, but she was still talking as if she were two people. And right in front of everyone! Her chest clenched as everything started to unravel. I am not a crazy cult person, she said to herself, *I am not a crazy cult person!*

"Don't listen to her!" Mack pleaded. "The dress is not proof of anything, she could have *easily* gotten a pink dress and League of Brave pins!"

"Break the seal, Heather!" Anna said, pushing Heather towards the large star. "Here, let me help you!" Anna grabbed the tools, and placed them in position. "Just chip off this seal, Heather. Don't be stupid. Stop shouting things at yourself! Just *do it!"*

"It must be done," Heather agreed. "Things need to be set right."

Mack struggled with her bonds. "Think about it, Heather. *Think. Use* your *head,* girl! Who stands more to gain by lying to you, Heather? Me or Anna?"

Heather's hands shook as she held the tools. She was in mid-swing, but she could not make her hand come down any further. These were not the tools that she should be holding. Her fingers needed to press something, pull something... small clockworks. Buttons. Small levers.

Mack acted upon her hesitation. "If you are true to anything, anything at all, you won't crack that seal. You won't expose that horror to your sister, or your parents, or — "

Anna screamed into Heather's ear. **"I know she is dead because I killed her, Mack! Do not fill her head with lies!!"**

Heather dropped the tools by her side. Light flashed back and forth through all the windows as the sounds of rain started to fill the cathedral. Above the water, a huge series of water spouts were now forming around the Southern Spoke. The floating platforms crashed into one another in the broiling waves.

Anna quickly realized her mistake and stammered, "No, I mean... no... I — "

Heather turned and faced Anna, her eyes red with rage. Mack sat up on the table, her bonds gone. She had done it. "It's over, Anna. You cannot summon whatever that thing is — "

"You can't tell me what to do, you can't deny destiny!!" Anna screamed, and pushed Heather aside. She grabbed the tools and started hammering away at the star.

"No, Anna, *wait!*" the Professor shouted. But with only a few blows, the star cracked and fell to the floor in a dozen pieces. The air suddenly grew thick like honey, and everything slowed down.

"Trolley... trolley... trolley..." the crowd started to chant. Each one had their battery held into the air, and the entire cathedral started to glow green. The line of blood mixed with trolley shot up and ran straight up the center of the blank wall. It was forming a bright crack. The people with the batteries removed the caps and let the gas flow out into the air. Many screamed as the gas tore into their flesh and filled their lungs. The rhythmic chanting started to collapse into chaotic peals of terror.

"Oh, fuck. Oh fuck, no no no..." Mack said, and ran to grab Heather. But Heather's body was trapped in some kind of trance. Her entire frame shook as she started to rise into the air. Mack grabbed her, and yanked downwards hard. "Come on, Heather! We have to go!" But Heather rose out of Mack's grip.

"I knew this would happen," Heather said. "I could not break the seal, but it had to be done. But trust me. The dreams have taught me what I can do. Stand aside as I fulfill my real destiny!"

"Heather..." Mack sobbed. "There is no destiny — that's all a lie the Waker cult made up. Please... no... Heather no..."

Heather's ghostly form looked down at Mack as she rose further into the air. "Trust me... for once... look into your heart and trust me."

The wall shuddered open, and a hideous, bloated, giant monstrosity blocked the crack of light as two huge claws started to pry the two halves apart. Pieces of the cathedral were crumbling as the lectromag roared outside in a maelstrom of arced light. Huge sections of the floating city were plowed by raw light that set blocks ablaze; even in the pouring rain and crashing waves.

"Mack!" Heather shouted up to Heather. Mack crawled on top of the stone table to avoid the trolley gas that was slithering up the altar. The gas was solidifying, turning into huge tentacles barbed with hooks. They were attaching themselves to the leviathan behind the collapsing wall, pulling it into their world like thousands of dock workers with hundreds of ropes. Small trails of water fell from cracks in the strained glass, pouring on the decaying corpses scattered over the pews. Green worms that turned themselves inside out to move were slithering out of the ripped holes in their bodies to greet their hideous master.

"Trust me...!" Heather shouted from above.

Mack closed her eyes, and looked deep into her heart. Morgana's face stared back at her. "I want you to be okay," she said. "Please trust your twin sister. Just this once. Heather has to do this. Thank you for thinking of me at the very end. Thank you for the letters. I don't know who Mack is, but I know Heather would never let the world end. She is weird, but her heart is good. Please... trust her."

Mack opened her eyes. The gigantic creature was already halfway out, an unsettling bouquet of worms and rot. It wasn't so much a solid thing like an animal, but more like a quivery mass of unspeakable evil. One giant kidney-shaped fish eye emerged, rotating in its pustule-like socket to stare directly at Heather as she floated only a dozen feet in front of its stare. The pupil was so large, it nearly eclipsed Heather's shape in its shadow. There was no way Heather, or anyone, could stop this thing now. The few remaining people who had come to their senses had climbed to higher ground. Most were screaming and clawing at their own eyes to shut out the vision before them while others just wailed in weeping insanity. They had all gone mad in the end, and Mack did not pity them for they could never be saved. Anna had been crushed beneath the creature and her flesh corroded like wet tissue paper into sloppy mats of brittle, sizzling bone. Chang had impaled the Professor with the golden blade, where it wobbled awkwardly in the gushing wound, As the Professor went through his last death throes, he stuffed Trolley down Chang's throat, where it burned a hole through his neck, mixing with his blood and turning it a dull amber hue.

"Trust my twin sister..." Morgana's voice said in her heart.

Mack bent down from the stone table and pulled the golden blade from the Professor's wound. She didn't know why she did it, but it ... felt right. "Do what you have to do," she called out to Heather. She looked up at the giant eye oozing towards her and held the knife above her head. **"Do it now!"**

At that moment, the huge stained glass ceiling shattered, and thick dark curtains of thundering sea water poured into the cathedral, narrowly missing the stone table. Just before the waves crashed over the altar, lectromag dove into the opening, grabbing Mack's hand with the blade. Mack shrieked in pain, feeling the things she saw happen to the two workers at the difference engine. It wracked her body, soared from her burns, and arced across the altar to Heather's body. Heather held out her arm. The lectromag sprang from her arm with the choir of a thousand suns, tore into the beast like a hot knife, and sliced across its thick leathery hide like it was bursting seams off a bloated sack of rotting grain.

The entrails of the beast flowed forth, crashing into trolley-soaked waves, and spread like writhing eels among the foam and debris. The stone table Mack was on shifted, and water quickly rose to her ankles. The beast roared as the sea water reached his wound, tearing into the squirming gash with hissing froth. It looked at Heather and lurched forward, but Heather was gone. A giant waterfall separated the beast from Mack, but even through the thick blanket of pouring ocean, Mack could see the giant eye looking at her with the anger and hate that could only come from millennia of despair and anguish.

She knew it had been imprisoned by the Builders, and it was the folly of mankind. The cult of Anna Demure and Professor Gaylord had set it free from its bonds and released it to the world.

Mack could barely stand to look into the malevolent gaze of the creature, but she could not look away. As it slid from the gap in the wall, its entire body, stories tall, was squat and bloated. Its worm-like torso was flanked with scaled arms and in place of its head was a gigantic octopus with two large fish-eyes with kidney-shaped lenses that bulged in terror as it tried to right itself in the rising waters. With each attempt to rise, its skin was torn asunder, and muscles slid off bones like overcooked boiled chicken sliding from a roasting pan.

"It can't form," Mack realized. "It can't form without trolley."

With one final, desperate lunge, the monstrosity raised its sloppy and grotesque bulk above the water and dove at Mack through the waterfall, howling deep from a primal place where mankind dared not listen. But Mack was not a man.

She was a woman.

That woman jumped from the table and plunged the golden blade into the creature's eye before being overcome by the rotting lime-green filth that erupted from it.

 Twenty
The Destiny

Heather rose from a grating where seawater was pouring into unseen drainage systems. She gagged and choked on the water in her lungs, pulling herself out of the flow that tugged at her skin.

Heather had no memory of how she had gotten there. One of the first things she did was try to assess her ability to stand in the pitch darkness of what she assumed was a huge drain pipe. Rushing water echoed off the walls for quite some time before she managed to stand up and stagger into the darkness away from the grate. She was completely naked, and the only thing she had on her was some kind of heavy cane or handle which dragged across the metal floor.

Heather stumbled randomly forward. She had to get away from the roaring noise. Strange, fleeting memories of a head wound in the darkness of a lab crossed her mind's eye. There were symbols and feelings, but nothing concrete. She didn't know if she was even upright, but knew that she had to keep moving. She had no idea how long she'd been walking, but she held her hand along the smooth sloping wall and had distant, quieter echoes to guide her.

Abruptly, the wall stopped at another wall. She groped around that wall for a bit, until she found a raised surface with a small lever. Without thinking, she pulled it down. A strange deep click and a hum followed, and a small steady amber light came to life above her. In front of her was a lever and a small slot with the picture of the knife above it. She looked at the object in her hand, unsurprised that it was the same knife. She pushed it into the slot, and turned it like a key.

There were distant thumping sounds, more clicks and deep hums, and the wall before her slowly began moving up. A huge, cold draft poured into the space and she shivered. As the gap widened, Heather ducked under the rising wall's edge, walking into a large and gas-lit room.

The room itself was an amazing display of wonder. Like the world's largest museum, the strangest artifacts bedecked its walls. There were portraits, models of ships and devices she had never seen before, skeletons of exotic creatures in domed glass, and huge stacks of books crammed into every space and nook. They piled on the floor, threatening to topple next to walls and assorted cabinets.

Heather slowly walked among the brick-a-brack, pausing at the distorted pale reflections of her skinny and scarred frame in the dusty and yellowed glass. The air was dry and stale, as if the place had been sealed for centuries, perhaps even longer. As she fingered the dusty papers scattered about, they were brown and brittle. She absently grabbed a large tablecloth and wrapped herself in it, feeling the coarse and fragile texture scrape against her burns.

There was a deep clicking, and Heather heard something begin to whir. Suddenly, a deep and booming voice echoed something rather loudly from ah unseen tube, and it scared Heather rather badly. She squeaked in fright, and then started sobbing uncontrollably at herself. The voice continued as she wept. She was spent, confused, frightened, and unsure what had just happened. She was only barely aware that she was calling out to her mother to end this terrible nightmare. A strange amnesia coated her thoughts like a protective cloud, but her soul ached with despair and terror. She collapsed to the floor on her hands and knees, drawing the cloth around her and wailing.

Then she heard her name. It came from the voice, which said a lot of nonsense, but she recognized her name repeating every now and again. She composed herself, then moved to sit cross-legged on the stone floor. When she heard her name again, she said, "I am Heather January!"

The voice stopped. More clicks.

"Can you understand what I am saying, Heather January?" said the voice in Korisan.

"What?" asked Heather, pausing her sobs.

"Can you understand what I am saying, Heather January?"

"I can understand what you are saying now," she replied. Where was this voice coming from?

There was more clicking. Then, "Heather January, can you come forward towards the wall with the bench? Please sit on the bench if you can understand me."

Heather paused, but then slowly stood up, and sat on the bench. The bench shifted, as if it was in a slot. Her weight must have depressed a plate, she thought.

There were more clicks. "This bench is going to move backwards after the third bell. Please be aware that it will move backwards, so you do not fall off of it." A small chime sounded.

At the third chime, the bench lurched backwards, and Heather struggled to remain on the bench as it slid behind the wall and into a dark tunnel. On the walls were lit several shadow pictures, but they moved like she was looking out a window. It was almost like watching a shadow puppet play with actual pictures. They seemed to be coming from lights attached to the opposite wall. As she raised her hand into the light, she saw the shadows of her hands move across the projected images.

"Before you are scenes from the history of your planet. Some of them may seem familiar, while others might seem more alien. These are the collected memories of [click click] thousands and [click click] thousands of years," the voice explained.

"Where am I?" Heather asked.

"If you are wondering where you are, you are in the root machine. This tunnel you are passing down was created to explain to future generations the purpose of this journey."

"What happened to me — "

"[click click] Please do not interrupt this process with questions, as you must listen. This is a recording that will not be able to respond adequately to your queries. The voice that made this recording has been dead for quite some time now," the voice continued, sounding a little sad. "Since I am not a real person, by the time you listen to this, I must convey to you that your arrival here means something grave has happened."

Memories started to come back to Heather. The water, the beast, the cult... her stomach heaved at the return of the burden.

"This planet was colonized [click click] thousands and [click click] thousands of years ago by a group of people that built the root machine. The purpose of the machine was to contain a variety of horrible creations that can neither be destroyed nor permanently hidden away. If you are on this journey and can speak our original language, this means that one of these creatures has broken free. The giant metal ring around your world is what we call an electrical generator. It forms a force field that keeps these creatures locked away. But over time, these monstrosities of man's own arrogant creation find a way to break out of every bond we have created for them. So we built this giant living prison and populated it with our ancestors to adapt and adjust the prison as necessary."

Heather was entranced by the moving pictures. They showed men and women in various costumes doing mundane activities like playing hoops, drinking tea, working on machinery, and other aspects of daily life. As the voice had said, they were both familiar and alien. In a few of them, there were machines that could fly without a large hydrogen bladder or strange giant lights that did not flicker like gas lamps. In others, they showed women working on machinery just like Heather wanted to.

"The root machine checks on the various activities of the planet from the view of the ring. We observe various aspects of civilization and shape it as needed. Part of how we can do this is the selective breeding of various bloodlines and control of the places where these creatures are imprisoned. But as time erodes even the largest of mountains, so do the bonds of these creature's imprisonments. People, however, are far more adaptable. You are the end result of a bloodline started over [click click] three centuries [click click] earlier. Your name is Heather January. You are a direct descendant from a strain of ancestors who were skilled mechanical engineers."

Heather understood. Somehow none of this shocked her. Her chest swelled with a sense of pride and accomplishment. She had fulfilled her purpose. Only... now what?

The bench stopped suddenly.

"Please disembark from the bench and follow the glowing white path down the tunnel to your left," a woman's voice commanded.

Heather hopped off the bench and followed the small tunnel. The floor was lit with a strange, rubbery glass with bright steady white lights under them. When the tunnel ended, she found herself in a warm room where dozens of these strange shadowbox pictures displayed various creatures on the wall. Her stomach heaved in fear. There were over a hundred of these pictures, and she knew that this was a display room of some kind. Looking around, she saw one picture in red. This was the creature she had just seen.

"Heather January?" asked another voice. This one was also female, but had a deeper tone not unlike her mother's.

"Yes?" she answered.

"You are now in the root machine central control room. One or more of these displays is outlined in red. Please say the word 'affirmative' if you understand what I am saying."

"Affirmative," Heather said. She thought the accent of the woman was much like Terry's; a combination of southern Palachian and diver, but with a hint of Yurpan pentameter. Then her heart grew heavy at Terry's memory. He... she... would have loved to see this. The central control room of the root machine itself.

"Please sit down in the chair in the center of the ring in the raised area of the middle of this room."

A strange altar rose from the floor. A series of short work benches with countless non-flickering lights and tiny levers covering the tops made a large ring around a padded chair. Heather walked up the small steps, and was in the chair before the altar had stopped moving upwards. From this vantage point, she was able to see all the pictures of all the creatures. Another one went red, and a horrible siren wailed.

"Specimen number [click click] 14 [click click] has just broken free," said yet another female voice from somewhere far away.

"Heather January," said the last voice again. This time it was coming from a large dome over Heather's head instead of some large distant tube she couldn't see. "Please lower this helmet over your head so your training may begin."

Heather did as she was told. Two goggles in front of her eyes lit up. Strange lines appeared that formed a picture of what looked like the rotting surface of a fruit. There were puffs of white covering a mottled brown and green curved surface.

"This is your planet. We call it Turopa. You may have a different word for it now. What you are seeing is the vantage point from the Observation Ring: the inner ring of the electromagnetic generator."

"... lectromag..." Heather whispered in realization.

"You can zoom in on any point of the planet's surface...." the voice continued. But Heather knew how it worked. Somehow, she knew. Something in the Korisan language clicked in her head and made sense. She grabbed two levers with each hand outside the helmet and when she crossed them a certain way, she could magnify her world's surface. Her face grew hot as parts of her mind awoke and took over her muscles.

"If our training was successful, years of dream implants have made these controls second nature to you. If you are able to control your vantage point, focus on the third spoke of the — "

Heather zoomed in on the Southern Spoke. It was covered with the white fungus-looking material, which she realized were clouds. Then a red light appeared.

"If you see any red dot, this is the location of one of the specimens that have been reported missing from their containment. On each control lever, you will find a small button. If you — "

Heather pressed the buttons with her thumb. Huge bolts of lectromag filled her vision with a hot white light, and slammed into a drifting city platform, shattering it with a horrible explosion that sent pieces for mile around. But the red dot was unaffected, and kept moving.

"Specimen number [click click] 38 [click click] has just broken free," said the alert voice.

What had Anna done? Heather realized. She must have started a chain reaction of some kind, setting lose these creatures on her world. Anna wanted control of the very root machine Heather was sitting in, and instead, subverted the design of the root machine itself. If these creatures were traveling under the water, or underground, the lectromag would never get to them. There had to be another way.

"How do I get creatures that live underground?" she wondered aloud.

There was a clicking noise. "I do not understand the question," the voice said.

Heather paused. Had the machine heard her? "Is there some-one alive in there?"

More clicking. "The question you have asked is not in our li-brary. Remember, these are recordings made a long time before you were born. We listen to your voice pattern, and give you a response based on a matching pattern. Please keep all questions simple."

Of course, Heather thought. The clicking must be when the record-ings change. The root machine would listen to her question, then use her voice like a punch card used in the Deosil-Widdershin gear exam.

"Question," she stated. "How to hit creature under water?"

After the clicking, the voice answered, "The electromagnetic beams cannot work through deep water or under a layer of a non-ferrous substance."

For a while, Heather kept trying to figure out how to hit the creatures with this machine, but the voices were crude, and not unlike talking to her younger brother Neil. Finally, she removed the helmet in frustration and looked at the control panel in front of her. Most of the buttons were unlabeled. Sometimes when she pushed on or pulled a lever, an alarm sounded, but most of the time, they did nothing. Her eyes focused on the projection on the wall. There were now 13 creatures labeled as escaped.

Heather sighed in frustration, and kicked the control panel. She felt she should know how to get rid of the creatures, but they were all hiding under the water, escaping one at a time. And what made things worse is that they weren't just escaping from the wall by the Southern Spoke. Many of them seemed to be escaping from all over the globe. Her stomach felt sick from the anxiety and growing help-lessness of the situation. She knew she must have some answer. She tried to think of the ceremony, and any clue that could be gained from the cult. Most of it was nonsense. Then she remembered some-thing that nagged at her: there was no Korisan word for trolley.

"Question," she said. "Trolley."

"There is no word in our library that matches that term."

"Trolley..." she said, with a deep northern Palachian accent, giving it a Yurpan sing-song spin. It sounded different to her that way, but seemed slightly more Korisan.

"Petroleum," said the voice.

That sounded Korisan, she thought. There was a word that was similar that meant, "pollutant" or "waste." Heather's chest swelled with renewed vigor. "Define petroleum."

"Petroleum is a waste by-product that occurs in areas mined around the geothermal connections. Given the planet's radioactive core, this crystallizes as a green mineral that when exposed to air, flame, or electricity will degrade or explode violently."

Heather's skin crawled. Trolley was a waste byproduct? Suddenly, things started to make sense.

"How are creatures trapped?" she asked.

"Creatures are trapped in an energy-like state and require a physical energized medium to assemble."

"Creatures and Petroleum?"

There was a lot of clicking. Then a male voice said, "This recording was made in the year of our King, 4538. It will play if someone asks about creatures and petroleum. Please refer to my notes which should be under the chair on the control panel."

Heather excitedly looked under the chair and found a thin and strangely-bound book coated with dust. She opened it and read the first page. Its charcoal lines were badly faded and hard to read in the yellowish light, but she did what she could.

"These notes were written by the Chosen One in the year of our King, Aldonius the Wise, 4538," it started. The Korisan was crude and poorly written, and reminded Heather of the scroll the Professor received. She did not know what year 4538 was, as her year was

1117, but given the brittleness of the pages, she assumed the book was very, very old. She skimmed the pages looking for an answer, but found herself drawn to the story Aldonius had left behind.

A young, effeminate man born of a lower caste, Aldonius was not allowed to work on machinery because in his society, people of his caste were not permitted to touch machines. But he found a way through deception, and ended up working for a small group of men who were trying to eliminate trolley. In his time, trolley was considered a poison that was being used by various cults to create weapons. Most of these mines were in and around where the root engine reached the surface: along the spokes and throughout several points around the world. One cult in particular called "The People of the Golden Blade" had figured out a way to open one of the walls that kept the monsters at bay. For years, several of these creatures rampaged his world, nearly destroying civilization with their horror.

"I have written this after a long fight trapping the creatures that scoured the caves and seas of our world, in hopes that if a later Chosen One has run into the same problem that they would not waste countless years and millions of lives. These creatures are using trolley to keep their forms. Once you eliminate trolley, they have no substance to escape their entrapments. Using the giant ring that hovers above the clouds, I was able to charge it with its own electricity and anything and everything connected to it would explode when trolley came into contact with it. There was mass devastation. Entire continents were erased. Deep valleys were dug and water filled them. Civilization was only spared because it was far away from trolley deposits at the spokes of the Sky Ring."

Heather's bones grew cold at the thought. Trolley was everywhere in her society. Not just in a few places, but it powered their machines and anything under the surface. If she was to do that, she would completely unravel all of human civilization in a series of violent explosions. But if she didn't... those creatures would. Those creatures were using the trolley present everywhere to form and gain power. In Aldonius' world, he only had to contend with a few small isolated mines, but Heather's world had scattered trolley everywhere. It powered nearly every underground machine except the root machines. She looked at some of the drawings in the book of what the world looked like before the incident and after. The continents from Aldonius' time were reduced by huge amounts. Her thin little world of Palachia was once three times as wide. Two of the spokes were not bound by surrounding ocean. The lectromag must have been devastating.

She looked up at the projections, and saw that nearly 70 creatures were now free.

"The number of creatures getting free is [click click] rapidly increasing," the voice said. "If this number reaches the total number of imprisoned creatures, the root machine will self-destruct. The entire planet will be irradiated, killing all life. It is important that these creatures remain on this planet and are not released to the universe. They will eventually eliminate all living things."

Heather had very little time. But she knew what must be done. She had to destroy trolley. But how?

"You must fulfill your destiny," said Mack. "You knew this was coming."

Heather sighed. "I thought you would be gone," she said with a weary voice.

"I will never be gone, Heather. Look at the last page of the book."

Heather gasped at the last squiggles of text.

"It is my hope that my writing will live on in spirit," it said. *"Signed, Aldonius Velicio, aka Mack Van Horn."*

"Yes," said Mack. "Every alter ego I take, the name ends up being Mack. I have never died, only existed in this machine, as the ... soul of this entire planet. I was the daughter of one of the last original builders. Every few thousand years, we have to eradicate those who have escaped and rebuild from the beginning; we will have to do this again if you cannot do this for yourself. It was always the plan that you cleanse the planet of all the beasts that corrupt and pollute it. I was the first. You won't be the last. It is our burden and destiny as punishment for building these horrific monsters during an interstellar war long, long forgotten."

"How can this be?" Heather asked. "How can... how can you exist?"

"You chosen folk don't understand your role. How can you? How can you... measure what you don't know about which you don't know? It is nearly infinite. Each time your society is rec-reated and resurrected, you start from a new root. But eventually the plant has to die, and its seeds take its place. The sun and moon spin around the ring, the stars lights up and die. All of them are in their own teeny world, just like you, and unaware of their affect on other places and peoples, It is like a gear that has no knowl-edge of the vast machine around it that depends on it and all the other gears. You are like me; I just am. I cannot explain how I am speaking to you now, or how your brain was genetically constructed to bring me back from the dead. Am I a hologram? A spirit? Who knows? I merely exist as part of the process."

Heather looked at the shadowbox shapes of the escaped creatures.

"Heather, I don't have to tell you what you will do. We both know what our destiny is."

"Will I be remembered?" Heather asked.

"Hard to say. Do you remember the Builders?"

"No, I suppose not. But I see their creation. I do not have such a legacy."

"Aldonius Velicio became immortal with a stick of charcoal and an old notebook. Anything can happen."

Heather looked at Mack. "I want to be remembered. But not as the destructor of civilization. I want... I want to be a builder."

"You have always wanted that, Heather January. And so it shall be done as you must complete what you set out to do."

Heather climbed back in the chair, and pulled the helmet down over her head. The red dots were rampaging everywhere, and she knew even if she fried them on the surface, they would reform in the presence of trolley just like the enormous creature she'd defeated had done at the wall. She began weeping and her hands trembled.

"Will I ever see you again, Mack?" she asked, starting a large sequence of events with several knobs and levers.

"I think so..." Mack said. "But you'll have to find your sister first."

Heather understood. "I'm sorry," she said, looking down at the world. "I am sorry for what I am about to do."

She pointed the lectromag gun at the base of the Southern Spoke. It started building up immense power. Warning sirens and alerts started sounding, and the room filled with hot steam as the charge kept building and building. The root machine, which had been steadily churning away, was now speeding up. Massive charges were building up deep in the machine's core miles below the ground. The entire Sky Ring started to glow blue as arcs of lectromag danced between the spokes. Heather's hair stood on its end as she tasted copper on her tongue. She hoped that whatever happened, it was for the common good of all. She was glad Morgana was already dead. And for the first time in Heather's life, she felt at peace and accepted death. Just as her dreams foretold.

She pulled the trigger and light filled her body.

Epilogue

"We have a visitor," said Neil, his voice heavy with concern. He noticed from the windmill roof that a figure had been traveling down their farm road for a few minutes. The figure was hunched and worn, carrying what looked like a lute on her back, and wearing a motley assortment of Yurpan clothing. She looked to be approaching the house with a direct purpose, albeit not easily on the uneven terrain of their dirt road.

"Who is it, grandpa?" asked his grandson Heath, who was helping repair torn canvas of the windmill blade.

"Heath, why don't you go see who it is. It looks like an old woman. Be careful now," he warned.

"Grandpa, people are not as mean as they used to be — "

"Still, son. Make sure to bring a heavy tool with you..." he called out, but Heath was already running down the road. "Foolish, foolish youth," he said. But his grandson was probably right. Violence on the open roads hadn't happened for a while, except near the city centers. Still, a stranger was a stranger. Neil watched his exuberant grandson as he started chatting with the woman, and remembered what it was like to be so bold and fresh as a young man. Nothing but positive energy and optimism.

That optimism was destroyed in Neil like so many others when the Lectromag Cataclysm descended from the skies. It was hard to believe that it was almost three quarters of a century since civilization had ended. Nobody knew why. Crazy green monsters tearing around machinery, forcing people to the surface. Lectromag descending from the sky, scarring the land with deep craters. "Just the power of nature," said the youth of today. But Neil, like most of his generation, was certain it was something more sinister. All of civilization had seemed to explode at the seams and stop, and for many years those that survived became mean and brutal. The survivors from the ruined underground cities were forced to the surface, where the older farm folk did not take kindly to them. Many battles were fought. Neil himself had lost his parents in a riot at a grain storage facility when he was a small boy. He became an indentured servant to a series of abusive owners where he had witnessed some of the cruelest acts humanity had to offer.

It took nearly two decades years before the deaths leveled off, and another few decades to get things back into stability. The underground cities were abandoned and closed off as cave-like prisons for whatever horrors had come from the deep, and the superior Northern Palachian way of life became the world's way of life. Trolley was gone, lectromag dominated the skies, and things had returned to a simpler and less sophisticated rural existence.

Like many of the former "gearbacks," Neil tried at first to restore things to a semblance of civilized sanity, but repeatedly was thwarted by lack of basic needs of clean water, sustainable food, and decent sanitation. Eventually, he survived by becoming a surface dweller who was good at repairing things and traveled from village to village trading his skilled hands and strong back for water and food. After many years, he'd become a simple landowner of a series of windmills and watermills that did basic tasks like powering grindstones or sawmills. He raised a sturdy family, and turned his back on his southern Palachian past. While many of his generation spoke of the former glory days, Neil spit upon them. And if this old woman was from this generation, she could bring trouble to the comfortable shroud of forgetfulness he cloaked around himself.

"Grandpa!" Heath yelled back, nearly dragging the woman off her feet towards their house.

"Careful now!" he shouted back. "You're a young man, Heath. Not a boy anymore. You can't go dragging old ladies around like they are a pull toy!"

The old woman didn't seem to mind, though. She laughed as she tried to keep pace with the boy. Neil climbed down from the roof and went to meet the stranger, dreading the eventual small talk that would probably lead to "remember when civilization took care of everything? That was nice..." He had enough of that depressing nostalgia from his senile older sister.

"I am sorry, we don't get many visitors near the pumping stations," he said, wiping off his hand and offering it to her. "My name is Neil. Neil January. I manage this windmill plantation with my son and his family."

"Pleasure to meet you, Neil. January is an old southern Palachian name, is it not?" She was answered with silence. "Well, my name is Aura Claviger. I am a wandering storyteller."

"Oh," Neil said, a little surprised. "I have heard of you! You have come through town many times."

"I have. But I decided to come here, because I am in need of rest."

Neil was suspicious. He was pretty far from town for such visitors. He knew Aura because she was one of the older storytellers who would bring news and reconstruction ideas from village to village. Oral storytelling was finally waning because of the slow return of printed publications, but Aura had a special gift and unique perspective. Unlike many women, she had traveled nearly everywhere and had a lot of innovative ideas. Neil himself had used some of her teachings to improve the structure of his sawmills, but it had been a long time since he had heard of her, and he wondered about the veracity of this stranger. "Aura... that's a Yurpan name, is it not? I was told you had died."

"Southern Yurpan, and the news of my death is a bit premature, although it's not the first time this wretched cough has spawned a rumor of that type," Aura said, coughing into her sleeve.

"You are not — "

"Rest easy, my fellow builder. I am not contagious. I am merely old." Aura then chuckled at some private joke.

Neil stood up stiffly. "I am afraid I cannot pay you on my wages. But I can offer a shared meal and a bed."

"That is all I require. Plus a little time to bend your ear and answer a few questions I have. Perhaps we can trade a story or two..."

Neil laughed. "I am afraid all my children and grandchildren are grown, and past the storytelling age."

Aura smiled. "I am here for different stories."

"I see. Well, Heath will show you the way."

"Interesting name, Heath," Aura said. "How did you come about this name?"

"It was my sister's," Neil said. "Her name was Heather."

The woman nodded. "Was?"

"Heather died during the Great Lectromag Cataclysm," Neil said with a stone expression.

"Is that what that noise was?" Aura said with a smile and a wink. "Nearly scared me out of bed!"

Heath laughed heartily. "Oh, such wit!"

Neil frowned. "Yes, quite."

"You survived from below — "

Neil stamped his foot. "Forgive my abruptness, but I do not wish to speak of those times. Those are days long gone, and serve no purpose but narcissistic reflection." For some reason, Neil felt the old woman's face showed more than a casual interest, and the resentful pang of loss from a long-gone age unsettled him. "Old men and women who managed to survive the horrors from the skies become lost in their own demented minds — "

"Neil, do not be so serious about things. Life goes on. You survived to have a wonderful family."

"Yes, that I have..." Neil said. "My sister will be a little annoyed that we have unexpected visitors, so I apologize if she takes your — "

"Your sister?" Aura said with a puzzling look. She stopped in mild-walk.

"Yes. My sister Morgana. She's a rather ill-tempered woman that... are you all right?"

Aura stood in place. She was shaking. "So you... do... have a sister..."

"Yes, Aura. Is that so unusual? I don't mention her much, it's true, but I don't think you should have such an incredulous look."

"No. No... well, maybe. Is she your half sister?"

Neil rolled his eyes. "Not that it's any business of yours, but no!"

"I am sorry," Aura said. "I am old, and sometimes become a little dotty. I can't wait to meet her."

"Heath January!" Morgana shouted as her great nephew thundered into the house. "I don't want you coming into this house with those filthy shoes and — oh, we have a visitor?"

Aura stood by the door; her face drained of color. "Morgana?"

"Yes?" Morgana said.

Aura stood dumbstruck. "I... I don't understand. You're alive!"

"And regretting every day of it. And who might you be?"

"I... you look so much like ..."

Morgana was in no mood for this. "Heath? Who is this scatter-brained old lady?"

"Aura Claviger, mum. Storyteller."

"You invited a storyteller to our house? What are you, a small tot who wants to hear fables?"

"No mum, she came to us. Needs a place to stay."

Morgana walked up to Aura. "And what do we get in return?"

Aura swallowed. "I am at a loss for words, but I think I may have something to give you in return. Please, may I stay for just the night? I need to ... collect my thoughts."

Morgana went back to her cooking. "A storyteller at a loss for words! That sounds like misfortune for your line of work. Well, can you cook or clean? Everyone earns their keep in this house!"

"I can," Aura said.

Aura was silent for the rest of the evening. She swept and set the table, dusted the mantelpiece, and did what she could to earn her keep. Morgana was annoyed that Aura would pause and stare at her for long periods of time, so she avoided her gaze and was grateful Aura didn't try small talk. After a dinner where Neil's family talked about their mundane day's work, Aura broke her silence and asked everyone to sit in front of the evening fire and listen to something she had to say. Neil and his two sons were there, along with a few grandchildren. Morgana sat in an old rocking chair, staring at the fire.

"Let me begin by saying that I have spent most of my life wandering," Aura said. "And in my travels, I have heard many tales. I have been from Rokasia to Yurpa and back — "

"Rokasia? Is anyone in that country even left?" Neil asked, puffing his pipe.

"Oh yes. No longer the huge power of mechanical wonder anymore, Rokasia had so polluted their soil and waters that they are nothing more than a series of scattered fishing villages."

"The Lectromag Cataclysm changed everything," Morgana said, her eyes not leaving the light of the hearth fire. "Destroyed all that was good in the world."

Aura smiled. "Not everything."

"I wish to change the subject," Neil said. "It is well known that you have some great ideas in manufacturing — "

"I agree. I wish to change the subject. Morgana, are you married?"

Neil huffed. "Aura, that is an unusually personal question for a guest — "

"No," Morgana said, trying to swallow sadness. "I am under the care of my brother."

"Pity," Aura said. "I always figured you the marrying type."

There was an uncomfortable silence where only the crackling of the fire interrupted.

"What is in your bag, Aura? A lute?" Heath asked. Without asking, he opened the bag an gasped at the huge golden blade. "What is this?"

"Thundering heavens, Heath! Don't go snooping about another person's things!" Neil exclaimed in horror. "I raised you better than that!"

Aura smiled. "It is a key, Heath. A key to places that help me get to other places. But I need to ask you this, Morgana. How did your... final days before the Cataclysm go?"

"What an annoying question!" Neil snapped. "If there's one thing I can't stand is old people moaning and crying about how great things used to be. I won't have that sort of nostalgia in my house!"

"Do you miss your sister?" Aura asked, ignoring him.

Morgana gasped as tears welled up in her eyes, she turned to her hateful guest. "I don't see what... **what gives you the right** to ask such a thing?"

"Because I miss mine, Morgana. I spent a long time thinking she was dead." Aura's lips were trembling.

"Aura, we have all had our own burdens," Neil said sternly. "It is time to let the past rest. You have upset Morgana with your banter, and I think you're a rotten storyteller so far."

"Perhaps," Aura said. "But I am here for something else. Morgana... I need to know what happened at the League of the Brave parade. The last one you attended."

Morgana wiped away a few stray tears. "What?"

"League of the Brave," Neil said. "That's a name I haven't heard in a long time. I wonder what happened to them through the Cataclysm? Fat lot of good they were. You know for years, I heard people saying that the League would save them, and that — "

Aura waved him quiet turned Morgana's chair to face her. "After your sister left with the Professor. You attended one last parade."

Morgana sighed. "No, I did not. I don't know how you knew about those days, but your facts are way off. I was actually grounded for that parade, if you must know. And my best friend took my pins and dress and went instead. She died in a horrible parade disaster. Trampled, burned, and as she tried to get help... some... horrid person stabbed her straight in the chest, stole my dress, and let her die from Trolley asphyxiation; a guilt which I was forced to burden even through the Cataclysm thank you *so* much."

"It wasn't you! All this time, it wasn't you!" Aura said excitedly. Tears began to dribble down her wrinkled face.

Morgana recoiled slightly away from Aura. "What are you talking about?"

"Oh, silly Morgana! It's me, Heather!"

The sound of a teacup hit the floor.

"Heavens abound..." Neil said. "Heather?"

Heather grabbed her sister's weathered face and scanned it, trying to erase the years that had separated the. The two of them stared deep into each other's eyes as tears trickled down their faces. Heather unleashed a gasping whimper of gratitude as she said, "Morgana? Oh my goodness, sis... I... I was in town last week, and I heard Neil's name and I wondered if it was my younger brother — "

"Oh my sister... my dearest Heather. I have missed you so!" Morgana said, finally breaking free from her stunned silence. She collapsed into sobs and the two of them held onto one another hugging and grasping at their weary bones in attempt to pull themselves as close together as possible.

"Aura the storyteller was... is... my sister Heather?" Neil asked in shock.

Heather looked up, scanning the glow off everyone's faces.

"Oh look at you all. Morgana, you look just like mother! Neil you look just like father! And your children.... what happened to Kye?"

Neil shook his head. "The University was one of the hardest hit by the cataclysm due to the amount of trolley inside and its closeness to the surface."

Aura nodded. "I have seen the crater many times. It's a lake now. I was hoping... but still, Morgana...! Morgana how I have missed you. I didn't think I'd find you until the ends of time. Have our parents...?"

"Mother and father both died in a riot," Neil said, wiping away a tear of his own. "I found Morgana quite by accident when I worked for the same house where we were both servants. We have been traveling together and eventually, Morgana settled with us. She was the only old family I thought I had left." A chortle escaped his throat.

Heather nodded. She went back to hugging and gripping Morgana as they cried and rocked each other in comfort.

Hours later, Heather tucked her sister into bed. Morgana seemed so old and frail in comparison to her sister's thin and wiry frame. Heather's face was tan and taut with expressive lines, while Morgana's face was pale, and dragged in any direction her sagging jowls lay.

"How come you never married?" Heather asked quietly. She was absently stroking Morgana's hair through her fingers as Morgana breathed softly with closed eyes in bliss.

"I never had the chance," she replied with a chuckle. "My life became complicated and too worrisome for children."

"Are you still hoping for a Lance Worthingheart?"

Morgana chuckled and covered her face in a regrettable memory. "Oh, Lance. There's a name I have not heard in... quite a long time." She sighed, and for a second, her childlike bliss overtook her. "I might have married him. I wonder whatever happened to that man?"

Heather remained silent. She could not remember, but felt that perhaps this was for the best.

"Please... lie next to me and hold me?" Morgana asked. "Just like we used to as sisters?"

Heather smiled and crawled under the covers next to her sister.

"Your skin is so dry and leathery," Morgana said. "But part of you feels the same."

"I have traveled for decades, wandering lost, and you were here all along. I missed you dearly, Morgana... The things I have seen, the places I've been."

"I missed you too," Morgana said sleepily. "I held onto your pneumatic tube letters for as long as I could... but I was never... a good... reader..." she drifted off into memories she had long since put away. Then, she started to snore softly.

Heather hugged and hugged her sister with all her waning strength. Falling asleep next to her sister was the best thing that could have ever happened to her after the Cataclysm. It was almost like it had never happened.

"It's time to go," said a young voice by the doorway. A 12 year old girl, dressed in worker's clothes, stood enveloped in a heavenly glow.

Heather looked up from her sister's chest. "No! I just found her. You were right, Mack! She was alive! Please let me spend more time with her."

"Your time in this world is finished. I led you here so you could have some final closure, as I promised."

"I have so much more to teach! These people still need me! They need to know how to rebuild what they have lost. The Yurpan people are using lectromag for so many wondrous things. I can teach them the telegraph and the electric light and — "

"They will learn when they are ready," Mack said with a smile. "You have done well. Your journey is finished." She held out a hand. "Come, Heather. It's time to rest. To become part of the root machine."

"No! I missed her so much — *please* let me stay! Please give me more time! *Please*, Mack??" Heather whined as she clung to her sister.

Morgana opened her eyes and squeezed Heather's shoulder. "Heather," Morgana said gently, smiling the same way their mother did. "I will go with you this time. I am your twin, remember?"

Heather wept through laughter. "F-fraternal twin!" she snorted through her tears.

The twin sisters hugged one another, and joined Mack in the enveloping light.

Neil didn't know what happened that night, but he thought it fitting that wherever they went from now on, they were finally together. After the funeral, he placed the golden blade over the fireplace. For centuries, the strange golden blade was handed down from generation to generation until one day, a thin man in a green suit bought it at an estate sale.

"That's an odd one," the head of the auction house mused, stamping his check. "The writing on it is completely mystic. Nobody knows what it means."

The thin man nodded. "It's an ancient language called Korisan," he said. "Our ... archaeological group has been collecting Korisan artifacts." There was a trace of a smile on his lips as he fingered a small stone star on his necklace. "I think we will find this useful..."